## PRAISE FOR BETH WEBB HART

"[I]ntelligent and promising."

—*Publishers Weekly* referring to *Adelaide Piper*

"It really speaks to the heart while tackling tough issues."

—www.epinions.com referring to *Adelaide Piper*

"[E]njoyable, contemporary reading that is entertaining . . ."

—Jodi Kuhrt, Christian Book Previews.com

"[*Grace at Low Tide*] is unabashedly about the presence of God in the midst of pain and hopelessness. It is a gentle coming-of-age story with a warm, tender slant."

—Sonia Coffin, *The Charlotte Observer*

"*Grace at Low Tide*, Hart's first novel, is an aromatic bouillabaisse of Southern manners, island life and God's redemptive love. Readers who love Oprah's book picks will find this title in keeping with the best contemporary fiction."

—Lynn Waalkes, *CBA Marketplace*

"Beth Webb Hart's storytelling is as rich, complex, and detailed as the intricate Southern landscape she describes [in *Grace at Low Tide*]. Mercy and grace flow from the pages of this coming-of-age novel. A glorious debut."

—Patti Callahan Henry, author of *Where the River Runs*

# Adelaide Piper

# Adelaide Piper

## Beth Webb Hart

WestBow
PRESS

A Division of Thomas Nelson Publishers
*Since 1798*

visit us at www.westbowpress.com

Published in Nashville, Tennessee, by WestBow Press, a division of Thomas Nelson, Inc.

WestBow Press books may be purchased in bulk for educational, business, fund-raising, or sales promotional use. For information, please e-mail SpecialMarkets@ThomasNelson.com.

Scriptures quotations are taken from the *Holy Bible*, New Living Translation, copyright © 1996. Used by permission of Tyndale House Publishers, Inc., Wheaton, Illinois 60189. All rights reserved. The King James Version of the Bible. The New King James Version, copyright © 1979, 1980, 1982 by Thomas Nelson, Inc., Publishers.

Publisher's Note: This novel is a work of fiction. Names, characters, places, and incidents are either products of the author's imagination or used fictitiously. All characters are fictional, and any similarity to people living or dead is purely coincidental.

### Library of Congress Cataloging-in-Publication Data

Hart, Beth Webb, 1971–
    Adelaide Piper / Beth Webb Hart.
      p. cm.
    ISBN 1-59554-027-X
    1. Young women—Fiction. 2. Women college students--Fiction.
  3. Authors—Fiction. 4. Campus violence—Fiction. 5. Southern States—
Fiction. I. Title.
PS3608.A78395A34 2006
813'.6—dc22
2006011841

*Printed in the United States of America*

06 07 08 09 10 RRD 6 5 4 3 2

*This book is dedicated to my tenacious cheerleader and devoted father, Joe W. Jelks III.*

## *prologue*

# Swimming Lesson

I had just turned six the afternoon my father peeled off my water wings to show me I could swim. We were spending the last week of summer on Pawleys Island, and the August tide had built a gully four feet deep and almost twenty yards wide that was flanked by a sandbar on the ocean side and beds of crushed shells along the beach.

"Come on in, Adelaide," he said, motioning with his good arm as I stood at the edge of the gully, fingering the dime-sized mole in the center of my forehead. My jewel, Daddy had named it, and because of him I believed it was a precious stone that marked my distinction.

As I stepped ankle-deep into the warm, salty water, I glanced back over the dunes to the front porch of the beach cottage where my paternal grandfolks, Papa Great and Mae Mae, were already sipping their gin and tonics while Mama spooned pea mush out of a little jar that Dizzy, my younger sister, refused to eat. And I imagined the pop and sizzle of Juliabelle frying up shrimp and hush puppies in the kitchen, though I knew she was watching me out of the corner of her eye.

"If you make the swim, I give you a piece from the secret stash, eh?" she had said. She hoarded bubble gum in a brown paper bag beneath her bed, and I hounded her for a piece whenever I got the chance.

Daddy was near the middle of the gully now, the murky green

licking his washboard belly. He dived under for several seconds before turning over and floating on his back, his broad chest rising out of the water. He spit a fountain of green from his lips and said, "Sure feels good!"

I would have splashed right in after Daddy if I'd had a flotation device. A few days ago he had shown me how to paddle in my water wings over to the sandbar at low tide, and I had filled my bucket with bachelor's buttons, hermits, and a horseshoe crab that was shuffling across the surface in its heavy armor. But yesterday Papa Great dared me to go on my own (no Daddy and no life jacket), and I had sunk into the dark, soupy depth at the center of the gully, swallowing what felt like half the Atlantic Ocean until Daddy caught hold of my pony-tail and yanked me to the surface.

Now I moved in to my knees and planned to take every second of the time he was giving me to get my courage up. There was a quick drop-off after the next bed of crushed shells, and I knew that in a few short steps the water would cover me whole.

"Don't push her too hard, Zane," Mama called from behind the screened porch. There was a murmur among them that I couldn't make out, but even at that tender age I could guess that Mae Mae was saying, "Let her try," while Papa Great concluded, "Fear's got her by the scruff."

Fact was, I wasn't afraid of what was *in* the ocean. Why, a man-of-war had wrapped its tentacles around my second cousin Randy's calf two mornings ago, leaving thin red burn marks, as if he had been caught in one of the wild hog traps Daddy set along the swamp. And even after Mama numbed Randy's leg with meat tenderizer and let me touch it, so I could feel the heat rising off his seared skin, I still jumped right back into the gully that afternoon.

And just this morning, Papa Great had caught a sand shark longer than my leg on his fishing line, and I had touched its leathery belly with the tip of my big toe as he held it between his knees and pulled the hook out of its snout. But right after, I went back in with Daddy to venture to the sandbar and collect my treasures.

No, it wasn't fear of what was in the water. Seems to me I just didn't want that dark and covered feeling. Not knowing which way was up. Not knowing if Daddy would find me.

The water wings were swirling in the breeze along the beach now as I stood knee-deep in the gully, and since I prided myself in keeping track of my belongings, I stepped out to chase after them. To pin them beneath Daddy's beach chair.

"Don't worry about those, gal!" he said as he stood back up in the water and shook his head so that his soaked hair looked like two fins above his ears. "Now, *come on in*."

The water was a gray-green broth, and when I stepped back in, I could feel the sand and shells stir up for a moment, but I couldn't see through the clouds to whatever was swirling around my legs now.

All of a sudden, Daddy moved forward and pulled me out by my elbow with his only hand. He smelled like sweat and coconut suntan lotion, and I had to paddle quickly with my other arm beneath his fiery pink stump to stay afloat. The stump was wrinkled at its very tip from where a doctor had sliced off his forearm in an army hospital in Than Khe, Vietnam. Sometimes I asked him what the hospital had done with his other arm, and he winked and said they fed it to the dogs before admitting that he didn't have the foggiest idea.

Now I was flailing my arms and gasping for air as we reached the gully depths, and he said, "I'm going to let go, all right? I'll be here if you need me."

He released my arm, and I tried to touch bottom just to get my bearings. To get a nice shove up and out of the water. Some momentum. But as my foot searched for the sharp shells that lined the floor, I was already sunk, and when I breathed in the water, it stung my nose and throat.

"Easy now," Daddy said, lifting me above the surface for a moment so I could cough it out. Then, "Here we go again, gal." And he dropped me down and stepped back fast.

I tried whirling my arms and legs into a motion that would buoy me, but before you could say "boo!" I was covered in the dark soup again and holding my breath.

One Mississippi.

Two Mississippi.

Covered in darkness.

Water rushing into my nose.

He found my shoulder this time, pulled me up, and dragged me onto the shore, where I coughed for dear life and rubbed my burning eyes. My heart was pounding like the wings of the hummingbirds that sipped from Mae Mae's feeder most afternoons. And the tiny bits of crushed shells were clinging to the backs of my legs and gathering in the folds of my bathing suit.

"You're my little fish, Adelaide," Daddy said.

Papa Great had given him the month of August off so that he could vacation with us, and as long as I had his hand and a float, I'd go way out beyond the waves and let the current push us down the beach toward the pier.

"I know you can do it," he whispered now.

"Dinnertime!" Juliabelle called from the screened porch. I could see her long, thin neck craning to check on me. She never went near the ocean. Her younger brother had drowned in the surf when she was a girl, and she said it would do me good to know how to keep myself afloat. But I guessed even she was concluding that I couldn't do it. Not this year, anyway.

The porch door slapped once as Papa Great ambled out onto the boardwalk to holler down at us.

"Maybe next summer, son," he called to Daddy as he caught a mosquito in his fist and examined the small heap of blood and wings in the center of his palm. "Y'all come on in for supper now."

The pink sun was sitting for a moment on top of the ocean as if it were a beach ball floating on the surface. A mullet jumped up from the gully, and Daddy squeezed my shoulder before exhaling, "Let's go in, sweetheart."

His first steps toward the boardwalk left a shower of wet sand along the small of my back, and a newfound fury started rising inside me. When I spotted one of my water wings flying over the dunes toward a neighbor's cottage, the fury stoked itself into a hot fire in my throat as if I had just swallowed the popping grease from Juliabelle's iron skillet.

"No!" I said.

I wanted to cry and hit something, but I knew what I had to do, and when I ran back into the gully, I tripped over the shells and splashed clumsily to the deep center.

More salt water in my throat now. A burning in my nose. But still I twitched, thrashed my arms and legs with all my might, and managed to keep my head above water for a few seconds.

Twitch. Kick. Slap. Slap. Breathe.

Kick. Slap. Reach. Breathe.

Daddy turned back to see what the commotion was about, and then he called, "Look!" to the porch, though everyone was already inside for dinner. Then he ran into the gully and stood feet in front of me as I made my way to his outstretched hand.

"That's a girl!" he said as I paddled for him. "I *knew* you could do it!"

He stepped back a few times the closer I got to him, and when I had made my way past the boardwalk and the crab trap and Papa Great's fishing lines, he caught me, lifted me up onto his shoulder with his good hand beneath one arm and his stump beneath my other, and spun me around twice before plunging us backward into the murky water.

He was a former college football tailback for the University of South Carolina, and I loved his burly horsing around, so when his shoulder hit my lip in this celebratory pitch, I didn't mind the pain or the metal tang of blood on my tongue. And I laughed the sweet laugh of victory because I had proved us both right, and because I'd believed, like when my teacher had discovered I was seeing letters backward, that I could force things back to where they belonged.

Mama handed us each a towel before we took our seats in front of two heaping plates of battered shrimp topped with two lopsided balls of fried corn bread.

"Like to have fooled me," Papa Great said as he sucked a shrimp out of its tail and slurped his toddy.

He motioned to Mama's swelling belly and said, "Let's hope this third one's a boy. Then you'll see determination, son."

Papa Great. Ugh. He put the "pig" in "male chauvinist pig"; he even looked like a hog with his upturned nose rooting out the weakness in everyone.

"She's been swimming all summer long," Mae Mae said as she searched the table for the cocktail sauce.

If he was a hog, then she was a peacock, tall and here for no reason at all except to be beautiful. She had a way of looking down her beak at him, and I liked that about her.

"Somethin' for sweet in your mouth," murmured Juliabelle under her breath as she put a Bazooka square beside my plate and patted my back.

Then Daddy, the greatest cheerleader anyone could hope for, said, "Adelaide's got determination, Papa. You watch what I tell you."

That night, beneath the sheets of the roll-away bed that sat flush against a window opened to the porch, I watched Juliabelle smoke her pipe at the edge of the boardwalk, with a shotgun propped against the wooden rail. Spooked by the snakes and the remote possibility of a gator skulking out of the marsh and across the gravelly road, she had taken one of Daddy's old field guns and learned how to shoot it. And we all understood that no one and nothing should disrupt the pleasure of her evening smoke.

She was lanky but strong, and I loved her as much as my mama, who was going to be even farther from me now with the birth of a third child. I'd stolen a picture from Mae Mae's photo album of Juliabelle holding me as an infant and hidden it in the lining of my suitcase. How I looked forward to curling up in her bony arms on the hammock in the early mornings and smelling her sweet tobacco smell as she rocked me on the porch and hummed "Eye on the Sparrow" before anyone else was awake. Her skin was loose and darker than the coal funneled into the furnace at the Williamstown steel mill, but her palms were a chalky pink like the tip of Daddy's stump or a square of Bazooka bubble gum, and she would cup them around my cheeks in those first minutes of daylight and say, "Good morning, my Adelaide."

I didn't want the summer to end. The guidance counselor had labeled me "learning disabled" because of the dyslexia, and I'd have to share a classroom with Averill Skaggs, the ringleader of a mean generation of mill village lowlifes, for the first years of elementary school. He'd throw spitballs at me and trip me and ask me if a bird had crapped on my forehead. My jewel.

*De-ter-mi-na-tion.* I had no idea what it meant then, but over the next twelve years I came to understand that it was something I must cultivate if I had any hope of getting out of Williamstown County and the open-air asylum that we called home. I had found it that day in the gully, and I would bridle it and use it to turn the letters straight, to help Mama raise up my younger sisters, and to bodysurf in the storm tide as the hurricanes gnawed along our South Carolina coast.

On the porch I could hear Daddy singing, "Like a rhinestone cowboy . . . ," as Mae Mae shuffled the cards and dealt out another hand of seven-card stud. He was humming the refrain to the rhythm of clinking poker chips, and I focused on his voice and the sound of the hammock creaking where its chain met the wall until my eyelids were weighted and the dull roar of the ocean nearly lulled me to sleep.

I played possum a few minutes later when Daddy popped his head through the porch window to kiss me good night.

"You're my gal," he whispered as I pretended to sleep. He still smelled like coconut suntan lotion, but it was mixed with beer now, and the stubble from his chin tickled my cheek and nearly gave me away.

"You can do anything you set your mind to," he added before Papa Great called him back to the game.

As he ducked out onto the porch, I turned back toward him, caught my swollen lip between my teeth, and grinned.

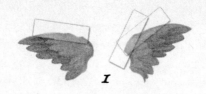

*I*

# Home

### Williamstown

The paper mill's
two fingers
of smoke
rise
out of the
thick gray sky.
They coat
my throat
with their stench
and when I swallow
I have sipped
the sewer.

Run your finger
across the
layer of soot
on the corner
of Main and King
and taste

the steel mill
whose furnace
devours
one ton
of coal
each week.

Look in the inlet
where the dye
is dumped
from the textile mill
and you might see
a stained brim
belly up
from what
some folks call
industry.

A poem by Miss Adelaide Piper, Grade 10,
Williamstown High School
Published in the *Palmetto State Paper* on November 5, 1987

By high school, I was a poet, if you can believe that. And the very words that had stumped me as a child became my strongest allies. I stumbled upon the art form quite by accident. I mean, I'd always loved music and the sounds of words when you put them together. But when I panicked over a creative writing assignment from Mr. Gaskins—a new and handsome English teacher I suspected was an environmental activist—I wrote the poem above to get into his good graces.

Before I knew it, he had submitted it to the state paper's student contest, and after it was published, the Williamstown Chamber of Commerce hated my teenage guts, and Papa Great (my grandfather, my father's employer, and the head of the textile mill) all but disowned me.

∽

Two years down the road it was by default that Principal Dingledine asked me to give the valedictorian address in the crumbling gymnasium one June morning in 1989. I was actually third in the Williamstown High School senior class, but the rightful valedictorian, Georgianne Mayfield, was six months pregnant, and the would-be salutatorian and my senior dance date, Lazarus Greene, had moved to Norfolk on account of his daddy's port transfer. So it was up to me to address the faculty and students whom, to be honest, I hoped I'd never see again.

"Pickaninny's girl," Charlene Roe said as I made my way to the front of the class processional.

My cheap turquoise graduation gown was open at the bottom, and when I reached down to pull it closed, the first page of my speech slipped out of my folder and landed at the foot of the second-biggest Philistine in the class, Bubba Ratliff.

"Pipe down, Piper," he said, eyeing me hard as I snatched the paper out of his hand.

Averill Skaggs, the ringleader of the bunch, had coined that catchy chant when I ran for class president our freshman year. My campaign (which focused on creating a healthier learning environment) threatened to move the smoking section to the back corner of campus so that every member of the student body wouldn't have to walk through a cloud of burning cancer sticks on the way to class.

Averill and his smoking-section hoodlums hated this idea, as well as my plan to curb the dust from the shop class, where he spent most days feeding pieces of pine through dangerous machines to build gun racks and boxes for his snuff. He had been the first to raise his hand with a question during that freshman-year campaign assembly, and if I closed my eyes, I could still see him standing at the top of the bleachers, his peach fuzz of a mustache tucked between his pursed lips as he called out, "What's that on your forehead, Piper? Bird dropping?" The freshman class had erupted with laughter.

I lost the race. And I often blamed Averill for the fact that no boy from my class ever asked me out. With one glorious exception, the only head I'd ever turned was my second cousin's, Randy Stubbs, who finagled his way into most family gatherings and tried to woo me with fishing stories, Gamecock football trivia, or his copious collection of country music.

Thankfully, I could boast of one truly romantic evening last summer at the Charleston Governor's School, where a young Italian violinist from the Spoleto Festival orchestra took me to dinner after attending my poetry reading.

Luigi Agnolucci. *Mon amore.*

He bought me a palmetto frond that a black boy with a gold tooth had sculpted into a rose before pushing us on a porch swing at the end of the Water Front Park dock. And there, beneath the dull lights of Fort Sumter and the thin sliver of the Carolina moon, he cupped the back of my head with his long, gifted fingers and pulled me in for the kiss of my life . . .

Since Luigi was an ocean away and I refused to take my cousin to the senior dance, I'd bucked protocol and asked my favorite male classmate, Lazarus Greene, to be my date to the senior dance. He was the editor of the yearbook and my study partner in AP English, and he always made me laugh with his impersonation of Principal Dingledine's morning announcements, so I figured, why not?

You wouldn't have thought that in 1989 a white girl asking a black boy to a dance would have caused a stir. But Williamstown, a once-honored city of the country's Founding Fathers, had nose-dived during the industrial era into a backward village of cretins, and the mill boys made sure that all eyes were on me and my bright and handsome friend when we entered the gymnasium door five weeks ago. Me in a strapless lilac gown that Mama copied from a Jessica McClintock advertisement, and Lazarus in a white dinner jacket with a coordinating lavender bow tie and cummerbund.

Now Principal Dingledine motioned for me to hurry up and take my place behind the flag bearer who led the procession. I quickly reorganized the papers of my speech and didn't flinch when I heard Averill Skaggs call a simple "Don't brick!" from the back of the line.

Philistines. Cretins. I was so ready to be rid of them.

And I had my ticket out.

It had come in the form of a thick, gold-crested acceptance letter from Nathaniel Buxton University, an elite liberal arts college in Virginia. Ever since it arrived last March, I had pictured the red-brick buildings with their mammoth white pillars as the answer to all that I longed for: knowledge, wonder, enlightenment, and a worthy environment in which to tear open the cocoon I was in and start *living*.

I took my place on the stage by my friend and Miss Williamstown High, Jif Ferguson, who kept flipping her golden bangs and asking me to look between her teeth to make sure a poppy seed from her breakfast muffin wasn't lodged somewhere in there.

"Beep." Jif sounded her alarm. "Holy Roller alert. Beep."

Shannon Pitts, my best childhood friend turned born-again Christian, leaned down and whispered in my ear, "God be with you, Adelaide," before taking her place behind us.

*Thanks, Miss Wear-My-Faith-on-My-Sleeve,* I thought to myself. *But this one is in the bag.*

Principal Dingledine was the first to address the audience with his uninspired thank-yous and watered-down best wishes for our futures. We had plumb worn him out, and it was common knowledge that he would retire with the class of 1990 next year.

Now, me, I was no troublemaker in the conventional sense, but I did cause a bit of a stir with my choice of a date for the senior dance.

When Averill's crew tried to pick a fight with Lazarus on his way to the parking lot the night before the dance, Principal Dingledine had called me into his office.

"I'm not saying those boys are right, Adelaide," he'd said. "But I don't know why you have to go and throw gas on a fire."

And then there was the pollution poem. After it hit the state paper, some of the Williamstown business executives (including Papa Great) had a sit-down meeting with Principal Dingledine, and before I knew it, the creative writing class was off the curriculum and Mr. Gaskins was teaching below-average English to Averill Skaggs and the rest of the lowlifes.

I came out of the whole matter unscathed. In fact, the poem's publication earned me an invitation to the prestigious Governor's School summer program for the arts, and before you knew it, I was a poet sent off to hone my craft each summer at my state's Emerald City of history and culture, Charleston.

Now I was standing before my classmates on this beautiful Sunday morning in June, and I was worrying more about whether folks could see through my white linen dress than about the merits of my speech.

"Good morning, Principal Dingledine, Vice Principal Chalmers, faculty, family, friends, and most important, the class of 1989."

A cacophony of throat clearing began, and I repositioned the thinly covered mortarboard that Juliabelle and Mama had safety-pinned to my head, not caring whether my jewel was showing or not. As the rusty air conditioner rattled above the bleachers, I took a deep breath and began.

"Our historic Williamstown makes up the heart of the tidelands where four rivers converge on the intracoastal waterway before pushing out into the Atlantic Ocean.

"Like the rivers that quietly begin behind the ridges of the North Carolina mountains, each of us has cut a different path to this momentous day. And our lives have converged for four years before, like the rivers that empty out into the ocean, we pour into that unchartered abyss known as adult life.

"Today, as we walk across this stage to receive the formal document that marks the end of our river days, and step through the creaking gym doors into the outside world, we must not forget this place where we came together.

"Remember the classroom where the encouraging words of a dedicated teacher stirred the current in our minds? Or the pat on the back from a friend who dried our tears with the stiff hand towels in the bathroom after a typical teenage trial? That pat showed us we were not alone on our journey to the ocean.

"It wasn't all bliss, of course. There were failed tests, detention hours served; there was that close Williamstown Dolphins football game where we lost the state championship in overtime, and, of course, those cruel words doled out by peers that, like the harbor silt, weighted down our very bones.

"But even the challenging times taught us how to brace ourselves for the big water that is coming. A vast frontier where we can only guess that high seas and strong winds may threaten our very existence."

(Count 1 Mississippi, 2 Mississippi, 3 Mississippi; then posture for main point.)

"While we expect the big water to be daunting at times, we also trust that it will be a life lined with many a calm surface day, and we await with great expectation those glorious sunrises on the horizon that give us reason to keep on as the tide pushes us farther out to sea.

"As I see it, we are on not a hapless journey, but rather a *quest* for the answer to these two crucial questions before each of us: one, who *am* I? and two, *where* am I going?"

(Count 1 Mississippi, 2 Mississippi, 3 Mississippi—you're home free. Now push it on through to the finish.)

"Search with all your might, my fellow classmates, to find the answers to these two questions that propel us day and night from the bottom of the seabeds of our souls.

"And when the darkness comes, retain the memory of this gentle tideland where we came together for a moment in time before moving out to sea.

"Bon voyage, class of 1989. Congratulations! I honor you."

It did feel like a moment of convergence when the applause broke out and Principal Dingledine breathed a sigh of relief that a third-string girl like me didn't use the microphone as an environmental soapbox and that no one had yelled out a racial slur.

Nostalgia crept up in my throat like indigestion as I took my seat. Jif read my body posture and thumped my thigh as if to say, "Now, come on, Adelaide. You have *no* intention of looking back to the tidelands."

Then Principal Dingledine started to call out the graduate names in alphabetical order, and just as I was about to make a mental belch, I glimpsed a shadowy figure ducking out from the audience and through the gym doors. I could tell by his uneven shoulders and his purposeful gait that it was my friend Lazarus Greene.

It should have been him giving this speech instead of me and my mouthy maritime metaphors. What a louse I was to have added the third strike against him. (The first was the color of his skin, and the second was his above-average intelligence, which landed him in the small honors classes with the uppity college-bound white girls, not to mention the president's scholarship to the University of South Carolina, where he would be come fall.)

Lazarus and I did go to the senior dance, and we had a great time swaying to the tunes of Liquid Pleasure and gawking at the slutty gowns and creepy tattoos our classmates sported. But he wasn't at school on Monday, and when he came back on Tuesday, he moved to the back of the English class and avoided me. I figured Averill and his mill village thugs must have threatened him. I'd known he was moving to Norfolk the next week because of his daddy's port transfer, but he didn't bother to say good-bye. And I hadn't heard from him since.

The last joke of the day was on Averill Skaggs when the local newspaper called a handful of graduates back for the class superlative announcements and a photo shoot for the front page of the *Williamstown Times.*

Jif was voted Best All Around, along with the popular black basketball point guard, Cedric Gibbes, who had a scholarship to Clemson come fall.

I was selected for Most Likely to Succeed (though it would have gone to Georgianne if she'd been here), and what should have been Lazarus's went to the dullest crayon in the box, Averill Skaggs.

When the vice principal named him Most Likely to Succeed, Cedric laughed out loud and slapped his diploma on his knees in disbelief. Jif smirked and I guffawed, and Averill looked this way and that like a trapped bobcat on center stage as the clueless newspaper photographer took him by the elbow tip and led him over to where I was already sitting beneath the lights in front of a Williamstown Dolphins backdrop. He bit his lip and flicked a piece of gray fuzz off his crudely tattooed forearm as the photographer asked him to take a seat.

"Y'all are next," the photographer said as he set up the tripod and held a tinfoil board over the camera. I waited for what seemed like whole minutes for Averill to insult my speech or poke fun at my jewel. First, I avoided eye contact and stared down at his metal-tipped boots. Then out of curiosity I tried to make out the image on his arm, which was supposed to be some sort of web with skulls in the center, but looked more like a crooked tic-tac-toe board with blurred X's and O's.

Still, he said nothing.

I cleared my throat, and the question came to the tip of my tongue before I even had a chance to resist it. "So where are you going to be come fall, Averill?"

I didn't exactly know where that was going to be, but I guessed that at best it was the North Myrtle Beach Technical College, and something in me wanted to make him say it.

He wiped his arm across his nose and said, "Forget this." He had not yet looked me in the eye, and now he stood up nonchalantly and walked away from the backdrop, thumping the camera on its tripod before trotting down the stage stairs.

As he tucked his diploma somewhere beneath his gown, my face reddened with a mixture of guilt and satisfaction. Mama always told us two wrongs don't make a right, but she also said I was a chronic stirrer of the pot.

"Mr. Skaggs?" the photographer called out to him in disbelief. "We haven't taken the photo yet."

Averill turned back long enough to give him the classic bird right in front of Principal Dingledine and Vice Principal Chalmers, then kept walking toward the shaft of light from the open gym door.

"What's with *him*?" Jif said, blotting her pink lips on a Kleenex after I said "college" four times into the camera.

"I don't know. Guess he was picked as a gag."

"Ya think?"

"Yeah." I shrugged. "That, and I asked him where he would be next year."

Jif watched the shadow of her profile as we walked off the stage before turning to me.

"Don't you know what he's doing, Adelaide?"

"Nope."

"He's working at the steel mill, Miss Rivers of Convergence. Third shift."

"Ouch," I said. My cheeks reddened, but it was only from guilt this time.

Sure, I had wished Averill Skaggs to Hades more than once in my life, but shoveling coal into that furnace every day seemed the grimmest fate on earth. Not to mention dangerous. Two men had been killed there in the last nine months. One was actually incinerated in the fire after passing out from the heat. I had written a poem about it. About the man's very cells floating over our city, settling in the oak trees and the slate roofs and the salt marsh.

Jif and I walked out into the gravelly parking lot where the asphalt had been chewed up by the Friday afternoon drag races and the roots of some grand live oak trees that refused to be tarred over. It was a glorious Sunday morning. The mills were closed, and there was no black smoke or rotten-egg stench settling over the town.

Out of the corner of my eye, I saw Daddy and Papa Great waiting for me by Mae Mae's white Cadillac (anyone over fifty with two dimes to rub together drove a Cadillac). She, Juliabelle, and Mama had scurried home to get things ready.

"See you in a little while," Jif said as she fluttered to her car, letting the hot wind open her gown so that her short floral sundress billowed out above her tanned knees.

"There's my valedictorian!" Daddy said, waving me over to them. He had recently been fitted for a prosthetic, and he looked like all the other fathers today, his arms filling out the sleeves of his seersucker suit.

"Not exactly," I said.

It was awfully humid, as usual, and Papa Great was patting his forehead with a yellowed handkerchief before loosening his suspenders.

"Let's go," he said to me as he tucked his handkerchief into the back pocket of his orange linen pants.

At best, I puzzled him. Like a doe that runs into an open field at dusk, even though a shot has been fired in the distance. At worst, I was the symbol of his life's greatest disappointment—no grandsons to keep the mill going after Daddy's generation.

"Going to bite the hand that feeds you?" he had said my sophomore year, slapping the state newspaper with my poem in front of me one Sunday. "I'm going to jerk a knot in your tail next time you pull a stunt like this, young lady.

"Mouthy girl," he whispered before storming out of the dining room. "Juliabelle! Bring me mine in front of the television!"

Now a screech from the back of the parking lot made me jump, and when I made a visor over my eyes, I could see that it was Averill Skaggs hot-wheeling around in his jacked-up pickup truck. He hurled full speed toward us and our Cadillac, and I could see that his gown was off and he had donned a gray work suit with a name patch beneath the left collar. A steel-mill uniform.

"I am so proud of you, I could burst," Daddy said, hugging me tightly, oblivious to the truck as my eyes met Averill's from behind the windshield. If my football legend/Vietnam vet father had not been holding me, he might have run right over me, but instead he took a hard right just before us and flew out of the parking lot.

"What the heck?" Papa Great looked over his shoulder to see what the screech was about. The smell of burned rubber seemed to sting his nose, and he shook his head as Daddy turned to him.

"Now, come on, Papa—didn't I tell you this girl would do good?"

Papa Great snorted and tried to think up a compliment while I watched Averill's truck disappear beyond the curve. "Sure she did," he said to Daddy, opening the driver's side door. "Now let's get to that brunch Mae Mae has been planning all week before your uncle Tinka eats all the deviled eggs."

"All right," Daddy said, knocking his plastic hand on the hood of the Cadillac. But he couldn't dim his pride. "It was something, though, Papa. My gal got Most Likely to Succeed too!"

It had taken only a moment for the hot sun and the humidity to take their toll, and I could already feel a ring of perspiration forming under my turquoise gown as I opened the back car door.

"Get in!" Papa Great said.

While the Cadillac spewed out its smoke of cold air into the backseat, I spotted a red-tailed hawk landing on a live oak limb at the edge of the school gates.

I pulled my folder close to my chest and pictured Averill shoveling coal as I nibbled on shrimp and deviled eggs.

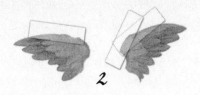

# Rattlesnakes and
# Brunch at Mae Mae's

There were only three places to eat in Williamstown. There was Ryan's Restaurant with the mega bar, McDonald's with the Big Mac, and the run-down country club where I once found a cockroach in my fruit salad. So Mae Mae invited the family and some of my closest friends over for a graduation luncheon.

She and Juliabelle had been polishing silver and dusting off the crystal all week. The fine linens had been pressed, the shrimp had been peeled, and the house was decorated with beautiful homemade flower arrangements—pale pink roses, Queen Anne's lace, and greenery from the garden—in a variety of silver urns.

Mae Mae and Papa Great's house was next to ours, divided only by thirty yards and a wall of pittosporum shrubs. There was a well-worn footpath between the two properties, with an opening between the branches big enough for Daddy's shoulders to plow through. The two homes (which had been in Mae Mae's family since the 1870s) were at the end of the historic district, overlooking the salt marsh and a narrow creek that poured into the Williamstown Harbor, where shrimp boats and barges of steel and paper made their way out to sea.

We had a piddly crab dock barely big enough for one hammock because the creek was really shallow on our end, but Papa Great and

Mae Mae had a large covered dock with rocking chairs and a floating dock for their boats and for us girls to sunbathe on while dipping our fingers into the dark water.

One morning when I was sunbathing at the edge of the floating dock, the splash from a pelican dive left a cool spray on my shoulder, and I thought this wasn't such a bad place to cocoon. And I often walked through the shrubs and over to my grandfolks' to watch the pelicans dive for food and hear about the grand old days of Mae Mae's ancestors, whose Carolina Gold rice provided a beautiful life of culture and refinement that this country has not matched since.

One dead-and-gone native son and state poet laureate, Archibald Rutledge, said every life has its azaleas and its razorbacks. The bygone era's razorback was slavery, which every thinking person around here knows is wrong, but its azalea was an unspoken code of chivalry and honor among the plantation pioneers, and I loved to imagine those grand plantation dinners where men like Thomas Lynch Jr. mustered up the courage to sign the Declaration of Independence and Francis Marion pieced together the ragtag militia.

Another local planter and colonel of the continental army, Christopher Gadsden, designed the "Don't Tread on Me!" flag with a rattlesnake poised to strike the British, who would not let our New World be. Mae Mae and Papa Great flew that flag from the end of their saltmarsh dock each Independence Day, and we ate watermelon and hot dogs beneath it and thanked God for men with more guts than sense.

Ever wonder if you were born in the wrong place or the wrong time? Sometimes I did. Williamstown in the mid-eighteenth century would have been my first choice of places to live. I would have secretly left food out for the Swamp Fox in my kitchen or hosted George Washington on his tour of the South.

∿

Mama ran out from the kitchen with her apron tied around her beige linen suit. Her hands were white from flouring the biscuits.

"Are you exhausted, darling?" she asked with a light embrace. "Your daddy was so proud, I thought he was going to pop the button on his suit!"

"I feel good," I said, accepting a mimosa my sister Dizzy brought over to me.

Dizzy was a sophomore at Williamstown High and a dedicated member of the Goth fringe set, but today Mama had forced her to wear a blue sundress, and she looked good despite her dyed black hair and ghastly white makeup.

My baby sister, Lou, was growing up too. Already in the sixth grade and sporting her first bra. She hugged me tightly and rested her head on my chest. Her speech impediment kept her from talking at the speed of her mind.

"R-r-really. G-good, Ad!"

The back garden looked beautiful. There were five round tables draped in fine linens and decorated with flowers in crystal vases, silver, and gilded china.

Uncle Tinka, the black sheep of the family (who refused to go to Vietnam or marry or work for Papa Great), came up to hug me.

"You brought down the house today, sister. Don't tell Papa Great, but I think you're the smartest member of the family."

I pushed his shoulder. "Go on."

"Now I'm going to put you to work for me—after I hog-tie the old coot," he said.

Uncle Tinka, a car mechanic by trade, was going to town with a new network marketing business called Bizway, and he was trying to talk Daddy into going in with him, though Papa Great had made it clear his textile job would be in jeopardy if he even considered such a thing. Mama had said, "You know better than to ruffle your daddy's feathers, Zane."

I craned my neck to look for Juliabelle and Mae Mae, who had put on this exquisite spread. I was so thirsty that I downed my mimosa and went inside to find them.

Mae Mae kissed me on the cheek as Juliabelle put a pan of her buttery biscuits in the oven. Mama had harvested the first of her homegrown tomatoes of the season and had sliced them up on a big silver platter with a dollop of mayonnaise on top of each one. The smell of sautéed shrimp and hominy grits filled the kitchen, and it was all I could do to stay away from the two large skillets on the stove.

"Don't even talk to us right now. We've still got work to do," Mae Mae said.

Juliabelle laughed and looked up at me with a wink as she closed the oven door. She had sat between my daddy and Mae Mae when I gave the graduation speech, and I hoped she was proud of me.

"Go freshen up, upstairs in my powder room!" Mae Mae added. "Your cousins are ravenous, so we've got to act fast."

The bathroom window was open and overlooking the party, so I gazed out and onto the garden before I sat down at the vanity to re-apply my lipstick. Below me Daddy was pouring mimosas with his new metal pinchers, and Uncle Tinka was taking my cousins down to the dock to check the crab traps. Mama was setting her homemade strawberry preserves on the tables to go with the biscuits, and my sec-ond cousin Randy was talking to Jif and her snobbish Charleston boyfriend, boring them with Gamecock football trivia, no doubt. He hadn't made the team this year, but he would be trying again for next.

Papa Great and Dizzy were right below the bathroom window, rocking on the chairs of the back piazza.

"Well, my big sis pulled it off, didn't she?" I could hear Dizzy say. We were often at odds, but we were united in that we liked to show Papa Great he had a skewed vision of the gender divide.

"Yeah," he said. "A fresh start up at college will do her good, I believe." I hid behind the drapes to listen as he leaned in toward my sister and said, "Sometimes I wondered why she never went on a date with a boy."

"Slim pickings, I suppose," Dizzy said. "Ad's a little picky, you know?"

"Yeah," he said, puckering his lips in concern. "Sometimes I wonder if maybe she's one of those who likes other girls, you know?"

"*What?*" Dizzy said before giggling in disbelief.

"You know," Papa Great said, gaining strength, "what do you kids
call it—a lesbian, right?"

"Adelaide, a lesbian?" Dizzy said. "I don't think so, Papa Great."

And the fury rose up in my throat.

*Dern if that hog nose isn't trying to burst my bubble at the loveliest
gathering I have ever attended.*

I almost stuck my head out the window to spit down on him or
to say, "Have you ever heard of a thing called discerning taste?
Selectivity? And have you ever heard of a hottie named Luigi
Agnolucci? A prodigy violinist with the strongest, longest fingers
you've ever seen? I'm cocooning, for heaven's sake! Saving myself so I
can get the heck out of this hades hole you call home!"

But I didn't say a word. Instead, I rushed downstairs and stormed out
onto the back piazza and between their two rocking chairs. Then I
walked right over to my second cousin Randy, who was pretending to
throw a football, and I grabbed his face and kissed him hard on the lips,
tongue and all, before wiping my mouth with one of Mae Mae's linen
napkins and dropping it in Papa Great's lap.

He patted it against his wet forehead and said, "Well, that answers
that."

Dizzy laughed at my response. "Since when did your ears become
bionic, Adelaide?" she asked as I ran back into the house and up the
stairs to reapply my lipstick.

Dizzy. If I was a pot stirrer, then she took the pot, shook it with all
her might, and hurled it in her victim's face. She had more gall than
me, and she drove Daddy crazy with her smoking and witch clothes
and poor grades.

But this was my day. And I decided not to let Papa Great or Dizzy
rattle my cage as I blotted my lips and brushed my thick brown hair
out of my eyes. I took off my gown and stared at my long white
sheath of a linen dress that hung from my knobby shoulders. I could

fit in Jif's snug miniskirts, and I could nearly fill out her strapless summer tops, so I suspected I must have a somewhat decent figure. I didn't have the blonde hair or the blue eyes, but I did have olive skin that browned in the summer, and Mae Mae said that when I pulled my hair back out of my face, I looked like her grandmother, for whom I am named—Adelaide Rutledge Graydon. Her parents were building her a lovely spinster home (which is now our house) on the harbor next to theirs when she surprised everyone by accepting a wedding proposal from a French portrait painter who was working for her family, and she left Williamstown for a beautiful life of travels across America before settling in Paris and painting her own cityscapes. The house is called "The Spinster" in all of the Low-Country tourist books, and occasionally we have a busload of vacationers peering into our back garden or snapping a photo of the jasmine that frames our wraparound porch with its sweet white blooms each spring.

Adelaide Rutledge Graydon's elegant debutante portrait hung over the sofa in Mae Mae's living room, and I hoped I would possess a remnant of her grace and beauty next Christmas when I performed the ritual of curtsying before the Camellia Club in her long white gown (which was wrapped in yellowed sheets at the back of Mae Mae's closet).

Making one's debut was one of the last remnants of the refined society that once existed in Williamstown. Ever since I was a child, Mae Mae had told me about the importance of the ritual of a young lady being presented to society, and I was not about to miss a chance to be acknowledged as a local treasure who was crossing the threshold into womanhood.

The brunch was divine, despite the heat, the no-see-um bugs, and Randy's following me around the rest of the afternoon like a puppy dog. Toward the end of the party, he ambled out to the dock where Jif, Dizzy, and I were sharing a platter of lemon squares and a glass of

champagne as we dipped our toes in the dark water and watched a
school of mullet break the surface of the outgoing tide.

"Beep," said Jif. "Drooling cousin. Nine o'clock."

Randy slipped off his loafers, sat down beside me, and put his arm
around my waist to draw me close.

"No offense, Randy," I said, stiffening, "but we're cousins."

"Second cousins," he said.

"*Kissing* cousins," Dizzy added, kicking her feet so that a few drops
of dark water hit my shoulder.

And it was true; many folks in South Carolina did marry their second cousins. Heck, in this state, it was legal to marry your *first* cousin!

Anyhow, Randy had been smitten with me since the September I
turned thirteen and we harvested oyster bushels along the riverbank at
low tide. I nearly lost my bathing suit top while cutting away at the
shells with the tip of a shovel, and when I looked up to tie the string
back tighter, I thought he was going to keel over into the shell bank
in awe. He was fourteen and utterly stupefied over the recent changes
my body had undergone.

That night at the family oyster roast, he found a black pearl the size
of a pea inside his delicacy, and he gave it to me after holding it up in
the moonlight and whispering, "You are a pearl to me."

"I was just proving a point to Papa Great, okay?" I said to him now.
"Let's forget it happened. I didn't mean to send mixed messages."

Randy sighed and removed his arm, setting both hands on his
knees.

"I don't know why you didn't take that scholarship to Carolina," he
said, shaking his head. "We'd have a good time together."

Jif spit a sip of champagne out into the marsh and laughed through
her coughing fit. "Randy, if you haven't noticed, it's been Adelaide's
life purpose to get out of South Carolina."

"Yeah, didn't you hear her speech today?" Dizzy said. "She's *ocean-*
bound."

"I don't understand why," he said, looking me in the eye. He
motioned to the harbor, where the sunlight was dancing on the water

as a sailboat let the hot breeze and the outgoing tide carry it toward the sea. (Randy had just bought his own boat earlier in the summer and, like a good Southern boy, named it after his mama.)

"Now, what could be better than this?" he said.

On one level, Randy was right. The harbor on a summer Sunday was more than picturesque; it was like a Low-Country Eden with porpoise fins lifting up out of the water and herons perched on the green marsh banks. But if you looked back toward the city and the drums of the furnaces and the black smog of burning coal and molten iron, you might as well have been in a wasteland.

Now, Randy loved his home. He was an avid hunter and fisherman and an active church member, and he had just finished his freshman year at Carolina. So I didn't want to snub the place where he would surely build a decent life. But I knew this much was true: if you wanted to get out of Williamstown, you had to leave the godforsaken state; otherwise, it pulled you back into its forceful, homespun grasp. The kids who went to the University of South Carolina always came back home to do their laundry and eat their mama's rice and gravy, and before they knew it, they were trapped, falling in love with some girl down the street and working in her daddy's mill for the rest of their lives. But the ones who went off to school, especially in the direction of the Northeast, escaped, and they rarely came back to stay.

"I want to see what's beyond here," I said. "I mean, Randy, don't you ever wonder?"

"Not so much," he said, nodding up the intracoastal waterway. "There's more to explore in this thirty-mile radius than I could ever get to—barrier islands, rice fields, the swamp . . . Heck, you could fill books of poetry with what's around you. Right?"

"Well, maybe, but I want to go away. I just know it's best for me."

"Oh, I hope they pluck *me* from the waiting list," Jif chimed in with a whine. She wanted to go to NBU, too, but as it stood, she was headed to Clemson. "I mean, can you see me dodging cow patties and sporting orange?"

I laughed at her dilemma, kicked my feet, and splashed everyone in the process.

Randy cupped his hands with dark water and sprayed Jif and me. "Just what my cousin needs. Encouragement."

Then he splashed us both so hard that a streak of dark water and mud stained our dresses. "You two snobs don't know what you're missing here."

"Spare us, Randy," Jif said, dabbing her sundress with a napkin. "You know, you really ought to work for the state tourism department." Then she splashed him back, and so did Dizzy, and before I knew it, we had all toppled into the water and were coated with pluff mud. I even lost my sandal in the dense, dark marsh, and a blue crab snapped at my pinkie toe before Randy lifted us one by one back onto the dock.

When we walked into the garden, Uncle Tinka was writing out a Bizway chart for Daddy, looking up every so often to make sure Papa Great was still snoozing in the rocking chair.

Then Juliabelle met us with the hose.

"And just when you think they've gone and got some sense," she said before spraying us down.

After we folded up the tables and piled up the linens, Juliabelle stopped me on the back piazza with a small box tied in one of Mae Mae's perfect white ribbons. She had taken off her apron and looked very elegant in the peach suit with pearl buttons her cousin had lent her and with her hair pulled back tightly in a braided bun on the top of her narrow head. At graduation she had stood out in the audience in a white hat with white feathers that swayed in the draft from the air conditioner.

"You made the grade real good," she said, holding my chin up with her long, skinny fingers. "Here's somethin' worth totin' on your journey."

When I slid back the ribbon and snapped open the gray velvet box, I saw a silver medal of St. Christopher carrying the Christ child across the churning waters. After I read the words inscribed on the outer rim, "And Go Your Way in Safety," I reached up and squeezed her long neck so hard that her pointed chin left a red mark on my shoulder.

Other than the childhood picture I had stolen from Mae Mae, it was the first tangible thing I had of Juliabelle.

"Thank you, thank you, thank you," I said as she laughed her quiet laugh and hugged me back.

"You know I'll make the prayer for you, my Adelaide. I'll be here making it every time you come to mind."

She watched me as I carried my bags of gifts and a bouquet of flowers through Mae Mae's flower garden and the shrubs and over to my house, where the backyard was littered with plastic lawn chairs, an abandoned playhouse, and fiddler crabs crawling sideways in and out of their holes along the mud banks. We didn't have a gardener like Papa Great and Mae Mae did, so the kudzu was always threatening to swallow our yard, and Daddy fought it every few months with an array of chemicals as it crept toward the tomato vines and the dock.

Now I put down my stuff in the dirt by the playhouse and walked out to the mildewed hammock at the end of the crab dock and swung myself out over the creek, smelling the ripe tomatoes and the fishy low-tide mud as the sun baked me dry.

That night I flipped through my NBU course catalog and highlighted the literature and philosophy classes I planned to take come fall. Josiah Dirkas, a prizewinning poet I'd studied at Governor's School, was going to be the writer-in-residence there, and I was going to do all in my power to finagle my way into one of his upper-level workshop courses. If I could get my chapbook in front of him, maybe he would let me in.

The phone rang, and when I answered, I was surprised to hear the familiar voice on the other end of the line.

"You did good today," he said.

"Lazarus! I saw you! It should have been you, not me."

"Nah," he said. "It should have been Georgianne, but things happen, and you sure pulled it off."

"Why didn't you tell me good-bye?"

"I didn't want to bring trouble on you. You know, Skaggs and all."

"Did he threaten you after the dance?"

"Tried to," he said. "But it didn't bother me. Taught me something, though."

"What?"

"I don't want to go to school down here. I mean, Adelaide, they still fly the Confederate flag over the statehouse, you know? I turned down my scholarship, and I'm moving up to DC. to live with my uncle who teaches at Howard University. He's got some contacts at Georgetown, and he thinks he can get me into their journalism program."

"You'll do great, Lazarus. You deserve every shot at what you want. I'll look you up if I head up to DC. It's only a few hours from NBU."

"I hope you will," he said. "You're my friend, and you're going to find the answer to those two questions you posed today."

"You think?" I said.

"One way or another," he said before he hung up the phone with a final "Take care."

~

The next morning, I jumped up, kicked on my slippers, and raced downstairs to see the class superlative photos in the paper.

But when I opened the front door, it was to see a bird hanging in a noose from the front gutter and what looked like human feces on the newspaper that was open on the doormat. Someone had added horns and a beard to my photo in the class superlatives. And scrawled across the column in black marker was the familiar sentiment, "Pipe down, Piper!"

I wasn't all that surprised by the cruel prank, but I couldn't keep my heart from speeding up, and before I knew it, the hot tears were coming.

"What's wrong?" Daddy said as he shuffled down the hallway, half asleep and perplexed by my weeping.

When he got to the door, he saw what had happened and closed it shut before pulling me into his arm.

"Put this out of your mind, gal. Just some jealous no-goods, is all."

Now, I should have known better than to poke a stick at Averill. Like the serpent on Gadsden's flag, he would strike if provoked. But I wanted to be a rattlesnake too. After all, it became the very symbol that united the colonies around their greatest asset: freedom. Then I remembered an old superstition Juliabelle had told me about: a snake that has been cut into parts can come back to life if you join the sections together before sunset.

And I couldn't help the poem that was forming in my mind . . .

*Piece me*
*back*
*together*
*as the day*
*fades,*
*and I will*
*twist away*
*before the dust*
*settles.*

3

# Off to College

$L$et's take the scenic route, gals," Daddy announced. His prosthetic hand swatted the carefully unfolded maps of North Carolina and Virginia out of Mama's grasp.

He was growing a rebellious streak as he entertained Uncle Tinka's new business venture, and we were beginning to learn it was sometimes best not to cross him. But I'd been waiting my whole life to get to college, and I couldn't stop myself from leaning across my two siblings to thump Mama's shoulder.

"Take the *scenic* route, Zane?" she inquired before collecting her highlighted interstates from the floorboard. I knew she had mapped out our route several days ago in preparation for taking me the 325 miles into the mountains of Virginia. She had even marked the rest areas on the highway where we might want to grab a Co-Cola and stretch our legs.

"With three daughters, someone *always* needs to go," she had said with a wink a few nights before while she ironed preprinted tags that read in a graceful cursive "This belongs to Adelaide Piper" into all of my underwear and T-shirts.

Mama. She worked herself silly for us girls.

"Oh, just live a little, Greta," Daddy said now with a boyish innocence as he squeezed her knee. "'Member that show we watched on PBS the other night? The one about the Blue Ridge Parkway? Heck, I think they said that it can take you all the way to Lynchburg. Now, don't you want to show these girls the beauty of the mountains where their big sister will be living and learning?"

"Humph," Mama said. She patted her brow with a handkerchief before twisting the knob that controlled the air conditioner, turning it up one notch and then another. Her shoulders tightened at his insistence of our new route, but he had been on a "let's do what *I* want for a change" kick since his secret meetings with Uncle Tinka, and I guessed she was deciding to choose her battles. The big one was coming, and she was stockpiling her strength for the day she'd say, "No way will I go along with this hoax of a new business, nor will I allow you to jeopardize the security of our three daughters."

And if I were a betting girl, I'd put my money on Mama.

Dizzy and Lou were already arguing over their space in the back of the station wagon. Without looking back, Mama opened the glove compartment, pulled out the masking tape, and handed it back to Dizzy, who unfairly marked off the space between them. Little Lou was so flustered that all she could do was cross her arms and purse her lips.

It was *really* hot, I began to admit to myself as my hair frizzed and my freshly applied makeup started to melt. Could something be wrong with the air conditioner? It groaned then sputtered every few seconds as if possessed by the morning heat of the Low-Country August. When Mama positioned the vents toward the backseat, the air covered me like a thick wool blanket. At this rate, I'd look like a greased pig by the time we hit Virginia.

Now, Daddy said I had an overactive imagination, but it helped me cope from time to time. So instead of patting my brow or watching the paper mill's smoke litter the sky, I pretended that I had an ejection button beneath my seat like the kind the fighter pilots have, and that I could press it and go flying out the top of the wood-paneled Country Squire station wagon, fly over the Blue Ridge Mountains, and descend gently onto the pristine quadrangle of Nathaniel Buxton University in a holler north of Roanoke, where the new life I yearned for could finally commence.

Ever since I'd received that acceptance letter and then an encouraging call from an upperclassman, I trusted that Nathaniel Buxton University on its high hill would end my longing for a raison d'être and fill the gaping hole in my heart.

Laughing over a Cherry Coke at Campbell's Pharmacy last spring, I had named it for Jif and Georgianne Mayfield: "It's like an itch—the itch of the soul."

"We *all* have that, Adelaide," Georgianne had assured me. "Every thinking person in the world has *that*!"

Then Jif concurred by charging three fashion magazines and candy bars on her daddy's credit card. "Here," she said, handing me a *Vogue* and a Snickers. "These give me temporary relief."

We all nodded in unison and spent the rest of our afternoon devouring the sweets and the gorgeous people who lined the glossy pages.

Now, without warning, little Lou, trapped in the middle, dodged a shove from Dizzy, and my chin caught the full impact of her sharp, eleven-year-old shoulder.

"Get *off* me, Lou," I said, my eyes narrowing toward Dizzy, the space miser and the perpetual destroyer of my peace. "Can't you make this an endurable ride, Diz? After today, you're not going to lay eyes on me until Thanksgiving, you know?"

"*Hallelujah!*" she shouted in a Juliabelle tone of voice, hands raised in an act of worship.

I chuckled as my fifteen-year-old wild child of a sister feigned a sudden interest in the rotting mill village that marked the outskirts of Williamstown. Dizzy had dressed in a black lace getup (much to everyone's dismay) for this road trip, and I could see the sharp kohl streaks around her eyes beginning to soften.

Dizzy scratched her itch with nicotine and rebellion, I thought to myself as I watched her finger the Marlboro Lights in her backpack. Daddy would have had a *fit* if he knew she had brought those along!

Then I paused to take my own last look at the mill village. The small shotgun houses were propped up on cinder blocks, with weathered cars in the dirt driveways and Confederate flags flying from nearly every third roof. One had suffered a recent fire, its marred shell of a home staring back at me like a black eye. I could not help but notice the melted cuckoo clock hanging on the singed wall or the wrinkled newspaper that was trapped beneath a sofa and lifted in a breeze as we drove past.

Next door to the burned-down house, I spotted a young woman with flat brown hair and dull eyes peering at me from the front window, and I shivered even in the August heat of the suffocating car when our eyes met.

"Good-bye, Williamstown," I muttered, and I might as well have said, "Good riddance!" Or "See ya; wouldn't wanna be ya."

I was over this sad Low-Country town that had entrapped me for eighteen years. I knew I'd be back this summer for the debutante teas and luncheons that Mae Mae's Camellia Club had planned, and I'd be back during the holidays from time to time. But in the end, I had my escape route: college two states away, and, as my uncle Tinka said at our family dinner last Sunday afternoon, "She'd be doggoned if she isn't going to take it!"

"M-M-Mom," Lou stammered between her standoff with Dizzy.

"Whatcha need?" Mama whipped her head around, her oversized purse poised to provide Lou with whatever she wanted: baby wipes, bottled water, chewing gum.

"It's kind of h-h-o-t," she said, rubbing her rich brown eyes. Though Lou was crossing the threshold of adolescence, she still had the most beautiful baby face I had ever seen—those chubby red cheeks and long black lashes. A grosgrain bow pulled her thick hair back, and her pretty little forehead glowed like one of those Madame Alexander dolls we all had collected over the years.

I would miss reading with Lou at night, trying to rehearse how it would go when Mrs. Spicklemeyer, the middle-school English teacher, called her name in the class and the other children snickered to see if she could make it through the next two paragraphs of the textbook. I jokingly called Lou's teacher "Mrs. Despicablemeyer" during our rehearsals, but this got Lou's tongue so twisted when she attempted to say it that she even laughed at herself.

I would miss curling up on opposite sides of the den couch with her, watching sitcoms and, occasionally, a teenybopper movie. I'd feel guilty every time a four-letter word made its way across the screen, and I'd say, "Now, Lou, don't you ever say that, okay?"

"I've heard them all from D-Dizzy, a-anyway," she'd answer, then, "Don't w-worry, I w-won't say them, Ad."

Now I pulled out my new journal and began to write poetry. This was one way to scratch the itch, and a marvelous method of escape. The journal was a graduation present from Shannon Pitts, that former best friend who went born-again Christian on me two summers ago at a Young Life retreat in Colorado. Shannon tenaciously evangelized even our most minor conversations, and it was downright wearisome.

"Thank God she chose the women's college in North Carolina," Jif had said, "so we can have a break from her!" Otherwise, every college question or problem would have been answered by her rote, Holy Roller lingo: "Give it to God . . . Take it to the Cross . . ." What in the world did *that* mean, anyway?

And what about this: Shannon talked about Jesus as if He'd just left the room. As if He had been sitting with us, drinking a Co-Cola, and walked to the kitchen to get some tortilla chips! I was bewildered by the nonchalance with which she referred to the Son of God. It was startling, if not irreverent. Who would dare to assume that they knew *Him* in such an *intimate* way?

Goodness knows *I* wasn't on a first-name basis with the guy. I'd heard about Him at the High Episcopal church my family attended, with a Communion that was more fashion show than sacred. I could remember praying when I was a young girl. I could even recall a kind of supernatural peace when I lay in bed at night and recounted my day

—the things I did right, the things I did wrong, and the things I would try to do right tomorrow. It was my own little litany of repentance, and it brought me a wonderful kind of lightness at the end of each day. But I gave it up somewhere around adolescence when my body changed and my mind raced and the itch gnawed away at me. Instead, I filled myself with schoolwork and poetry and crushes on teachers or upperclassmen who had a little something going on upstairs.

Nonetheless, it was nice of Shannon to notice how I spent my time these days—writing. No one else seemed to. I'd spent this last summer once again at the Governor's School at the College of Charleston, where my favorite professor, Penelope Russo, gave me fresh insight into my craft. I had learned from Penelope (she let us call her by her first name) that poems didn't have to rhyme or have punctuation and that short stories could transport you anyplace in the world: the streets of Harlem, a café in a Paris alleyway, or even a foxhole in Vietnam, where my own daddy lost his arm and two friends when a well-aimed grenade was hurled their direction.

Penelope Russo had taught me more than just the art of writing—she had taught me how to look within my heart and examine the itch. How to pin it under a microscope and probe at it with the point of a pencil. And for me to name what I longed for on paper provided some relief, and for that I was immeasurably grateful.

I scribbled down a poem as the wagon steamed up the foothills of the Blue Ridge, looking up every few minutes to see if I could lay eyes on the "You are now leaving South Carolina" sign.

> Good-bye Williamstown.
> Farewell gloom
> in the window
> of a mill village
> home.
> Every mile
> toward Virginia
> takes me closer

*to what has to be*
*my destiny.*

*Thank God they let us retake those SATs because of the noise of the elementary-school carnival last autumn,* I thought. On the second try, I had purchased those Kaplan books and stared at vocabulary words and algebra problems until I could hardly see straight. I raised my score 240 points, which opened a spot with a minor scholarship for me at NBU, the small and prestigious liberal arts college "nestled in the Blue Ridge Mountains," as the brochure boasted. Now I was bound for an institution that judges, senators, and Pulitzer prize–winning authors were proud to call their alma mater.

I'd had to do some fancy footwork to convince my parents that this was a better opportunity than the full scholarship I received to the University of South Carolina. I can remember walking the magnolia-lined brick path up to Papa Great and Mae Mae's front door for a change, to sit down in their living room and ask if they would further convince my parents by splitting the remainder of the tuition bill of my academic dream. Thankfully, the old pig considered it a good investment in family relations (i.e., another way to keep Daddy happy and working at the mill), and so they agreed to contribute. Sometimes I felt a tinge of guilt knowing this would hem Daddy in to his mill job another four years, but I was in claw-my-way-out mode, and nothing short of an act of God could stop me.

The Governor's School, fashion magazines, and MTV—these were my only vistas into what lay beyond Williamstown. I was a bug in a jar, and I was counting on NBU to take the lid off so I could fly. I could hardly wait to register for classes, to smell the insides of the hardbound books that would expand my horizons.

And there was more that I would experience, I was sure. I might even fall in love in college with a bright and cultured Mr. Right. That's how my parents met, in fact. My mama, a socialite from Charleston, yearning for a slice of what she called the "All-American Life" (which I had come to realize was just an amalgamation of Southern culture and small-town charm), had fallen in love with Zane Piper, the star tailback of the University of South Carolina football team, their sophomore year. (He was a kind of legend, even today, because the Gamecocks have not had as good a season since his class graduated more than twenty years ago. Sometimes people came right up to him on the streets and said, "You were the one who gave us the taste of victory, Zane." Or they honked and yelled, "Go, Gamecocks!" from their cars when he jogged along the interstate, his stump keeping time with his good arm.)

But I certainly wouldn't let romance knock me off track, as it had Georgianne Mayfield. Poor Georgianne, the honest winner of that valedictorian race of the Williamstown class of 1989, was about to give birth to her first child. She had been accepted at Princeton and Wellesley and even offered a full scholarship to Davidson, an above-average college in the right direction, but before she could make up her mind, she started feeling queasy in the morning and had to face the fact that her future would take a dramatically different turn.

It was Peach Hickman who had sucked my dear friend back into Williamstown with his good looks and his fifty-yard-line seats at the University of South Carolina football games. He was a junior at Carolina, but he came home every weekend, and Georgianne had thought it was so romantic the way he would pick her up on game days with a picnic basket filled with his mama's pickled okra and pimento cheese sandwiches. I tailgated with them on occasion in the corporate field where his daddy's tractor company was a sponsor. I did a lot of thumb twiddling and daydreaming as Peach and Georgianne threw the football back and forth and snuggled beneath the blankets when the temperature dropped.

Now Georgianne wouldn't be a scholar or a debutante. She'd married Peach Hickman just three weeks ago. Jif, Shannon, and I threw a bridal shower for her at the country club, and I cried tears of grief over her future with every Pyrex dish and cookbook that she unwrapped. I made such a scene that Georgianne pulled me into the powder room for a reprimand: "This is not a funeral, Adelaide. It's not even an original story, Miss Smarty-Pants Poet. You ought to know that much. Now, buck up and give me a little support here!"

I nodded to appease her, but to me Georgianne was living the worst nightmare I could ever imagine. I did not know how I would survive the stifling life of casseroles and dirty diapers that awaited her. Maybe it was a good thing that no boy at Williamstown High had ever asked me out.

Nobody in my class ever talked about sex. And no one's parents ever talked about it, and the school never talked about it, and neither did the church. So we were all clueless as to what it was all about and how a tragedy like this could sneak up on you unawares. I put it together—the mechanics of what actually happened between a man and a woman—in eighth grade after watching a *Little House on the Prairie* episode in which one of the town's girls was attacked by a man in a clown mask. It came to me like a great revelation at the end of the show, and I went and told Dizzy about how it must work. But, of course, she already knew all about it from a classmate named Angel who had spelled it out to her the summer before.

Not me. I would not succumb to this fate. In fact, if an NBU guy got the hots for me (and let me tell you, one had *better*!) I would keep him at arm's length until I knew where I wanted to go. I'd worked too hard to get caught in that old trap.

Yes, I was up for adventure, I longed for romance, and I wanted desperately to know the meaning behind the collage of terminology that spilled out of Penelope Russo's mouth: words like *postmodern, deconstructionists, existentialism,* or names like Kafka, Beckett, and Proust. I had to study Shakespeare—anyone who seemed remotely cultured was always quoting him. I had to read Virginia Woolf—heck, there was a whole play written about her! I had read it at Governor's School but had no idea what it was about.

What I did know was that there were mysteries all around me— and more than this, there were moments of downright splendor. Like when my daddy took me fishing in the Santee River by the old rice fields, and the sun set behind the cypress swamp, leaving a backdrop of red and orange, and the gnarled limbs of the oak trees reached up to the sky like open arms. Like when I found an abandoned kitten in the packing room at the mill and brought it home to our infertile house cat, Marmalade, whose breasts miraculously swelled with milk so that she could nurse him back to life.

And like the time I ate a bad oyster and my throat closed up so I could hardly breathe, and Juliabelle made Daddy drive me over to Berkeley County, where they carried me through the Francis Marion Forest and over to the artesian well by Huger Creek. Juliabelle filled an empty Co-Cola bottle with the water from the spigot, and when she handed it to me, she said, "Drink up. This is the tonic." When that cool underground water coated my throat, I swear I could breathe again.

The explanation of such splendor and more opportunities to experience them had to be in books and colleges and heated discussions in coffeehouses, and NBU had to be the place where my journey would begin.

Penelope Russo had applauded the poem I wrote a few weeks ago at the end of my summer session:

> There has to be more to this world
> than climbing the Williamstown water tower
> and drinking cheap, tasteless beer
> at the end of the frontage road.

She'd asked me to read it during the closing ceremony of Governor's School in the College of Charleston auditorium. It upset my parents that I looked as though I was a drinker and a water-tower climber when, in fact, I couldn't stand the taste of beer or anything other than champagne, and I was hardly the daredevil, tower-climbing type. But my parents didn't understand that you could write something from the heart even though it wasn't from your own personal experience. I had concluded that Zane and Greta Piper were, sad to say, unenlightened.

Now, I was no fool. I realized that one could not mention the splendor of this world without acknowledging the sadness.

Just a mile from my home, I had once wandered over to Cousin Randy's farm when cows were being slaughtered. I could see the bloodstained walls of the cinder-block building and the carcasses piled up behind the barn with flies swirling around them in their buzzing frenzy. The smell made me so weak in the knees that I swore off hamburgers for a year.

And once, when I was cleaning up a back road for a school service project, I saw a man hit a woman so hard that her lip bled. When he walked to his truck to leave, the woman chased after him, hugging and kissing him and begging him to come back inside their mobile home, which he did.

And what about the old car in the kudzu-covered woods behind my house? Dizzy and I had found it one morning when we were playing hide-and-seek. It looked like those first Model Ts. There was a spring popping out of the backseat cushioning, spiderwebs around the steering wheel, and a woman's black high-heeled shoe caught in the door handle. What made someone abandon a car like that? Did they win the lottery? Did they fall into the swampy quicksand? Or had they been swept up in a hurricane, their remains spread out across the marsh, only to be picked apart by the vultures I saw from time to time circling the sky?

> Definitive queries:
> Is there a point
> to my life?
> Am I missing it?
> Why so much brokenness
> and wonder all
> in the same place?
> Give me
> more,
> more
> splendor!
> And less

*of the cracked
and spoiled.*

The problem was, I could not shake the feeling that I was created for a reason. That I had a specific role to play on the stage of the world, as Shakespeare (I think) suggested. But what? I could reel in daydreams about it for hours. Was this God's hand on my life, as Shannon had once argued? I had not ruled out that possibility. But the ivory tower was where I was going to look first, and as I watched the nose of our car tilt toward the mountains, my heart delighted to know I was moving closer to it, mile marker by mile marker.

Oh, and I couldn't wait for my sweet reunion with Peter Carpenter, an NBU student from Williamstown, who had promised to show me around once the fraternity rush that he was directing was over. Peter was two years my senior and as responsible and bright as they come. He had tutored me in geometry when I was a freshman in high school, and I'd had a huge crush on him. I can remember his rugged hands with the ruler and protractor, marking off the angles and degrees of squares and triangles. I could see a pulse in the vein on the side of his neck and composed a little poem in my head while we worked.

*Peter Carpenter is so alive,
Look at his pulse,
His geometrical drive!*

Dizzy, sensing my crush, embarrassed me greatly by announcing during one of our lessons, "Sister says you're the best-looking guy in Williamstown!"

My face had lit up like a ripe tomato, but somehow, this moment sealed our friendship, and he always went out of his way to say hello to me on our summer breaks while he was mowing lawns or coaching the country-club swim team. He had even met with me and Daddy last October in the NBU snack bar after our campus tour. He bought us a Co-Cola and gave us pointers on my admissions interview while nodding out of the corner of his eye to an assortment of fraternity brothers and girls who meandered by, their backpacks hanging from one shoulder, their unwashed hair sticking up in all directions. I remembered wondering why they were all underdressed for the cold, whipping wind, in their tight midriff T-shirts and low-riding blue jeans. How I yearned to be one of them!

Now I had permed my hair just for Peter Carpenter, and I thought it looked nice despite Dizzy's reaction when I walked into the kitchen: "Figured you would have lost the poodle look by high school graduation."

But it was 1989 and the era of big hair in Williamstown, South Carolina, and I thought I would knock Peter Carpenter's socks off with my curls and bubble gum–pink lipstick. I had daydreamed about our meeting all during the summer. I could picture us studying together on the college colonnade on a sunny afternoon or throwing snowballs at each other across the quadrangle when winter set in. I had high hopes for Peter Carpenter and my college social life.

These daydreams willed me to eat sparsely during the last two weeks in an effort to drop a size. It had been painful to drink water instead of Co-Cola, and eat Special K instead of pancakes and bacon, but it was worth it. Poor Mama was distraught when I wouldn't touch her tomato pie or Mexican casserole (my all-time favorites) during my last night as a permanent resident under her roof. But I took one look at the grease rising from the ground beef and cheese, pinched my waist, and said, "No way, Mama." (Though late into the night, when everyone else was asleep except for my moaning belly, I snuck downstairs for a few cold bites of the leftovers and a bowl of Mama's delectable banana pudding.)

We'd been traveling awhile now, and I was still looking for that "You are now leaving South Carolina" sign. I wanted to put my eye on it.

I mean, South Carolina. Ugh. We're talking about a state where cockfighting is as common a crime as theft and where Strom Thurmond will never lose a senatorial election though the old geezer has made a pass at nearly every woman in the state. It's a world where blacks—and women, for that matter—are still secretly considered second-class citizens by some. There is a lingering prejudice that still has its hooks in the region. Ku Klux Klan descendants are still around—albeit tight-lipped. And the public education system ranks the lowest in the country.

Ah, but in her glory day she was a strong, feisty state. Standing up against the British and later the Union. Problem is, like an old lady with dementia, her rebel brand of courage seems to have perverted itself into a crusty pit of backwardness, and in a lot of ways she has failed to progress.

Except for making my debut, I didn't plan to come back. New York City is where I hoped to land. Mae Mae took me there when I was twelve, and I kissed the dirty sidewalk of Broadway and Lexington and said, "I'll be back!" before we hopped into a cab to go to the airport. In my mind's eye I was there, writing poem after poem on a dirty park bench in Washington Square about the Southern world from whence I came—its curse and its blessing. But, so help me God, I would no longer be *in* it.

Before I knew it, the station wagon had made its way up to the Blue Ridge Parkway, and I admired the gaping view of the valleys below while my ears popped from our ascent. There were cabins perched on the sides of the mountains and homemade signs for apple cider on the edge of the road. A mountain man was sitting on a wooden chair on the front porch of a run-down sweetshop at the top of a nearby hill. He stared through us at the clouds.

"It is burning *up!*" Dizzy shrieked before pulling the back of Mama's hair. "Ice Lady, *do* something."

"Zane," Mama said ever so gently as the wagon passed a sign that read "Welcome to the state of Tennessee." "It is a bit hot."

"Did that sign say Tennessee, Daddy?" I pointed out in horror.

"Heck no, darlin'," Daddy answered. But I knew he was

unreasonably optimistic and would not entertain the thought that we were headed up the parkway in the wrong direction.

It amazed me that after all he had lost, not one shred of doubt or pessimism entered his thoughts.

Zane Piper and Greta LeVan Wimmer had married in August 1968, two months after they graduated from the University of South Carolina. Zane had just signed a handsome contract with the Washington Redskins, but feeling a call to serve his country, he enlisted in the marines in September, and they shipped him off to Paris Island and then Vietnam, where he joined a reconnaissance group, some of whom had watched him play college ball on TV for years.

"Are you nuts, Piper?" Gil Galbraith, a fellow classmate, had asked him when their paths crossed on a base west of Chu Lai.

But while Uncle Tinka fled to Toronto to dodge the draft, Papa Great had greatly influenced Daddy's view of serving in the war. The Hog didn't serve in WWII because the Piper Mill made the fibers that went inside the military tires that served the war effort. And he deeply regretted not going over to the Pacific Theater. He had lost a brother and a cousin there, and somehow he was ashamed to stay in Williamstown making tires—coming home every night to Juliabelle's okra soup and pecan pie while his friends and brothers spilled their guts across the ocean to thwart the plans of the evil powers of the world.

When Daddy landed in the Boston airport on his journey home from Vietnam, he was shocked to see people his own age spitting on the troops as they walked through the gates. The antiwar protests had not yet reached the insulated life of Williamstown or the trenches of Than Khe, and he had no idea what their fury was about.

"They wouldn't spit on me, though," he had recalled to me count-less times on fishing trips off Pawleys Island and vacation drives to Myrtle Beach. He had given his arm and his football career to the war, and he reckoned their consciences wouldn't let them do that.

Anyhow, he told the Redskins he couldn't run the ball without an arm, and he took a job at the Piper Mill, where he pushed papers as a vice president and daydreamed about a life in which he didn't have to sit behind a desk and wear those uncomfortable coats and ties.

He would have loved to have been in sales, and I think that's why he was flirting with the idea of joining Uncle Tinka's Bizway venture. But Papa Great wouldn't have any part of his calling on businesses. My family was big-time in the little town of Williamstown, and Papa Great was grooming Daddy to be the president of the mill, though everyone knew that the Southern industry was dwindling as every sort of textile became cheaper to make overseas.

My daddy was bound by social status, parental control, and the limitations of only one working arm, but even with all these constraints, he was the most optimistic person I knew.

He could be happy and hopeful just sitting on our crab dock, drinking iced tea. He'd look around at one of his daughters or his petite, well-dressed wife and say, "We've got it good, don't we?" And then, "Let's go down to the Dairy Cream and get a sundae, just for the heck of it!"

"You're the one I'm countin' on," he'd told me a few nights ago beneath the fluorescent light of the kitchen. I had forgone an evening of hanging out with Jif and Georgianne to finish my *Catcher in the Rye* novel because Penelope Russo had referred to it countless times in Governor's School. To my disappointment, it was a fatalistic novel about the loss of innocence of a teenage boy, and I hoped that every book didn't depress me this way. The thought dawned on me, *Could Penelope Russo not know the meaning of life?* But I pushed it aside to listen to Daddy.

"Lou has learning problems, and Dizzy is as wild as a goat, Adelaide."

He shook his head and squeezed the top of my hand with his good arm. "Heck, I just want to get her to adulthood in one piece."

He looked me square in the eye without a blink. "But *you're* the one who is going to make it, sister. I can just feel it, you know?"

"Yes, sir," I said, and I wanted to believe him.

"Now, I know you like poems and that sort of thing, but you've

got to promise your old man that you'll pick a solid major and get a
job that can support your dreams: lawyer, doctor, you name it. You
can have it all, baby—work, family, and poems—but you've got to
get the solid stuff first, okay?"

"Yes, sir," I said, turning my hand palm up to squeeze his back.

"Thing about it, I never understood that when I was your age. All
I did was chase your mama and run the football, and it hurt me not
to pay more attention to my books." He tugged at his paisley tie to
indicate his failure. "You want to have choices."

"I understand, Daddy."

"I think you do," he said as he walked toward the den. "Now I'm
going to get your mama to help me put on my fatigues and relax."
(He could not unbutton his shirt without her help.) Then he turned
back once as I stared at my letdown of a novel, and he said, "I love
ya, sweetheart. And I'm pulling for you."

When I looked up, he had walked out of the room.

Now Mama, whom Dizzy had unfairly nicknamed "Ice Lady,"
handed each of us a cup of ice from the minicooler at her feet before
consulting her map.

Her nickname came a few years back when she handed out icy
treats at the Williamstown children's charity run. She stood at the
corner of Main and Mill Street and gave Dixie cups of sweet crushed
ice and frozen orange slices to the participants as they flew past.
There was a picture of her on the front page of the state paper that
was in town to cover the event.

"If it weren't for that ice lady," one of the runners said, "I wouldn't
have made it to the finish line."

And there was a letter to the editor that read, "Thank you, ice
lady!" and recounted one overheated woman's blurred vision during
the race, cured only by the sweet, icy oranges that a lovely lady in a
large straw hat handed to her at the busiest intersection in town.

But while I refused to call her by the nickname, I could see the
second truth in it. Greta LeVan Piper was emotionally distant somehow. I couldn't remember her ever spontaneously hugging one of
us—or Daddy, for that matter. And she didn't shower us with kisses

or "I love yous" the way I saw some mamas do. Now, I knew we were her very life, but she showed it to us by what she *did* for us. Works of service—that was her love language.

"You have to admit she's kinda frigid," Dizzy had said to me one afternoon when Daddy coaxed Mama to an overnight in Myrtle Beach to attend a Bizway meeting. She didn't want to go, and she was terrified that Papa Great might find out what they were up to. When she was leaving, she couldn't bring herself to kiss us good-bye, not even Lou, who had been stung by a bee on her top lip that afternoon. "Oh, girls," she'd said, wringing her tough little hands. "I've made you spaghetti and a salad, and you can call Juliabelle if you need anything."

"Loosen up and have some fun at MB, Mom!" Dizzy said.

"Yeah," I said, putting my arm around Lou. "Take a walk on the beach and pretend you're on vacation."

Mama shook her head in dismay and walked through the door, head down, before muttering, "Bye-bye."

Now, I suspected that Mama had a story and a half to tell if she could ever get the words out. She was raised mostly by a nanny named Rosetta in the thick of Charleston high society. Her aristocratic mom was prone to nervous breakdowns, and her daddy, a famous German physician at the medical university, didn't pay her much mind. Mama hated even going back to the "Holy City" and asked me to take Zane to his doctor's appointments at the veterans hospital. She said that the Charleston skyline, with all of those steeples stabbing the clouds, just made her stomach turn.

Mama was also a master escape artist, and she had taught this craft to me, which I honed through my poetry and excessive daydreams. When my allergies flared up during childhood and I scratched the backs of my knees until they bled, Mama calmed my nerves by saying, "Imagine you are somewhere else, sweetheart. An opera singer on a stage, or a mermaid in a deep-sea cave." And I could *do* it; I could nearly escape the present and go somewhere else in my mind. What a wonderful trick to be transported like that!

Once, during my third-grade bedtime routine, I asked her, "What is heaven like?" in expectation of a great imaginative journey. To my surprise, Mama stood gulping back tears and said, "I don't know. No one ever told me about it." Then she scurried out of the room, sending Daddy in to kiss me good night.

Mama was an orphan in a sense, and she did all in her power not to make the same mistake with us. The dedication with which she approached her role as mother ranked head and shoulders above that of the other moms in town. She was always the first in line to pick us up from school. The napkins in our lunch boxes had stickers or smiley faces on them each day, along with a thought: "I am thinking about you!" Or "Smile!" Or "I love you." (It was much easier to write it.)

Motherhood was the role she had always wanted. Domesticity was her territory, from the tomato vines to the laundry room, and she claimed it as best she could.

Maybe that's why Juliabelle was in my life. She was a widow, and she didn't have any children or grands of her own, and she never saw me that she didn't cup my face and tell me that she loved me.

~

"I'm afraid Adelaide's right, Zane," Mama said now while he forcefully turned the air-conditioner knobs and held out his plastic hand over the vents as though the cold, hard machinery of his prosthetic could feel the hot air.

He pulled reluctantly over on the side of a mountain and puttered into a run-down Exxon station. After a few minutes of conversation with the gas station manager, he bounded back to the car, shaking his head in defeat.

"Well, we went up the parkway in the wrong direction, and we're in Goodloe, Tennessee."

"Good grief!" Dizzy shouted. She maniacally caressed the cigarettes in her backpack with the tips of her black-painted nails and asked to go to the bathroom. Daddy gave her one stern look because he knew what she was up to.

"If I ever catch you with one of those in your mouth, I'll tan your hide, Dizzy! Now, hand 'em over!"

She pulled out a half-empty pack of cigarettes, and he snatched them with his good hand and threw them in the trash can behind him.

"You might think you're a renegade," he said to her angry eyes, "but I'll have you tamed yet, and we can do it the hard way or the easy one. That much of it is up to you, sister."

No one moved for a few seconds so that his point could sink into her hard head.

Then Lou whimpered, "Can I g-get a Co-Co-Cola, Daddy?"

"Me too!" Dizzy added, taking her eyes away from his.

"Okay. Co-Colas and Nabs for everyone; then we've got to head back down the mountain and get on the interstate if we're going to get Adelaide to her convocation on time." And then he added, "If the air-conditioning is broke, no one at this place can fix it, so I need y'all to press on without it."

Back down the parkway we went, with Mama reorganizing her maps so that we could make up the lost time on the interstate. Daddy and my sisters were quiet, enjoying the sweet, dark bubbles and peanut-butter crackers that rolled down their throats. When we crossed over into Virginia, I marveled at the runaway truck ramps on our way through the mountains. Could a truck get going so fast that it needed a runaway ramp to slow it down? I scribbled this notion down in my journal as a metaphor for a future poem.

Dizzy was like a runaway truck, speeding out of control by way of drinking and smoking and dressing in funeral attire, and Daddy would step up to serve as the ramp that she needed to stop her in her tracks.

As for me, I was still a parked truck that had never left the lot. Sure, I'd had my minor run-ins with Averill and the no-goods and my romantic night with Luigi Agnolucci, but all in all, my life had been mostly uneventful. I had a tank full of gas, but what I needed was for someone to turn the ignition key and get me rolling. Surely college would lift the heavy speedometer needle of my boring life above the 0.

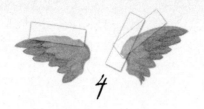

# 4

## Orientation

A handsome, towheaded boy met us with a clipboard as we entered the campus gates. The grounds were lush and manicured, and the air was refreshingly crisp. Nathaniel Buxton University transcended the August heat, and the cool air that spilled through the open car windows left goose bumps on our arms and legs.

We looked like the Griswolds with the full-sized storage box on top of the station wagon and our carload of frowning faces. I could see the boy grimace as Daddy awkwardly put out his left hand (the good one) to say, "I'm Zane Piper, young man."

"Bo Hagerty, student council vice president," he responded before glancing in to pick me out of the group.

"Brought the whole family with you?" he said with a half grin, his straight white teeth standing out against his tan skin. He looked as if he had spent the summer on a beach.

He scanned down his list until he found my name. "You're on the third floor of Tully, Miss Piper." Then he pointed the way around the bend to the freshman dormitory.

"Thank you," I called from the backseat, but he was already talking to the inhabitants of a sleek Range Rover that had pulled up behind us. (He was *so* not South Carolina!)

"Bo Hagerty is Beauregard," I said to Dizzy with a thump on her knee as we made our way around the bend. We had always been able to find a common ground when it came to good-looking boys.

"If you like the preppy, stuck-up type," she said, still licking her wounds from the Exxon episode. She seemed envious of my pending escape.

"Look at it this way, Diz: you and Lou will have the whole backseat to yourselves on the way home. You could practically stretch out and sleep."

She shrugged, then couldn't help but gawk at the beautiful green campus that opened up before us, its weeping willows and oaks waving us in. NBU was on the edge of the quaint valley town of Troutville, and beyond the campus gates and the three-block town, there were rolling hills with pastoral vistas of barns and silos and cows grazing on patches of emerald. Rising up above the hills were the colossal Blue Ridge Mountains that surrounded us as far as the eye could see.

Daddy lifted his hand out the window to feel the cool air.

"Isn't this something, girls?"

Mama cooed in agreement as we passed the colonnade and the quadrangle with its bright red bricks and Corinthian columns. A bearded professor in a stereotypical tweed jacket stopped to chat with a circle of students who were tossing a hacky sack. And a girl with a golden retriever at her feet napped on a rocking chair in the center of the quad.

"Adelaide, I think these mountains are like wise sages calling you to learn, baby!" Daddy said.

"I guess so," I said with a chuckle. He was poetic in a Geechee sort of way, and so I had him to thank for that gene.

"This ought to be an incentive to get those grades up, Dizzy," he added. It was an untimely remark that hit below the belt.

Dizzy flicked a Nabs wrapper onto the floorboard and rolled her eyes. At this rate, she'd be lucky to get into Myrtle Beach Technical College, and we all knew it.

"Don't hold your breath, Daddy dearest."

Thankfully, I knew my roommate, Ruthie Baxter from Gastonia,

North Carolina. We had shared a cabin together at Camp Greystone a few summers in a row and had set out to room with each other when we found out we had both been accepted.

And good old beauty queen Jif had gotten her wish: she had been plucked from the NBU waiting list and would forgo her Clemson scholarship to join me in the class of 1993.

Now another strapping upperclassman with his hair pulled back in a ponytail, of all things, met us at the steps of the dormitory and helped Daddy carry in the luggage. *This place is extremely organized,* I thought as the Range Rover pulled in behind us and another boy ran out to grab its belongings.

Out of the corner of my eye, I could see some sort of demonstration going on at the rear of the quadrangle. I saw a map that read "Beijing," and a gravestone that read "For the thousands killed in Tiananmen Square," and thousands of plastic forks were sticking up from the ground with different names inscribed on them. *Where is Tiananmen Square, anyway?* I thought to myself. I had become so engrossed in my literature that I was certainly not up on current events. *It must be somewhere in Asia.*

Intimidation crept up on me like a rash. Was I already in over my head? Was I country-come-to-town even in my first hour on campus? I had to remember that just because I was near the top of my class in Williamstown didn't mean my chops were up to some of the sharpest kids from around the country.

Upperclass girls from the NBU Student Wellness Committee greeted me at the foyer with a pink care package that included bubble gum, Band-Aids, Tylenol, an instruction manual about how to check for breast cancer, and, much to my shock, a pack of condoms. There was a floral notice taped to them that read "Practice safe sex! Come See Ms. Eugenia in the health clinic if you need birth control pills" on one side and "A health and wellness seminar will be held in the Tully lounge on Friday at 4:00 p.m." on the other.

Daddy's eyes met mine as I peered up from the bag. I could tell he was weighing his words carefully before he spoke. "Now, Adelaide, you're going to be exposed to a lot of outlandish ideas up here, you know?"

"I sure hope so," I said, unable to fully sense his anxiety over shelling out thousands of dollars to a place that already threatened his daughter's innocence. "I mean, that's why I'm here, right?"

Meanwhile, someone had mistaken Dizzy for a freshman and handed her a pink bag too. She pulled out the condoms in great delight, waved them between Daddy and me, and said, "Guess you're not in Kansas anymore, big sis!"

Daddy grabbed the bag from Dizzy with his metal pinchers and threw it into the trash can at the bottom of the stairwell. Then he gently grabbed my shoulders with his hands (one metal, one bone) and said, "We're trusting you to keep your head on, sister."

"Yes, sir," I assured him. "I've kept it on so far, and I'm not about to lose it now."

He nodded in relief and patted my back. Just behind him Dizzy was making a gagging gesture and pointing to a sign with rainbows and pink triangles that read, "Harmony, the NBU Gay and Lesbian Society, welcomes you to our campus."

She came over and whispered, "I'll tell Papa Great they have a society for you."

I rolled my wide eyes. Even her teasing couldn't stop the gnawing that had begun in my gut. I was overwhelmed by the new names and faces; the boys cut out of granite, lugging my belongings up three flights of stairs; and the talk of politics and sex at every turn. Was someone burning incense? I peered into an open dorm room where a girl and a guy were smoking cloves and tapping their feet to a folksy-sounding song. There was a black tapestry over the window, with a picture of a grinning skeleton wearing a top hat, and it blocked out the afternoon sunlight.

Suddenly I was afraid to climb the three flights of stairs to my new home. I stood at the bottom of the stairwell as if paralyzed and watched my family clomp up ahead of me. Was I up for this? Should I run back to the University of South Carolina and beg them to return my scholarship? *Cousin Randy, here I come! Football, cockfighting—don't start without me!*

Dizzy looked back and then ran back down and squeezed my elbow. "You can do this, Ad," she said. "You've been waiting your whole life for this." I looked my sister in the eye and bit my bottom lip to ward off the fear. When she offered her arm, I took it and held it all the way up the cold concrete stairs.

The cinder-block walls in my dorm room seemed gray and sad. *Twenty-six thousand dollars a year in tuition for cinder-block walls?* Ruthie and I had coordinated our room in a soothing periwinkle and white, and Mama had made some adorable curtains that she draped around our one and only window to brighten the place up. After we frantically hung posters and pictures and piled notebooks and pens on our little wooden desks, the room warmed up a little. Mama, Dizzy, and Lou spent time fussing over the organization of my closet drawers, racing to get me settled before the convocation ceremony, while Ruthie hung pictures around the room of prom and college parties she and her boyfriend had attended together.

Ruthie's hometown boyfriend, Tag Eisley, had come along with her parents to settle her in. Tag was a junior at the University of North Carolina, and Ruthie had already circled in red on her desk calendar all of the game weekends during which she would drive down to Chapel Hill to visit him. They had dated since her freshman year in high school. Now he and Daddy paced and bristled at the invitations to fraternity rush parties that upperclassman boys were handing out up and down the halls.

"Come on by tonight," they would say as they slid the flyers under the doors.

Ruthie hugged Tag hard after crumpling each invitation and tossing it into the trash.

"I won't be needing these," she said.

*Great,* I thought. *Ruthie's going to be no fun.*

A bulky upperclass girl named Beryl Dunlap dropped by to introduce herself as our small-group leader during orientation. She sported a yellow men's polo tucked into red plastic workout pants. Out of her crinkly-sounding pocket, she pulled a flyer for some kind of athletic team tryout.

"Play lacrosse?" she asked.

*Huh? Never heard of it.*

"I don't think so," I told Beryl, who had been playing ever since her sophomore year at Miss Porter's.

"I'll pick you ladies up in an hour and a half and escort you to the convocation," she said. "It is best," she announced to all parents, "if you say your good-byes before then."

Tears filled Mama's eyes when Daddy said, "It's time, Greta." She put the last sweater neatly in my drawer and could not even look me in the eye to bid me farewell. I reached across the threshold and hugged her. "It's okay, Mama. I love you, too, and I'm going to be just fine. Don't worry."

"You'll go to the cafeteria and eat something after convocation," she urged. "It's open until seven fifteen."

"Yes," I said. "I'll do it."

"I saw the menu," she said. "They're going to have lasagna and green-bean casserole, and the salad bar looks really fresh. And I left you some tomatoes in your minifridge and even some leftover Mexican casserole that I brought up in the cooler, and there's a microwave down the hall by the lounge."

"I'll eat. It's a primary need. Don't fret."

I could tell that she just didn't know what to say or what physical gesture to give to express the joy and sadness this moment brought to her. I guessed that she was thinking of every diaper she had changed, every runny nose she had wiped, every multiplication table she had called out, and every science project she had stewed over, and now she could hardly bear the rite of passage that was before her firstborn.

I kissed her on the cheek. "Mama, I'll be okay."

Though Lou didn't fully understand what was going on, she knew enough to hold my hand tightly all the way down the steps and out the dorm to the station wagon. Dizzy understood exactly what was happening, but she had more pressing issues to attend to.

"I'm starving," she called to Mama and Daddy as she puckered in the mountain air and reapplied her jet-black lipstick. "Can we stop at that Hardee's on the way to the highway?"

"Yes," Daddy said in a hushed tone, while Mama wiped her eyes with his handkerchief.

After a last farewell, I watched as the wagon drove out of the Tully dorm parking lot and over the speed bumps that led down the hill and to the tall brick gates of Nathaniel Buxton University.

"Good-bye," I said to myself, and I was surprised by the lump in my own throat.

"C'mon, Adelaide!" Ruthie called from our dorm-room window. She was already in a church dress with her hair in a French braid. "Convocation starts in twenty minutes!"

The NBU convocation was held in the stone chapel in the center of the colonnade on the top of the great green hill. The college president, Dr. Neil G. Schaeffer, addressed us from an opulent mahogany pulpit that seemed miraculously suspended in the air, eye level with the balcony.

Jif, Ruthie, and I were on the left side of the floor-level aisle with members of the class of 1993 surrounding us. We lifted our chins up toward the pulpit to hear the speech.

"The mission of NBU is to cultivate intellectual growth in its students in a setting that stresses both the importance of individual honor and integrity and the responsibility to serve humanity through the productive use of one's education," he said without looking down at his notes. He was a tall, stately man about the age of Papa Great. His deep-set eyes had a way of looking into a student's core, and his facial expressions and hand motions were confident and controlled.

*Honor. Integrity. Serving humanity.* Now, these were words I could get inspired by, I thought as I gave a peripheral glance at the members of the class of 1993. A lean, buff brunette to my left tilted her head to ponder the notion, and a peculiar boy to my right was snorting loudly every few seconds as though he had a nervous tic. Could someone get that poor guy a Kleenex? As I thumbed through my purse to see if I had one, President Schaeffer continued. When I looked up, he was singling me out with his black eyes.

"How will you take advantage of this opportunity, scholars?"

My purse dropped to the stone floor when he said that. I loved being labeled a scholar, and I wanted to hear more.

"Will you join the archaeological dig that Dr. Weston is leading in Mexico this summer? Will you run for a position on the school judiciary committee that enforces the honor code and a no-tolerance policy for cheating and plagiarism? Will you serve at the Troutville soup kitchen on Saturday mornings or take a biological study trip with Professor Ereckson to the Galápagos Islands? How about our award-winning *Shenandoah Valley Review*? Will you help Dr. Hirsch with the selection of poetry and essay submissions?"

*Yes! Yes! Yes!* I was saying to all of his questions as he continued to single students out with his stare. My heart was racing, and I looked around to see if everyone else was as exhilarated as me, but most folks seemed to be staring dully at the altar.

I started tapping my foot with excitement, but Jif squeezed my knee as if to say, "Get a grip," though I could tell that she was stirred, too, at all the possibilities of how the four years before us would unfold.

After President Schaeffer concluded his address and made a regal trot down the steps of the pulpit, taking his place behind the altar, the dean of student life, Dr. Josephine Atwood, addressed us about what was in store over the next two days of orientation, and I took another moment to survey the class of three hundred freshmen.

Jif, Ruthie, and I were by far the most dressed up in the group. We had on bright makeup and church skirts, and we had donned pink-and-purple-colored pumps and carried purses that matched our tops. Almost all the guys were in khakis, some form of casual loafer, and a wrinkled oxford shirt. The girls were in tight-fitting earth-colored blouses and either pants or miniskirts that showed off their impressive figures. They had lean, muscular arms and tight calves as though they had been training for a triathlon.

As hard as it was to get to NBU, I was surprised at how attractive most of these people were. I would have expected them to look more bookwormish. Not all of these suntanned, straight-teethed preppies. Beauty and brains—Renaissance folks, I supposed. I really was in over my head.

It was dusk when we filed out the arched chapel doors and into the crisp mountain air. We were at the highest point on campus, and the sun was setting behind the first mountain peaks against a backdrop of orange and pink. Beyond it were the little ridges of blue that fanned out around us farther than the eye could see.

As the mass shuffled down the colonnade and turned toward the quadrangle behind it, I tried once again to make out the group. There were side conversations all around me, and it seemed as though many of the freshmen knew one another. They chuckled and slapped hands and pushed each other down the stone path. Had they arrived the week before and made friends?

"Andover, right?" a stout but handsome boy said to another.

"Yeah. We slaughtered you in lacrosse last year," the other said.

"Don't remind me."

Their accents were unfamiliar—such precise pronunciation that was sharply clipped at the end of each word. Northeastern, I supposed.

"Going out for the team?" the stout boy said to the other.

"You know it. And I'll see you at the Sigma Alpha house tonight."

"Yeah. I hear rush is one abuse after another. But hey, it'll be our turn next year."

Sigma Alpha? Fraternity, I guessed. (NBU had only started admitting women in 1983, and so there weren't sororities yet.) And what was it with lacrosse? I had never heard of such a sport. In South Carolina it was football, football, football. There were a little basketball and a little baseball, but no mysterious game called lacrosse. Every time the word came up, I pictured a grumpy Frenchman.

"I'm from Westchester, New York," I heard the beautiful brunette who'd sat next to me say to another lean girl with straight blonde hair that grazed her shoulder blades.

"Greenwich, Connecticut," the other one said, pulling her hair back and twisting it into a knot. Thin little wisps formed around her perfectly proportioned face. "Want to get something to eat in town?"

"Yeah. And then let's go to the Sigma Alpha house. This junior said they're having a bash and to come by."

They were so natural and attractive. Buff yet feminine, well-bred and, as I was already beginning to see, *privileged* as they scurried to their Jeeps and BMWs in the parking lot of the dorm.

Jif, who had a keener sense of style than me, gave me a worried face as she surveyed our outfits and big, curly hair. She put her hand over her mouth and tried to temper her Low-Country drawl. "We've got work to do, Adelaide."

It would be two whole days until we registered for classes, and I knew she would whip herself into the subtle, sporty look in no time. She had the raw material to do it, but I wondered how Ruthie and I would fare.

But even though these folks were intimidating, I could not squelch the thrill of being immersed in the environment that President Schaeffer had just described. A place where honor was encouraged and justice was enforced. A place where learning was expected. This was just what I wanted, and I couldn't wait to roll up my sleeves and dig in. Finally, I was beginning to feel that maybe I wasn't born in the wrong place at the wrong time. There would be no Averill Skaggs lobbying for the cretins in this place.

The crowd parted at the tall bronze statue of Nathaniel Buxton in the center of the quadrangle as some headed toward the Randolph dorm and others to Tully.

Like Thomas Lynch Jr. from Williamstown, Nathaniel Buxton had been a signer of the Declaration of Independence and was considered a Founding Father. He served on the cabinets of both George Washington and John Adams, and he was one of the leading commanders of the ground troops during the Revolutionary War. His family and even his horse were buried on the cemetery hill beyond the colonnade. I'd seen a photo of his gravestone fenced in with wrought iron and dripping with wisteria in the application, and I planned to make a pilgrimage there before classes started.

Now his statue seemed to be looking down on us with a thoughtful stare as he held his battle gun in one hand and his coat in the other.

As the class of 1993 continued to move through the quad and into their dorms or automobiles, I wondered which one among them would be a Pulitzer prize winner in twenty-five years. Which one would be a senator or a Supreme Court justice? Which one would discover the cure for diabetes? Though most looked more like athletes than scholars, NBU had produced leaders who had influenced the country and the world, and each year they became more and more selective, so chances were these folks had something exceptional to offer.

"*Who* are these people?" I said to Jif and Ruthie as I spun around twice, embarrassing them both. I jumped up on the steps of the commerce school, made a clumsy arabesque, and shouted, "And *where* are they going?"

Jif acted as if she didn't know me and made a beeline for Tully. Ruthie looked around at the other students chuckling at my accent.

"Get down, Adelaide!" she said through gritted teeth. She reached her arm up and pulled me off the steps.

"Nice hair," a pudgy girl said with that clipped voice.

"And accent," her tall waif of a friend added.

# 5

## Student Life

That night as Ruthie and I were catching up and thanking God that the dorm floors were staggered girl-boy-girl so we could walk around in our nightgowns, Jif knocked on our door with a hot iron for straightening hair, a stack of fashion catalogs, and a two-liter bottle of Diet Coke.

"We need a new look," she said, opening the glossy pages. "Mama said she'd give me her credit card, so go on and help me decide."

There were laughter and the slap of feet on stone in the quadrangle as the darkness set in. We looked out the windows and tried to make out the freshmen scurrying from Tully and out into the night. The girls had changed and were now in tight male-cut Levis and brown patterned halter tops that showed off their bronze shoulders. They didn't take pocketbooks or backpacks, and they wore brown leather sandals with square heels.

"Where are they going?" Ruthie asked as Jif poured us a soft drink.

When the telephone rang, I answered.

"Adelaide, it's Peter Carpenter."

"Hi, Peter!" I said, winking at both of them.

"Tone down the accent," Jif whispered firmly.

"Welcome to NBU, girl!" Peter said.

"Thanks," I said in my usual drawl, taking up at least two syllables. "I'm looking forward to seeing you." I stuck my tongue out at Jif and waited for Peter's response.

"Say, we're having a rush party at the Kappa Nu house in a little while. Why don't you and your hall mates come down and say hello?"

"A party?" I said, looking across the room at my two friends.

Jif was nodding excitedly as if to say, "Let's go," but Ruthie bit her lip in loyalty to Tag and mouthed a "No."

Meeting at a fraternity house wasn't exactly how I'd envisioned my first rendezvous with Peter. I'd had more of a dinner-and-a-movie vision in mind, but all I could see was the speedometer at "0" and a little voice inside the cocoon saying, "Why the heck not?"

"Great," I said. "Tell us how to get there."

Next Jif opened my closet and pulled out a yellow sundress.

"Cut the top off of this and put on some blue jeans," she said. "I don't know *what* we'll do about shoes!"

I had four pairs in my closet. A turquoise pump, my Keds, a leather flat, and a black patent-leather pump for dressy occasions.

"Just put on the Keds, I guess," Jif said.

"First of all, I am *not* cutting off my sundress, Jif Ferguson. Mae Mae just bought that for me, so you can forget it."

"Okay," she said, pulling a white oxford out of the closet. "Put this on and tie it in a knot above your jeans."

"Glad we've got the fashion police here," Ruthie said.

"You should be," Jif said. "Adelaide's gonna be thanking her homely stars I'm not at Clemson."

We all chuckled, and she ran to her room to cut her own sundress apart. She put on tight jeans and some brown Moses sandals her mama had bought for her at Bob Ellis in Charleston, and off we went, down the great hill, through the quaint and hilly mountain town of Troutville, and to the Kappa Nu house.

Peter's fraternity was at the bottom of the hill of Troutville's Main Street. It was a three-story brick house with white columns that mimicked the NBU colonnade, and there was a piazza on the second floor

where a Confederate flag flew below the two large gold-and-garnet letters *KN*.

I made a little mental *humph* when I saw the flag of the Confederacy. I mean, I wouldn't exactly associate what it had come to rep-
resent with an ivory tower of enlightenment. But then again, this was
the homeland of Robert E. Lee, and perhaps the KNs were more interested in the history of the flag than in its current connection with big-
otry and intolerance.

"You think too much," Jif said, guessing my thoughts as I eyed the
blue *X* and its white stars. "Loosen up, brainiac. You're going to have
to if you ever expect to have some fun."

I took a breath and exhaled, "You're so right."

"Fresh meat," an unshaven, heavyset upperclassman called from
the front porch when he spotted us on the lawn.

"What did that guy just say?" I asked.

"I don't know," Jif said, pulling me by the wrist toward the house.
"Let's find Peter."

Five or six boys rushed out to greet us before Peter called from the
piazza, "Adelaide! I'll be right down."

"So are you ladies from South Carolina?" a brawny boy named
Derek inquired. He had on the fraternity uniform: a well-worn polo
shirt, khakis that were frayed at the bottom, and dark hunting boots.

"Williamstown," Jif said. "And what about you?"

"Houston, pretty girl. The Lone Star State. This is the Southern
fraternity. Why don't you let me get you a beer."

"All right." Jif winked to me as Peter ran down the stairs and out
onto the lawn. He gave me a big squeeze and spun me around. He
smelled like beer and smoke and sweat, but I was thrilled to have the
warm welcome.

"It's so good to see you," he said. His eyes were sincere, but a little
glazed over. "Hey, come on inside and I'll introduce you around."

Jif was already on her way inside with Derek. The other boys ran
farther down the lawn to meet a new heap of freshman girls who were
waddling by in tight jeans and halter tops.

Inside was a zoo. Wide-eyed freshman boys were nervously sipping from plastic cups of red punch served out of trash cans as they met the upperclassmen. A heavy heat was rising from the crowd, and every forehead across the room seemed aglow. The music, which seemed like nothing more than the pulse of a bass guitar and some deep whines, pelted the walls with its steady beat.

A short guy with a thatch of blond hair and a light case of acne whom I recognized from the freshman floor below us spotted me and said, "Hey, you're third-floor Tully, right? I'm Frankie Wells, second floor."

"You're here to meet the fraternity brothers, Pizza Mug," Peter reminded him. "Not girls. Just because you're from Georgia doesn't mean you're a shoo-in, so get to schmoozing."

"Yikes," I said as Wells scurried away. "He was just introducing himself."

Peter chuckled and tugged on a strand of my permed hair, then whispered in my ear, "I just have to mess with these guys, you know? It's part of the rush chairman's job."

"Ah," I said.

"Hey, what's with the big hair?" some tall guy with a beard shouted, and I think he was pointing at me.

Peter rolled his eyes, and I started to rub my jewel nervously.

He grabbed my hand, pushed through the crowd, pulled us through the kitchen door, and grabbed a beer with a picture of a moose on it from a cooler hidden in the pantry.

"Try this," he said, thumbing through a kitchen drawer for a bottle opener. "And when you're finished, I'll show you how to inaugurate your first visit to the Kappa Nu house."

I had been at the house for less than five minutes, and I was already a fitting character for some cheesy after-school special. I didn't really drink—except for champagne on special occasions—and I could barely stomach the taste of beer. Was this a worthy environment in which to step out of my cocoon?

Then I thought about Jif telling me to loosen up, and I let Peter pop off the cap and hand the green bottle to me.

"I guess I'll try a little," I said.

He grinned and his lips glistened with saliva beneath the fluorescent kitchen lights. His eyes were bloodshot, and he had a thin outline of a beard growing around his jowls.

"So Mama told me you gave the valedictorian address," he said before sipping from his own green bottle.

"Yeah. You heard about Georgianne?" (Peter's family home was just two doors down from the Mayfields'.)

"Knocked up, right?"

"Yeah."

"And she was a promising one too," he said. "But Peach had to have her."

"Well, I hope they'll be happy."

"Carpenter, where are you?" a voice hollered from the microphone in the main room.

"That's Yates, the frat president. He wants me to address the rush candidates. Come on out to the party, and I'll find you in a few minutes."

"Okay."

When I pushed through the kitchen door into the darkened haze, I looked for Jif or anyone remotely familiar from my dorm. Out of the corner of my eye, I could see Peter taking the stage with the guy who made the comment about my hair. They were welcoming the freshman boys who were coming out for rush before naming the reasons why Kappa Nu was the house of choice for the true Southern gentleman of NBU.

Frankie grinned sheepishly at me as I made my way through the crowd. "I'm from Milledgeville, Georgia," he said, holding out his hand. "What about you?"

"Williamstown, South Carolina," I said, giving his hand a gentle shake. "So you wanna be in this fraternity?"

"I don't know," he said. "It's my first day here. My uncle was in this fraternity, but I don't know what the heck I'm doing."

"You and me both," I said, smiling at him.

The heavyset upperclassman I'd seen on the porch suddenly appeared and pulled Frankie away from me by his earlobe, and he waved good-bye. I looked around for Jif. Not seeing her, I started to sway to the music like everyone else and watched Peter grab freshman boys and haul them up the stairwell. After what seemed like an hour of pretending to know people and nursing my unsavory beer, I finally made my way to the line for the bathroom in hopes of coming across someone I knew.

⌒

It took twenty minutes to get in there. A petite and fair-skinned black-haired girl in line before me was hardly able to stand up. She was a drunken Snow White, and when she finally made it into the bathroom, I could hear her getting sick behind the door.

"You think she's okay?" I said to an upperclass girl waiting behind me.

"She's road cheese," the girl said, flapping her hand as if she were swatting away a fly. "Don't concern yourself."

*Road cheese,* I thought. What in the world did that mean?

Finally, the girl's friend, a made-up blonde with big breasts and the largest diamond-stud earrings I'd ever seen, pushed through the door to help her friend. They barely made their way across the threshold, Snow White as green as the wicked stepmother now.

"Let's hit the highway," the blonde said. "Just hold on till we get to the car, Isabelle."

I watched as they stumbled out onto the porch. No fraternity brother or NBU girl offered them any help as they made their way onto the dark lawn and toward a red, new-fangled Ford Explorer.

"Waiting for an invitation?" the upperclassman said to me as she pointed at the empty bathroom door.

"Oh, right," I said as I hurried into the smelly room, locked the door, and turned on the light.

My stomach caught itself in my throat as I saw the pornography that lined the walls. Picture after picture of centerfolds bearing unnaturally large breasts and tight, round fannies were taped haphazardly to the walls. There was a stack of magazines on the back of the toilet, and the tile floor was covered in a layer of water and grime. The sour smell of vomit burned my nose, and though I really needed to urinate by this point, I didn't know if I could do it.

I stuffed my blouse over my nose, loosened my white Keds from the sticky floor, and thought of President Schaeffer's speech about honor and integrity. Had it fallen onto deaf ears at the Kappa Nu house? And though I really had to go, I couldn't bring myself to sit on the toilet where Snow White's puke and Lord knows what else had recently been expelled.

As I retied the knot on my blouse, I spotted a little floral bag on top of a roll of toilet paper by the sink. I opened it; inside was a fifty-dollar bill, a condom, a tube of fig-colored lipstick, and a Louisiana driver's license with a picture of Snow White.

"All right then," I said as I tucked the bag in my back pocket and walked back out into the foyer, my bladder about to burst.

"That was fast," the upperclassman girl said.

"Have you been in there?" I asked, trying to warn her.

"Yates is my beau," she asked. "I practically live here." Then she grabbed my shoulder and added, "This is college, Wide-Eyed. Time to grow up. Boys will be boys and all that."

"Ouch," I said, too afraid to come up with a thought-provoking rebuttal about the danger of exploiting women.

As the girl slammed the bathroom door, I finally spotted Jif in the living room. She was trying to peel the Texan's bulky arms off her.

"Help," she mouthed to me, and I came over and made like I was sick.

"I'm not feeling so well. I need you to walk me home, Jif," I said.

"Where's Carpenter?" the boy said, tightening his grip on my friend.

"I don't know. Fulfilling his rush duties, I suppose."

"I've got to go, Derek," Jif said, wriggling out of his arms. He pouted before taking another gulp from his green bottle. Then he bit his lip in frustration and narrowed his unibrow before adding, "Suit yourself, Fresh Meat."

"Wow, you really know how to woo a girl," Jif said sarcastically and turned from him so fast that I think she swatted his nose with her bouffy hair. I could hear him sneezing as I followed her speedy exit. We scurried down the porch steps and out onto the lawn, where Peter was conducting a belching contest with three rush candidates.

He looked up and ran over to me.

"You aren't leaving?"

"Well," I said, "that guy, Derek, kind of had an unwelcome death grip on Jif, and you seem pretty busy. We can catch up later."

"I apologize for all of the craziness, Adelaide. The brothers are blowing off a little steam before classes start, you know? I'll tell Derek to lay off. Why don't y'all hang around a little longer?"

I felt the pulsing of my full bladder and added, "Also, um, the decor in the guest bathroom kind of made me ill."

He looked perplexed for a moment. Then it dawned on him, and he gave a grin that was somewhere between guilt and empathy.

"Adelaide," he said, gently taking my hand and lacing his fingers through mine, "I've always been attracted to your spunk."

I liked that he took my hand, but I couldn't stifle my opinion. "And one more thing: it's not exactly appealing to be referred to as a slab of flank steak or something." I looked to Jif, and she nodded in agreement. "Am I wrong?"

"I don't think y'all are flank steak," he said, rubbing his thumb across my palm. He pinched my cheek with his other hand. "Filet mignon, I could accept. But definitely not flank steak."

I pushed his chest, not knowing if I should be offended or flattered. He pulled me gently toward him. "Rush will be over at the end of this week," he whispered into my ear. The stubble on his chin tickled my neck as he held me close. "Then I'd love to take you out for dinner. I've really been looking forward to having you here."

"Get a room, Carpenter!" the heavyset guy called from the porch. He threw his empty bottle into the shrubbery and demanded that a freshman boy get him another.

Through the window I could see Derek with his arms around

another young girl. His big hand was under the back of her shirt, and he was pulling her closer.

"All right," I said, pulling back to smile at Peter. He was my only male friend at this point, and I had to give him the benefit of the doubt. After all, he was my geometry tutor and one of the finest boys ever to come out of Williamstown. So I had good reason to hope that he wasn't the alcoholic-porn-gazing type that a portion of the KN brothers appeared to be.

"And, Jif," he said before we stepped onto the sidewalk, "Derek's your typical egomaniac Texan. His daddy's some bigwig lawyer, and he thinks he can have whatever he wants. Forget about him. I'll set you up with a gentleman, okay?"

"Okay," she said, flipping her hair and correcting her posture.

As we walked up Main Street, we saw several freshman boys downing drinks on the green lawns of frat houses and upperclassmen with young girls on their arms, hollering at the rush candidates to continue.

"Well," I said, "I'm not sure what to make of all this."

"Yeah," Jif said. "Derek was a *creep*. He must have asked me to walk upstairs to his room five times."

"This can't be the only social life at NBU. Surely there's a lot more going on than just fraternities, right? I mean, who are those activists who put up that Tiananmen Square display? We've just scratched the surface."

"Let's hope so," she said.

"And what is road cheese?" I asked, pulling the floral bag out of my pocket to show to her. "This girl was getting sick in this porn-laden bathroom, and no one was helping her. She left this behind. I didn't exactly think that the KNs had a lost and found, so I thought I'd turn it in to campus security tomorrow."

"Road cheese means they're from one of the pricey women's colleges," she said. "There are three or four of them on the outskirts of Troutville, and NBU is where they go to meet guys. The hall counselor told me they were here to get their MRS degrees."

"Ah," I said. "The NBU girls snub them for staking out their territory."

"And the guys just have more and more fresh meat to choose from," Jif said.

"Aren't they fortunate?" I said.

~

When we returned to the dorm room, Ruthie was talking in lovey-dovey tones into the telephone receiver as she gazed longingly out the open third-floor window into the starry mountain sky.

Jif, a little freaked out by the Derek experience, pulled her mattress down the hall into ours, and we fell asleep to the distant sounds of music spilling out of the frat houses and shrieks of either laughter or horror. I couldn't tell which.

~

Orientation. Ugh. All of the freshmen were instructed to meet in the gym for a series of icebreakers with Dean Atwood and her entourage of assistants and coaches.

"Find everyone born the same month as you," the dean would holler in her perfectly pressed pin-striped suit. Or "Find everyone with the same color eyes."

I scurried through the crowd, trying to follow the rules that she called out from the microphone. I had never felt so short. What was in the water across the rest of the country that was creating this tall, earthy race of natural blonds? Seventy-five percent of the class was a head taller than me, and very few chose to duck down to ask the brunette with the poodle hair when she was born.

Many of the boys looked green from the fraternity rush. After an hour, Frankie Wells excused himself from the gym, which was hot from all of our nervous energy, and went outside to get some fresh air. I could see him lying back on the emerald lawn, holding his head.

"You all right?" I asked stealing away for a moment to bring him a sip of water in a paper cone from the gym cooler.

He lifted his head and said, "Am I in hell?"

"Just college," I said. He laughed and said, "Go on back in. If a KN sees me talking to you, he'll get me good tonight."

Another freshman boy came out of the gym, put his head between his knees, and took deep breaths.

"That guy's on my hall," said Frankie. "He's going for KN too. Hey, what's your name, bub?" he called over.

The boy wiped his watery eyes. "Brother," he said. He picked at the sculpted green shrubs beneath the gym windows and spit. Then he kicked some wood chips over his mess and sucked on his teeth before coming over to lie down next to Frankie. "Brother Benton. I'm from Tuscaloosa. What about you?"

"Frankie Wells from Milledgeville, Georgia, bub. And this is Adelaide from South Carolina."

I waved and offered him the last of the water as Frankie continued, "This rush is something, huh?"

"Tough," he said with eyes to the ground. "But the KNs aren't as bad as the Sigma Alpha house. Those guys are from up north, and they really whip your tail. My roommate's still in bed. He couldn't even stand up this morning."

"Man!" Frankie said. And as he said this, a coach from the athletic department knocked on the gym window with his fist and said, "The dean wants you all back inside."

"Do y'all not find this such a cliché?" I asked, shaking my head and reaching out to Frankie Wells to help him up. "So, like, *Animal House* passé, you know?"

"I guess so, Miss Adelaide," Frankie said, patting me on the back and chuckling at my Southern twist on a French word. "You're a philosophy major, right?"

Brother Benton sat up and looked at me for the first time and smiled. He looked like five miles of bad road, but he had dark curly hair and the greatest smile I think I'd ever seen. White teeth and a dimple on the right side of his cheek. His brown eyes were alive, and they glistened in the white light of this mountain morning.

"I'm just here to get my journalism degree," Frankie said to both of us. "My uncle says if I make it here, he'll let me write for his newspaper in Atlanta."

"Will you publish my poems?"

"Why not?" he said.

"What about you?" I said to Brother. "Are you prelaw like the rest of the frat boys?"

"Nah," Brother said, shaking his brown curly hair. "Literature, my lady. Guess we're all left-brain folks. I'm going to write a novel and camp out in front of a publishing house until someone notices me. But mostly I want to get out of Alabama."

"If you survive rush," I said, walking back to the watercooler to fill up the cone. "And if you want out of Alabama, I wonder *why* you're choosing to join the Southern fraternity."

When I brought the water over to him, he flashed me that smile again.

"Same reason you were there the other night," he said. "It's the only place I know someone from home."

I blushed, glad to have been noticed by this handsome, literary freshman. Yes, this is what I'd expected from college—sailing out of the Williamstown Harbor and into the sea where the fish were bigger and brighter. At last!

As he took a sip, the coach tapped on the window again, and I said, "See y'all later."

Before I opened the gym door, I overheard Brother say to Frankie, "I'm going to marry that poet, Wells. You wait and see."

I smiled with my back to him and bit my bottom lip. How nice it was to be wanted!

Then I heard Frankie's reply. "Carpenter's got dibs on her. You'd better lay off for now."

"I'll bide my time," Brother Benton said. "We won't always be freshmen."

It was at the class of '93 orientation social the next afternoon on the front quadrangle that Jif, Ruthie, and I were officially relegated to country bumpkins amid the naturally beautiful girls from the Northeast with their nature-oriented, androgynous names: Heath, Rivers, and Park.

They all looked like J.Crew models in those cropped oatmeal sweaters, worn blue jeans, and sporty hiking boots. Was it possible to have legs so long and thin? It must have been. And what about the golden (untreated) hair that draped their backs? Dern Dizzy had been right—not another perm in sight!

Yes, we faced up to the fact that we were a sight that day on the green and handsome campus that surrounded us with its great history and wealth. We had attended the social all dressed up in bright pink and turquoise outfits with matching leather flats. I had tried to straighten my hair with Jif's iron, but all that did was make it frizzy and then stiff as a corpse in its thick coat of hair spray. And the hot-pink glittery lipstick covering Ruthie's lips was like a sign that blinked *Redneck* with every smile she flashed.

Frankie and Brother were nowhere to be found. And the rest of the shabbishly preppy freshman boys gradually made their way to the fresh flock of earthy girls while a sophomore nerd named Ned Crater from Abingdon, Tennessee, cornered us with his inane tales of life on a tobacco farm and ended with a dinner invitation that extended only to Jif. Even in her bumpkin state, Jif's blonde and blue-eyed beauty could be recognized (and Ned would make numerous attempts to win her affection during our freshman year and beyond).

Except for my brief rendezvous with Peter earlier in the week, I felt virtually invisible. I had never known this feeling back in Williamstown, and it stung my heart more than I could admit. Didn't anyone know that I was a published poet? That I gave the valedictorian address, attended Governor's School, and pondered the meaning of life in my journal late at night? I had thought that I was too good for the back-home set to pay them much attention, but now I was low man on the totem pole at NBU—Geechee and gaudy, with big brown hair and stubby legs.

At the end of the social, I ducked back into Tully, stopped to check myself in the hall bathroom, and for the first time in my life, looked in the mirror and experienced shame. I was horrified by my jewel, as if it were a final blow from the ugly stick, and from that day on I vowed to conceal it by coating it with makeup and fashioning my bangs just so until I could save enough money for Jif's daddy (the only surgeon in town) to snip it off.

The next day I woke up early, showered, made another attempt to straighten my hair and tone down my makeup, and went straight over to the English department to a meeting that was set up with my pre-ordained adviser, Dr. McSweeney. I had heard through the grapevine that he was elderly, formal, and had never quite gotten over the fact that NBU had decided to admit girls, so I wore a skirt and wrote my questions in as concise a manner as possible. I wanted to ask him about the creative writing workshop with Josiah Dirkas and where to begin with my literature studies. I had outlined all that I was interested in, from Shakespeare's theater to modern poetry, and I had already thumbed through the books in the college store, devouring the Emily Dickinson poems and one by Sylvia Plath in which a panther stalks her mind.

I didn't want to be late for my appointment, so I took a few sips of Diet Coke from the dorm kitchen and ate the remnants of a leftover bag of popcorn before I scurried over to the Humboldt Humanities Building on the colonnade. I sat on the bench of the quiet hall for whole minutes, daydreaming about Peter Carpenter, before I looked around at the quotes by C. S. Lewis and a photo of a large man named Chesterton. There were applications for a mission trip to Honduras on the bulletin board and a listing of all the chapel services as well as a student-run study of the book of John in the main hall on Monday nights.

*Wait a minute.* A look of panic came over my face as a man in a green bow tie posted a course description titled "Religion and Social Justice" on the bulletin board. Then he turned around to greet me and said, "I'm Dr. Shaw. Can I help you?"

"Is this not the English department?" I asked, realizing that I was now five minutes late for my appointment with McSweeney.

He grimaced. "You went one floor too high. This is the third floor. English is on the second."

"I'm late for my appointment with Dr. McSweeney."

"Ah," he said, understanding the panicked tone in my voice and nodding his head. "Let me show you to his office."

He walked me down the stairs and into the English department.

"It makes sense if you think about it," he said as he held open the door. "History's on the first floor—all that is past. English is on the second—man's reflection of his life experiences. Religious studies on the third and final floor—man's realization of what is above and beyond him."

I nodded my head, still befuddled about being late to my appointment.

Unlike the religion department, the English department was crowded, and many nervous freshmen were milling about. A bearded man in Birkenstocks was wheeling his bicycle into his office, and an overweight, unkempt lady was smoking a cigarette while making copies and taking a slug from a twenty-ounce bottle of Diet Pepsi.

"Tell me your name," Dr. Shaw said as he knocked on McSweeney's closed door.

"Adelaide," I said. "Adelaide Piper."

From behind the thick door, someone cleared his throat and said, "You may enter."

"Morning, Randolph," Dr. Shaw said. "A Miss Adelaide Piper seemed to be turned around this morning and waiting to meet with you on the third floor. I'm just showing her down to your office."

"I see," said Dr. McSweeney. He motioned for me to enter, and I thanked Dr. Shaw before taking a seat on a wingback chair that swallowed me into its cracked, dark leather cushion. I looked up at Dr. McSweeney, who was staring at my name and social security number.

"So you want to be an English major?" he said before looking up and flaring his nostrils at the sight of me. "Tell me, what's your area of interest?"

He looked like a bull with his ruddy face and bushy eyebrows. His head rested on his wide shoulders as though he had no neck at all, and I half expected steam to come out of his dark, round nostrils as he waited for my answer.

"Poetry," I said, handing him my chapbook from the Governor's School.

He thumbed through the book before handing it back to me. I couldn't see his feet behind his stout mahogany desk, but in my mind's eye I pictured strong hooves scraping a hole in the worn Oriental rug.

"To begin with, contemporary poetry is like entering through the back door, don't you think?" He narrowed his eyes and furrowed his brow. "How can you presume to write poetry, Miss Adelaide, without a formal studying of the poets who came before you?"

Ugh. Dr. McSweeney. He was charging, and I hadn't even given him a reason to. What in the world could I say to chill this bull out? I needed him to sign off on the Dirkas workshop. I'd been pining over it all summer, and I had been reworking poems I could hardly wait to submit.

"Well, sir," I said, "that's why I'm at NBU. To learn the background and take a crack at the present. Can't I do those simultaneously?"

He pushed his colorless lips to one side and brought his two index fingers up to them in mock contemplation.

"Miss Piper, Expository Writing is a freshman requirement. I recommend you take that as well as Seventeenth-Century Poetry. From there you can work your way up in chronological order. If you make it through, *then* I'd recommend taking a poetry workshop your junior year."

"But—but I don't want to miss this Dirkas opportunity. I've been working toward it all summer. I can still take Seventeenth-Century Poetry and Expository Writing along with it."

"It's an upper-level, and I think you should wait until you have a firm literature foundation to stand on. There will be other visiting writers."

I shook my head in disbelief. Why couldn't I have gotten the crunchy Birkenstock professor for an adviser or the fat lady with the cigarette? What was this old bull (who should have been put out to pasture a decade ago) trying to do to me?

"You know, Miss Piper, there is nothing new under the sun. There are only new ways to say it. How do you know you're not mimicking someone who came before you, if you don't, in fact, *know* what came before you?"

I was more shocked than dismayed, and I couldn't think of a coherent rebuttal. "Point taken, Dr. McSweeney."

"Then we're settled," he said, signing his name to my class registration form. He nodded once before crossing through my name with a yellow highlighter and moving on to the next.

I stood and looked out the thick glass panes of his office window. To the right it was framed by a great Corinthian column, and to the left was a downward view of the quadrangle, with freshmen scurrying across with their registration papers. Beyond the canopy of pine lay the outer quadrangle where the steep and craggy mountain ridges pushed at the sky.

McSweeney cleared his throat as if to say, "Don't let the door hit you on the way out," and I gathered my bag and walked solemnly across the threshold of his pen.

# Ivory Tower

Brother Benton died in the wee hours of a Sunday morning two weeks after classes started. Though the reports were somewhat inconsistent, the gist of the story was this: Brother was in the middle of the KN initiation weekend when he refused to walk across the quadrangle in nothing but an NBU baseball cap. For his insubordination, he was ordered to drink a pint of whiskey, after which he stumbled home arm in arm with Frankie, where they both collapsed in their respective dorm rooms on the third floor.

Brother got sick sometime in the night, and like the rock stars you hear about on the VH1 specials, he choked on his own puke without a soul between the stone walls of Tully knowing his struggle.

For a month I felt what was like a brick in my gut, and I sat from time to time in the library, weeping over the waste of Brother Benton's life as the campus slowly cranked back up again (though the KN house was under investigation). I had driven with Frankie down to Alabama and watched as they lowered Brother's mahogany casket into the earth behind the First Presbyterian Church of Tuscaloosa while his daddy held his mama, who sobbed and sobbed through the service. Mostly I looked away from the hole in the patch of soil he had wanted to escape and instead watched his seven-year-old sister, whose hair was pulled back in a bun outlined with purple pansies. She blew dandelion fluff into the damp grass and looked at the weepy adults around her as though they were strangers.

I wrote this in the margin of the church bulletin as Frankie drove us back up into the mountains:

> *Alabama air*
> *thicker*
> *than kudzu vines.*
> *Your mama's*
> *graveside cry*
> *shriller*
> *than a wren.*
> *You*
> *my potential*
> *suitor*
> *whose shirt*
> *still holds*
> *your scent*
> *gone*
> *(for what?)*
> *at eighteen.*

Yates, the KN president, was waiting in the dorm lobby when we returned from Tuscaloosa. Frankie held up his arm and said, "I'm not joining your godforsaken fraternity or any other. Brother's gone, and I think KN is partly responsible for his death."

To that Yates held up his arms, shook his head in a kind of solemn frustration, and turned toward the door.

I didn't hear from Peter Carpenter again, though I had tried to call him a few times. I ran into him once on the colonnade. His eyes were

bloodshot, and while he balanced a biology book on his hip, he seemed
to have no idea where he was going.

"Peter, you okay?"

"Adelaide," he said. "I'm sorry I haven't called. It's been a rough
time."

"I'm sure," I said, and we stood there, silent, as the chapel bell
tolled for Seventeenth-Century Poetry.

"Can't be late for class," I said, patting his shoulder. He didn't
move a muscle as I scurried into the humanities building.

In my heart, I didn't know if the KNs were responsible for Brother's
death. It was rumored that Peter had given the order to drink at Yates's
command, but I wondered why Brother didn't refuse it.

As the leaves on campus turned a ruddy orange and I fought to
keep my grades high so that McSweeney would sign off on a creative
writing course for the spring, I filed Brother's death away in my mind
as a sad, horrible, freak event, and I didn't expect anything like it to
happen again.

But I had a bird's-eye view from my Expository Writing class that
October when the Troutville County police pulled Peter Carpenter out
of the Burroway Science Building and charged him with manslaughter
right there on the front quad beneath Nathaniel Buxton's statue as a
handful of nervous students gathered around the outlying columns and
patches of emerald landscaping.

They handcuffed him on the spot and read him his rights, and he
dropped to his knees and began to bawl.

As they led him to the police car, a surge of nausea crept up my
throat, and I bolted out of my classroom, where my professor was in
midsentence, and ran to a weeping willow tree to get sick. How I
wished Mama or Juliabelle were there to hold my hair back and wipe
my eyes. There was a sour churning like lava in the pit of my stomach, and before I knew it I was running to the chapel to see if I could
ice it down with a prayer.

When I walked into the arched doors of the sanctuary, I remembered the convocation speech in which President Schaeffer had told

us we were on a mission to cultivate intellectual growth in a setting that stressed the importance of individual honor and integrity. And then there was his bit about our responsibility to serve humanity through the productive use of our education. Humph.

"How will you take advantage of this opportunity, scholars?" he had said right into my eyes.

I had toiled to get here. I had kicked and scratched my way up through Williamstown High and put my daddy's dreams on hold. And for what?

I didn't realize how loud I was weeping, but before I knew it, the stout and elderly man who ran the chapel bookstore came up, offered me a tissue, and sat beside me as I blew my nose.

I flung myself into his soft little chest and cried. I didn't even know who he was, but he was nice enough to bring me a tissue, and he patted my back and told me not to worry. Not to worry.

He smelled like mothballs and Tic Tacs, and by the time I pulled away from him, the pocket of his starched oxford shirt was soaked.

A tourist interested in purchasing a postcard of the chapel had come in the middle of the outburst, and when she cleared her throat, he had to excuse himself to ring her up.

Mostly, I felt alone. It was only autumn, and it was colder than any winter Williamstown had known, and the two young men who had remotely noticed me were gone—one in a graveyard in Tuscaloosa and the other handcuffed and headed for the Roanoke County Jail. What was going on?

The tissue the sweet man had given me was shredded now, and when I reached in my backpack for another, I felt something smaller than a coin and pulled it out to find that it was the St. Christopher medal Juliabelle had given me on my graduation day. It was oval, and on the outer rim it said, "Behold St. Christopher—And Go Your Way in Safety." In the center was the hulking saint leaning on a cane and looking back at the sacred passenger on his shoulder.

I rubbed the medal and thought about my commencement speech and the "out to sea" adventure that I proclaimed would make up our post–high school life. I thought about Juliabelle's promise, "You know I'll make the prayer for you, my Adelaide. I'll be here making it every time you come to mind."

The "Go" in "Go Your Way" was in my mind now, and I mouthed it more than once as the little man came back and asked me if I'd like him to walk me to the counselor's office.

"I'm okay," I said to him, and he smiled a dear and sympathetic smile at me.

"You're welcome here anytime, miss."

"Thank you," I said.

*Go my way.* I mean, I couldn't give up now. Okay, *two* freak things had happened—Brother Benton was gone and Peter was in trouble—but I still had to hold my future by the scruff and not let go. That fury rose inside me like the day on the beach when Daddy wanted me to swim. I could hear him say, "C'mon, sister!"

I inhaled, buttoned my coat, and walked out onto the great hill as a flutter of the fiery-colored leaves loosened from their hinges and fell onto the green grass.

On the quadrangle I could see Dean Atwood pacing the colonnade with President Schaeffer as two media trucks from Roanoke and one from Richmond raised their large antennae for a press conference in response to the arrest. I walked right toward them on my way to Tully, and I gave President Schaeffer the mean eye for the crock of dung he had spewed at us at the convocation. Heck, this wasn't the ivory tower, set apart from reality. Rather, it was its own little warped world tucked in the mountains.

A thought was coming to me. Maybe a title for a poem. I was trying to remember the name of that book I'd read in tenth-grade English class in which a group of young and well-bred boarding-school children devolve from civilized to barbaric after they are stranded on an island.

Before I knew it, a lady in a red suit with gold buttons approached me.

"What year are you, ma'am?" She spoke into a black microphone that had "WKIV-ABC News" sealed across it.

"Freshman," I said as a camera wheeled around to my left.

"What do you think about the arrest that just took place here?"

"I think it's sad," I said. "I know the boy from home, and he is a good boy."

"Oh, so you know Mr. Carpenter?"

Dean Atwood was racing toward me with her finger making a mock slash across her mouth as if to instruct me to button up. The reporter, sensing the urgency, shoved the microphone closer to my lips. "Give me your reaction of the events that have transpired here over the last few weeks."

"I can't make heads or tails of it, miss. I worked my whole life to get into a school like NBU"—I nodded toward the colonnade—"and now the highest-caliber person I know is on his way to jail."

Then the thought came to me! The title of the book was on the tip of my tongue, and I had to spout it out.

"*The Lord of the Flies* meets *Animal House* is how I'd describe it here so far. And this ivory tower is beginning to look more and more like the pig's head on a stick."

Dean Atwood furrowed her brow, then narrowed her eyes at me. She pinched her fingers over her lips in her own version of "Pipe down, Piper!"

But I was too riled up not to finish my thought. I looked away from her and into the camera. "How are we supposed to thrive in an environment like this?"

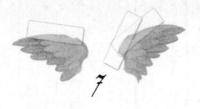

# Freshman Spring

**W**hen Devon Hunt asked me out, I believed it was a turning point in what had been a remarkably tough year.

The shock and horror of what happened to Brother and the subsequent arrest of Peter were the cornerstones, and so was Dean Atwood's sharp letter to me saying that my remarks to the press would adversely affect NBU's reputation and requesting that I leave communications up to those who were trained in that area.

But, moreover, a thin layer upon layer of rejection and self-loathing was what really walled us in.

We all gained our fair share of the freshman fifteen. Pizza was easy to come by. In fact, it was everywhere—in the lounges of the dormitories for every meeting or social, on the quadrangle on Friday afternoons, and even in the foyer of the library at midnight on Wednesdays. This fed the self-loathing that was being birthed in me, and when the button of my favorite pair of jeans popped, I went into the dormitory shower to cry.

Unexpected Weight

*The blonde girls*
*hit their tennis balls*

*back and forth*
*across the net.*
*The calories*
*they burn*
*rise up*
*like mist*
*above the court*
*before the*
*mountain wind*
*ushers them*
*through the crack*
*in my window.*
*They affix*
*themselves*
*to my roommate*
*and me*
*while we sleep,*
*and the next morning*
*we spot them*
*beneath our chins*
*as we peer into*
*the bathroom mirror.*

Jif, the one with the most means and a keen eye for style, refused to be an outcast. She shed her fifteen pounds by eating Raisin Bran for every meal and walking briskly around the campus twice each day. She made regular trips to the tanning salon to put on the appearance that she spent her life outside, and her dorm room was packed with J.Crew and Brooks Brothers catalogs; she studied them and circled her choices and added up the price tags on her calculator. Once she was armed with her mother's credit card number, a package containing an addition to her carefully chosen wardrobe arrived in her PO box weekly. She even refined her Southern dialect so that she sounded more like Scarlett O'Hara. Jif remade herself into a thin, preppy, earthy beauty, and before long the girls from the Northeast befriended her and invited her into their blonde and beautiful world.

As for my academic life, I found the 101 classes to be monotonous and unnecessarily complicated. My only light in the academic realm was the Josiah Dirkas workshop he asked McSweeney if I could audit after reading the poems I slipped under his door and, to my surprise, a religion class about social justice that I stumbled upon during my spring term.

When I called my born-again friend, Shannon, to tell her that I was studying Christianity, she shrieked with delight, "Yes!" to which I rolled my eyes and said, "Don't get too excited, Miss Jesus Freak." Then we both chuckled, and I was grateful that Shannon had not surrendered her sense of humor to the cause.

Overall, I continued to be surprised by how little college had to do with academics. Fraternity parties dominated most conversations among classmates, and as far as I could tell, they appeared to be simply higher-budget versions of the cul-de-sac episodes I had reluctantly attended in Williamstown. Though I'll admit I wanted to be invited out from time to time.

After witnessing a game of keg rolling in the street that had inadvertently crushed one of my Chaucer professor's beloved old house cats, I wrote:

> The majestic
> houses
> with Greek Letters
> branded
> on the piazzas
> encircle the campus
> like a noose.

Frankie published it in the college paper he was now working on, and many a frat folk gave me a cruel stare as I made my way to classes each day. But other than the activist/newspaper types whom Frankie took up with and the Harmony Society, the Greeks were the only place to build a social life, so I still hung out there from time to time.

Every other weekend there were bars on the frat house lawns with men from the hill country serving cocktails and crawfish. There was always live music spilling out their open windows, and occasionally the brothers wore coats and ties instead of blue jeans in an attempt to appear civilized.

During the Winter Formal, Ned Crater set me up with an overweight fraternity brother nicknamed "Behemoth," and I reluctantly danced with his fat arm around me the whole night, his sweat dripping on my black sequined dress—the one Mae Mae had bought for me at Saks Fifth Avenue during a precollege shopping trip she took to Charleston. I looked longingly at Ned and Jif, who gazed into each other's eyes. They danced closely as Ned professed his love every few minutes, causing someone somewhere to yell, "Get a room, Crater!" And I wondered if anyone would ever gaze longingly into my eyes.

"Two hundred and fifty bucks for a sweat rag!" I chuckled to Ruthie as I hung up my dress at the end of the evening.

"That's probably not what your grandmother envisioned," Ruthie said before taking a bag of popcorn out of the microwave and setting it before me.

"Behemoth is nice," I said, munching on the buttery treat, "but I sure hope he doesn't call me."

When Peter was found guilty of involuntary manslaughter one Thursday in April, I threw my Chaucer book at the wall and dissolved into tears. Sensing my despair, Ruthie postponed her trip to Chapel Hill for the weekend, and Jif told Ned that she'd better stick around the dorm, too, and the three of us spent the weekend together.

They drove me to the Pooshee Pass, where we picnicked by the river, sunning on blankets and swinging on a rope swing that whisked us out into the black water, where there was no choice but to let go.

"I know you're down, Adelaide," Ruthie said as we sat on our blankets, sipping Co-Colas and waiting for the sun to bake us dry. "This whole Peter Carpenter thing is definitely freaky. But I just have to believe that life here is going to get better for you and for all of us." (Ruthie's parents had refused her request to transfer to the University of North Carolina, and she was deciding to make the best of things at NBU.)

"Freshman year is supposed to be the hardest of all, right?" Jif said, flicking a horsefly off Ruthie's shoulder. "I know some of it has bothered you, Ad, but next year we'll be sophomores, and we'll know what to expect. And I can surely guess that this whole arrest thing will make the administration take a look at some of the backwardness of the Greek world here. Ned told me that President Schaeffer is investigating all of the frat houses personally and giving them strict instructions about what not to do during initiation."

"You're probably right," I said, my eyes on the moving water as it rushed over the rocks, making them slick and slippery. "But you know, this is just not what I expected college to be like."

"What do you mean?" Ruthie asked.

"I mean, I worked so hard to get here—even got that little scholarship and some help from my grandparents that really sealed the deal. I was counting on this place to transform me into a brighter, better person. But instead, I'm nothing but a country bumpkin. And a reviled one at that."

Jif tucked a strand of wet hair behind my ear, and Ruthie patted my back.

"Don't you think it's like this at most colleges?" Ruthie asked. "I mean, at Chapel Hill, some pretty backward stuff goes on."

"Well, yeah, bad stuff goes on in pockets of every college, but we're so small and secluded here."

They both nodded in an attempt to hear me out.

"But it's more than that for me," I said. "For one thing, you both have people who care about you in the midst of it all." Jif shielded her eyes from the afternoon sun, and Ruthie dug her toes into the black river mud.

"You've got Tag and a place to escape to," I said to Ruthie. And to Jif, "You've got Ned pining all over you—inviting you to every social event that comes down the pike and walking you safely back to the dorm each night."

Jif looked down to her pink toenails and nodded.

"The only person who has so much as looked my way this year is Behemoth!"

Then we all laughed and put our hands over our mouths to hide our full-blown grins. Even me. My ears reddened with embarrassment.

Behemoth had called me every other week for a few months to ask me out, and I always made some half-baked excuse about a paper to write or a friend coming from out of town. Finally, he stopped calling, and I was relieved.

"I'm alone," I said, feeling the familiar sting in my eye.

"You're not alone," Jif said, squeezing my shoulder. "You've got us, for one thing."

"And you've got your poetry," said Ruthie. "Dirkas just asked you to join that upperclassman workshop next semester. You aced that religion class, and the professor called to tell you that he wanted you to submit your last essay to a religion magazine!"

When I was honest with myself, I had to admit that I'd had some positive experiences at NBU: I had joined the community service program and served food at a soup kitchen twice a month on Saturdays. My creative writing teacher, Professor Dirkas, had been hired as a permanent professor. He liked my work and invited me to join the graduate class next fall. The social justice class was taught by Dr. Shaw, that wise and gentle minister who helped me find McSweeney's office last fall, and he had us all over to his home, where his wife cooked us spaghetti and let their three children sit in our laps while we discussed writings of Niebuhr and Ryan. As I held Molly, Dr. Shaw's joyful and precocious three-year-old, I wondered what the Shaw family did to take cover when the kegs started rolling in the streets.

And I had to admit that there were students in Dr. Shaw's class who didn't seem like barbarians, and I was thankful to know that they existed. One of them even invited me to a Bible study, and I winced at the sound of it but peeked in the chapel once on my way to the library; they were having an intense discussion about the *The Great Divorce* by C. S. Lewis. The discussion had something to do with Lewis's assertion that earth was actually a region of hell, and that piqued my interest for a moment. Certain portions of my freshman year at NBU could pass for a region of hell!

"I'm fat and alone," I said now, unwilling to depart from the pity party I was hosting with my friends. "My mom is going to *die* when she sees me. I mean, she's been buying me party dresses for the deb season I won't be able to fit into! At this point, I can't even get my big toe into them!"

"Okay, stop right there!" Jif said with a determined look in her eyes.

She squeezed both of our wrists and continued, "I think a diet is what will make us all feel better. We've got six weeks until we go home for the summer, and I think we should each try to drop ten pounds before then."

"How?" Ruthie asked.

"I'm practically an expert on this," Jif assured us. "Laird and Jenna do it all the time." (Laird and Jenna were Jif's two newest friends, and they were both from quaint Connecticut towns outside Manhattan. They were pencil thin and usually dressed to kill.)

So Jif and Ruthie and I spent the rest of the afternoon at the Pooshee Pass concocting a college-budget crash diet that included Slim-Fast, ramen noodles, chewing gum, and diet pills. Ugh.

When Devon Hunt asked me out at the Wednesday coffeehouse social, I thought things were finally looking up. Devon was a first-year law student at the University of Virginia, and his father was the provost at NBU. He was an alum and came down frequently to see his folks and old friends at the Phi Kap house.

On the night that we met, I was tapping my foot at our table with

Jif, Ruthie, and my new friend Vera, an exchange student from Vienna, Austria.

Taking Jif's lead, I'd toned down my makeup, depermed my hair at the local salon, and begun the painful process of dieting so that my debutante dress would fasten when I went home for the summer. I felt lighter, having shed the first few pounds of pizza and ice cream that had attached themselves to my rear end over the last eight months. I even stood up to dance when the guitarist played my favorite song, "Brown-Eyed Girl," and moved with a new kind of exuberance and hope, before Devon made his way over to extend his hand in an introduction.

It was my first real date since Luigi Agnolucci (if you didn't count my asking Lazarus to the senior dance and being set up with Behemoth), and my friends were as excited as I was. They brought in all their new spring dresses and sandals for me to try on.

He wanted to take me out to dinner instead of a frat party. And he had said something about a movie or a drive up to Buxton Hill to look through his telescope at the stars.

"I'm so excited for you!" Jif said, and she pulled out a pale pink sundress from her closet that still had the store tags dangling from it.

"That's your Kentucky Derby dress," I said, waving it away. (Ned had relatives in Louisville with box seats, and he had invited her to attend the event with his family. She had ordered it from some fancy New York boutique that Jenna had told her about, and had searched all over Roanoke for the perfect hat and shoes to accompany it.)

"I'm *not* going to wear that before you," I said. "And besides, there is no way I could fit into it."

"This is your color, Adelaide, and I know it would look great on you," Jif persuaded. She waved the dress forward and backward so that it billowed out as though a breeze were bringing it to life. Then she threw it to me, and I had no choice but to catch it.

"Now, if you spend the next two days before the date on a liquid diet . . . ," Jif said.

"I *can't*," I protested. "I've got that McSweeney paper to write before finals, and I don't have the stamina that you do. I need food to write papers!"

Jif had already proved she had the will to diet. Over the last two weeks she had followed our Tully Dormitory Diet to a tee and had lost six pounds. She had even climbed Kiki Mountain with Laird and Ned in the middle of it all, and she had made a B+ on her American History paper.

I held up the lovely pink dress my friend had thrust in my arms before looking back to Jif, who was raising her eyebrows in a familiar expression of determination. We stood this way for one whole minute until I agreed to a liquid breakfast and lunch.

"But I have to eat dinner," I said as she took the liberty of grabbing the dress and hanging it up in the center of my closet.

I didn't drink at my dinner with Devon Hunt—I wasn't old enough, and it was my little test to see if he would be interested in a girl who didn't partake. Not to mention the fact that all my stomach had seen during the last twenty-four hours was coffee, water, and orange juice so that I could squeeze into Jif's dress. It fit me perfectly, and I was glad to have made the extra effort to wear it, though my fingers were trembling with hunger by the time the waitress brought my pasta primavera.

I had even consented to a Correctol laxative that Jif sent in an envelope to my room the night before.

"This will do the trick," she had written. "I've tried it before, and Laird does it all the time."

I took it reluctantly before falling into bed and spent much of my afternoon on the library toilet instead of in my study room.

Devon Hunt had one beer and a steak sandwich and told me stories about law school at the University of Virginia and the good times he'd had at NBU.

"So what do you think you'll major in?" he asked.

"English with a creative writing focus," I said.

"I was an English major. What do you want to do with it?"

"I want to be a poet, as impractical as that sounds." I swirled the pasta around my spoon as I waited for his response.

"Hey"—he shrugged—"somebody's got to fill the bookshelves with new stuff. Why can't it be you?"

"Yeah." I grinned at his optimism. I looked him in the eye and wondered if someone true was beneath the surface.

Just then one of his friends stopped by the table to say hello.

"And who's the lucky girl this evening?" the boy said, stretching his hand out in an introduction.

"Adelaide . . . um . . . ," Devon said, and I could tell he couldn't remember my last name, though Jif, Ruthie, and I had said his full name over and over all week long. We had even looked up his senior photograph in an old yearbook. He was sitting on a rocking chair on the front porch of the Phi Kap house, reading *Tender Is the Night* by Fitzgerald.

"Piper," I said as Devon searched my face.

"Right," he said, wiping his brow. Then he reached over to squeeze my hand. "This is my lovely date for the evening, Miss Adelaide Piper."

I had seen Devon's friend before. He was a seasoned senior and was often seen sitting on the lawn, drinking a beer or throwing a Frisbee. I'd taken note of him once on a Saturday night in an argument with a girl I did not know. When the girl scurried away from him, he threw his beer bottle against the column and it shattered into tiny pieces of sharp brown glass that caught the light of the moon as I walked by. It gave me a funny feeling. I would have loved to have had a man break glass over my departure. Heck, I would have settled for an "Oh, stay a few more minutes."

"It's called being whipped," Frankie had said to me when I related the incident. It was something that happened on a rare occasion at NBU. A boy, even a cool frat boy, would fall hopelessly in love (usually with one of the prep-school blondes), and he would become nice and sweet and do anything she said. A senior had become whipped over Laird, Jif's friend, and he brought her roses and took her home to meet his parents over Christmas break. He even decided to attend the NBU law school instead of the higher-ranking Yale where he had been accepted so that he could be closer to her.

Maybe Devon would fall like that. I hoped *someone* would break glass over me one of these days.

"Don't let him fool you, Miss Piper," the boy said. "He looks quite the part of the intellectual with his books and telescope, but behind the smoke and mirrors he's a typical Phi Kap."

"I'll remember that," I said (wondering what the take-home message was), and the boy patted Devon on the back and took his seat with a group of seniors toward the back of the restaurant.

Devon rolled his eyes at his friend's departure.

"So, an English major?" he said. "I remember the days. Have you taken McSweeney's American Poetry class?"

I had a paper due to him day after next, and I was delighted that my date was familiar with the course.

Devon had concentrated on American literature, and we remarked about McSweeney's bizarre obsession with Robert Frost, whom he had known during his days at Dartmouth. McSweeney had shared a few lunches with Frost during his college years and recounted their conversations about twentieth-century poetry over and over to his classes. He was an obvious chauvinist, Devon agreed, and he reenacted several cruel remarks he had made toward female classmates who attempted to dissect the poetry he adored.

I admitted that I was writing a paper about William Carlos Williams, another one of his favorite poets, in order to maintain my B average, though I really wanted to write about Marianne Moore, whose nature poems seemed the most compelling of anyone I had studied.

During a quick bathroom break, I ran into Miranda Thompson, an upperclassman from my social justice class. Miranda was from Columbia, South Carolina, and we had shared a few friendly conversations about our misfit state and the Governor's School, which Miranda had attended for science and math.

"Hi, Piper," she said as I applied the subtle rose-colored lipstick Jif had selected for me. "You look terrific," she said. "What's different?"

"I've lost a few pounds."

"Good for you. That freshman weight can be a bear."

"Don't I know it," I said. "I've gotta lose a few more before I head home so my parents won't think I'm some evil dorm mate who ate their daughter."

Miranda chuckled as she readjusted her blouse in the mirror. "So what do you have going on tonight?"

"I'm out with a graduate—Devon Hunt. I met him at the coffee-house the other night."

She raised her eyebrows slightly. "Isn't that the provost's son?" she asked.

"Yeah," I said. "Know him?"

"I know *of* him. I knew a girl who used to go out with him."

"Oh," I said. "Well, he seems like a nice guy."

"Yeah," Miranda said; then she turned around to face me. "Just take it slow. I wish someone had told me that my freshman year."

"Don't worry," I said. "My pace is comparable to a snail's."

We both laughed, and Miranda wished me luck on my finals.

"I won't see you until next spring," she remarked.

"Why?"

"I'm taking the London abroad semester in the fall."

"How great," I said, and I imagined myself flying to London in a few years to study British literature (though that would definitely take another private trip to Papa Great and Mae Mae's house).

I said good-bye and headed back into the dining room, where Devon was waiting with a smile.

⌒

Devon remarked about the clear spring sky as we walked out of the restaurant. Then he handed me a peppermint and tried to persuade me to let him drive us up to the Buxton family cemetery hill on the outskirts of campus where he could set up his telescope and give me a good look at the constellations.

I had told him over dinner that I had signed up for Tuttle's astronomy class in the fall, which was one of the more popular science courses on campus, and he said that he had loved it so much that his parents bought him a telescope for graduation.

"I probably shouldn't," I said. "I've got to work on that paper for McSweeney tonight, and my time is ticking on a study room." I had reserved one of the private rooms in the library, and I envisioned my stacks of papers and reference books as they lay open and sprawled across the table.

Also, I was still shaky with hunger. I'd gotten only a fourth of the way through my pasta primavera before the waitress whisked it away, and I was already planning a trip to the Hardee's drive-through on the way to the library.

Devon pointed to the sky, and I saw hundreds of stars staring back at us.

"I'll have you back before the clock strikes ten," he said, "or I'll turn *myself* into a pumpkin."

Suddenly I remembered Jif and Ruthie waving me good-bye earlier in the evening with their fingers crossed.

"Now, don't be so uptight," Ruthie had advised. "Let yourself have some fun, Adelaide. It's okay."

I had put in a lot of preparation for this date to have it over already.

"All right," I said to Devon as we walked toward his car. "Perhaps it will inspire me."

He drove me up the hill in his old Volvo station wagon. The telescope rattled and scraped across the back window as we made our way up the gravelly incline. Much to my embarrassment, my stomach began to groan in protest of the Tully Dorm Diet, and I felt a little light-headed.

"It's a clear night," he said, not seeming to notice the noise. "Perfect conditions for stargazing."

"Great," I said, basking in his attention and the romantic notion of peering at the stars together. If I could just get my stomach and head to hold on a little longer, I would give them what they needed in less than an hour.

Devon set up the telescope and pointed me in the direction of Virgo. He stood behind me, gently directing me on how to use the apparatus. Yes, I could see it, the outline of the maiden who, Devon told me, announced the harvest when the sun passed through her in mid-September.

"I've spotted it!" I said.

"She's the second-largest constellation in the sky," he said as he spread a blanket out on the grass just outside the cemetery gates. "She's one of the zodiacs too," he added while pulling out a bottle of red wine from his backpack, "but I'll let Tuttle fill you in on all of that."

As he unrolled two delicate glasses from a dishrag, he sheepishly admitted they were from his mother's kitchen.

"I'll have just a sip," I instructed. "I don't really drink, and I do have to get some work done tonight." *Loosen up, Adelaide.*

I sat up Indian-style as he reclined on his elbows and the crickets called to one another in every direction. After we stared into the Milky Way in an attempt to catch a falling star, he leaned in to kiss me and I moved away instinctively. I was startled by this sudden move, and things were beginning to go a little too fast for my taste. I hadn't kissed anyone since Luigi Agnolucci, and that was two summers ago.

Did I get a fear of physical intimacy from my mother, or was I right to want to take things slow? Shannon believed in abstinence before marriage. But Ruthie was physically active with Tag—at least I assumed so after seeing a condom fall out of his wallet one day while he was buying us ice cream in downtown Troutville. I hadn't made up my mind about such things, but I knew it would have to be a serious relationship. *But one kiss can't hurt,* I thought, and when he leaned in again, I responded nervously.

We took a few more sips of wine, and he smoked a cigarette, which seemed somehow out of character. I hadn't figured him for a smoker.

My stomach groaned again. I needed to eat something soon. The smoke from his cigarette made my head pound, and I was beginning to think about all of the work that was waiting for me in my study room. I had reserved it only for the next twenty-four hours.

"We'd better head back, Devon," I said. "That paper for McSweeney is due day after tomorrow. The time is ticking in my study room."

When I said this, he gripped my shoulders firmly and pressed me hard into the ground.

"That hurt," I said, pushing him away. I was shocked at his sudden physical aggression, and I gritted my teeth and said, "Let me *up*. Get *off* of me!"

But he didn't. And he didn't look me in the eye when his fists pounded my chin as he ripped open the top of my dress. The metal taste of blood filled my mouth, and my jaw ached with pain. When I screamed, he punched me in the stomach and pinned my neck down with his forearm. I could feel the blood from my lip sliding down my cheek and into my hair as I gasped for air.

∽

It was over in a matter of minutes. He had taken my virginity away by force in no time at all while I hit his back and scratched at his face before giving up and going somewhere else in my mind: the salt-marsh creek behind my house where I caught my first spot-tailed bass and put its slippery body back into the water. Daddy had removed the plastic portion of his hand to reveal the metal pinchers in an effort to get the hook out of the fish's mouth. "Hurry now, Daddy," I had called. "Get it back in the water!"

"Let's get you home," Devon said after standing up, adjusting his pants, and rubbing his hands together as if to keep warm. "I'll give you a lift back down to campus." He nodded toward his car, where the telescope was still pointing in the direction of the stars.

I kept my face buried in the quilted blanket and let out a muffled cry.

"Get away from me," I said when he extended his hand to help me up. "I wouldn't *dare* get in a car with you!"

"C'mon, now." And I could tell that he couldn't even recall my name in all the excitement. "How are you going to get back to the dorm?"

"Get away from me," I said again with an intense wrath in my voice that did not register with him.

"Suit yourself." He shook his head as if I were a supreme disappointment.

Then he drove back down the hill, his taillights blinking like a warning that comes too late.

When I found myself in complete darkness, I wept and wept for what seemed like hours while a dog far away let out a howl. The crickets were making music, and wisteria buds were forming in the vines that lined the cemetery.

I gathered the quilt around my shoulders when the security guard made his way up the hill on his usual late-night rounds to lock the campus gates. His flashlight blinded me for a moment; then I sat up and waved him toward me. He did not seem altogether surprised to find me there, and he ushered me to his car and down to the infirmary after guessing what had happened by my muffled weeping into the quilt.

Ms. Eugenia, the nurse, met us there in her bathrobe.

I squinted in the fluorescent light of the examining room, the grass-stained quilt draping me like a shroud.

It was the death of many things.

I had studied William Blake's *The Songs of Innocence* and *The Songs of Experience* in Penelope Russo's class, and I knew now what they were about. My virginity was gone in one brutal moment, and so were my wide-eyed innocence and trust of other human beings. What would move in, in their place, was fear, anxiety, and bitterness. These things were taking root in my heart even as I waited for Ms. Eugenia to direct me.

"Do you want to talk about it?" she asked.

"No. I want to be examined by the doctor, then just go to my room. I have a paper due tomorrow." I felt a sense of urgency to turn back the clock and remember what had been my focus just minutes before I was raped.

"The doctor is out of town until tomorrow afternoon," Ms. Eugenia said. "Why don't you take a bath and spend the night here in the infirmary?" She handed me two pills that she said would calm my nerves.

"I want to go back to my room. Isn't there a backup doctor?"

"I'll write your professor an excuse," she said as she reached to pat my shoulder.

Jumping back from her, I cried, "If there is no doctor around, please let me call my roommate to come get me."

"All right," Ms. Eugenia conceded, "if that will make you feel better. But you should come back tomorrow to see the doctor. They usually don't, but you really should."

Jif and Ruthie picked me up within ten minutes. They took me home and sat in the bathroom with me while I took a long, piercing-hot shower.

In less than three weeks my folks would be here to take me home for the summer. Mama had already sent me copies of the debutante tea and luncheon invitations, and she was making a scrapbook of them and ordering dresses from Talbot's and Laura Ashley for the occasions.

I pondered all of this as Jif and Ruthie quietly guided me into my pajamas before I curled up in my creaky bed and stared at the grooves around the blocks in the wall.

Depression set in like fog on the mountain peaks as my freshman year concluded. My period came two days after my date with Devon Hunt, and I didn't return to see the doctor at the health clinic. The books sat in the library of my reserved study room gathering dust all week, and I barely passed my exams and received a D on my McSweeney paper, which I changed at the last moment to an examination of the poems of Marianne Moore.

# Debutante Summer

When Daddy picked me up at NBU the last Saturday in May, he was too excited about a successful Bizway meeting he'd had in Roanoke the night before to notice the dull glaze over my eyes. Not that I would have let him see it anyway.

My daddy! He pulled me close with his stump and his arm on the front steps of Tully, where he had pulled the station wagon up to the loading zone and opened the wide, wood-paneled trunk door. He smelled like a mixture of aftershave and vitamins, and I would have wailed if I'd let my guard down. But I didn't.

He'd gone back to the habit of pinning up the long sleeve of the amputated arm instead of wearing the prosthetic, and when he nuzzled my head, I could feel the safety pin and the fabric from his blue oxford across the back of my head and then on my ear when he pulled back to examine me.

It had been three weeks since the rape. I had failed most of my finals, jeopardizing my scholarship, and had managed to gain back a fair portion of the weight that I'd lost on the Tully Diet, and though he didn't say a word, I could see a look of concern register on his face.

"You all right, sister?" he asked.

"Yes, sir. Just ready to get home."

"Now, I never thought *those* words would come out of your mouth."

Then he loaded our car with my typewriter, books, and hanging clothes, laying them carefully on top of the Bizway vitamins, air filters, and cleaning supplies that took up a good portion of the trunk.

There were no handsome young bucks carting my stuff down the three flights of stairs and into my car this time. Just my one-armed daddy and me, straining to carry the boxes of books and sweaters through the dorm doors as pockets of giggly freshmen hugged one another good-bye. I took one glance around at the colonnade and the grass, which seemed as though someone had spray-painted it a vibrant shade of jade each night while term papers and coffee beans danced in our heads. If I got word over the summer that my scholarship was gone, I'd probably never come back.

On the drive down the mountains, we listened to training cassettes of Bizway gems who had built lucrative businesses by signing up folks underneath them who purchased products. At one point Daddy pounded the steering wheel and said, "Now, doesn't this excite you, Adelaide?"

*Excite me?* I thought. *Winning the Nobel Prize in poetry wouldn't excite me at this point.* I was all but numb to the core.

As Daddy talked about the plan and how he wanted to make a run for it, wanted to become a diamond and collect a $12,000 paycheck every month (not to mention the speaking fees), I tuned out and wondered how I could avoid revealing to Mama and Juliabelle what had happened to me. They would be the two to sense that something was wrong, so I'd have to be a heck of an actress to convince them otherwise.

∾

When we pulled into the driveway of my white clapboard house that afternoon, I was struck with the thick, moist air and the syrupy scent of jasmine that was in full bloom along the sides of the house and the front porch. Lou jumped up from the rocking chair and ran out to the car barefoot, her face lit up like a jack-o'-lantern.

"Adelaide!"

She ran up to the passenger side and put her hands on the window before she jumped up and down.

"She's here!" she shouted to the house, and in seconds Mama and Dizzy were running down the porch, clapping and smiling and saying, "Welcome home!"

When I got out of the car, they crowded around me, even Dizzy, and embraced me. They smelled like perfume and tomatoes and cigarettes and pluff mud, and it was all I could do to bite my lip and try not to fall apart in front of them.

Daddy gave everyone a job in unpacking the car, so I was relieved that I didn't have to look anyone in the eye too long.

It was Juliabelle who took notice of me a few minutes later. She caught my eye that afternoon as she was packing up Papa Great to move him out to Pawleys Island for the summer while Mae Mae and Mama went debbing with me. I was hauling two pillowcases of dirty clothes when I spotted her running across my grandparents' front garden and over to mine to greet me. She had a Pyrex bowl full of pickled creek shrimp that she'd made for me.

"Adelaide!" she said. "Look at you, child!"

She hugged me, dirty clothes and all, rocking me back and forth in her skinny arms. I could feel her jaw working her bubble gum, and the sweet smell of it reminded me of all that was good about my home life.

I thought about the St. Christopher medal and the prayers she'd offered for me daily, and I vowed I would do all in my power to keep the awful secret of my defilement from her.

Then she cupped her pink palms around my flabby cheeks and took a look into my eyes. At first, I turned away toward Mama's hydrangea blooms, but she wouldn't let me loose. Then I glanced back at her and tried to make my face say, "Nothing. Nothing is wrong here."

She stepped back and put a clenched fist over her mouth and blinked hard. It was the same thing I'd seen her do the summer she spotted a gator that had drifted out of the river and into the surf at Pawleys Island. And she had done it once when Papa Great told Mae Mae to fire the gardener who had shown up late.

"Adelaide," she said through her lips, "you come talk to me when you can."

I shook my head as though I hadn't the faintest idea of what she was talking about and gulped back the tears. I had never been so relieved to see the round shadow of Papa Great as it surfaced on the driveway.

I turned away from her to greet him.

"Well, the college girl's home," he said, pinching his nostrils together before snorting once for good measure.

He patted my back, then looked me up and down and said, "Well, gotta lose that weight before the debutante ball. Adelaide Rutledge Graydon had a slim figure, you know?"

I didn't know whether to slap him or hug him for changing the subject.

"Hope the year treated you right," he said; then he looked over to the Cadillac that was packed to the brim with Co-Colas and bright linen blazers and fishing rods and buckets.

"'Bout ready to head on?" he said to Juliabelle.

"Yes, sir," she said as he started back toward the car.

"Come visit us when you get a break from all the parties, Adelaide," he said.

Juliabelle put her long fingers back on my chin. "I'll give you a few days. But then I 'spect you to come out to the island and talk."

I looked beyond her at the two fingers of smog billowing out of the paper mill and then down at the cracks in the driveway where the spider grass was pushing through the bricks and oyster shells. Papa Great was starting the engine, and she reached to the top of the station wagon where she'd rested the bowl of shrimp, handed it to me, and walked back across the garden.

Before I could stop them, tears were streaming down my face, but Daddy was so busy telling Mama about the Bizway meeting that Lou was the only one to notice me.

"A-Ad?" she said. "What's wrong?" She looked up at me with three pronounced worry lines across her shining forehead.

"Just missed you is all," I said. Then I handed her a pillowcase of laundry. "Want to help me wash clothes?"

I didn't look back at the Cadillac as it drove out of the historic district and toward the bridge. But I could imagine Juliabelle in the backseat by the fishing tackle, her big dark eyes bearing down on me.

When I walked into the house, Daddy was throwing one of Mama's ripe tomatoes against the wall in the kitchen. It hit the bright striped wallpaper by the pantry and slid down the blue and yellow lines, landing right at Mama's feet.

"You're a *fool* to jeopardize your job, Zane Piper," Mama was whispering harshly to him. "When he finds out, then you tell me where we'll be!"

They both looked up at me as I tried to make myself scarce and head toward the stairwell.

"Adelaide," Mama called to me in a sweet, strained voice, "I'll have your lunch ready in just a minute, darlin'."

It helped to be home for the summer. There were times when I could forget for whole minutes about what happened with Devon Hunt on the campus hillside, but the anxiety never left me completely. I could get lost watching the dust dance in the morning sun that poured through my bedroom window or Mama tending to her tomato vines, but when someone tapped on my door with a breakfast invitation, dread seized me once again. It ran up my spine and made every muscle in my back tighten.

When I looked out into the kudzu-covered field that met my backyard and ate everything but the marsh, I remembered learning in a high-school botany class that the unyielding vine grows a foot each day during the summer months and sixty feet each year, snuffing the life out of trees that need sunlight and overtaking any abandoned vehicle or building in its path. I knew I was a meager tree in the center of that field, and I had no way of stopping the vine of fear from darkening my days.

Ruthie and I were glad to have left that dank dorm room with all its bad memories and move on to our debutante summers. Ruthie would be receiving tea and chicken salad at her own "coming out" luncheons at the Country Club of North Carolina, while Jif and I did the same in the handful of once-grand homes that lined Third Avenue in downtown Williamstown.

In a sense, our transition into womanhood (which was what the debutante season was supposed to be about) was a thick piece of iced pound cake. There was a certain charade about this rite of passage passed down from our English ancestors, but we had it easy compared to girls in other cultures or other time periods. We didn't have to bind our feet like a Chinese girl in the thirteenth century or mutilate our bodies like the young women in the northern and western parts of Africa do even today. Instead, we just learned to ballroom dance, socialize, eat mayonnaise-laden chicken salad at the country club, and write warm and witty thank-you notes on monogrammed stationery.

To the South of the 1990s, this was what prepared you for becoming a grown lady in good standing. And this summer was all about social engagements of every sort, where we were to gain confidence in each facet of Southern etiquette—to include table manners and small talk with little old ladies who were most proud to have an opportunity to put their fine china and silver to use. It was a tradition that had been passed down since the plantation days, and, like the Confederacy, it would not be forgotten.

The Williamstown summer debutante season was our formal introduction to society, and it concluded with a ball the following Christmas, where we would first lift our floor-length white gowns with the tips of our long kid gloves to curtsy in front of our parents and grandparents and then march up and down the corridors of the Magnolia Club as if to say, "Here is the next generation of well-bred Southern ladies! We're of age, so have at us!"

⌒

"How was your first year at Nathaniel Buxton?" Mrs. Zapes asked me during the first luncheon of the season.

"It was good," I flat-out lied. I knew it just wouldn't do to say, "Horrible. The classes were monotonous, the students took no interest in me, and to top it all off, I was raped by my one and only date a few weeks before the year concluded. By July, I'll know for sure if I've lost my scholarship, so chew on that with your chicken salad and fruit tarts, Mrs. Zapes!"

I caught my eye in the gilded mirror of the musty drawing room. I felt ridiculous in the paper-white dress and patent-leather flats that Mama insisted I wear. I looked like a doily or a handkerchief in one of Mrs. Zapes's beaded purses.

"That's a fine institution," the widowed Mrs. Kitteridge chimed in. "My husband, Padgett, was proud to call NBU his alma mater, and I can still remember my first dance with him there at the Heritage Ball beneath the starry Virginia sky. What a romantic evening that was!"

"But did you all hear the awful news about the Carpenter boy who was in school up there?" Miss Pringle crooned. She was the old maid of the town and loved to talk about other people's business, particularly their falls from grace. "Juanita, their next-door neighbor, says his mama has not taken a single visitor. Says she's utterly inconsolable, bless her heart."

"Yes," Jif jumped in to save me from the conversation. "That was really awful, Miss Pringle. It looks like Peter made a very poor judgment call that will cost him dearly. But the NBU administration has taken great strides to enforce fraternity hazing rules so that nothing like that will ever happen again." And then to Mrs. Kitteridge, "They still have the Heritage Ball and an outdoor dance floor on the front quad like always. My boyfriend, Ned, and I danced barefoot there into the early hours of the morning just a few months ago. You're right; it was truly romantic."

Jif. Ugh. She was charming, and everyone admired her. She was dressed to the nines in a blue linen pantsuit and strappy sandals that snaked their way up her ankles, and she brought to the deb parties a kind of style and freshness that I envied. *How could she have come out of her freshman year at NBU unscathed?* I wondered. Just three doors away on the same floor of the Tully dormitory, and we were in completely different places.

Jif's mama, Marny Ferguson, looked like a million bucks too. She had grown up in the mill village and had made her way out by becoming a beauty queen. First Miss Williamstown, then Miss South Carolina, but she downplayed this, as beauty queens weren't necessarily debutante material—too made-up and flashy for a well-bred gal. But Marny's life mission was to show the Mrs. Zapeses of the world that she did know the difference and was certainly able to ascend to the height of the social order of Williamstown.

She'd had the good sense to marry up with a local boy, Teddy Ferguson, while he was in medical school in Charleston. She persuaded him to switch his focus from pediatrics to plastic surgery, and he was given credit for improving the looks of every well-off woman in a sixty-mile radius of Williamstown. Thin as a rail and enjoying the benefits of her own first face-lift, she was sitting in the corner with a bird-sized plate of chicken salad, her tan Ferragamo shoes catching the sunlight.

Marny Ferguson was proud, it was easy to see, of the way NBU had sharpened Jif's sense of wit and style. She encouraged her to keep her freshman weight off by taking her to an aerobics class once a day, and she introduced her to the meal-replacement bars and shakes that were selling at the new health-food store outside Columbia. She had even bought Jif a snug and gorgeous designer deb dress from a pricey Atlanta boutique to entice her into keeping her weight down.

Mrs. Kitteridge patted her wrinkled lips with a monogrammed napkin and began again. "Of course, they weren't admitting girls at the time my Padgett was there."

"This conversation is dying a slow death," my eyes said to Jif from across the drawing room.

"No, that didn't happen until 1982," said Jif, flicking a fruit fly off her tart before sighing and giving me an "I tried" look.

I scanned the room to see what the other debs were up to. What an odd assortment of girls we were. Poor Winkie Pride was caught between a conversation with her mother and the mayor's wife, Flo Kuhn. Winkie had quite a flamboyant name for such a mouse of a young lady. She had been homeschooled all of her life and was still living with her folks and commuting to the USC satellite campus at Myrtle Beach. Whenever I spoke with her, she emitted a squeaky, nervous laugh, and she had a significantly delayed response to any question or comment I posed. It was downright *work* to carry on a conversation with her, and the worst part was that Winkie seemed to be all too aware of her verbal shortcomings. She had warm green eyes that pleaded, "Please don't leave me here with no one to talk to," but she had no idea how to help herself.

Now I could tell that Winkie was relieved to have caught the attention of Mrs. Zapes's house cat, as this somehow excused her from conversing with anyone. She petted him the rest of the luncheon and whispered who knew what into his fuzzy ears.

Nan McCant was an excellent conversationalist, but she tended to get on my nerves. She attended Converse College and was as petite and preppy as they come with a round, cursive monogram on everything she owned, from her earrings to her pocketbook to the backs of her pastel sweater sets. Jif and I joked that Nan would have monogrammed the hood of her zippy white convertible if she could have. Of course, she couldn't resist personalizing her license plate with KN ROSE (she had been chosen as the sweetheart of the Kappa Nu fraternity at Wofford College), and she frequently pulled out her framed picture of the frat composite to point to whatever boy had come up in her frivolous chitchat. And there was her photo in the center of the group of handsome young men, right between the cook and the mascot, a chocolate Labrador retriever named Leroy.

This left Jif and me as the last of three debs. Georgianne would have made four, but she was a mother to Baby Peach now and a wife to Peach Hickman, who worked at his daddy's tractor company. Georgianne's mother declined any invitation to the events, and I was certain Georgianne never received one.

The third deb had not yet graced us with her presence, as she was on a trip to France with her family. Her name was Harriet von Hasselson Hartness, and Jif and I hadn't laid eyes on her since she was in grade school. She was the granddaughter of Mrs. Marguerite Hartness, the wealthiest lady in town, who lived at the end of Third Street in the house where in 1825 the Marquis de Lafayette stood on the second-floor piazza in the dark of night to greet more than a thousand Williamstown residents during his tour of the thirteen states.

Harriet had grown up in some charming Connecticut town, and all we knew about her was that she went to the pricey (not to mention *liberal*) Sarah Lawrence College outside Manhattan. Our imaginations had run wild with suppositions about the pretentious snob she would likely be.

"Harriet von Hasselson Hartness has a driver and a personal assistant who gives her manicures and massages," Jif and I joked as we swung in the hammock at the end of my crab dock and flipped through Mae Mae's fancy hand-me-down magazines.

"Harriet buys all of her clothes from Neiman Marcus," Jif said, pointing her finger at an ad in a *Town & Country* that was dated 1984.

"She has an account there," I added, slapping at a giant mosquito that was nibbling on my knee. The air was still, and not a strand of the summer-green marsh grass was moving.

"Her thank-you note stationery is stamped with a family crest," Jif joked, but I didn't even know what a family crest was.

"She has a tennis bracelet and a double strand of pearls that her grandmother bought for her in Japan," I said, fanning the thick air. (I had heard about gifts like that from the Northeastern girls at NBU.)

So Harriet von Hasselson Hartness became a caricature of the ideal debutante. She was a modern-day princess with an endless supply of beauty, brains, and wealth. Moreover, she was everything that was beyond our grasp, and she grew larger than life each day she was absent from the social functions.

"She has thin ankles, and she wears a D-sized bra," Jif said as we sipped on Cherry Cokes at Campbell's Pharmacy on Main Street one afternoon.

(We were B cups at best.)

"I've got it!" I said in an inspired moment, as a streak of ash from the steel mill descended upon the store window. "She didn't gain any weight her freshman year of college."

"Oh, how I hate her!" Jif had screamed with a half-crazed laugh.

"You girls are so fortunate to live in the time that you do," Mrs. Zapes said now, concluding the first luncheon of the season as she signaled someone in the kitchen. "You can go to the finest schools and expand your horizons in a way that we couldn't. Isn't that right, Edwina?"

"It's true," Mrs. Kitteridge responded, and her eyes glazed over as she peered beyond my shoulder into some bygone daydream of how her life would have turned out if she'd been born in the generation the world was about to label "X."

*Would she have been sitting in this parlor, nibbling on chicken salad? I had to wonder. Or did she have her own itch that she couldn't quite get to? And now, in what could very well be the last decade of her life, has she resigned herself to the fact that she will never reach it?*

Mrs. Kitteridge woke up from all the possibilities and wiped her watery eyes to look me straight in the face. "As they say, the world is your *oyster*, my dear."

"That is what they say," I responded, though my world had become a cramped cell with stone walls.

I suddenly jumped with fright when the housekeeper came up behind me with a silver tray full of teacups and saucers. My strawberry tart slid off my plate and landed upside down in my lap, leaving a dark smudge in the center of my paper-white dress.

~

The anxiety hatched all sorts of unfounded suspicions in my mind. I couldn't stand for someone to come up behind me without warning, and I *never* wanted to be left alone.

When the serviceman at the gas station filled my tank, I locked the doors. When I drove by the mobile home where I saw the woman harshly slapped a few summers ago, I picked up speed so that I could get by quickly. I avoided the mill village on the outskirts of town where the young woman had given me that haunting look on my way to college last summer, and when I had to go by there on a fishing trip with Daddy, I simply closed my eyes for a whole minute until it was out of sight.

I didn't like to drive by myself at night. I didn't like to be home alone. Ever. I wouldn't go to the movies by myself or loll about in the city library the way I had for so many summers, falling into one fictional world after another on the worn-out sofas that smelled of pencil lead and used books.

When I saw Averill Skaggs and Bubba Ratliff shuffling down Main Street in their mill uniforms, I ducked into Campbell's and buried myself in a newspaper until they passed.

"What is *with* you?" Dizzy pried one evening after I begged her to stay home and play gin rummy.

"Well, Lou's at a slumber party, and Mama and Daddy are going with Uncle Tinka to that Bizway meeting, and I just don't want to be here by myself."

"Adelaide, this is ridiculous," Dizzy said as she pulled a cigarette out of her purse. Though she knew everyone was out for the evening, she looked behind both shoulders only to find Marmalade, the cat, stretching out her paws on the sofa. As she took her first drag, she said, "I just don't get this, sis. Nine months ago you were the most independent girl I knew. You wanted to sail out into the world and make your way and become a great poet or something, and now you're home from college and afraid to spend an evening alone in the house?"

Dizzy exhaled a cloud of smoke in my face and added, "This is Williamstown, for God's sake! Nothing bad happens here, because nothing *ever* happens here! You remember that much, don't you?"

My face flushed with frustration at my own absurd fear. "You've changed," Dizzy said before ashing into a watery glass of orange juice that someone had left on the coffee table and pronouncing, "Something must have scared the socks off of you up there."

I nodded, but I didn't have the strength to recount my pain with my younger sister. I didn't want *anyone* to know what had happened. It would have shattered my family's image of me and made the debutante season, which Mae Mae and Mama cared so much about, seem like the farce that it already was for me.

As for Dizzy, I was supposed to be the positive role model on the path ahead of her. The wild child was still up to her tricks of partying well past her curfew, getting poor grades in school, and dressing (as Mae Mae had so aptly described it) "like death warmed over" in her Goth dresses and hair dyed the color of coal. I had watched her spend an hour in front of the mirror one morning as she powdered her face with stark white makeup and painted ebony circles around her eyes.

My folks told me plainly that they were counting on me to talk some sense into Dizzy over the summer. Next year, she would be in the twelfth grade, and this was her last chance to pull her grades up so that she could attend college.

As June passed, I lost my grip and began to blame myself for what Devon Hunt had done to me. How could I have been so dense as to assume that he had my best interests at heart when he took me up that hill to view the stars?

There was a force at work in me, as voracious as the pollutants and the kudzu that were eating the town and even stronger than the fury I could once muster. I'd thought I would have vengeful fantasies of driving up to UVA Law and painting "rapist" across Devon's apartment door, but I resented myself more than him. And this force convinced me that I would never be worth the attention of a man who would treat me decently. The diet pills, the laxative, the glass of wine—these were all really stupid steps that I took to contribute to what had happened. But worst of all, I had assumed something about his character—that he was nice and good and safe. I chided myself for how foolish I had been and concluded that the world was more dangerous and unpredictable than I had ever suspected.

I had lost something in addition to my virginity that spring. And something even more precious than my trust in my fellow man. I had lost the hope I once had for my purpose in this world, and I grieved this more than anything else. Before that dreadful night, my expectations for my future had made up my entire reason to exist, and now that they were gone, I didn't know how to make my way without them.

So I avoided Juliabelle, Mama, and all mirrors, and I went through the motions. I wrote thank-you notes to Mrs. Zapes and Mrs. Kitteridge and everyone else who hosted a deb luncheon on the thick white stationery Mae Mae had selected for me. I invited my second cousin Randy to the coed deb events: the casino parties, cocktail parties, and shag parties. And I even let him kiss me from time to time while he talked on the front porch about saltwater fishing and turkey hunting and the future we could have together in Williamstown. I stopped short of telling him that I'd probably lose my NBU scholarship and join him at the state university, but with every hand squeeze and gaze into my eyes, I knew he was hoping that was how the next year would unfold. And sometimes I thought a life with him might be just fine. I even loosened up and drank cheap beer at the end of the frontage road with Jif and the others and laughed while the boys climbed the water tower for the umpteenth time.

But when the darkness came into my room late at night, I was haunted by thoughts that convinced me of my worthlessness. I hated being in my own skin, and I did not welcome the dawn or the new day set before me.

If there was an itch to be scratched or a void to be filled, I knew that I was so far away from it now that it would never be in my grasp again, and so every time I tried to write, even about my pain or self-hatred, the page came up empty. What did *I* have to say?

*What a haughty joke of a third-string valedictorian I was,* I thought as I drove by the old high school one morning on the way to a deb brunch.

Who *was* I? *Nothing.*

And *where* was I going? *Nowhere.*

⌒

At Mama's strong suggestion, I did babysit for Willa, a three-year-old girl down the street, four days a week to earn some pocket money. Being around children eased the pain, if only for a moment. Their motives were pure, even their selfish ones, and their little minds were not jaded by the dark edges of the world around them. Willa didn't know, for instance, that a trip through the woods in bare feet might result in a rattlesnake bite or that she could bust her head open if she jumped too closely to the edge of her bed. She didn't know that a stranger could swoop her up off the sidewalk and do away with her before sunset in whatever wicked way he desired.

When I took Willa to pick some of Mama's tomatoes and smell the flowers in Mae Mae's rose garden, I chuckled to see how she planted her nose as deep as it could go into the center of an open bloom to enjoy the fragrance. All I could see was the back of her head and her little ears while she breathed in the yellow and pink blossoms that the summer heat had opened.

When I took Willa to the Kmart, I couldn't stop her from waving to the stranger in line behind us. "I'm Willa," she would say with a coquettish grin. Then she'd hold up her fingers and count. "And I'm one, two, three years old!"

One afternoon, a migrant worker who stood behind us in the checkout line grinned back at the little girl and whispered something in Spanish that I assumed was sinister. As he scratched his unshaven chin with the tips of his dirt-encrusted fingernails, I shot him a cold look before studying his face: small dark eyes, scar in the center of his nose, mullet.

"C'mon, let's go," I said sharply to Willa. Then I grabbed the receipt from the checkout lady and hurried past the candy machines and the grimy plastic rocking horse that I had told Willa she could ride after we'd finished our shopping.

When we were unlocking the car door, Willa cried, "Horsey ride!" Then she threw her sippy cup onto the filthy asphalt that was cracking in the summer heat and screamed, "You promised horsey!"

"Not now, girl," I said as I buckled her tightly into her car seat. "You mustn't talk to strangers, Willa. They're dangerous." Of course, Willa had no way of understanding, and she kicked and screamed in disappointment until we reached her neighborhood.

When we got home, I gave her a Popsicle as a consolation gift and rocked her on the porch until she fell asleep in my arms.

Willa was the only person I could stand coming into physical contact with. And I held the little girl tightly for the rest of the afternoon and wept in anger at the terror that now framed my thoughts.

I visited Georgianne and seven-month-old Baby Peach in the late afternoons. Georgianne lived out beyond the mill village in a new little subdivision where all of the cookie-cutter homes looked as though they were built out of paper and might tip over in the next big storm. We would sit on the back patio of the house and blow bubbles or fill a plastic pool with water and watch Baby Peach splash around in it until his fingertips shriveled up like raisins and the mosquitoes started to bite.

Neither of us talked about the elephants in the kitchen as Georgianne prepared a casserole in her Pyrex dish. That is, Georgianne's derailed education and defunct debutante status and my nightmare of a first year as I continued my schooling and squinted in the spotlight of the Camellia Club of stinky old Williamstown.

My emotions were mixed as I watched Georgianne boil the macaroni for another batch of tuna surprise or wipe little Peach's runny nose for the umpteenth time of the day.

As sad as I was for Georgianne's change of plans, Baby Peach was a dear, and I couldn't get him out of my mind. I even brought him gifts: a rattle from the dollar store or a stuffed animal from Kmart. It was obvious that he was going to be bright like his mother. He was so alert and already learning to crawl. Just yesterday he'd planted his fat little feet on the ground and lifted up his rear in a pike position as if he would prefer to walk if he could just get himself upright.

When Big Peach came home from work at the tractor company, he would kiss Georgianne softly and tickle his son's underarms until he turned red in the face and wet his diaper. Georgianne never seemed to tire of lugging him back to the changing table or bathing him or reading him nonsensical books as he cackled in his crib before bedtime. Was the hole in Georgianne's heart filled now? Was the itch scratched? At times it appeared so, but I didn't have the nerve to ask her straight out.

Now Mama could tell that something was wrong, but she wasn't very good at talking, so how could she pry when I was closed tighter than a periwinkle snail? Instead, she busied herself on my behalf by cooking my favorite summer dishes: tomato pie, sweet creamed corn, and peach ice cream. She cut beautiful blue hydrangea blooms from the yard and put them in a vase on my bedside table and invited me on a trip to the outlet mall in Myrtle Beach to shop for sundresses. I declined the invitation. There were too many mirrors in dressing rooms. And when it was just the two of us rocking in the hammock as the sun went down beyond the marsh, I couldn't bear to explain my despair. It would break many places in Greta Piper's carefully guarded heart.

My childhood friend Shannon also could tell that something was different, and she had the gumption to come right out with it.

Shannon was not an official debutante. Her parents were fairly new to town. That is, they arrived fifteen years ago. But she was invited to some of the social engagements because she was friends with me, Jif, and the others, and we often added her to the guest list.

Perhaps because Shannon had "found Jesus," she knew how to cut right to the heart of any matter. So one day when she and I were in the powder room at the country club, full from shrimp salad and Jell-O molds, she asked me, "What's wrong with you, Adelaide? Something has happened. I *know* it."

I was so tired of pretending that I broke right down on the pink-and-green-striped love seat and went into a crying frenzy right by a rack of golf clubs.

"Can't say," I said to Shannon, who gently patted my shoulders until Mrs. Kitteridge came to the door to announce that our ride was waiting for us.

"That's all right, Mrs. Kitteridge," Shannon said. "We'll just walk."

And so we sauntered the two miles to our neighborhood together as I recounted what happened to me on that clear night in May and all the rest of what had burst my bubble last year at NBU while the pink sandals that Mama had just bought nipped sharply at my heels. Shannon just listened and wept for me from time to time during the account. I was greatly relieved to tell the story to someone I trusted. Shannon had been my closest childhood friend, and no matter how much of a Jesus freak she had become, she still had a backstage pass into my head.

"How awful, Adelaide," Shannon said, "that you had to go through that. It was wrong. What that boy did to you was wrong. I'm so sorry."

*What-that-boy-did-to-you-was-wrong.* These words were like a flashlight in the shadowy corridors of my mind. I had spent so much of the last two months blaming myself for what had happened, but to hear that it was someone else's fault was a great reprieve. It felt true somehow. And it was contrary to the voice that chided me most days and nights.

I watched a blue jay take flight from a magnolia tree, and a little piece of hope rose up inside me.

Shannon said, "I know I've pushed too hard on this religion thing with you before." (We had missed the turn to Shannon's house and were going to continue this conversation the six blocks more toward my home.) "But I earnestly believe that God can carry you through this."

*God,* I thought to myself. I had a fuzzy memory of a sentimental Jesus cradling a lamb in His arms from a poster hanging in my childhood Sunday school class. I had not thought about *Him* in a long time, and I wondered if what Shannon anchored her life upon these days was actually real and could help me in some way.

I had resented my friend for overhauling her life a few years ago for what Jif and I called the "God Squad"—a group of college-aged men and women that dropped by our high school from time to time to invite the students to church and to mountain-climbing retreats at Windy Gap.

"Go, God! Beat the vices!" Jif and I cheered as we smoked cigarettes in her basement after the high school football games, and I imagined those zealous college folks jumping beneath Shannon's window in cheerleading uniforms and megaphones, coaxing her into their fanatical game.

Shannon had been drawn to the God Squad almost instantly after a knee injury on the soccer field that would blow a month of her junior year of high school and cost her the athletic scholarship to Clemson she had always wanted. Members of the God Squad would show up in Shannon's hospital room with her favorite candy bars and silly gag gifts. Then later, after she was on the mend, they carted her to the soccer games both in and out of town so that she could cheer her teammates on to the regional championships.

I had missed my best friend so much, had almost felt abandoned by her after her conversion. Shannon was no fun after that. She wouldn't gossip or tell a dirty joke or go to an R-rated movie or smoke cigarettes with me from time to time in the basement of Jif's house. And she had evangelized up a storm whenever we were together. She carried a Bible around in her backpack, for goodness' sake, and prayed out loud whenever I was worried about a test or having a bad hair day. Finally, I avoided her at school and stopped returning her phone calls.

"He's the one, Ad," Shannon said now. "He can restore your soul with a new kind of peace."

*Peace.* Despite her Bible-thumping diatribe, this was a word I had gained a much greater appreciation for now that I was without a shred of it. I woke up more than once in the middle of the night in a panic that made my heart beat madly until I oriented myself in the blackness of my hometown bedroom by making out the silhouettes of my bookshelf: my Madame Alexander dolls and a framed print of the Charleston High Battery where I'd taken many long walks during summers at Governor's School. On my bedside table I'd see the form of the small King James Bible—a baptism gift—with its silver pages that stuck together and my name embossed in gold on the bottom right cover. If Mama had left the porch light on for the night, the silver pages would glisten faintly in the darkness. I was not sure if I had ever opened it.

It was a long walk, and my new sandals were now pinching my toes and tightening around my ankles. Stopping to loosen them, I saw the glint of light during our heart-to-heart quickly eclipsed by something else—the voice that told me I was of no significance and responsible for my violation had returned, and it overshadowed the glimpse of hope I was squinting to see.

"I don't know about that stuff," I said to Shannon as we reached the driveway to my home.

Shannon looked dejected. Her life had changed forever at the Young Life camp in Colorado where she had so often told me that she officially "accepted Christ." She would have walked all the way to the country club and back to continue our discussion and share her true love with me. She was more excited than Uncle Tinka with his Bizway plan.

I was thankful for her friendship; it was a safe place to reveal what was going on in my heart. But I couldn't see entertaining all of that born-again Christian strangeness at a time like this. Aside from Shannon and the God Squad that had taken her away, all I knew about

vocal Christians were misfits and hypocrites like Jim and Tammy
Faye Bakker or the strange man on the television on Sunday morning who interrupted whatever I had hoped to watch with his dramatic preaching and healing scenes that seemed more theatrical than
holy. Papa Great had been ripped off by a preacher at a tent revival
outside Williamstown, and he vowed never to attend church again.
And it was common knowledge that Father Henderson, the former
rector of St. Anne's Episcopal Church, had a history of slipping into
the strip clubs outside Myrtle Beach.

But most of all, I didn't want to give up my life—the way I felt
Shannon had a few years back. It would not be *me* to refer to Jesus as
though He were sitting right beside me, stroking the strands of my
hair. It would feel silly to pray that my jewel would fade away or that
I would write a good English paper or have a nice time at the deb
luncheons. In my heart of hearts, I sensed that I would have to give
up too much to follow Shannon's path, and my heart recoiled at the
very idea of it.

All too aware of my vulnerable state, I feared being sucked into
something that would leave me worse off than before.

"I'm just in a tough spot," I said, "but I'll find my way through."

"A Rescuer exists," Shannon said lovingly to me as she patted my
shoulders. "I'm not going to push, Ad. That's backfired in the past, I'll
admit, but I'm here to tell you about it any time of the day or night."

"Thanks," I said, suddenly recalling those countless summer hours
we'd spent in Shannon's garage, reenacting *Charlotte's Web* during our
elementary years. And how, after reading *Black Beauty*, we spent most
of fourth grade pretending that we were horses and whinnying around
the playground in our shared imaginary world during recess. We had
even started our first periods within weeks of each other the summer
between sixth and seventh grades.

"I guess we're women now," I had said to Shannon when Mama
took us to the Kmart to pick out maxi pads.

"Yep!" Shannon said, giggling as she placed the bulky plastic package in our cart. "It's official."

Then we asked Mama to buy us a Diet Coke as we stood in the checkout line, forsaking our usual childhood request for a candy bar. We slurped the bitter drink all the way home, wincing at the aftertaste as if to toast our bodies, which were quietly undergoing the great transformation beneath our T-shirts and cutoff shorts.

I wanted to be a child again. Wanted to be swinging in the hammock with Juliabelle or in Shannon's garage, pretending to be Charlotte weaving Wilbur out of a fix with two simple words. But who could turn back the clock? Or better yet, allow me a second go at things? If only I could blot out the last year and start over. But I was spoiled. A strawberry tart stain on a white dress. Not just my body, but my mind too. My thoughts were out of control, and there was no way I could bridle them, much less express them on paper in what I had hoped would be my life's purpose.

I hugged my sweet, familiar friend at the edge of my driveway as the bees buzzed in and out of Mama's hydrangea blooms.

"Just let me melt down from time to time."

"Count on it," Shannon said. "You're a bright and wonderful person, Adelaide."

"I thought I was headed somewhere," I said, moving toward the front steps of her home. "What a fool I am."

"But if you'd just—"

Stepping toward the threshold, my ears shut down. I waved a final time, then walked into the house, the straps from my pink sandals popping the blisters beneath my heels.

"Adelaide!" Mama exclaimed. "You've scuffed up your new shoes, and you're bleeding on the Oriental rug. Run to the kitchen, sweetheart. I'll meet you there."

~

That night, Mama reluctantly agreed to host a dinner with what Daddy excitedly called some "Bizway diamonds" from Conway. I assumed that this meant some folks who had made it to the top of the business, but I kept picturing them as large round-cut stones who'd pierce the fabric of our antique chairs when they sat down to teach Daddy and Uncle Tinka the tricks of the trade.

~

"Pick the seven most influential people you know," said one of the diamonds, named Big Bugs Murphy.

He and his wife had driven up in the longest Mercedes I had ever seen. It took up half the driveway with its sleek white body and gold hubcaps that looked like the big coins I got for Willa at the Chuck E. Cheese in Myrtle Beach.

Mama feigned interest in the discussion, though I could tell she was more preoccupied with the fact that Bugs kept his elbows on the table and slurped his she-crab soup through the gap between his teeth. And when Mama served the beef tenderloin, Big Bugs's wife, Belinda, removed a piece of neon-green chewing gum from her mouth and set it on the side of Mama's gold-rimmed bone china plate. Good gravy, what manners!

Escaping to my room with a slice of mud pie, I heard them slowly migrate to the living room, where they talked vitamins and acquiring points and graduating first to precious metals and then to gems.

I couldn't resist pulling out my journal that night and searching my desk drawer for a nice ink pen to write with. Instead of thoughts or poems, I wrote questions about the God whom Shannon had brought up to me that afternoon. The God on the shoulder of St. Christopher on the medal I carried despite my unbelief. The God I had prayed to as a little girl each night and sang to with all my might during the one week of vacation Bible school I attended in grade school. The God someone—whoever had given me the silver-paged Bible—had hoped I'd get to know.

Yes, there was a part of me that worked to resist Him, but Shannon had infected me with the idea of hope this afternoon, and I felt an undeniable draw to dissect the idea with the tip of my pencil.

As I wrote, I felt sure that my questions were nothing new under the sun, but naming them kept me from exploring Shannon's post-saved world.

1. If there is a good and powerful God, how come there is so much pain and grief in the world? Even good people suffer (i.e., war and Daddy's lost arm and lost friends; Cousin Mina, whose one and only child was stillborn; Brother Benton, who died in the name of fraternity hazing; and Peter Carpenter, who didn't mean to hurt anyone).

2. Why is it such a mystery—the whole Jesus Messiah thing? The language is so cryptic. Why can't they just say it in plain English?

3. What about Genesis? If the world is only 7,000 years old, then how do you explain the Tyrannosaurus rex?

4. I mean, Jonah and the whale? Noah's ark? What is a thinking mind supposed to do with these tall tales?

5. Is every other religion wrong? Do you mean to tell me that the Muslims, Buddhists, and Hindus are all barking up the wrong trees?

6. And what about all of those bloodthirsty Crusades? Not to mention the modern-day hypocrites who steal money and molest children.

7. What does that horrific-sounding "die to self" phrase mean?

Closing my journal, I glanced over at that fancy Bible on my dresser. I flipped it open and saw the words scratched on one of the thin paper pages in Mae Mae's handwriting, *"To Adelaide on the day of her christening. From Juliabelle, November 1981."*

Juliabelle! She was stuck on Pawleys with Papa Great, and it was up to me to go out and see her. She must be worried sick.

I slid my finger down the silver pages before opening the book at random to a page full of *thees* and *thous* and verbs that ended in *-eth*.

"Can't be worse than Chaucer," I murmured as I read the first verse of St. John: "In the beginning was the Word, and the Word was with God, and the Word was God."

"Okay, definitely cryptic, but I like the poetry." I flipped through the chapter, and something stopped me at the reddish-orange words of Christ at the top of a page in the same Gospel, and I read the question that was asked to some crippled man at a pool in a place called Bethesda: "Wilt thou be made whole?"

My spirit quickened at the question. A sick body might be made well, but what about a crushed heart?

I jumped down the page and read more of the orange words: "Verily, verily, I say unto you, He that heareth my word, and believeth on him that sent me, hath everlasting life, and shall not come into condemnation; but is passed from death unto life."

Looking up from the book and into the mirror above my bureau, I guessed Mama and Daddy had bid the precious stones farewell. The house was quiet except for the faint sound of the eleven o'clock news in the den. And there was a distant ringing in my ears, but it grew closer as I stared back down at the words in red.

Suddenly, the ringing enveloped me. It was like a tingling heat that started at the back of my head and worked its way down to the backs of my knees. I wanted to collapse into the arms of it, but I didn't have the faintest idea how.

"'Passed from death unto life'?" I said aloud in a doubtful tone, but even through my sarcasm, I couldn't shake the sense that something was standing right behind me. Breathing on me. I looked back only to find the clouded eyes of my collection of dolls staring dully in my direction.

Then I went to my window to look out into the shadowy marsh surrounding Williamstown. In the corner of the sill, a large banana spider was tearing down part of its dusty web and reconstructing it again with fresh strands of transparent silk.

The phone rang, and I answered it.

"It's Shannon."

"Hey," I said.

"Just wanted to check on you."

"I'm okay."

"I'm here," Shannon said.

"Thank God," I said.

"Now you're talking."

I fell into the pillows on my bed and sighed.

"Wanna go with me to church on Wednesday?" Shannon slipped in without warning. "There's this lady who is giving her testimony, and I know how you love a good story."

"Not yet."

"Well, at least you didn't say, 'No, never.'"

I grinned at just the idea of passing from death to life. *Oh, that it were real. That it could actually be true.* Then I rested in the comforting lull of my childhood friend's voice as we chattered on about Bonnie Raitt's *Nick of Time* album and the Fourth of July coon-dog parade and a day trip we might take to the boardwalk in Myrtle Beach.

When we hung up, I put the journal on top of my bedside table and attached the nice ink pen to a clean page. If more questions woke me up in the wee hours, I would pen them down before they slipped through the dusty web of my mind and out into the thick black of the summer night.

# Harriet and Harvest Time

**H**arriet von Hasselson Hartness appeared the next evening at a sangria party for the debs on the back porch of Mrs. Bitsy Stillwell's house. Much to my surprise, she was built like a pumpkin on two sticks, and her dress style was a peculiar blend of hippie and grunge. She looked (and smelled) as though she had just stepped out of a circus tent or an extended Grateful Dead tour with her oversized men's tank top and her loose tapestry skirt. She wore a low-riding fanny pack cocked on her wide hip, and a frayed rope was tied around her ankle as though she had been shackled somewhere along the way.

"Harriet von Hasselson Hartness has *hairy* armpits," Jif whispered, after sizing her up at a distance while sucking on a potent orange from the sangria pitcher.

I chuckled as we marveled at the surprise of Miss Hartness. "It's refreshing," I said.

"All that *we* got right about her was the D cup," said Jif, "but I bet a week of Slim-Fast would get them down to a C." (It was all about calorie intake with Jif.)

"So we don't know so much after all," I said, strangely relieved by this realization.

Harriet looked bewildered and irritated as she tried to carry on a conversation with Nan McCant and Winkie Pride. She was a raccoon in the headlights of the quirky Williamstown social scene, and I hurried across the porch to rescue her.

"Hi, Harriet," I said, extending my hand. "I'm Adelaide Piper, and I've been looking forward to meeting you."

Jif was surely rolling her eyes somewhere beyond the chips and salsa.

"At least it's real sangria," Harriet responded, motioning to the table full of Mexican food, "but I'm a vegan, and I can't eat *any* of this stuff."

"A vegan?"

Harriet shrugged as if this word were an everyday one in Williamstown.

"Is that some kind of religion?" I asked in a hushed and considerate tone.

Harriet laughed out loud and explained, "It means I don't eat any animal products. And that I respect all life by eating only plant-based foods."

This remark seemed to grip the attention of most everyone in the party, and before long there was a semicircle of debs, mothers, and little old ladies who were trying to understand what *vegan* meant.

"You mean you're a vegetarian, dear." Bitsy Stillwell, who considered herself up on things, tried to correct Harriet.

"No," said Harriet as she wiped her nose with the back of her hand, "some vegetarians eat seafood and eggs. But they don't realize that they are contributing to the deaths of two hundred million male chicks a year."

"Oh my!" Mrs. Kitteridge crooned.

"Oh *yes*," Harriet stated with confidence. "Since a male chicken can't lay eggs, they serve no purpose to the egg industry and are killed shortly after hatching. The female chickens are kept five to a tiny battery cage and are usually killed before their second birthday to make way for the younger hens."

"Nonsense!" Mrs. Zapes said. She was known around town for her delectable deviled eggs, and her recipe had even made the state paper last Independence Day.

Harriet's mother didn't seem to be present, but her grandmother, Mrs. Marguerite Hartness, made her way over to Harriet in an effort to end the discussion by steering her out into the back garden.

"Dahlin'," she said as she placed an arm around Harriet's freckled shoulder, "have you seen Ms. Stillwell's garden?"

"You don't even want to know about the cows," Harriet said to me, and she nodded in the direction of the beef tacos in the center of the table before accepting her grandmother's invitation to the garden. "Or the leather soles of your shoes," she added over her shoulder.

Miss Pringle gasped, and the little old ladies murmured among themselves before inspecting the bottoms of their high heels.

I looked back at Jif and grinned with excitement. This gal was going to stir things up around here, and we were both going to enjoy it.

～

After touring the garden for a moment, I sat on a bench beneath the weeping willow tree. While my appetite for tacos had vanished, my mind was ingesting: if I had been so wrong about Harriet von Hasselson Hartness, could I be wrong about other things too? I pictured the journal on my bedside table and the childhood Bible on my dresser. What about Shannon and the invitation to the hand-raising church on Route 39? What did I have to lose in just going and hearing one lady's story?

I stroked this thought as if it were a smooth pebble plucked from the bottom of the Santee River. The katydid song upstaged the clink of china as the debs grazed on their Mexican buffet, and I heard a breeze pushing through the thick summer air. It dangled the tips of the weeping willow branches before lifting the wisps of hair on my forehead.

Toward the end of the evening, I had another refreshing conversation with Harriet, who turned out to be a movie buff and an English major who yearned to find the South in the Flannery O'Connor short stories she'd studied last semester at Sarah Lawrence College.

"Are there peacocks around here?" she asked. "I came here to see the peacocks and the busybody warthog ladies who spray down their pigpens and dream of a caste system in heaven. And the folks with gimp legs and the traveling Bible salesmen."

"Well," I whispered, "there are a few busybodies in this immediate circle, but to tell you the truth, you've landed in the wrong socioeconomic group. You need to go on down to the mill village or the mobile homes on Route 39 if you want to glimpse vestiges of that sort of thing."

"Will I really see it?" Harriet asked hopefully.

"You need to know," I said with a wink, as I recalled the O'Connor short story that had made a lasting impression on me, "a good, grotesque Southerner is hard to find." We both laughed until Harriet snorted.

"Gracious me," a warbly voice clucked somewhere behind us.

Then I motioned for Jif to come on over and join us, and we talked unreservedly about the highlights of our coastal town: climbing the water tower, rafting down the Santee River, picking the tomato fields after the migrant workers left town, and sucking on honeysuckle at the edge of Pawleys Island.

It seemed that Harriet loathed the well-to-do world of Greenwich, Connecticut, where she had been raised, and she was yearning for a drastic change. Her parents had split when she was five years old. Her father, a psychiatrist, lived in Las Vegas, where he ran his own psychotherapy practice, and her mother, a depressed New York socialite with Southern roots, had remarried a Wall Street investment banker, forcing Harriet into a blended suburban family with his two perfect offspring, who were at the tops of their classes at a New England prep school and an Ivy League institution.

"Ever been to Darlington?" Jif asked with a gleam in her eye.

"Can't say that I have," Harriet said.

"Well, you haven't seen the South until you've seen NASCAR," Jif informed her. "I've a cousin who lives there, and he'll take us around before the big race. His daddy sells T-shirts for Richard Petty."

"For sure!" Harriet said before taking some sort of soybean snack from her fanny pack and offering it to us. "I just knew this place would be brimming with life."

"That's one way to put it," I replied, though the irony was not lost on me: Harriet had sought out sooty old Williamstown to find the wonder while I had fled to NBU for much the same reason.

When I got home that night, I called Juliabelle first to say, "I'm okay. And I'll be out in a few days to see you."

Then I called Shannon on a whim and said, "Okay, I'll go."

"Go where?"

"To hear the lady at your church."

"Awesome!" Shannon said. "Now, it's a little different than what you're used to in a church."

"I'm game."

"Then I'll pick you up Wednesday afternoon at five thirty."

When I hung up the phone, I heard Daddy calling out to Dizzy from the front porch. She had shimmied down the magnolia tree in the front yard and was scurrying toward a car just beyond the hydrangea bushes whose motor was running though the lights were off.

"Where do you think you are going this time of night, Dizzy?"

"Ah, crap!" she said, turning around toward him. "Daddy, I'm sixteen years old. Every sixteen-year-old in the county goes out this time of night."

"Everyone but you," Daddy said, walking past her and toward the car that suddenly turned on its lights and drove around the bend toward Main Street.

"Get in your room," he said, pulling the purse off her shoulder and crumpling the pack of cigarettes and matches inside.

"Just because your life is miserable doesn't mean mine has to be," she said.

"Don't you talk to your daddy that way," Mama said. She was on the porch in her nightgown, and I could make out the outline of her petite little body through the white cotton eyelet.

Dizzy stormed past them into the house, ran up to her room, and turned on her Cure CD full blast. I heard her screaming the lyrics to "Just Like Heaven": "You-oo-oo, lost and lonely . . ."

"So you still back me up on some things?" Daddy said to Mama as he pulled her close and rocked her back and forth, keeping time with the churning of the steel-mill furnace blasts beyond Main Street.

She nuzzled beneath the crook of his shoulder, kissed his chest, and said, "I want what's best for our family, Zane."

"I know you do."

∽

Two nights later, Shannon and I made our way into the gravelly parking lot of Harvest Time Assembly Church. The cinder-block sanctuary was a former barbecue joint on Route 39 (as I had suspected), and it was run by some "church planters" by the names of Dale and Darla Pelzer. Shannon had taken great pains to explain to me the Pelzers' mission and how she had come to know them. She had met them once at the Young Life camp where she gave her soul away and then again at a Fellowship of Christian Athletes meeting at the University of South Carolina last semester, where they shared their vision for starting churches in poor communities all over the South. Williamstown was their first stop, and their plan was to share the gospel with the migrant workers and the leftover families from the mill villages.

*A church with a social conscience,* I thought as we made our way to the outskirts of town, and I pictured the sullen girl staring back at me from the old mill home the day I went to NBU. I felt a twinge of guilt as I recalled the poem I wrote in response to that exchange. Had I ever made an effort to reach out to anyone in the struggling section of my hometown? Nope. All I ever wanted to do was get away from them.

"Now, it's a covered-dish dinner," Shannon had told me when we stopped at the Piggly Wiggly on the way to pick up two gallons of sweet tea. "After we eat, we'll hear the testimony, and that's all there is to it."

"Sounds pretty painless," I had said, "and a far cry from St. Anne's." We had both laughed as we envisioned the pristine Tudor-style Episcopal church where I was baptized and confirmed, with its sterling silver chalices and ornate stained-glass windows.

"It's a bit earthier than St. Anne's."

"'Earthier' is putting it mildly," I now joked as I read the letters on the marquee outside the crude sanctuary: "Exposure to the Son can prevent burning."

Shannon handed me a gallon of tea and prodded me out of the car. "Sometimes it's necessary to get right to the point. Now, keep an open mind, O Enlightened One."

When we entered the cinder-block building set on its thin concrete slab, I felt a kind of energy envelop me. Then my mouth began to water as I scanned the wobbly card tables filled with fried flounder and tamales and banana pudding. *This sure beats country-club chicken salad,* I thought to myself as a large lady named Charlie Farley greeted me with a soft, warm hug that smelled like sugar and baby powder. She was the female version of the Pillsbury Dough Boy.

"Shannon told me you were coming, and I'm so happy to meet you, Adelaide."

"Thanks," I said hesitantly as I flashed Shannon an inquisitive look, but before my friend could respond, a young Mexican lady pulled her away for counsel.

"I'm the parish greeter," Charlie Farley said, "and I've got a place set for you right by me so that I can introduce you around." Then she whispered into my ear, "The Lord is *moving* in this place, and your presence here is another great blessing He's given us tonight."

Before I could say, "I think you've confused me with someone else," Charlie Farley had gathered a group of five middle-aged ladies, who encircled me as they spouted out their questions: How did I know Shannon? What part of town was I from? What did I like to eat? After one lady offered to fix me a plate, a couple of college students from neighboring small towns came over and introduced themselves. Teddy Mee was enrolled at Columbia Bible College, while Sarah Spicer and Rob Marjenhoff were upperclassmen at the University of South Carolina. They were all helping the Pelzers get this church going, and Teddy was already planning the next mission field in the little towns of Mullins and Greeleyville.

"You'd think we wouldn't need churches in the Bible Belt, Adelaide," Teddy explained, "but there's a lot of poor folks who are displaced and haven't ever heard the gospel before. Take the migrant workers, for instance. They have been right under our noses every harvest season, but nobody has taken the time to share the Word with them."

"Dale and Darla have a heart for these folks," Sarah Spicer added. "This is their calling."

"And we're just trying to do our part in carrying out the Great Commission," Rob Marjenhoff said, and they all nodded in unison.

*The Word? The Great Commission? Having a calling?* I had no idea exactly what they were talking about, but I was curiously drawn to their fervor for what they were doing. *I sure would like to know what the heck my calling is!*

Shannon, who had made an attempt to make her way back to me, was now off in a corner, praying for the young Mexican lady, who was wiping her wet eyes with the heels of her hands.

"Sit right over here by me," Charlie Farley called. An older woman had piled my plate high with food and set it in the center of the table.

As Dale Pelzer got up to say the blessing, everyone took their seats, and I scanned the rest of the room to get my bearings.

There was a group of migrant workers who could barely speak English in the front corner. Shannon had told me that the church was partnering with Habitat for Humanity to help construct permanent homes for them so that the wives and children could put down roots and get a steady education. And Dale and Darla were taking Spanish lessons from my high school Spanish teacher, Señora Barker, so that they could better communicate with them.

The Mexican man with the mullet from the Kmart line was there, and he was sitting next to a woman who was likely his wife, holding her hand. *Am I paranoid or what?* I thought as I recalled grabbing Willa out of my cart and running away after he tried to speak to us. Ashamed, I vowed to take Willa back to the store the next day to ride the scuffed-up rocking horse.

What struck me as I passed the biscuits and butter around my table and explained who I was and who had brought me were the vigor and exuberance that each person seemed to share, from the college student to the migrant worker. They all had some remarkable source of power that they seemed to be mutually tapped into, and I caught glimpses of it in the gleams of their eyes. I had never known people like this, who had fire in their gazes and I hoped that the explanation of it would be given in the talk we were about to hear. *Keep an open mind, sister.*

When Darla Pelzer got up to give her testimony, I was mesmerized. Though she had poor grammar, an accent as thick as syrup, and an unsightly outfit with sequined butterflies that made her look like a beauty pageant contestant who was past her prime, her story gripped my heart. She had grown up in an alcoholic home. At the age of eight, a teacher had told her that she was unsightly and dense, and those words broke her heart and destroyed her sense of self-worth. Her stepfather had raped her at the age of thirteen, and when she told her mother what had happened, she was promptly thrown out of the house. She left town and married at seventeen, and that ended in divorce less than two years later. She contracted herpes from her first husband, which invaded her body monthly and destroyed whatever shred of self-respect she had left.

Then she "met Christ" in a women's shelter outside Atlanta when an evangelist couple named Boochie and Laura Beth Day came through with a message about forgiveness, mercy, and being washed clean in the blood of the Lamb. After her baptism, she enrolled in secretarial school and took a job as a receptionist for a construction company, and that was where she met Dale. He was working on the site to put himself through Bible school, and he married her knowing that her disease could infect him and the children who might come from their union. He prayed over her body on their wedding night, and she had not had any herpes symptoms since that prayer seven years ago, but they had never been able to conceive a child.

She said that we all have a God-sized void in our hearts and that we try to fill it with all kinds of things—money, alcohol, infidelities, you name it—but that only one thing can fit there: God.

This hit a nerve.

"The itch of the soul," I wrote down on the paper napkin in front of me. Could Darla be suggesting that *God* was the remedy for this longing? Surely the *cure* for the emptiness I felt could not actually be found in a cinder-block church on Route 39 in the trashiest part of Williamstown, South Carolina. I had made my pilgrimage to NBU to fill the void, and I would be furious if it had been under my nose all along.

Still, I kept listening.

Next Darla said that God had a life purpose for each person in the room. That He had created them and bestowed upon them gifts they were to use for His glory and that worshipping Him and putting those gifts to use for Him were our chief reasons for existing.

Then she warned that we couldn't act upon our purposes without understanding the price that Christ paid on the cross for our lives and accepting this as the payment for the debt of our sins. Once we realized this, we were set free from the pasts that bound us and transformed into children of the Light, who would have abundant life in the here and now and eternal life with Christ in heaven. That is, we would rise from the dead the way He did.

She said that God had been speaking to people in the room in all kinds of ways all of their lives. She described a double rainbow she saw in the Blue Ridge Mountains when she didn't have two pennies to rub together and had nowhere to lay her head. She mentioned a kind word at just the right time from a social worker who encouraged her to go hear what Boochie and Laura Beth Day had to say. And just last year she had seen a beautiful baby girl in a vivid dream, and she believed God was giving her hope that she would one day be a mother.

I thought about the wonder that I had been in pursuit of. That I had written about in my poetry and dissected in the works of Marianne Moore and William Blake. Could the One on the shoulder of St. Christopher scratch the itch of my soul? Could He have been talking to me in all those moments of splendor that I could recall: the Pawleys Island sunsets, the adopted kitten, and the well water that took the swelling out of my throat?

These thoughts were quickly overshadowed by a concern related to my rape that I had buried during the last few months. Darla had forced me to remember again.

⌢

"What a story," I said as we closed the car door and pulled onto the dark road.

"What'd you think?" Shannon asked eagerly.

"I was blown away," I said. "She seemed sincere, and her life has been so hard."

Shannon seemed to breathe a sigh of relief. "I hoped it wouldn't shock you. I mean, she has had a pretty tough road."

Shannon swerved ever so slightly to miss a possum and asked, "Did her message *speak* to you?"

"I don't know. I'm a little curious about it all, I have to admit. I even wrote some questions down the other night that I'd like to talk over with you. But something else is on my mind now."

"Okay. Tell me."

"Darla's talk opened up the one fear that I'd managed to keep at bay since what happened to me a few months ago."

"What's that?" Shannon asked in a gentle tone.

"Sexually transmitted disease. I mean, with what happened to me at NBU, don't you think I should get checked out?" My voice cracked on the last two words. I could be carrying who-knew-what awful disease in my body, and I was beginning to brace myself for another painful blow.

Shannon thought for a moment; then the light flashed across her eyes.

"Let's go see my aunt Bernise in north Charleston. She works in women's health at Trident, and she can run all of the tests to make sure you're okay."

"That would be great," I said, exhaling deeper than I had in months. As frightening as it was, it felt right to finally address, head-on, another source of anxiety that had been secretly weighing on me.

Shannon's friendship truly touched me, and I wanted to give her something in return.

"Maybe after we get through this, we can sit down with some people at Harvest Time and just go through some of my questions about this whole Christianity thing."

"I'd love that," Shannon said. "I can set it all up just as soon as you're ready."

When we reached the driveway, she asked, "Can I pray for you now?"

"Why not?"

Shannon gripped the steering wheel and asked God for peace and a total healing for my mind, body, and hurting heart. When she reached out to touch my shoulder at the end of the prayer, I was surprised at the emotions that churned inside me at just the momentary thought of being made well again, and I wept for many minutes while Shannon fished for Kleenex and continued to pat my back.

Entering my quiet home, I was not surprised to find Dizzy and Lou asleep in front of the *Father of the Bride* movie in the den. I tapped little Lou on the shoulder and walked her to her bedroom. When I returned to do the same for Dizzy, I paused to smile down at my younger sister, who was curled up on one end of the sofa, still in her grave clothes and makeup from her night on the town. She had two round crystals around her neck—both with a tarnished silver claw that held them in place—and her fingernails were painted black. The fading white powder on her face revealed the rose tint of her freckled cheeks. Dizzy looked as though she were a grade-school girl dressed up for Halloween. It was only a few years earlier that she had worn the pink-and-purple floral pajamas that Lou now sported.

What had happened to Dizzy? And why did she want to dress like death?

As I bent down to nudge her, I could smell the marijuana and alcohol, and I wondered where in the world she had been earlier in the evening. I tapped her leg until she arose from her grogginess and shuffled to the kitchen for a glass of water.

"How was the Holy Roller night?" she asked, her gray eyes squinting in the fluorescent kitchen light.

"It was something," I said.

"I'm too beat to hear about it," she said, yawning. "You can catch me up tomorrow."

"You know, you smell like trouble, Diz. You'd better take a shower before Mama and Daddy catch a whiff of you."

Dizzy rolled her eyes and turned away from me as she shuffled toward the stairs.

"Like they have anything other than Bizway on their minds."

"If you keep going on like this, you're going to get yourself in a fix," I warned. I was never a partier like Dizzy, but I knew that trouble could sneak up on you before you could plan an escape, and I didn't want my sister to mess up big-time by making one bad decision or finding herself in the wrong place at the wrong time.

"You're preaching already, Adelaide?" Dizzy said midway up the stairs, and before I could think of a good response, I heard the slam and lock of her door.

When I walked back into the kitchen, I noticed for the first time a bouquet of wildflowers and an envelope with my name on it.

Adelaide,
    This has been the best summer I can remember. Thank you for spending it with me.

                              Love,
                              Randy

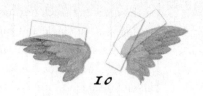

# 10

# New Moon

The following week, Shannon drove me to Charleston to see her aunt Bernise at Trident Hospital. Before we even chose a magazine article in the waiting room of the women's health center, Bernise called us to her office, where she took my blood and sent me to the bathroom with a little plastic cup that would hold the answer to my future in forty-eight hours.

After Bernise quizzed me on symptoms of which I had none, she said, "Some don't show up for a long while, but let's be optimistic, girls."

Looking to Shannon, I guessed that Bernise was addressing the greatest of the unspoken diseases: HIV. A college graduate had come to a dorm meeting at NBU once to share the story of how she had contracted it, and it had frightened me, not so much for my own mortality (I had planned to be a virgin until Mr. Right came along), but for Ruthie and Jif, who I suspected were in physical relationships with their beaus.

"You want to tell me about what happened?" Bernise asked me as she labeled little plastic tubes *A. Piper*.

I had met Bernise several times before at Shannon's annual family reunions on Lake Summit. She was the one who brought a seven-layer chocolate cake that we looked forward to devouring in our wet bathing suits as we sat on the dock and stuck our toes into the cold black water. Bernise was religious, but single and fun, and she had always been willing to cart us over to the movie theater in Saluda on rainy days when we just had to get out of the house.

"It's too hard to talk about," I said, and my eyes pricked before I decided that I could not recount the story.

Shannon squeezed my shoulder, and Bernise looked me straight in the face. "There is mending for you, Adelaide. I don't know what happened to you exactly, but I do know that God can mend your heart."

"You guys are ganging up on me," I said to both of them. Then, to Bernise, "You're a Jesus freak too?"

"Oh, sure I am," Bernise said. "Do you think I could work in this place without faith?"

"Okay, okay," I said, putting my hands up as if to say, "Enough."

"One thing at a time," Shannon whispered to Bernise, slowing her down.

"Yeah," I said. "First let's see if I've got some fatal disease; then we'll go from there."

Bernise was sweet and hopeful. "Sorry if I push too hard. It runs in our family." She gave Shannon a wink that made us all chuckle, albeit nervously.

Then she gave Shannon a twenty-dollar bill and told us to get a warm lunch on our way back to Williamstown and not to worry too much.

"Call me after noon on Thursday," she said; then she patted the top of my hand. "All of the results will be in by then."

∽

"Let's put it in God's hands," Shannon said as we scarfed down fried okra and creamed corn at the Lizard's Thicket just off Highway 17.

"Do I have a choice?"

I wondered how God would feel if I started to pray to Him about this after keeping my distance for so long.

"So did Bernise play a role in bringing you to your faith?"

"I suppose she planted some seeds, but it was really that Young Life retreat that made it clear."

"Right. Where you 'met Jesus,'" I said and immediately realized it came out more sarcastically than I meant for it to. "That phrase cracks me up, because I see this man in a white robe and sandals charging toward you with his arm outstretched for a firm handshake. You have to admit it sounds hokey."

Shannon chuckled. "Yeah, I need to work on my lingo. Christian-speak can turn people away. That's one of the things Dale and Darla have been teaching us."

"What made you decide to do it?"

"A few things, I guess," Shannon said as she buttered her corn bread. "My father's death, for one."

I had forgotten about that. Frank, Shannon's stepfather, had been with them since they moved to Williamstown, and Shannon even referred to him as Dad. But Shannon told me once in the deep of night that her real father had been killed in a car accident when she was in kindergarten.

"Frank is great, but it wasn't the same. I wanted to know where my dad was. Then the knee injury sort of pushed me over the edge. I mean, it sounds stupid, but I had put all of my time and effort into that soccer scholarship to Clemson, and so it was a real blow when it didn't happen for me." She pondered a misshapen piece of fried okra on her fork and added, "But I guess the main thing was the way those guys loved me."

"The God Squad?" I said, chuckling at my picture of the college cheerleaders with the fuzzy letters "Go, God!" across their polyester chests.

"Yeah," she admitted. "And they had a kind of life in them that seemed better than anyone else's around. Then when I was at that camp, it just became clear. A man named Danny Powell was talking to us, and it just seemed right. Something, like, nudged me, you know? I still have a ways to go, but it's been the best thing that has ever happened to me. I have peace. I know where my dad is. I don't have to take my identity from a sport. Or from being a part of the Camellia Debutante Club. Or anything else."

Now, I had to admit that some of the vines of fear had loosened their grip since my trip to Harvest Time. I sensed a kind of hope that just wouldn't go away. It was like I was being courted by Shannon, Charlie Farley, and perhaps God Himself. But why?

It was nice to be pursued. But it was all so out of the blue. And *so* Williamstown.

∽

With only a half hour before Randy was picking me up for a deb shag party, I raced up to my bedroom, locked the door, and got down on my knees.

"Please let me be okay. I don't deserve to even talk to You, much less ask You for Your help, but here I am anyway, doing just that. If You're as merciful as people say You are, then You can understand my position. I'll go meet with Dale and Darla and hear this thing out, but please let those test results be good."

"Are you getting ready?" Mama called up the stairs to me as I became aware of the many minutes I had been kneeling. My thighs ached, and the carpet left large indentions on my knees as I stood up to say, "Yes, ma'am."

∽

The deb party was at Mrs. Hartness's house, which was at the tip of the Williamstown Peninsula, facing the harbor, and it was in honor of Harriet. Marguerite hired the Catalinas, a famous beach-music band, and ordered two trucks full of sand from Pawleys Island to be dumped in her backyard so it would feel like we were dancing on the beach.

Harriet was nervous about the whole thing. Her grandmother had sent her to a two-day crash course to learn the dance steps, but she was as clumsy as an ox and utterly frustrated by the whole endeavor.

She didn't know a soul to bring to the coed events, so she'd made friends with the assistant manager at the Blockbuster video store next to the Kmart. He sported a diamond stud earring and a goatee and seemed to get a kick out of having all the socialites stare at him.

Jif and I had been bonding with Harriet over the last few weeks. She was so different. Like a shot of Texas Pete in your hominy. And yet she was earnestly trying to be a part of our world. We'd gone tubing down the Santee and gone to the county fair, and plans were well on the way to take a day trip to Myrtle Beach.

"Why aren't you at some fancy dude ranch this summer?" I had asked her one evening as we sat on her porch eating vegan molasses cookies.

Harriet let out a guffaw and said, "They eat a lot of red meat on those ranches." And then, "But seriously, this place is charming, and, hey I like to have parties thrown in my honor."

"Mmm," Jif said as she stamped on a palmetto bug that was scurrying toward them. "I hadn't looked at it that way."

"Don't they have debs in Connecticut?" I probed.

"At home, I am a palmetto bug," Harriet said as Jif kicked the creature into Mrs. Marguerite Hartness's sculpted shrubs. "My mother is, like, brain-dead from her alcohol consumption, and my stepfamily chooses not to acknowledge me—the butt-ugly, freak-show vegan who takes up space in their nearly perfect home. Sometimes I think they actually want me to hide when they bring their friends home."

I furrowed my brow and looked down at the floorboards.

"Whatever." She shrugged. "At least I have Marguerite. I mean, she's a small-town snoot, and her house reeks of mothballs, but she thinks I'm the bee's knees. Who can say why, but she always has."

"Wonder if there's a good vegan diet out there," Jif pondered as the fireflies began to light up the front yard.

"Don't start," I said. "The answer to everyone's problems is not in a thinner waistline."

"Seriously," Harriet said as she handed us each another tasteless molasses cookie. "I'm built just like my dad, so there is no way of getting rid of this barrel-on-stilts shape."

Jif pulled out a half-eaten Twix Bar from her pocketbook and said, "If I'm going to be bad, it might as well have some flavor."

The three of us grinned while Mrs. Hartness called out from the kitchen to offer us some lemonade.

Now, as the sun made its way down, Randy and I made our way onto the sandy backyard, where we shagged barefoot and without reserve beneath the string of white lights that were draped from her roof to the blooming magnolia trees that framed the end of her garden. Randy had more moves than an eel in a croaker sack. He was spinning and dipping me, and I would have bet anything he'd been practicing with his mama.

Harriet looked great. She'd pulled her hair up in a free-form twist and sported a simple black sundress that was cut just so in the back so that you could see a tattoo on her left shoulder: a "yin and yang." Much murmur commenced about this among the parents and older social folks who danced around her in their preppy madras pants and floral skirts. But it didn't seem to bother Harriet. Rod, the Blockbuster guy, had become quite adept during their shag lessons last week, and he led her around the backyard all night as she stepped-two-three with pride and smiled toward her grandmother.

Marguerite presided over the party in a white linen suit. Three heavy gold bangles accented her right arm, and her silver helmet hair was styled just so. Even she took off her sandals and danced with Rod, then a few deb fathers, as we gathered around the punch table to whisper and laugh.

Shannon was there with Teddy Mee from Harvest Time, and they seemed to be having a great time too. As a group of townspeople gathered around him to hear about his mission, Shannon pulled me aside and said, "How are you doing?"

"Okay. Even said a prayer this afternoon."

"Sounds promising," she said, then squeezed my wrist.

Randy came up behind me and said to Shannon, "May I have my date for a minute?" Then he grabbed my hand and pulled me through the garden and the covering of live oaks and magnolias and toward Marguerite's dock, where the harbor lights glistened across the glassy water as the last pink streaks of daylight faded.

"Look," he said, sitting down and patting a place beside him before he dipped his toes into the water. Three porpoises were feeding along the marsh bank near the dock, and they would slap their tails along the shallow water, trapping the schools of mullet for their sunset dinner. The seagulls and terns were flapping furiously toward their roosts, but the pelican took her sweet time above us. She flapped her wings for a moment, then let the wind carry her as long as it could before she exerted herself again.

The coast guard station trumpet rang out taps, and I sat down beside Randy and dipped my feet into the warm water. The ripples from my ankles grew larger and larger across the glassy surface.

"Could you ever get tired of this?" Randy whispered, interlocking his large fingers with mine.

The porpoises zigzagged from one bank to another as we looked on. The thick Low-Country air hung around us like the Spanish moss framing our vista, and if I didn't look behind me at the puffing towers of mill waste, I might have confused this with a subtropical paradise.

Randy turned to face me.

Randy. Mmm. He had become a man, and only now was I cluing in. His shoulders had broadened during the last year, and he was at least a foot taller than me now. He had even been recruited as a second-string kicker for the University of South Carolina football team, and I had seen him practicing in the Williamstown High School field in the early morning, kicking the oblong ball through the goalpost time and time again.

And he was a good man. He took his little brother and Lou fishing every Sunday afternoon, and Mae Mae or Mama was always calling him over to fix things: Lou's bent bicycle rim or the leaking dishwasher. Even Papa Great had noticed his worth, and with no male heirs in the direct line, he was bending Randy's ear about joining the Piper Mill after college.

Despite my weight gain and my skittishness, he continued to put the full-court press on me. He was as loyal as a Labrador, and I was grateful to have him as my debutante escort. I hadn't ever felt anything more than friendship for him, but I wondered if that would change.

"Come home for good, Adelaide," he said to me as the porpoises blew air like breathless swimmers.

The Catalinas were singing, "Well, you're more than a number in my little red book. You're more than a one-night stand. Babe, I think to tell you that I've been hooked. You're more than a number, baby, in my little red book." The dull roar of the party wafted through the oak trees and out into the harbor.

"Randy," I said, but I had no idea what to say next.

His olive-colored eyes looked down on me as though I were the football itself and he did not want to lose focus. "You can't tell me that college in Virginia has done you any good, now, can you? What with all of the crazy stuff going on there?"

"You don't know the half of it," I said. And I knew that if I told it all to him, he would take me in his arms and say, "You are still the pearl for me."

"Transfer back to Carolina. Come home and be my girl, and I'll build you a house on Pawleys Island and marry you, and you can write poetry until your fingers go numb."

A blue crab skittered sideways into the water, and I wondered if it was warm enough for molting season. If the moon was new, the timing would be right—the male crab would swing his claws and kick up sand with his hind legs to get his mate's attention. And after she acquiesced, he would carry the female in his claws for up to a week until her shell softened and they mated. Then he'd hold her again another two days, until her back hardened and she was no longer in danger.

"Don't make me an offer I can't refuse," I said, nudging him with my elbow. (Harriet had told me the other day that Albert Einstein and Charles Darwin had married their first cousins, so it couldn't be that bad to fall for your second.)

"Remember that day you kissed me last summer? On your gradua-tion?" he said.

"Yes." I felt a tinge of guilt for how I'd used him that way to get at the Hog.

Randy had long eyelashes, and his green eyes glistened in the light of the harbor. Even I had to admit that with his new football physique, he really was striking. He lifted the hair off my forehead and rubbed my jewel with the tip of his thumb. "There's not a day that's gone by that I haven't thought about that kiss and prayed to the good Lord to make you mine."

I sucked on my teeth and wondered what to say to all of this. Randy had *real* feelings for me, and I didn't want to drop-kick his tender heart. Should I relax into his embrace?

After a minute went by and I didn't reply, he nodded. The air was so still that the no-see-um bugs were starting to nip at our scalps.

"Just think on it," he said, taking my hand and pulling me back through the tree covering and toward the music. "But know this: I'm going to do all that I can to convince you."

When we came back to the sand-filled garden, we danced. We shagged and spun and dipped until our foreheads glowed, and we traded partners and laughed and kicked at the soft grains until the last note was played and the band loaded their equipment into their shabby van.

Randy had all but proposed to me, and I was flattered to be loved like this. If I'd lost my scholarship, I might do just what he said—move back and make this my life. It might not be the worst fate, after all.

Shannon called me every morning and every night over the next three days, and she even left an encouraging note in my mailbox one day with a verse about not being anxious and gaining the peace that passes all understanding.

Now, I didn't have that kind of peace, but I did manage to survive the wait for the test results. I even ate three meals a day, though every time I let my mind go back to it, my stomach churned and the vines of fretfulness tightened their hold on me.

When the time arrived for me to contact Bernise, I rang her from the pay phone at the Piggly Wiggly before a deb luncheon at the country club.

There I stood in my pink linen suit and pearl earrings, wiping off the gritty receiver and sliding in the proper change. Two whole minutes went by before Bernise made her way to the telephone. As I was scrounging up more change from the bottom of my purse to feed to the pay phone, she picked up the line and said, "Well, go ahead and breathe yourself a sigh of relief, 'cause they all came back negative."

"Negative?" I said, suddenly aware of the cars whizzing by. A truck pulled up just in front of me, and the driver began unloading cartons of Co-Colas through the side door of the grocery store.

"You're clean as a whistle, Adelaide."

"Are you serious?" I wanted to hug Bernise through the telephone. "Thank You, God!"

"Now, stay that way for me, okay?"

I sighed with relief, and a new hope seemed to fill my lungs as I inhaled again.

"No problem. I can *guarantee* you that."

After hanging up the phone, I walked a few steps over to a shaft of light that was hitting the wall of the store and the concrete slab beneath the awning. And there I stood in my patent-leather pumps, the dark stains of discarded bubble gum and spilled soft drinks beneath my feet as I let the sun fall on me.

Had God answered my prayer? Did He have a place for me in the palm of His hand? The world was a filthy and dangerous place, but there might be another side to it after all. A side where mercy and pardon existed.

"Thank You," I said, peering above the crumbling asphalt of the parking lot and squinting into the morning light that was cutting through the mill smog. If He was real and had reached out to me, I certainly wanted to give Him the credit He was due.

⌒

Early that afternoon, Shannon and I snuck into the country-club powder room after a decadent deb lunch of honey ham, tomato pies, and blackberry cobbler with ice cream. As we were celebrating over my medical results, Jif stumbled out of one of the stalls with a pink face and watery eyes. She popped a mint into her mouth, but that could not cover up the sour smell of vomit.

"Jif," I said, "what were you doing in there?"

She dabbed at her eyes with a Kleenex and straightened out her designer dress. "That lunch must have had two thousand calories," she said, not looking at either of us straight on. "I've got to keep my weight down if I'm going to fit in my gown."

"That's ridiculous!" I said. "You look terrific, and you could stand to put *on* a few pounds."

Jif shook her head in firm disagreement.

"Jennifer?" Marny Ferguson's snappy voice penetrated the bathroom door. "Time to go if—"

"Coming," Jif called back to her with a froggy voice.

I stepped in front of the door and stared Jif down. As she began to look me in the eye, Marny said through the door, "Time to go if we want to make our eyebrow appointment."

"Chill, Marny!" I called from over my shoulder.

"What in the world?" she said, then cleared her throat dramatically. "Who said that? Is that you, Adelaide? A deb doesn't speak to anyone's mother in that tone."

"Don't you fall into this trap," I said, grabbing Jif by the shoulder. "You look great, and you need to eat."

"I eat," Jif assured me. "Just not tomato pie and blackberry cobbler with vanilla ice cream." Then she shooed me out of the way and ran out to meet her mother.

Shannon and I stared at each other, our eyes widening. Jif was a diet freak, but I didn't know she was making herself sick over it.

Marny was waiting to get a good look at me when the door

opened. She stared me down like nobody's business, as if there was something about me that had always bugged her and it was all she could do to keep a lid on it. As if my ancestry weren't really Graydon-Piper but some backwoods brand of swamp kin who would raise a girl who mouthed off to her elders. I stared right back at her for what seemed like a whole minute until Jif pulled her away.

"I'll try to talk some sense into her," I said to Shannon.

We peered out the powder-room window as the two sets of long, skinny legs in high-heeled mules hurried out to their candy-blue Mercedes.

Marny was a bit of a cheesy pageant gal turned Gucci mannequin, but I didn't think she would be happy to know that her daughter was willing to puke up her lunch in the Magnolia Club bathroom to keep her weight down.

I pictured the fashion magazines that Jif pored over regularly with the abnormally thin fashion models, and then I envisioned Jif's father with his scalpel, ready to slice her into perfection when it was time.

"You could get that thing snipped," she'd told me last March as I rubbed my jewel in the dorm-room mirror.

She stood at the sink next to mine and examined her nose. "Dad will give me a nose job if I graduate cum laude."

"There is nothing wrong with your nose."

"Maybe a boob job, then," she said, pushing out her thin chest. "So long as they don't make me look fat."

What was more barbaric: a thirteenth-century Chinese girl bending the bones in her feet or a twentieth-century American slicing open her breasts and shoving water balloons inside them?

"So what about meeting with the Pelzers?" Shannon asked as Jif and her mother pulled quickly out of the parking lot.

"For Jif?"

"No, for *you*," Shannon said. "We're celebrating your good news, remember? The summer is nearly over, and I want you to see them before you head on back to school."

While my grades were bad, I hadn't gotten word about my

scholarship, and I wondered where I'd be come fall. *Lord of the Flies* or the sweet and loyal arms of Randy, the Gamecock kicker?

"All right," I said, "I'll meet with them, but I can't promise that this whole thing is for me."

"I know," she said, but I could tell that she was already hopeful her spiritual mentors would persuade me to take a walk down their well-worn path.

When I walked out onto the terrace of the club, I spotted Mama waiting for us in the station wagon. She was writing down a grocery list of my favorite foods, since this was my last two weeks to be home (as far as she knew). As Shannon and I plopped down in the seat, the hot vinyl stuck to the backs of our legs. Mama patted me on the knee and said, "Now, think about all that you want to do before you head back to school. I want to have that Mexican casserole one night, and we could have your friends over for a picnic one afternoon. Randy said he wants to take you out someplace special."

I was thankful that Greta Piper was my mama. She was safe and caring, and she wanted me to be healthy and happy, and that was about it.

"Want to cook out with us tonight?" she asked Shannon. "Zane wants to listen to the Braves game on the radio."

"Yes, ma'am," Shannon responded. Then I turned on the radio and found the new and horrendously maudlin Bette Midler song, "Wind Beneath My Wings." Shannon and I belted it out all the way back to our neighborhood.

Juliabelle was waiting for me on the back steps of my house when we pulled up. Papa Great had sent her to town to get some of Mama's tomatoes, and she was sitting with her sun hat on her lap when we pulled up. She had a glaze of perspiration down her neck and a half-filled carton of water at her feet.

"Not coming out, eh?" she said to me after Mama dropped me off and headed on to the Piggly Wiggly.

"Sorry, Juliabelle," I said, taking my place beside her on the steps. "I don't want to talk. Nobody in the family knows. And I don't want to upset you."

She bit her lip and crinkled her nose. She reached out to rub my cheek and said, "That bad?"

And when I felt the pads of her fingertips on my face, a grief rose up in my throat, and I went straight from composure to complete meltdown. My face turned darker than Mama's ripest tomato, and I wept, hitting my fists on the brick steps until the skin on my knuckles was raw.

She held my arms at my sides until I gave up my hitting and rested my head in her lap. As she rocked me, she spoke in a hushed tone, and her words were an entirely different language. A powerful one that moved fast and had a kind of strength to it, a language I could feel in my gut. I stopped my crying and listened. Her eyes were closed now, and a drop of perspiration from her chin dropped down on my forehead. I closed my eyes again, rested my head in her lap like when I was a girl, and let her strange words stream out of her mouth and wash over me like rain.

How did she come upon that secret language? Was it making me feel better?

Our breathing became synchronized as I listened, and I remembered where I had heard it before. It was during the one trip I'd ever taken to her house. I had been nine, and she was supposed to be keeping Dizzy, Lou, and me for a week while my folks and grandfolks went to a textile convention. Normally, she would have kept us at our house, but she was tending to her aunt Scripty, who had recently suffered a stroke, so we packed our bags and went to her house. She lived far down a dirt road off Route 39 on a bluff near the Santee River, in the same house where her mother used to live. (Her mother had worked for Mae Mae's mother.) A few of her cousins had houses along the bluff, and they all had meticulous gardens with fences around them where they grew cantaloupe and honeydew melons as big as your head. And Juliabelle had woods behind her home, full of sweet grass that her husband, Nigel, and Aunt Scripty wove into baskets, which they sold at a roadside stand to the tourists driving from Charleston to Pawleys Island.

Nigel would take us girls out into the woods in the early morning to gather the grass and the pine straw. And he'd climb up his ladder to the tops of the palmettos, where he'd throw down palm leaves we tried to catch in his big gray trash can. Then he'd tote us and his supplies over to the stand by the highway, where we'd play kick-the-can and eat melon and smile at the tourists who inspected the baskets as he'd pierce an opening in the center of the sweet grass knot and weave the palm leaves and pine straw through the coil.

Sometimes he'd send me with a wad of money back to the house to report the sale of the day to Juliabelle and Aunt Scripty. Once, when I had seventy-five dollars in my little hand and a guarantee from Nigel that he'd take us all to McDonald's for supper, I ran through the woods and onto the porch and peered through the open window, where I could see Aunt Scripty propped up on her bed, staring ahead at the muted fuzzy television screen while Juliabelle stood over her, her hands cupped around Aunt Scripty's head, speaking loudly the same mysterious tongue she was speaking over me today. I can remember Aunt Scripty's nostrils flaring as she breathed in and out, in and out, as if she were trying to suck up the incantation itself. As if she would starve without it.

Now, I wasn't about to interrupt to tell them about the sale of the day. Instead, I sat down on the bed Juliabelle had made for us on the screened porch and intently listened to the sounds and syllables blending together like a power-wielding poem, like the coke and the iron ore that are heated together and poured out into a fiery lava before being molded into sheets of steel.

They didn't have telephone lines out there, so when someone wanted an update on Aunt Scripty, Juliabelle would stand on the edge of the bluff and call the news, and the neighbors would pass it on down the river, calling to one another as the wind carried their voices along.

That afternoon it was Aunt Scripty herself moving out to the water's edge, her hands around her mouth to say, "I'm betta now." Then she clapped her hands in a strange rhythm as she stomped to her garden.

As Dizzy and I followed her, she sang, "The Spirit and the bride say, 'Come!' And let him who hears say, 'Come!'"

Then she let us yank the largest honeydew off the vine, which she cut into sweet cubes for our evening dessert.

It was Aunt Scripty who tucked us into a king-sized bed on the screened porch that night, and we drifted off to the sounds of the crickets and bullfrogs while she and Juliabelle smoked their evening pipes at the foot of our bed and Nigel weaved another fruit basket to replace the one he'd sold that day to a couple from Pennsylvania.

Today, when Juliabelle stopped talking in the strange language, I opened my eyes and reached out to the carton beside her.

"What's this?" I asked.

"Tonic," she said. "From the well, remember?"

Yeah, there was more than just that time my throat had swelled from a bad oyster and she made the trip to Huger Creek to get me some. And now I remembered that she had bathed Lou with the water when she contracted such a bad case of chicken pox that it lined every crack and crevice of her skin. And once when Daddy was suffering from an awful case of insomnia, she had taken Dizzy and me with her into the Francis Marion Forest and had us hold a bowl while she pumped out the drink that would help him rest.

"Can this help a hurting heart?" I asked as I fingered the carton lid.

"Might be," she said, and she rubbed my back gently.

"Okay, I'll drink some," I said, sitting up again. "And one day I'll get the strength to tell you."

"Every time I think on you," she said, reminding me of her prayer promise of last summer, knocking her shoulder against mine.

"Thank you," I said, embracing her again. I rested in her arms for whole minutes, smelling her powder-sweet perspiration and staring down at the fresh dirt from the forest that lined the edges of her sandals.

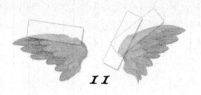

# 11

# End of Summer

The next day I drank a cup of Juliabelle's water with my breakfast, and an hour later I found myself in the Harvest Time pastor's office (which in its previous life had been a bathroom for the barbecue restaurant that the building once functioned as). The Pelzers had laid down some pieces of scrap carpet and hung a few cheesy sunset and rainbow posters on the tile walls, but there was still a floor drain in one corner of the office and a random sink beside Dale's desk.

"C'mon in, girls," Darla said to Shannon and me as she popped her bright blue chewing gum and patted the place beside her on the secondhand couch while Dale pushed his swivel chair from around his desk to face us.

"Hi there, Adelaide." Dale extended his hand, and when he smiled, I could see that he needed braces something awful.

He popped a mint-flavored toothpick into his mouth and began to gnaw on it, and I could just hear Mae Mae whispering, "What terrible manners!" (I mean, these folk could give the Bizway diamonds a run for their money in the etiquette department.)

After a lengthy prayer in which Darla supported Dale's words with several moans of agreement, Dale straightened out his blue jeans and leaned in toward us, saying, "Now, Shannon tells me you're a thinker, and that's a God-given blessing. You ask me your questions, and Darla and I'll try to answer them the best we can. We're not the sharpest tacks, but we believe we have the answer to life's most important question. What's been revealed to us is the truth of the Almighty, and it's good news indeed, Miss Adelaide! As Christ Himself said in Matthew 11:25 and 26, 'O Father, Lord of heaven and earth, thank you for hiding the truth from those who think themselves so wise and clever, and for revealing it to the childlike.'"

Darla offered a four-syllable "Amen" and began to roll her cheap beaded bracelets back and forth across her wrist as I found the right place in my journal.

*What am I doing here?* The sharp thought suddenly nipped at my mind as I looked down at my questions. *Do I belong next to a lady who wears sparkly eye shadow at ten in the morning and a man who chews on mint toothpicks while he prays? Shouldn't I have gone to St. Anne's to ask these questions first before heading to this barbecue bathroom office?*

Though it took me a little by surprise, something in me was utterly repelled by Dale and Darla's evangelistic eagerness, and I had half a mind to just stand up and walk out. I didn't think I could contain my disdain for whatever their message was and whatever they expected me to do about it.

This newfound contempt was a surprise. It was so real and forceful that I could hardly speak. I suddenly recalled this same kind of repulsion when I was ten and attending my last year at St. Anne's vacation Bible school. How, when the music director asked us to sing a corny song about the steps of salvation and Jesus's making a home in our hearts, I muttered, "I won't do it," then stole away to the bathroom, where I waited for the bell to ring.

*I can say I'm sick,* I thought as we all waited for me to read from my journal. *I can tell Dale and Darla that I have just come down with a terrible virus and run out of the room and pretend to be nauseous.*

Mustering up the strength to sell this lie, I gave a side glance to the dear friend of my childhood, the girl who had practically carried me through this painful summer with her steady love and support, and I realized I didn't want to offend or hurt her. And what about Darla? The woman who had courageously spilled out her scandalous personal history a few weeks ago to me and a hundred other searching souls? The glow in her eyes burned even now.

Fighting off my rebellion, I rattled off my questions to Dale, who nodded as though they were thoughtful, but typical.

"Let me start with a visual analogy," Dale said as he pulled over an easel with a small chalkboard attached to it. "All my answers to your questions are going to build on this, so I might as well go ahead and lay this down as our foundation."

"Okay," I said, and I was breathing a little easier even now. I liked the classroom approach and was entirely comfortable approaching this as a brain exercise.

Dale took out a broken piece of chalk and drew a horizontal line across the middle of the cracked board. Under the left side of the line he wrote "man," and under the right side of the line he wrote "God."

"In the beginning God and man were together."

"Genesis," Shannon said in an effort to anchor me.

"Oh, like the Garden of Eden," I remarked.

"Yep," Darla added as her jaw worked her gum over.

Next Dale erased the middle of the horizontal line. Then he drew a vertical line at the end of the word *man* and another at the beginning of the word *God* so that they became two separate entities with a great gap in between them. He slapped his jeans so that two small clouds of chalk dust rose from his hips; then he wrote the word *sin* in the gap and stated, "Then sin separated man from God."

"The Fall," Shannon said, and I conjured up an image that had accompanied a John Milton poem in my freshman literature class.

"I get this," I said. "What happened when Adam and Eve gave in to temptation. I mean, they got thrown out, right?"

"Yes, ma'am," Dale said. "They and all of their descendants." Then he took his nubby chalk stick and pointed to himself, then Darla, then Shannon, then me.

*Sin?* I was mulling the archaic word over in my mind. I could already think of a few folks who surely did not have sin in them: (1) Mother Teresa; (2) Gandhi.

Now I was ready to stir the pot.

"Hear me out, now," Dale said, raising his chalky fingertips. He clapped his hands together once, and the white dust lifted for a moment like a cloud of smoke before him.

"But God had a plan to bring you and me back to Him." He drew a picture of a cross that filled in the schism so that one side could now get to the other.

"You mean Jesus?" I said.

"Jesus and what He did on the cross."

"He died," I said plainly, still not making the connection. Jesus-died-on-the-cross. These words were like wallpaper or a kind of white noise that had always been present in my small-town childhood. I had heard bits and pieces of the story over and over on the radio, in the pharmacy, in the strip mall, and at the gas stations, but it had never held any personal connection to me before. The words were part of the Williamstown culture, just another piece of the backwoods South, like tobacco or pork rinds, and I had always considered them as much superstition as anything else. In my mind, Jesus-died-on-the-cross was simply a notion that dim-witted folks relied on to get them through their hard and simple lives.

"Do you know what happened when Christ died?" Dale asked.

"I'm not sure I do," I said sheepishly. I was embarrassed that I had never followed this story all the way to its conclusion. Had I been asleep my whole life?

"Well, God Almighty's holy Son was sacrificed. He bore all of our sins—the ones from the beginning and the ones in the here and now and the ones to come—so that we could come back to God if we believe in what was accomplished on that cross."

I thought for a moment. Then I took out my pencil and re-created the illustration in my journal. I had to admit, it was a beautiful story, if not compelling. But still, I kept my spoon in hand. Where was the catch?

Life was painful, I'd concluded after my freshman year at NBU. Life smacked you in the face and left you sitting on the side of a cemetery hill with shame and a potential disease invading your body and destroying the future you had worked so hard to protect. I feared that even with a seemingly pure and simple situation like this salvation one, there was a catch.

"Jesus paid the penalty, took the shackles off our feet, and allowed us to enter back into fellowship with our Maker," Shannon added. Her voice cracked on the word *Maker*, and I could tell she was nervous. For years she'd been wanting to put a check by my name and write "saved" beside it.

"And not just that, darlin'," Darla said as her bracelets clamored together with her excited arm motions. "In this act of mercy, Christ conquered death. He rose again on the third day, and we will rise, too, if we believe."

*Rise again? Hold on!* I was just here to ask a few questions. I needed help coping with the here and now, not the afterlife.

"All who believe will have eternal life," Dale added, and the light in his eyes was bursting into a flame. It wasn't a *Carrie* horror-movie kind of fire, but rather a white light, like an electrical current, and I examined it with a kind of curiosity as it shot across his pupils.

*He really believes this stuff.*

"And in this next life," Dale continued, "God will be with His people. 'He will remove all of their sorrows, and there will be no more death or sorrow or crying or pain. For the old world and its evils are gone forever.'"

"That's from Revelation 21:4," Shannon whispered to me, and I wrote it down as if it would be a question on a test, but in truth, I was confused. What would some of that electrical light cost me?

*Let's slow down,* I thought. *Maybe I want to keep my speedometer at zero after all.*

"Back to the separation part," I said in an effort to take this thing by the horns and stand nose to nose with it. "Do you mean to tell me that Mother Teresa is separated from God or that Hitler could have been forgiven if he had believed this in the last moments of his life?"

"Yes'm," Dale said. "The Good Book says that no one is good—not even one. 'For all have sinned; all fall short of God's glorious standard.'"

"Romans chapter 3," Shannon whispered again.

What an encyclopedia of Scripture quotes she was! Weird. I turned to look at her as though she had two heads, and she grinned back at me.

Dale pressed on with an article that he removed from his second-hand file cabinet. "Mother Teresa says there are five words that explain the reason she picks those little orphans up out of the gutter in Calcutta: 'He Did This for Me.'"

"Really?" I said, raising my eyebrows as Dale handed me the article, where I read the very words he had highlighted.

*This is going to shatter the whole protagonist/antagonist literature prototype,* I thought. *I mean, if we're all bad guys after all . . .*

"And what about Hitler?" I said. "Do you mean to tell me that he was redeemable?"

"No question Hitler was evil," Dale said. "Somewhere along the way he turned away from God and became a mighty instrument of the enemy, but to say that he couldn't be saved would be to take away the value of the Cross, and I'm not gonna do that. So yes, Hitler was redeemable, but only the Lord knows if he chose that at the end."

Darla then added, "We are made right in God's sight when we trust in the shed blood of Christ to take away our sins."

As Shannon cleared her throat to cite the Scripture, I whispered back a little too loudly, "Take it easy, Miss Bible Beater," and we all broke out into laughter, relishing this moment of comic relief.

"It's so *simple*," I said.

Then Dale pulled out a book titled *Mere Christianity* by C. S. Lewis and handed it to me. "The Lord's given you a brain, and He wants you to use it, so try this on for size, and meet with me again when you come home during your next college break." He threw his frayed toothpick into the trash and added, "This'll be one for you to sink your teeth into. I never have gotten through it."

C. S. Lewis. I had loved the Chronicles of Narnia as a girl and had passed them down to Lou last year and even read them with her from time to time. Then I remembered peering into that Bible study at NBU where they were reading a book by Lewis—*The Great Divorce*, I remembered.

"Let me leave you with this thought," Dale said. He put his Bible down and rubbed his knees as he searched for the right words. "It's good to think this through, but it's also good to move ahead and commit when you sense it is right. You never know what tomorrow holds."

*Scare tactic*, I thought, the repulsion making its way back into my throat. *If this is an altar call, I'm not budging.* (I was beginning to feel bipolar.) Clearing my throat, I looked away from Dale and became suddenly conscious of the ticking of a bright yellow "Smile, God loves you!" clock behind his head. I imagined it was a bomb that would detonate any second.

"Let me put it another way," Dale said. "What could be bigger than eternal life, Adelaide? If you want to plan for your future, think about more than just the next seventy years. There was this bright fellow by the name of Pascal who came to the faith by seeing it in terms of a wager."

*Pascal's wager.* It sounded vaguely familiar, like a reference in a poem, but I couldn't recall.

"Anyhow, what Pascal said was, 'If God doesn't exist, it doesn't matter how you wager, 'cause there's nothing to win after death and nothing to lose neither. But if God *does* exist, your only chance of winning an eternal life is to believe, and your only chance of losing it is to refuse to believe.'"

Then Dale pulled out another yellowed file that quoted Pascal. He scratched the back of his neck and read, "'I should be much more afraid of being mistaken and then find out that Christianity is true than of being mistaken in believing it to be true.'"

*That's a thought, Mr. Toothpick,* I thought. *But then there's that whole "surrender your life" thing that Shannon brought up before and Darla mentioned in her testimony. My life belongs to me, and I'm not going to hand it over.*

Dale pointed the file at me and said, "I mean, if I'm wrong in believing, what did it hurt, but if I choose not to believe and I am wrong, what did I lose?"

"Everything," I murmured. Still, I wasn't going to budge. I looked into his fiery eyes head-on to let him know.

"But this is not wrong," Dale concluded as he stared back at me. "It's the truth, and we get confirmation of that every day of our lives."

I practically felt a breeze from Darla's and Shannon's strong head-nodding beside me.

If God had been courting me all of my life, then the splendor part was all about Him. My search had been for Him all along. Though I considered that this could actually be true, I wasn't ready to accept it.

I thanked Dale and Darla for their time and didn't say much to Shannon on the ride home. But late that night, I wrote the first poem I'd written since April.

> Could the chasm
> between us
> be bridged
> with two
> slats of
> wood?

∽

The Cold War ended later that week while my sisters and I drank cherry icees with Daddy in the backyard by the crab dock. We were listening to the proposal of the Western Alliance over a fuzzy portable radio as Daddy shot off the leftover Roman candles from the Fourth of July out over the marsh.

He was all excited. Uncle Tinka had just gone platinum, and he'd be next with just two more in his downline. He'd just returned from a convention in Atlanta where they gave him a standing ovation when he came out dressed in his star-studded marine uniform, his sleeve folded up to his ribs to show the sacrifice he had made. After that convention, several groups were calling to ask him to speak at seminars and meetings come fall. They ate up his Vietnam War stories, and they could easily weave his message of courage and hope into their own agendas.

But as the world looked forward to its newfound peace, the Piper family's pockets of resistance were gaining strength, and the first battle of a domestic war that would last for years was about to be waged.

It began on August 10, the same day that a letter from NBU arrived stating that because of my poor second-semester grades, my $6,000-a-year scholarship was in jeopardy. I had one semester of grace to pull up my GPA. After that, my parents would have to come up with the extra money to pay the full bill or I would have to transfer.

While Uncle Tinka had pushed Daddy hard to build his own line in Bizway, Mama lost any interest she ever had in the venture after attending a second convention at an Orlando resort where wives flaunted three-carat diamonds and husbands drove fully loaded limousines up to the front of the meeting room so that folks could gawk at their glittery wealth.

"Sure, they're rich," Mama told Daddy that night as they peered out their fourth-floor hotel window and watched the fireworks display from the Magic Kingdom light up the sky with its dazzling purple-and-gold fire. "But they pop their gum, and their mascara is all lumpy, and they're all overweight even though they're pushing vitamins and health shakes. Something doesn't add up here. And I'm tired of paying fifteen dollars for a hamburger in this godforsaken world of faux."

"You know what your problem is?" Daddy had said. "You're a small-town snob. Can't you for once try to let me *dream* a little, here?"

Mama had recently warned Daddy again not to upset his father (and employer) by admitting he was fully committed to the pyramid business. It was true that the American textiles industry was slowly collapsing because of cheap labor forces overseas, but Papa Great didn't see it that way.

Daddy had moved on in Bizway against his bride's wishes, and his plan was to work the business on the side until he could get free from the parental hooks that had kept him in an office job most of his adult life.

But on that swarmy summer night of August, Papa Great marched right up to the steps of my home with an ultimatum:

"Zane, you're going to be out of a job in two weeks if you continue in this harebrained pursuit," he hollered in the foyer. He had refused an iced tea or a seat in the living room. His face was red and bloated, and he pinched his nose so hard I thought steam might pour out of his ears.

"Papa, come on," Daddy said. "I've tried it your way for years, and you know I'm no good to the mill."

Papa Great glanced up to find Lou and me leaning over the banister, listening. He pointed up the stairwell in our direction while continuing to stare Daddy down. "And I will not put up the remainder of your eldest daughter's inflated college tuition, either."

Daddy rubbed his cheek with his stub. "You son of a—"

"I'm meeting with my attorney in two weeks to revise my will."

He turned back around as Mama cried out, "Wait, Papa!"

"No, Greta," he said, shaking his head. "You just tell your husband I sure hope it's worth it." Then he slammed the front door and shuffled toward the Cadillac, and I wondered where Mae Mae and Juliabelle were and if they'd had any idea what he was up to.

Before I knew it, I grabbed one of my Norton anthologies, opened my bedroom window, and threw it at him. "Hog!" I shouted.

It hit his right shoulder as he walked across the lawn.

He stopped in his tracks to look up at me.

I had my hands on my hips, and I strained to see the whites of his eyes.

"All that I can see you've gained from being away at that overpriced college is twenty pounds or so," he said, sniffing in the humid air.

I shifted my weight and did not take his bait.

"You know what I think, Papa? I think my daddy would have had two good arms and a pro football career if it weren't for you and your boorish expectations. It's time you let him be."

He sneered, then spit on my anthology.

"Uppity girl." He kept his gaze on me and shook his head in a combination of disgust and disbelief.

"Adelaide, don't you dare talk to your grandfather that way!" Mama was calling from the front porch. "Papa, now, you come on back inside and let's talk this out."

I gazed back at him.

He rubbed his shoulder, then pulled his hand away. "She hit me," he said to Mama, picking up the anthology and toting it to his car.

Lou started to cry from somewhere behind me, and by the time I turned around to check on her, he was driving down the street over the bridge to Pawleys.

If this wasn't bad enough, in the late hours of that same night, Dizzy was arrested for driving under the influence while swerving home from an all-day party on the river at her crazy friend Angel's house.

Zane Piper was madder than a hornet's nest when he wheeled the Country Squire out of the driveway to bail his wild child out of the city jail.

"I've had it with this one," he screamed after he hung up the phone from talking with a police officer. "She won't be leaving this house for months!"

Mama didn't say anything back to him before he left. She was melting under the pressure of the first day of war, and she cried into her pillow for an hour before her husband and her lost daughter appeared at the front door with long-term consequences to face for their wayward choices.

Poor Mama—all she wanted was a quiet, small-town life. An existence opposite her dysfunctional Charleston upbringing. Now nothing was going according to her plan, and she would have kissed Papa Great's thick, jagged toenails before releasing her Piper family vision.

You could hear a pin drop in the Piper house as Daddy locked the front door and turned off the last light at 3:00 a.m.

"Get up to your room!" he said to Dizzy, and she plodded up the stairs. "I hope you like it up there, 'cause the only time you're going to leave this house over the next three months is to go to school."

Lou woke up in all of the commotion, and I invited her to stay in my room for the rest of the night. When I went to invite Dizzy, I could not get her attention. Her door was locked, and she was blasting some kind of punk rock through her headphones.

⁓

Over the next few days I pondered God and my choices for the coming year: transferring back to USC as Randy proposed or taking out loans to cover Papa Great's half of my tuition, returning to NBU, and giving it another go. I had a call in to an admissions coordinator at Carolina, and she was working on piecing together some financial aid for me.

Mama had sided with Papa Great and refused to join Daddy at any Bizway meeting or convention. Daddy made his choice too—he was making a run for this new career, with or without his inheritance or his wife's support.

How I had yearned to curl up in my mother's arms on my last summer nights—to ask her about God and if I should accept the message that Dale and Darla had presented to me. I wanted to confide in Daddy as well, but he was distant and determined, making phone calls to vets and old football buddies, asking if he could come by and show them his new business plan.

Juliabelle was stuck out on the island with the old Hog, and I couldn't get to her, either, so I drank the last of her tonic and hoped for the best. (Little did I know that she and Mae Mae were going to bat for me in more ways than one.)

As my parents argued about the fate of Dizzy's next year—a rehab camp, homeschooling, boarding school, and the like—I drove her to the first of many Alcoholics Anonymous meetings that Judge Snodgrass had required her to attend.

"Will you come to the meeting?" Dizzy whispered to me. Her head was tilted toward the floorboard of the station wagon as we pulled into a space at Second Baptist Church. (She was not looking anyone in the eye these days.)

"Sure," I said, squeezing the back of my sister's hand. I, of course, had a million things to do and life-altering decisions to make, but I couldn't stand the thought of letting Dizzy down right now.

When we walked into the smoke-filled church gymnasium where the AA meetings were held, I quickly sensed the energy that I had felt at Harvest Time during that dinner several weeks ago. Dizzy and I sat down in the back row of seats as several kind and weathered faces nodded in our direction and personal stories about the battle with the addiction were told over a cheap and crackly microphone.

The AA steps were so reminiscent of my talks with Shannon and Dale and Darla that I was beginning to believe someone was trying to tell me something:

1. Admit that you are powerless.
2. Believe that a Power greater than yourself can restore you to sanity.
3. Make a decision to turn your will and your life over to the care of God.
4. Take a moral inventory of yourself.
5. Admit to God, yourself, and others the exact nature of your wrongdoings.
6. Become ready to have God remove all of these defects of character.
7. Humbly ask Him to remove your shortcomings.
8. Make a list of all persons you have harmed, and become willing to make amends to them all.
9. Make direct amends to such people wherever possible, except when to do so would injure them or others.
10. Continue to take personal inventory, and when you are wrong promptly admit it.
11. Seek through prayer and meditation to improve your

> conscious contact with God as you understand Him,
> praying only for knowledge of His will for you and the
> power to carry that out.
> 12. Having had a spiritual awakening as the result of these steps,
> try to carry this message to others who are hurting and to
> practice these principles in all your affairs.

The message was understandable. It was familiar to me by now, and yet I was not ready to take the leap of faith it required. It was as though I was aware of the battle that was being waged inside my mind, but I chose to side with the faithless faction because that came most naturally.

As prideful as it sounds, I was not convinced that if I took a moral inventory of myself, it would come up in the red. I was a victim, after all. A victim of a horrible attack. And before that, I was a victor: an above-average poet on my way to a promising future. *A sinner* was not how I described myself, frankly. Sure, I'd made a mistake here and there, but the overall picture was good.

Now Dizzy seemed lifeless in the meeting. She kept her head lowered and smoked the Marlboro Reds that had become her source of comfort and peace. If I was hard to reach, Dizzy was beyond the pale, and I feared that the only message my sis would receive in this meeting was that it was fine to chain-smoke and whine.

On our way home, Dizzy turned up the dark music that she had slid into the cassette player and rubbed her temples.

My folks had grounded her indefinitely until they came up with a plan to whip her into shape, and she hadn't left the house for at least five days. Knowing what it felt like to want to crawl into a hole and wither away, I wanted to do *something* to express my sympathy. Suddenly I turned off the music, made a U-turn in the middle of our quiet neighborhood, and headed out toward Pawleys Island. Dizzy gave me an inquisitive look before returning her gaze to the floorboard.

"Let's go to the beach. You could use some fresh air and a last look at it before fall comes."

Dizzy gave a deep sigh of relief and seemed to relax into the seat for the first time since we'd left the house. She looked out the window as the late-afternoon sun left a pink glow on all the weathered homes and the palmetto trees bent at curious angles along the gravel road.

We caught the end of the sunset when we parked at Boardwalk 11, and we scurried down to the gully's edge to dip our feet into the soupy pool just in time to watch three terns flap toward their roost in the top of an abandoned boardwalk as the purple sky faded into black. We lay back on the sand in the dark as the ocean slapped the shore and just listened.

The intracoastal waterway was the thoroughfare that had made Williamstown a wealthy shipping harbor during colonial times as the cotton, indigo, and rice were loaded here and carried on to Europe. And I thought about the four rivers that converged in the harbor and poured into the sea and the hurricanes that autumn brought and the ghost of the Gray Man that appeared before a storm to warn the residents to retreat.

Then I squeezed Dizzy's hand and said, "It sucks, but you'll get through. Don't roll over and die, sis."

"I've done worse than this," Dizzy said through a guffaw. "I've got a lot to change if I want to get back up again."

"Eh, water under the bridge, right?"

I tried to whitewash it, but Dizzy was ready to talk. It was as though she had weights on her chest, and she had to name them before she could consider lifting them off.

"I've carried drugs for people in my car, Adelaide. Drugs to *sell*."

"Well, that wasn't exactly a brilliant thing to do, but just don't do it again, okay?"

"Taken Ecstasy," Dizzy continued as we watched a barge stacked with red and black containers move out from the harbor and into the waterway. "And once, at Angel's house, I did acid. They had to tie me down to the couch because I kept wanting to jump off of the balcony and grab the moon."

Holding Dizzy's clammy hand, I rubbed my thumb across her knuckles.

"Besides all that, I've, like, totally been with guys before," she said before exhaling loudly.

A fish tail skittered before our toes, and I bit my lip. *What should I say?*

"Three," Dizzy continued. "Two of whom I haven't seen again."

The air was soft and moving enough to keep the mosquitoes at bay, and I heard the palm fronds knocking together behind us. A ghost crab scurried across the surf and into his hole. He went in and out again, staring us down with his beady raised eyes before moving sideways back toward the water.

"I've driven drunk, stoned, plenty of times," Dizzy continued. "I mowed down one of our neighbor's mailboxes last year and dented the station wagon so bad that I had to beg my friends to hammer it out."

Then Dizzy started to weep. I couldn't remember the last time my sister had let her guard down. My mind reeled with explanations: Dizzy had dyslexia like me, but hers had been a harder case to overcome, so she struggled in school. She had never found her niche in the academic or athletic worlds, and her class was made up of some world-class small-town losers.

"I, like, could have hurt someone," Dizzy said. "Driving as messed up as I was. Isn't that scary?"

"Yeah," I said, dabbing my sister's eyes with the arm of my blouse. "It can end here, though."

"Adelaide, do you believe in that greater Power stuff that they were talking about?"

"I'm working on that," I said. "I want to, but . . ."

Dizzy threw an oyster shell into the water, kicked at it, and added, "You might not need it, but I do."

I splashed back at her, and she kicked a clump of sand onto my belly, and before I knew it we were in a saltwater war, and our clothes were soaking from the gray-green soup. Dizzy laughed for the first time in days as she sat up and cupped the water in her hands. Then she poured it over my head.

"Thanks for listening," she said, and she looked up and met my eyes in the darkness. Her makeup was running, and she looked like a miniature Morticia Addams with a hangover.

"I love you, Diz," I said as I returned the head douse with a handful of water. "I want to help."

She stood first and pulled me up before throwing her arm over my shoulder. We walked back up the dunes to the station wagon, the sand clinging to our feet and ankles and our jeans making a squishing noise with each step.

We drove home, wet and itchy, on one of the last nights of the summer of 1990, our backsides leaving dark impressions in the plush car seat. It was the season we would later look back to and remember that our lives began to take a drastic turn in an unalterable direction. The Pipers would not be the same again.

As Iraq's invasion of Kuwait dominated the television screen and the last debutante dress fitting was taken before Thanksgiving, Mae Mae came over and said, "Pack your bags for NBU!"

"You know something I don't?" I asked. She was grinning from ear to ear, though all the Lancôme foundation in the world couldn't mask the gray bags under her eyes.

"We're back on for our half of the tuition," she said, tilting her head from side to side and tapping her thumb and middle finger together like a belly dancer.

"What about Papa Great?"

"Well, he got hungry and gave in."

"Huh?"

"Well," she said, winking at me, "Juliabelle went on strike last week after he took your scholarship away, and he hasn't had fried shrimp in seven days."

I smiled. "And what about you?" I said.

"We've had a few words, but I know how to open his eyes."

❧

Randy was disappointed, but he invited me on a boat ride the afternoon before I left. He brought a basket of wine and imported cheeses he'd bought in Charleston—stuff that I knew he never ate but thought I'd like.

"Ooh, doggie," he said when he bit into a piece of Stilton. He puckered his lips, drank a big gulp of wine, then pulled an anthology of Archibald Rutledge poems from the basket.

After we anchored beneath a live oak tree on the edge of Goose Creek, he read poetry to me. Rather maudlin poems about nature and love, but still, the gesture was dear.

When he pulled a little blue box out of his back pocket, I was scared to death he might be proposing.

*Oh, good gravy,* I thought as he snapped open the cover to reveal two perfectly round charcoal-pearl stud earrings. He handed them to me and said, "Three years isn't so long. And I'm not giving up now."

He kissed me long and hard; then he pulled out a folded piece of notebook paper from his pocket and read a poem he had just composed himself.

> *Every now and then*
> *While an oyster shell*
> *Filters salt water*
> *A few grains of sand come in.*

*After months of mud*
*The sand becomes a pearl.*
*Then I open the shell and find it.*
*Like my heart, it belongs to one girl.*

I smiled at his sincere effort and blushed at the sentiment. No one had ever written me a poem. And even though this one was terrible, I hugged him hard and thanked him for how much he'd meant to me this summer.

After kissing Randy a final good-bye on Mae Mae's dock, I went for a last summer visit with Baby Peach and Georgianne; then I loaded my suitcases into Jif's new car for our return to NBU.

The debs had gone on an informal farewell trip to Myrtle Beach the night before. Shannon had followed me onto my porch at the end of the night to ask me if I had gained any ground with *Mere Christianity*. Since my family turmoil, I had not cracked any book and had concluded that as wonderful an idea as it was, I just wasn't there yet.

"It's a lovely story," I assured her as the fireflies lit up the yard. "It's a beautiful notion. I mean, to think that God could have become human and died for mankind so that we could be reunited with Him. But . . ."

"Okay," Shannon said, unable to hold back a sigh. She seemed genuinely disappointed and concerned.

"I'm sorry to let you down, Shan. But hey, you can pray for me," I said, "that I will be able to function back at school and have a decent year there. My scholarship is in jeopardy, and heaven knows how freaked out I'm going to be when I get back there."

"You know I will."

"I know, Miss Holy Roller," I said, hugging her before tugging on her ponytail. "You have a good year too."

Shannon was headed back to the two-year women's college in

North Carolina while applying to other colleges where she would finish. I had never heard of Wheaton, which was Shannon's first choice,
but I could only imagine that it had a lot to do with religion.

Before the crowd broke up, Harriet gave us all an airbrushed
T-shirt that she had snuck off and purchased while we stood in line
at the Tilt-a-Whirl ride.

"Now, these are so deblike." Jif snickered as she held up a black
one with a pink-and-lavender beach scene and her name in a chalky
yellow cursive across the chest.

We donned them and squeezed into my porch swing while Dizzy
held the camera and Harriet hollered, "Say 'cheesy'!"

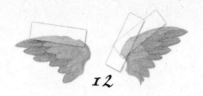

# Sophomores

As Jif and I made our way up the Blue Ridge Mountains, we learned every word to *Fun and Games*, the new Connells CD. It took our minds off our equally awkward family good-byes: I had learned on a trip downstairs for a late-night glass of water that Daddy was sleeping on the sofa, and Jif overheard her own mother in the bathroom after the farewell steak dinner refusing to come out until her husband agreed to schedule her for a tummy tuck before the deb ball.

"Marny," Dr. Ferguson had called to her harshly, "if you don't stop this foolishness, I'm going to call a shrink."

Marny Ferguson wanted Jif to have a car so that she could continue her beauty maintenance at a Roanoke salon, so she allowed her to take the candy-blue Mercedes to school.

"Nice wheels," I said when Jif rolled into my driveway earlier that morning. I had thought Jif was going to be driving the old Ford station wagon she drove in high school.

"It sort of comes with strings," Jif said as she helped me load my luggage into what little room was left in the trunk. (Jif was such a clotheshorse, but at least she wasn't stingy, and there were several tags hanging from suede jackets and cashmere sweaters that I looked forward to borrowing.)

"Let me guess," I said. "You're going to have to be in pageant condition when you go home for Thanksgiving."

"Something like that."

"Your mama is so misguided," I said, strapping myself into the passenger seat, "and I'm *not* going to let you puke your guts up all semester over this."

Motioning to the fancy dashboard with all of its knobs and gadgets, I looked at Jif head-on until she acknowledged my stare. "We're talking about your body, here, Jennifer Ferguson. Your health and well-being. You're certifiable if you're willing to jeopardize that for a second!"

"Yep," Jif said, nodding her head in a kind of resigned disgust at her mother's twisted priorities.

"Getting sick to lose weight is playing with fire," I said, waving away the Slim-Fast bar she offered on our way out of Williamstown. "You know that."

Before we veered onto the highway, I turned to face the old mill houses. Thankfully, there was no haunting face staring back at me. In fact, there were hints of life: a red geranium hanging on a front porch, a tricycle at the side door, and even a patch of grass here and there that softened the view of the shotgun homes, propped crudely on cinder blocks. What had changed—the village or my point of view?

Word around town was that Averill Skaggs had just married Charlene Roe, and I wondered if they were building their home here as their parents had. I half hoped to see them as I looked, but I didn't.

When we reached the picturesque NBU campus, Frankie was waiting for us on the piazza. He was leaning against a column smoking a cigarette, which was nearly a prerequisite for the campus newspaper staff that he had been invited to join. He hugged me hard after our car pulled onto the quadrangle lawn, then took my largest bag and said, "Let's get a cup of joe after y'all unload."

When we reached the top of the grand staircase to our sophomore dorm, we were thrilled to be reunited with Ruthie, who had shared a summer similar to ours as a deb in Gastonia and Charlotte. We'd moved up to West, an eighteenth-century dorm that faced the quad with an awe-inspiring view of the Blue Ridge and glorious afternoon sunlight. Things would *have* to be better this year, I proclaimed as we sipped our cappuccinos on the second-floor piazza and watched as wide-eyed freshmen walked fretfully back and forth between the building pillars, looking for their orientation classes as the upperclass frat boys sat on rocking chairs, scoping out the fresh meat.

In my caffeine rush, I leaned over the banister and shouted:

> *Freshman meat*
> *do beware*
> *poachers seek*
> *to devour*
> *you rare!*

Frankie bounded up and grasped the pillar beside me as a few folks stopped and took notice.

"It's the truth!" he said, shouting down on the emerald lawn. "Those Greeks'll eat you for lunch. Don't say you weren't warned."

Some upperclassman called back "Freak show!" to us, and some of the frat boys rolled their eyes, but a few of the KNs who knew Frankie from last year nodded to one another and discreetly made their way off the quad.

Daddy had told me plainly that if I didn't raise my grades by the end of the semester, my scholarship would be withdrawn and I would have to transfer to USC. There would be no asking Papa Great for the extra money, no matter how hard Juliabelle and Mae Mae strixed.

I had done well my freshman year before I botched my exams last spring, and I knew that I could make the grades with the exception of the mid-level calculus class that my liberal arts scholarship required. Tapping into that side of my brain was seriously tough for me, but I vowed to focus on the strange little Greek and geometrical shapes in those orderly algebraic patterns until my eyes throbbed with exhaustion. I had come too far to give up what I hoped were still positive opportunities for me here. For better or worse, NBU was my yellow brick road.

The semester got off to a good start. I kept myself away from the gravelly road that led to the graveyard. I didn't want to reopen that wound, because I had to stay sane in order to remain focused. *Bury it,* I told myself. Put it six feet under just like the Founding Father himself, Nathaniel Buxton, whose corpse was enclosed in that hill. Not to mention his favorite horse as well as his wife and children.

From time to time I thought I saw the silhouette of Devon Hunt out of the corner of my eye, and one night when walking by the provost's house on the way to class, I relished a fantasy that involved climbing the latticework to his bedroom window, cocking Juliabelle's shotgun, and pointing it toward his private parts while he slept.

Thankfully, my workload didn't seem to be as difficult as expected, and most evenings I had energy and time to spare, so I began reading the book *Mere Christianity* by C. S. Lewis that Dale Pelzer had given me.

As soon as I read the first chapter, I was riveted. Lewis's words were a wrecking ball, smashing through the walls in my mind. It was like a beautiful secret—this window into a brilliant and reluctant convert's head, and I came to savor those moments when I could curl up in a rocking chair on the quad or in one of the plush library sofas that overlooked the mountain stream and ingest his argument for the faith.

I bought a brown leather journal for such occasions and became determined to pin down what he was saying, to wrap my brain around the message. How I loved having to read the page over again before comprehending it. And when it finally set in, I would copy the idea down and then respond:

> There is a Law of Human Nature that is pressing in on us, but none of us are keeping it. We have failed to practice for ourselves the kind of behavior that we expect of other people. (p. 6)

> First, [the human race] is haunted by the idea of a sort of behavior they ought to practise, what you might call fair play, or decency or morality, or the Law of Nature. Second [they are haunted by the fact] that they did not do so. (p. 13)

> *Mr. Lewis,*
> *Do you mean to tell me that there is a universal moral code? And that a blueprint exists somewhere in the back of each of our minds?*

> I find that I do not exist on my own, that I am under a law; that somebody or something wants me to behave in a certain way. (p. 21)

> *I'm not an atheist. I mean, I don't think it's all a mistake. I'm just not ready to commit. Also, I don't think I'm all that bad, either. I try hard to be good, and usually I think that I am. Is that really obnoxious of me?*

When I got the nerve to ask Lewis the question that had been eating at me since the rape—that is, why does a supposedly good God allow suffering?—here is how he responded:

> You must believe that God is separate from the world and that some of the things we see in it are contrary to His will . . . A great many things have gone wrong with the world that God made and God insists, and insists very loudly, on our putting them right again. (p. 33)

And then:

This is a good world that has gone wrong, but still retains the memory of what it ought to have been. (p. 37)

*Why did it go wrong?*

Christianity agrees with dualism that this universe is in a war. But it does not think this is a war between independent powers. It thinks it is a civil war, a rebellion, and that we are living in a part of the universe occupied by the rebel. (p. 40)

*So we're on the foe's turf. That could explain a lot. I have to admit I'm rather snobby about this whole Christianity thing. My take has been that it is backwoods, cryptic, and superstitious. Not to mention, a social embarrassment. Am I wrong?*

About Christ who claimed to be God, I copied down Lewis's words:

You can shut Him up for a fool, you can spit at Him and kill Him as a demon; or you can fall at His feet and call Him Lord and God. (p. 45)

*Or you can just step away for a little while. Get busy with other things. Take your toe out of the water because you aren't ready for full immersion.*

*Sorry, you dear and charming Englishman, but I'm not going to lay down my arms just yet.*

I came to love my one-way conversations with Mr. Lewis. He was fascinating and convincing, but like an ill child who refuses his medicine, I remained stiff-necked.

Then the thought crossed my mind that there might be other respected writers who shared Lewis's view. In my creative nonfiction class, we had begun reading the Pulitzer prize–winning *Pilgrim at Tinker Creek*, in which a writer with a microscope on the natural world discovers wonder and God-created miracles at every turn. Upon further research on these lively nights in the library, I discovered that there were other notable writers who aligned themselves with Mr. Lewis's beliefs: Leo Tolstoy, W. H. Auden, T. S. Eliot, and Harriet's beloved Flannery O'Connor.

"Can you say obsessed?" Frankie whispered in my ear one Thursday night while I was intently writing in my journal. (We'd look for each other in the library around midnight to take a walk.)

"Let's take off. I need a smoke."

He was on a high this particular night. The paper had been put to bed hours earlier, and he needed to blow off some steam.

Regardless of what Harry had said to Sally earlier in the year in their famous movie, Frankie was my friend, and so far the sex thing hadn't gotten in the way. He knew about Randy, who was now mailing me a poem at least once a week despite his hectic travel schedule with the football team. In the verses Randy likened me to the moonlight or a magnolia bloom or a fiery fall leaf. (Randy. Humph. I think there's room for just one poet in a relationship, don't you?)

But even though Frankie and I shared a lot, I never could bring myself to tell him what happened to me on my date last spring, and he didn't invite me to where he went on weekend nights with the newspaper staff, who were an oddball combination of activists, hotheads, and Harmony Society members. Frankie was a social misfit. He wasn't in a frat, and he wasn't an athlete, so he'd become more and more linked with the fringe groups that bound together for survival.

"So, you finding religion?" he asked as he lit up his cigarette, grabbed my elbow, and began walking around the quad.

"Just exploring."

"More power to you," he said. Then he read me the three articles he'd written in the paper: one about campus recycling, one about a student who spent his summer working in a shelter for battered women in Philadelphia, and one about Iraq's military buildup in Kuwait.

He walked me back to the sofas in the library and lay down on the adjoining one to sleep. "Wake me up when you're ready to go."

Frankie. Hmm. Was he an active member of Harmony or just a really nice guy? The jury was still out.

Ah. Back to Lewis. When I opened the book, I could not help but feel that yearning I had felt that night in my room when I dusted off my childhood Bible for the first time and made out the mysterious messages in the book of John.

On weekend nights, while others were blowing it out on frat row, I found myself at the apologetics section in the library, where I would rub my fingers over the books that would come next: *The Great Divorce, The Screwtape Letters, A Grief Observed, Surprised by Joy.* Part of me wanted to devour them whole, make them settle in my innermost parts, and another part of me wanted to sample them and spit them right back out again as if they were one tray on a never-ending spiritual buffet.

I stared for whole minutes at Lewis's photograph on the first page of *Mere Christianity*—the warm eyes surrounded by fleshy circles of late-night thought and the itchy tweed jacket that surely smelled of pipe and English mist.

> I am smitten
> with a deceased
> Englishman
> whose words
> are more
> than manna.

It was not unlike me to become enamored with dead writers. Once I wrote a love letter to William Faulkner in which I confessed that if he invited me to the Yoknapatawpha County in his mind, I would make a life refilling the ink and stroking the top of his wide forehead as he foretold our region's doom. And when I chose to save a cockroach that scurried across my Governor's School classroom, I wrote a poem to Kafka in which I kissed the roach and became transported to early twentieth-century Prague and into the arms of a dark, delicate Jewish man.

But this new literary flame was pointing me and the rest of the sad world to a Source that was alive. A Source he claimed was at work even in the loss of his mother at a young age or the horrors of a world war in which he had served, and I couldn't help but hope that this Force was seeking me out against all odds as it had him.

Those evenings when Frankie and I would push through the library doors and out into the crisp darkness of the Virginia nights, I looked up at the very same star-studded sky I had watched with Devon Hunt on the worst evening of my life, and I wondered if my true suitor was this Force in the universe that was pressing in on me, and more specifically (as Mr. Lewis was persuading me), this Jewish carpenter who was either a madman or a Savior who laid down His life nearly two thousand years ago.

Yes, I might be destined to fall for a dead writer. (It was safer that way.) But this one, this Jewish carpenter, claimed to be alive somewhere out there in the night sky. Not just alive, but *resurrected* and sitting at the right hand of God.

Ruthie continued to steal away most weekends to Chapel Hill to see Tag Eisley. Exhausted from either her arrival or her preparation to depart again, she would draw all of the blinds and turn off the lights so that she could sleep most hours of the day and night. Between classes, she would sleep, before dinner she would sleep, and when she finally seemed to rouse herself from her cavelike condition around midnight, she'd order a pizza or Chinese takeout, which she scarfed down like there was no tomorrow while I held my nose and memorized my exponent rules or conducted my convergence tests.

*Calculus,*
*thou art*
*loathsome.*

"I can't come in your room past midnight anymore," Jif said to me as we walked toward the science building one blustery November morning. "It's too tempting, what with Ruthie ordering all of that fast food late at night. Does she know how bad it is to go to sleep having just ingested that many calories?"

Jif lifted her hand up like a claw and grabbed her own backside. "It's like asking a clump of lard to attach itself to your derriere."

"I don't know what's with her," I said. "It's the sleeping that gets me. She makes me feel weird if I turn on the light after supper to study. She groans and puts the pillow over her head, and it's not even time for *Wheel of Fortune.*"

"Does she *ever* crack a book these days?"

"Hardly," I said. "Maybe she's depressed. I mean, she gets sort of weepy sometimes when Tag calls. Think they're on the brink of a breakup or something?"

"Fat and lazy is how I would diagnose her condition," Jif said. (She had no sympathy for unexplained weight gain.) "See if you can get to the bottom of it, Adelaide, before she's too slothlike to curtsy at her deb ball."

As if Ruthie sensed our growing concern, she seemed to take great pains to avoid Jif and me during the remainder of the semester. She was asleep before I came back from the library most evenings, and she drove her car places late at night to get her fast-food fix. I dreamed about derivatives and logarithms as the stench of vinegar fries or chili dogs wafted across my sheets. And whenever the opportunity to talk presented itself, Ruthie packed her bags and headed down the mountains to Chapel Hill again.

Just before finals in early December, Ruthie seemed to fall into a real depression. It happened the day we all received our fine linen invitation to the State of North Carolina Debutante Ball, where Ruthie and six other young ladies from well-bred families across the state would make their debut at the beautiful Mountain View City Club in Charlotte. Her incessant munchies ceased after that day, and she didn't take calls in our room from Tag Eisley. Instead, she'd sneak down to the end of the hall and enclose herself in the phone booth, where they'd whisper well after I fell asleep.

One morning on our way to Intermediate French, I described to Ruthie the emerald dress I'd bought for her deb ball.

"Jif's going too," I said. "You know we wouldn't miss it."

Suddenly, Ruthie stopped in midstride along the path to the language building, sat down on a bench, and said plainly to me, "I'm pregnant."

Then her eyes brimmed with giant tears and her face went as red and contorted as a rotten tomato.

*Not again,* I thought to myself as I pictured Georgianne unwrapping those Pyrex dishes after the summer of our high school graduation.

Taking my place on the bench next to Ruthie, I rubbed the back of her head as she hovered over a little pool of tears that was forming on the sidewalk.

But then, and quite by surprise, I almost grinned when I pictured Baby Peach and his sticky little hands grabbing everything in sight: the remote control, a picture frame, the crystal candy bowl. As I was making the mental leap, with a kind of ease, to my roommate's wedding, Ruthie blurted out, "Tag wants me to abort."

The bell tower on the front quad rang out, declaring that we would certainly miss Intermediate French for the day. As grieved as I was about the premature turn my roommate's life would surely take toward domesticity, the notion of abortion shocked me even more. It made my stomach turn.

I had not considered abortion as an actual option for a pregnant woman in my circle of friends. Just the word sent shivers of dread up my spine.

"What do *you* want, Ruthie?"

"I want to keep Tag," she said as she crunched an orange maple leaf under her tennis shoe. "And I want for this never to have happened. I want things to continue the way I had planned—make my debut, graduate, marry Tag, maybe go to graduate school, *then* start a family."

I could tell that Ruthie was utterly tormented by her condition. She loathed what was taking place inside her, and she could hardly stand to be in her own skin.

After an official test at the college health center, Nurse Eugenia made the call to the Roanoke clinic and set the appointment for the second week of December. Exam week.

～

For seven days and nights, Ruthie begged me and Jif to go with her to the clinic. Jif had an easy out. Her chemistry final was the very hour of the appointment, and she couldn't be two places at once.

So I reluctantly agreed to go. Not only did I have no desire to partake in this course of action, but my calculus exam, the one that would decide the fate of my scholarship and my very future, was scheduled for that evening at six. The appointment was at two, and we would have to rush back in order for me to grab a bite at the snack bar and make it to my final.

My heart ached for Ruthie, who grew more and more paralyzed as the appointment approached. Her study room was littered with used tissues, and she had already made a D on her first exam.

"I can't make it through this without someone there, Adelaide," she had pleaded with me two nights before the appointment.

By default I was that someone, since Tag was preparing to take his MCATs and Jif was due at an exam.

The date of Ruthie's debutante ball was approaching fast, and her breasts were swelling with life. I endured the hushed calls to Tag in the middle of the night that always ended in groans of despair. Twice I told Ruthie that she didn't have to go through with it, that there were surely other options for her, such as adoption, but that seemed to make things worse, and she told me *not* to say that word again.

"Make me do it," she had whispered to me in our beds the night before our trip to the Roanoke clinic. "Be a friend, and make me go through with it, Adelaide, okay?"

A voice let out a late-night study howl somewhere down the hall. The whole campus was wired with caffeine and candy.

"All right," I whispered, half exhausted from the whole ordeal and trying to keep my faculties collected

But I was sad when those two small words left my mouth. Would I be the Gen-X depiction of Lady Macbeth tomorrow evening, unable to wash the spots off my hands? There seemed to be no way out of this trouble, and Ruthie was determined to cut off one of her own limbs in order to set herself free.

Still, I tried not to get too wrapped up in it all. I had to focus if I was going to make the B needed to keep my grade point average in good standing with the scholarship requirements. This was it. All my years of study had come down to this, and I didn't want to give my future away, either. Sitting in that clinic tomorrow would surely be the same as Ruthie sitting in the bathroom when I took my two-hour shower after my date with Devon Hunt. None of it was good. But I supposed we had to be there for each other if we were to survive. Right?

Mr. Lewis, whom I hadn't picked up in weeks, responded out of nowhere:

> There is Something which is directing the universe and which appears in me as a law urging me to do right and making me feel responsible and uncomfortable when I do wrong. (p. 22)

His words surfaced momentarily as I tried to fall asleep. *Now, how come I can never comprehend you when I want to, and then you pop up as familiar and easy as a country music song when I want to forget?*

I exerted my will and stuffed his words into the trash bin of my mind. Tomorrow night everything would be better, wouldn't it? We were in a race, in survival mode, and we had to press on.

⌢

When we arrived at the clinic, there were protesters holding graphic posters on the street beside the parking lot. Ruthie shielded her eyes with her hands and started to gag as the line reluctantly parted to let us drive in. I was sure that she wouldn't be able to get sick. She had hardly consumed a morsel of food in the last several days and had taken only a few small sips of water just to keep her strength. How she hated the life that was thriving in her body.

Tag's check hadn't arrived in time, so I had to ask Mae Mae to wire me some money on the pretense that I needed a dress for the NBU Christmas ball. In fact, Whit, from my social justice class, had invited me, but I would wear my standby black dress from freshman year.

Mae Mae was glad to help, but I learned during our conversation that Papa Great and Daddy hadn't spoken in a month. "He's lost his marbles over this pyramid scam," Mae Mae told me. "But even so, we're still your grandparents, and you can call on us with or without him in our good graces."

"Thanks, Mae Mae," I said, though I really didn't have time to dwell on the decaying condition of my family.

*Focus,* I told myself. *Roanoke clinic, calculus exam, then deal with the fam. Survival mode.*

Now, I was as frightened as Ruthie as we hurried out of our car and into the clinic, despite the piercing pleas of the protesters.

"No!" they called to us. "Don't end another life!"

I knew that abortion was a hot political topic that sharply divided people, but it had never come across my small-town path, and I had never made my decision about it. Certainly, Ruthie's body belonged to her, and she was on the edge of a nervous breakdown. But if I stopped for a moment to think about the other one—the little life growing quietly inside—I would make myself crazy.

As we sat for two hours in the solemn waiting room, listening to the muffled pleas from the street, there was a sadness in the very air that was palpable. The receptionist's face was like a cake that had fallen in on itself, and when she looked up to acknowledge the next people who walked through the door, her heavy eyes stared past them to a clock on the other side of the wall that ticked down her workday.

No one in the waiting room spoke or looked one another in the eye. But with my peripheral vision, I made out the clientele. There was a sweet-looking preteen girl not much older than Lou who was sucking on a strand of hair, with a woman who must have been her young mother sitting beside her. What was her story? There was a middle-aged couple off to the corner who would not look up from their respective newsmagazines. And a young professional-looking lady dressed in a designer suit and sitting alone, preoccupied with her workload. She might have been a lawyer preparing for a case, I thought, as the woman scanned a variety of file folders before writing notes fast and furiously on a yellow legal pad.

When a scantily dressed woman walked in with a bulging belly, bile rose in my throat. How far along was this one? Six months, perhaps. There was no denying it. The receptionist gave the woman a slow nod of familiarity and directed her to a seat across from me and Ruthie.

*What a messy world we live in, Mr. Lewis.*

Every now and then I was assaulted by the image of Baby Peach tottering around the patio, but I pushed it aside. This was hard. Much harder than I imagined it would be, but I had promised Ruthie I'd be here for her. My roommate was breaking down before my very eyes, and I earnestly believed that if she carried this life a moment longer, it would surely do her in.

Plus, there was the calculus exam. I still did not grasp the logarithm rules, and I had to get them straight before 6:00 p.m.

Another half hour passed before the thin door that led down the hallway opened and one of the New England beauties, Miranda Coates from NBU, scurried out as fast as her legs could carry her without looking at anything but the brown-and-purple pattern of the waiting-room carpet.

I watched Miranda as she bolted through the door, down the stairs, and across the line of protesters into an SUV where a handsome boy sporting a Sigma baseball cap was waiting for her, the car idling. He reached across the seat to unlock her door. Then he tossed out his cigarette through a crack in the window, and I watched it roll into the gutter after they drove off, its thin curl of smoke wafting up into the air.

Within minutes the nurse opened the door and called Ruthie's name. Ruthie had been fidgeting, blowing her nose and scraping down her cuticles. She refused a sip of water or a bite of the granola bar I had brought along.

When the nurse called Ruthie's name a second time, I nudged her, and she seized my elbow, pleading, "Go with me."

"What?" I whispered. Surely Ruthie did not expect me to go beyond the waiting room with her. I couldn't bear to be that close to the procedure. And I had to study. For heaven's sake, I'd driven her here and crossed a line of protesters. She had to do the rest on her own.

Without warning, Ruthie dragged me up to the door that the nurse held open. As we stood on the threshold, with the blank screen of an ultrasound machine to our left, Ruthie began to shudder at the droning noise of a device that was being used on a patient two doors down the hall. We could make out a faint whimper and a quick shriek, and with this Ruthie turned back and buried her head in my shoulder.

"I'm sorry, you *can't* bring a friend with you, hon," the nurse said in a hushed tone. She patted Ruthie's shoulder and added, "You'll be fine."

Ruthie looked up to me and did not move for whole seconds. We were face-to-face, a few inches apart, and she was searching my eyes.

I knew Ruthie was calling on me to address her second thoughts. To address the sound of that machine and the whimper of a woman on the other side of the procedure.

"Don't put this decision in my hands," my eyes said back to my friend. I was scared and angry, and I resented the fact that she was calling on me in this way. I glanced back to my seat. To the pile of calculus books.

The whole waiting room was staring at us now. We were a scene in an awful movie. The nurse was uncomfortable with the tension, and she tried to gently pull Ruthie farther down the hall.

"Sit down here and make yourself more comfortable," the nurse said, pointing to a reclining chair beside the ultrasound machine.

Ruthie wouldn't budge. Her eyes just kept pleading with mine.

Now I was furious. The young professional woman cleared her throat in frustration at this drama, and that was all I needed to distance myself from the situation. *This isn't fair,* I thought. I had reluctantly agreed to go along in a supporting role. Did Ruthie want me to suddenly make the decision *for* her?

*No,* I thought, but I didn't say it. *This is between you and Tag, and I'm not going to decide for you.*

How I wanted to escape into the maze of calculus problems at my chair—the center of a mass of inertia of a solid, the flow of water through a river, the rate of growth of bacteria in a culture. My college career was on the line, and I had only a few hours before the final. What more did Ruthie want from me?

"This way," the nurse entreated.

As Ruthie looked back at the nurse, I saw my way out, and I turned my back toward them and moved quickly to the waiting-room chair.

I was already escaping in my mind. Reenacting the little trick Mama had taught me. This time I was following the shrill cry of little Lou's voice down by the salt marsh behind our house. My baby sister had been playing there with a friend who had thrown a stick at a wasps' nest, and they were both wailing at the multiple stings on their arms and legs.

Ruthie took a step down the hall and then stopped to look back once more before the nurse pulled the door closed. I sensed her silent plea, but I didn't have anything left to give her, so I took my seat, picked up my textbook, and began to examine the logarithm rules. I didn't look up until I heard the door close and the muffled sound of two pairs of feet moving down the hallway.

We know that men find themselves under a moral law, which they did not make, and cannot quite forget even when they try. (p. 20)

As I stared at the dark grain of the closed door, I wondered, *have I failed Ruthie and that little life inside her?*

Now I was finding it difficult to even breathe. I placed my calculus book on my lap and tried to focus, but I could not get through the first question.

"'I have set before you life and death, blessings and curses.'" Shannon had recited those words from Deuteronomy to me last summer when I feared that the rest of my days were doomed by the anxiety that took control of me after the rape. As I thought on the words, I became aware of a resounding thump in my ears.

It was another hour before Ruthie emerged through the doorway. She was holding little round butter cookies, like the kind they served in Sunday school at St. Anne's. She was drinking a Hi-C juice box and looked like a little girl, except for the two boxes of Anaprox and birth control pills that she carried in her other hand.

She wept all the way home, writhing in pain and stopping at a gas station to puke up the butter cookies. Then she fell asleep in the bed and slept through dinner and on through the night while I failed my exam.

"I did it," Ruthie said to Tag when he called. I left the room to give them some privacy, but returned after hearing what sounded like Ruthie slamming the phone down on the floor.

Something awful had happened in that clinic in Roanoke. She was worse than she was before, according to Jif, who had caught her in the bathroom pricking her finger with a razor and pinching the incision until it bled. Her sociology professor and then the chair of the department called to find out why she wasn't showing up for her exams, but she refused to return their calls.

And I was suffering too. I was confused and afraid to consider that I had messed up and harmed my friend when I should have had the gumption to reach out to her in the clinic and say, "If you're unsure, don't do it." Or insisting, "There has to be another way through this."

Was there a darkness inside me that I had never faced before? I hadn't meant anyone any harm, so why did I feel so sick inside?

To what will you look for help if you will not look to that which is stronger than yourself? (p. 51)

"Shannon," I said aloud, my hands trembling across the open page of Lewis's book.

When she answered my call, I could barely speak.

"Can we talk?" I said through my cracking voice. "I'm desperate. Please meet me somewhere."

She took a deep breath. She was probably in the middle of exams herself, but just as I was about to say, "Never mind," she insisted, "I can meet you at the Appomattox truck stop off I-81. That's about halfway for both of us."

"When?"

"I can leave here in an hour," she said.

"Me too."

Jif promised she'd sit with Ruthie. She threw me the keys to the candy-blue Mercedes so that I could drive as fast as the German wheels would carry me down 81.

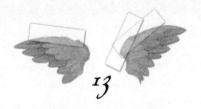

# A Contrite Heart

*Because of God's tender mercy,*
*the light from heaven is about to*
*break upon us,*
*to give light to those who sit in*
*darkness and in the shadow*
*of death,*
*and to guide us to the path of peace.*
Luke 1:78–79

I'm in trouble," I said through tears when we sat down at the truck stop and ordered two coffees. It was nearly midnight, and there were only three other people dining in the place, each at his own separate booth.

It had been an exhausting drive down the mountain. The sunset gave way to a foggy darkness, and there were times when I could hardly see a foot in front of Marny's Mercedes. I kept imagining a runaway truck knocking me over the side of the ridge. But I was determined, and I even prayed, *Help me get there.*

Squinting to make out the lanes and the guard rails, I thought about the doubts and questions I'd written in my notebook last summer and presented before Dale and Darla Pelzer, half wanting to know the truth and half wanting to trip them up and expose their unenlightened state of mind. I suspected that I could follow the maze of each question and each doubt for years until I made a decision.

But I didn't have time for all of that now. I had to get help.

"What's going on?" Shannon said from the other side of the booth.

I tried to talk, but when I opened my mouth, I wept so intensely that it was fifteen minutes before I actually uttered an intelligible word.

She moved over to my side and held me, wiping my dripping nose with coarse truck-stop napkins, until I could speak.

"I'm bewildered," I said. "I was doing better since last summer, but yesterday I took my roommate to an abortion clinic, and she's worse off than before, and I might be too."

"I'm sorry," Shannon said. She shooed away the waitress, who kept wanting to take our food order.

I wept without reserve in my friend's arms as bacon sizzled in the frying pan and trucks pulled in to fill up with gas or bed down for the night.

When I could look back up at her, I said, "I'm so weary."

Shannon took a deep breath. She was anxious and sympathetic, and I could tell she wanted hard for me to see.

"You don't have to be. You don't have to be alone, Adelaide."

I was beaten to a pulp, and I wanted to believe her. I was tired of the mazes in my mind about the reality of God. If there was any hope for me, I had to step over them now and get to the other side. What other choice did I have?

"Okay," I said. "What do I need to do?"

Shannon pulled me close beneath the fluorescent lights of the diner and prayed a simple prayer of my need for forgiveness and asked me to list silently the things that were weighing down my heart. Then she prayed for me to acknowledge and accept that Christ had paid the debt for the very things I'd just named and others that I might not even know about.

I muttered, "I accept," and Shannon thanked God for washing me clean.

Then she pulled a Bible out of her backpack and read a passage from Hebrews 10:9–10:

> He [Jesus] cancels the first covenant in order to establish the second. And what God wants is for us to be made holy by the sacrifice of the body of Jesus Christ once for all time.

"And that is that, Adelaide," she said. "You have received God's grace, once and for all time, in a two-minute prayer at a truck stop off Interstate 81."

I actually chuckled for a moment. She knew that was exactly what I would have said, and I loved her for that.

Though I still didn't fully get it, I stepped across that gaping chasm that Dale Pelzer had drawn on his makeshift chalkboard. Nothing overtly supernatural happened as Shannon prayed for me—no bright light or chorus of angels—but I guessed I didn't deserve any icing on the cake like that right now. What I hoped was that it was true, because it was the only thing I had. I had no choice but to accept the offer. And I was thankful for the chance to take hold of it.

Then Shannon gave me such a tight hug good-bye that I thought my eyeballs might pop out. I hugged her back just as hard, because I knew I had this old friend to thank for the slight relief I was feeling.

And though it was midnight, I scurried back to the car and started on my way back to school. As I started the fine-tuned engine and flicked on the high beams, I could see that the fog had dissipated and a Carolina moon was as clear as a prop in a play over the road before me. I rolled down my window and breathed in the cold night air, and as I exhaled, my own breath rose before me like burning incense before an altar.

Everything looked clear. So clear that I could almost make out the corners of the stars. The thought occurred to me that I had been seeing only shadows of the world until now.

⌒

It was two thirty in the morning by the time I got back to NBU. Jif was studying in my bed, and Ruthie was curled up with her knees to her chest. She was making a sound as if she were snoring, but her eyes were open.

"Hey," I whispered to Jif.

"Hey," she said. She nodded in the direction of Ruthie. "She's been cramping pretty bad, but she just took two Anaprox, and she should be out any minute."

"Thanks, Jif," I said.

"No problem," she answered. "I'm too tired to talk. Tell me about it tomorrow."

"Okay," I said.

⌒

The next morning I woke up and saw Ruthie taking a Band-Aid off her forearm and pinching the incision until the blood surfaced.

"Ruthie!" I felt such a strong mix of sympathy and frustration toward her that I thought I might explode. "We've got to talk."

Lurching, I grabbed the razor on her desk and threw it in the trash.

I knelt down beside her bed, grabbed her tepid hand, and said, "Forgive me for my role in what happened the other day."

"Don't—" Ruthie raised her hand as if to say she couldn't bear the idea of even mentioning that day.

"Hear me out," I pleaded. "That morning in the clinic, you wanted me to do something, and I didn't. I know you were having second thoughts when the nurse called you in, and I didn't do right by you by not asking you to reconsider."

Ruthie hugged her knees to her chest and shook with grief as I continued, "You were looking to me, and I failed you. I distanced myself. And I ignored you. I'm sorry."

Ruthie pinched her arm again until crimson appeared.

"Look, Ruthie," I said, pulling her hand away from her arm. "I'm not going to sit here and watch you mutilate yourself. It's *sick*! Now, I don't know what to do to make things better, but I know you need help, and I'm going to tell Tag that when he picks you up. And if he doesn't do anything about it, then I'm going to tell your parents."

Ruthie stared straight ahead, trancelike in the morning light.

I pulled her pajama sleeves down to her wrists.

"Jif said you went to meet Shannon," she whispered.

"Yeah," I said.

"Did it help?"

"I'm not sure yet, but I think so."

Ruthie let out a guffaw and then looked up at me as if she were the last canine at the pound, and I was preparing the injection with which to put her down for good.

I grabbed my roommate's knees and whispered, "Ruthie, there has to be a way out of this misery." Tears trickled down her face, and I went to the refrigerator to pour her a cup of orange juice.

She took a sip, then whispered, "When I close my eyes, all I can see is that heart beating on the ultrasound machine. That tiny organ in a sea of gray fuzz. I can't sleep. I can't eat. I can't walk by the mirror. What kind of person would take the life of her own baby? Just because it didn't fit into her neat and tidy future?"

Then she took the cup of juice and tossed it too hard in the direction of the trash can. It hit the open closet and left a streak of orange across her dresses and shoes.

"I don't deserve a thing."

Minutes passed as Ruthie shook her head and stared into the rumpled sheets beneath her feet. Then she looked up at me and was able to make eye contact, though her brow began to furrow before smoothing out again.

"What am I going to do?" she said, and it almost sounded like the tone of her old, strong voice before all of this awful stuff had happened.

"Tell your folks and get help," I said. And I sat with her as we waited for Tag to pick her up.

∽

When the phone rang, I answered it.

"Adelaide, it's Mrs. Baxter," she said. "Tag's car broke down on the way out of Chapel Hill, so I'm here to get Ruthie."

"I'll be down in a sec to let you in."

This turn of events was too good not to deny a guiding hand in it.

When I hung up the phone, I looked to Ruthie and said, "Your mama's here. Now, let's tell her what's going on."

Ruthie nodded her head in agreement.

∽

The chapel bell tower rang eleven times as Mrs. Baxter sat at the edge of Ruthie's bed and wept while she heard the account of the last few months of her daughter's life.

I was thankful that she didn't come at her with anger or disappointment. She could sense her daughter's earnest regret, and what she wanted was for her to forgive herself.

When Ruthie pulled up the sleeves of her pajamas to show how she had dealt with the last week, her mama held her tight and said, "We'll get you some help."

As Mrs. Baxter rubbed ointment from the dorm's first-aid kit on Ruthie's thin arms, Jif and I zipped her suitcases and lugged them down the stairs and into the car while big, papery snowflakes—the first of the season—lightly coated the quadrangle and the slate roofs of the buildings on the hill.

After they left, I took a shower, aced my French exam, and walked around campus one final time before Jif and I headed back down the mountain the next morning.

I was relieved to be alive. No, the sadness and regret over Ruthie's abortion didn't disappear, but I had confessed my part in it, and I honestly felt that I could breathe again.

As I treaded up faculty row and by President Schaeffer's house, I thought of the wonders that I had seen at NBU. The pastoral scenes of silos and cows grazing along the hillsides. The friendly voice of my creative writing professor, Josiah Dirkas, and the words of truth that Dr. Shaw, my religion professor, brought to life in his social justice class. A part of me would be sad to bid the place farewell, and I would tell those two professors as much if they were in their offices tomorrow morning.

I was headed to USC. No doubt about it. But the weight of the world wasn't on me at the moment.

Was forgiveness real? I hoped it was. And I hoped Ruthie could find it before she cut her way up her arm and toward her own pounding chest.

Had I "accepted Jesus" last night, like those seemingly wacko televangelists used to say as I flicked their voices away from me as fast as my remote control could carry them every Sunday morning since I could remember? Would my life be radically different from this point forward? Would I really care?

If I actually had been created for Someone's greater purpose, if my life was not really my own to begin with, then why not submit to the One who provided a way out of the pit?

As I walked by the gravel road that led to the campus graveyard on the next hillside, I felt that God had been drawing me to Him all along during the months following the rape. And maybe before that too. In every moment of wonder I had ever witnessed.

The snow was falling so fast now that the wall around the graves looked like a white gate surrounding a private garden.

I had been looking for a raison d'être when I went to college, and maybe I'd found it. It had been around me all of my life. If it had been a snake, it would have bitten me many times over. But now I could glimpse the dullest bit of it. I could put the pieces of all that I knew to be good together and barely see the edge of it.

I didn't really know how to pray or how to talk to God. I didn't even know much about the Bible except for the few stories I'd learned as a child. Of all these, I liked the miracle of the loaves and fishes best.

I remembered one morning in the run-down classroom at St.

Anne's when our teacher dressed up like Jesus and put two goldfish crackers and three oyster crackers into a basket covered with a paper towel. She lifted the basket up to thank God for the food, and when she pulled it down, it was filled with hundreds of oyster crackers and goldfish. What a great surprise!

So, on my walk around the snow-dusted campus that day, all I saw were those pieces of bread that were broken and broken again to fill the stomachs of the hungry listeners. *Can you take this loaf?* I said of my life. *And use it?*

I pictured each member of my family and their respective woes: Dizzy with her sordid high school history and DUI charges, Lou with her speech impediment and lack of self-confidence, Mama's emotional distance, and Daddy's decision to step away from the family business no matter what it cost his marriage or his relationship with his parents. I named each of them and my concerns for them, and then I envisioned placing them on an altar as I walked.

And I thought about Brother Benton's family and Peter Carpenter spending the first of many Christmases in jail after his manslaughter conviction, and I placed him on that altar as well.

As I ascended to the colonnade and looked out over the Blue Ridge Mountains, I was stunned by the beauty of the light on the patches of white atop the great masses of jagged rock. It was as though I was seeing them for the first time.

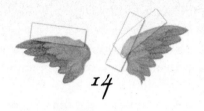

# I'm C-o-m-i-n-g Out

The next morning Jif and I made our way back down the mountains to Williamstown for the Christmas holiday and the Camellia Club Debutante Ball. I had said a final good-bye to my favorite professors.

On the way down the winding ridges, I told Jif about the last twenty-four hours,

"No lie," I said to her. "This God/Christ thing we've been hearing about all of our lives—I think Shannon was right all along."

Jif rolled her eyes. "*Please* don't turn into a Bible beater on me," she said. "I mean, don't misunderstand me; you sound better than you've sounded in months, and I'm happy that Ruthie's mom is clued in to the situation, but I don't want you to make my skin crawl the way Shannon used to. I mean, she totally changed, and we lost her."

Jif was sincerely worried that my personality would be sucked out by this newfound faith. It was the very thing that I had worried about, too, and I wondered how to make sure that didn't happen.

"If I change, I think it will be for the better."

"Time will tell," Jif said as she gulped down her Diet Coke and offered me a stick of Dentyne.

Jif was looking better than ever—like a Victoria's Secret model minus the full-sized breasts. After her exams, she shifted into high gear with her Tully Dorm Diet. For over a week she had been drinking ice water and lemon-lime Gatorade and eating only celery sticks and an occasional Slim-Fast bar. You never caught her without a piece of gum in her mouth in a constant attempt to suppress her appetite. She had even climbed up Kiki Mountain twice and attended two aerobics classes a day to burn-baby-burn those calories away. To Ned Crater's dismay, she was turning the heads of many a frat boy as she strolled through campus during the last days of the semester in her snug size 2 blue jeans and midriff sweaters.

But that was merely a fringe benefit of her pursuit. She was doing all of this for her deb dress. And she was going to make it into that tiny frock if it was the last thing she did. I just hoped that her obsession would end as soon as she marched her bony little fanny down the aisle at the ball.

When I arrived home to a half-decorated Christmas tree and no one but Marmalade the cat to greet me, I wondered what was going on.

Dizzy and Lou pulled up in the station wagon just after I hauled my suitcase to my room and informed me that my folks were at a Bizway convention (Mama must have caved) in St. Louis and would be home late that evening.

I hugged them both as though I hadn't really seen them in years, and I took them out to the new all-you-can-eat pizza joint, where we feasted on pepperoni pizza and slices of chocolate-chip pie as we caught up. Lou was sweet Lou, with a much better command of words that started with *r* and *w*, thanks to the new speech therapist at her school. And Dizzy seemed a thousand times better. She was still dressed like a witch, but she had stayed off the sauce and attended her AA meetings regularly, and she had even gone down to Harvest Time for a few services. She didn't think college was for her, but she wanted to go to cooking school. In fact, she had been cooking up a storm on the nights she would have normally been out partying, and Lou attested to the fact that her fettuccine Alfredo and tiramisu were true culinary delights. (Only she described them as "really y-yummy.") Dizzy had just applied to the Johnson & Wales Cooking College of Culinary Arts in Charleston, and if all went her way, she'd be enrolled come June.

As for Mama and Daddy, they were in a bad spot. Daddy was buying Bizway supplies like there was no tomorrow, and a box of vitamins or toilet paper or cleaning products arrived at our door daily as part of his building up the necessary points to make the next level—his part in becoming a "pro-sumer" instead of a "con-sumer."

Every time Uncle Tinka invited him to a new town to speak about the business and tell his war story about getting the Purple Heart, or his football tales of scoring the winning touchdown against Clemson in the fall of 1967, he'd come home with a wad of cash and three or four names scribbled down on a receipt, and he'd hound those poor souls until they agreed to sign up under him or were forced to change their number.

He was 100 points away from going platinum, and he was pumped. It was all a great adrenaline rush for him, and he was completely sold out to it. However, Mama (who had agreed to attend a few more meetings for the sake of her marriage) continued to disdain the business. She hated traveling. It was not at all a part of the small-town life she had always wanted and managed to have until now. She hated speaking and wearing sequined dresses and learning about how many cars someone owned.

Worst of all, she hated the fact that her husband was no longer a workingman in the traditional sense. She hated that he didn't wear a coat and tie each day and play the role of Ward Cleaver that he'd happily obliged her before. Not to mention the fact that he was at home all day, in the domestic domain that was hers to control.

Papa Great was still livid about the whole thing. He'd never wanted his black sheep of an offspring, Tinka, to go into the seemingly crooked networking business, and he certainly didn't want his war-hero son, Zane, to follow the same path.

"Daddy doesn't give a hoot about what anybody thinks," Dizzy said as Lou nodded in agreement while slurping down her second Co-Cola.

I guessed that he'd been doing what other people wanted for twenty-five years—and doing it with a good attitude, one might add. But this was his moment to shine, and he would not be denied.

"Papa asked Randy to take Daddy's place," Dizzy said.

"I had a feeling that was coming," I said. "But he'll have to cool his jets till Randy graduates."

When we returned home, Dizzy and Lou led me to a little shrine on the dining room table that Mama had created for my return. Next to a bouquet of fresh white roses and a pair of long kid gloves with pearl buttons, I saw first the framed invitation to the upcoming ball. The crest of the Camellia Club decorated the top line of the invitation, and below, in black engraving, it read:

*The Governors of the Camellia Club*
*request the pleasure of your company*
*at their annual debutante ball*
*Saturday, the twenty-seventh of December*
*One thousand nine hundred and ninety*
*at eight o'clock*
*The Magnolia Club*
*Williamstown, South Carolina*

And there was a thick linen insert with our names:

*Miss Jennifer Louise Ferguson*
*Miss Harriet von Hasselson Hartness*
*Miss Nancy Whitmire McCant*
*Miss Adelaide Rutledge Graydon Piper*
*Miss Winifred Powell Pride*

Also, there were less-formal invitations on little wooden picture holders to events that would take place over the next seven days before the ball: the curtsy tea, the final luncheon, a rehearsal dinner.

Gifts had arrived and were stacked behind the mounted invitations in polished white wrapping with white satin bows as if I were a virgin bride. I had to chuckle at the irony. I guessed the adults in my life didn't know that when a girl grows up in the postmodern, post–sexual revolution world, coming out often happens well before the ripe old age of twenty. Talk about a chasm.

Mama had even typed out my schedule for the next several days:

| | |
|---|---|
| Wednesday: | Dress fitting, 9:00 a.m. |
| | Shoe fitting, 11:00 a.m. |
| | Curtsy tea, 4:00 p.m. |
| Thursday: | Haircut, 10:00 a.m. |
| | Luncheon, noon |
| Friday: | Christmas |
| Saturday: | Portrait sitting, 10:00 a.m. |
| Monday: | Final fitting, 9:00 a.m. |
| | Rehearsal, 4:00 p.m. |
| | Rehearsal dinner, 6:00 p.m. |
| Tuesday: | Manicure, 2:00 p.m. |
| | Makeup and hair, 3:00 p.m. |
| | Debutante ball, 8:00 p.m. |
| | (must arrive by 5:30 p.m. for group and family photo session) |
| | Breakfast, midnight |

And she had laid out more of that white monogrammed stationery I would use to write thank-you notes to my hostesses and gift givers.

There was also a typed list of the family and friends who had responded to the ball invitation. My aunt Anna was actually traveling from Germany to make the event. And Daddy's kin from west Georgia too. Randy would be my escort, and I was relieved not to have to worry about him the way the other girls would about their out-of-town boyfriends coming in. I was looking forward to seeing him.

As I fingered the ball invitation and breathed in the thick perfume of the roses, I wondered what God thought about debutante balls and the formality and etiquette that went along with such social events.

*God,* I thought. *I hope You don't mind my being a debutante, because I think Mama would truly flip if I refused to go through with this.*

Late that evening, Randy called.

"I can't wait to see you!" he said. "When can you come with me out to the duck blind? You're going to love watching the birds come in to roost in the swamp."

"Sounds buggy," I said.

"No, they're gone for the winter. There's something I want to show you there. I can't wait to see you! When can I pick you up?"

I heard my parents pull up in the driveway, and I told Randy I'd call him tomorrow; then I ran down the stairs to greet them. There was nothing as comforting as the smell of Daddy's Aqua Velva after-shave and his prosthetic rubbing my back in a tight squeeze or Mama kissing my jewel as if I were the most precious treasure in the world.

I had much to tell them about my new faith and the likelihood of my transfer to USC, but they were so weary that they seemed relieved when I asked if they would rather catch up in the morning.

As I made my way back up the stairs and opened the confirmation Bible Juliabelle had given me, I heard my parents' angry words rico-chet off the ceiling below. I couldn't make out what they were saying to each other, but I detected the harshness in Mama's voice, and when I woke early in the morning, I found Daddy, again, on the sofa, still wearing his travel clothes from the night before. I wondered what could make Mama so angry that she wouldn't help him unbutton his shirt and get into his pajamas.

In between my fitting and my curtsy tea, I made the rounds to my odd assortment of local buddies. I went first to Harvest Time to tell

Dale and Darla about my newfound faith. They cheered and hugged me and called in Charlie Farley, who was in the receptionist area, answering the phone, and we all knelt down in the sanctuary to say a prayer of thanksgiving.

Dale and Darla sent me home with one of the hand-carved wooden crosses one of the migrant workers was making as a contribution to the church. I nailed it right over my bed beneath the print of Andrew Wyeth's *Christina's World* that Mama had framed for me a few years back. Christina looked paralyzed with fear as she sprawled across a field, looking at a drab farmhouse with dark windows in the distance. I imagined crawling into the painting and handing Christina the wooden cross. (Would I come down from this spiritual high?)

Next I went by Kmart to pick up a book of children's nursery rhymes and drove right out to the suburbs to visit Georgianne and Baby Peach.

"Let's get him started early on his poetry," I said as Georgianne opened the screen door with Baby Peach cocked on her hip. "If I have anything to say about it, he's going to be the next James Dickey. Minus the alcohol, of course."

Then I strolled with them over to their neighborhood park, where I marveled at how well the toddler boy could climb up the stairs and zoom down the slide and rock himself back and forth on the tire swing.

As he plopped down his pail and shovel to dig in the sandbox, Georgianne invited me to sit down on a park bench, where I promptly grabbed her arm and said, "Forgive me for freaking out when you got married a few summers ago."

Georgianne grinned, recalling the scene in the bathroom of the country club. "So where is this coming from?" she asked as she held a rubber band between her teeth and pulled her hair back.

"It's just . . . a lot of crazy things happened to me at college. And let's just say I learned the nobleness of your decision to carry Peach and raise him up even though it wasn't what you had planned."

Georgianne's eyes settled on me.

"Thanks," she said, and then she looked away to check on Peach.

"That means a lot to me. I mean, it's no cakewalk raising a kid and going to college at the same time. But it's what happened, and I'm going to see it through."

"I'm not trying to romanticize it or anything, but I just want you to know I think you made the right decision."

"Me too," she said before making a visor with her hand to get a better look at Peach. "I've missed a lot, Ad. But I wouldn't take the world for him."

We both looked on as he patted the full pail of sand with the back side of his shovel and blended a medley of toddler songs that started with "Twinkle, Twinkle, Little Star" and ended with "The Farmer in the Dell."

"Oh, and just in case you are curious, you aren't missing a thing when it comes to the Camellia Debutante Club. It's just a bunch of old ladies and chicken salad."

"I figured," Georgianne said as Baby Peach brought a fistful of sand to his mouth. When she scurried toward him screaming, "No!" he looked up at her with a Cheshire grin and opened his chubby fingers to let the grains spill out and onto his knees.

"So how's school going?" I asked Georgianne when she returned.

"Pretty well, actually. I got into the honors program, and I'm going to double-major in math and biology. Peach wants me to go premed, but I think I'd rather teach."

"Boy, I could have used you a few weeks ago when I took my calculus exam."

"Bad?"

"Lost my scholarship over it. I'm coming back here for school."

"Hey, that'll make Randy's day."

"Yeah," I said.

"But if they let you retake, come see me. I aced calculus."

When we looked up, Baby Peach had decided that the sand looked too delectable not to sample, and we both ran over to him and tried to teach him how to spit, which he took to surprisingly well, and he spit just for fun much of the way home in his stroller.

That afternoon, I threw on a tweed suit and raced over to the curtsy tea with Jif. We were delighted to see Harriet and even the socially awkward Winkie and the obnoxiously preppy Nan.

"What's different about you?" Harriet asked as I bit into a cinnamon scone. She squinted her eyes as if to singe my veneer, then handed me a linen napkin to wipe away the clotted cream on the corner of my mouth. "You look better," she said, tapping her hand on my cheek. "Come over to dinner at Marguerite's tonight and spill the beans."

"Okay," I said as Mrs. Percy got our attention by tapping her silver spoon on her delicate china teacup. Her gardener and housekeeper rolled an ancient television set, complete with tinfoiled rabbit ears, into the parlor and propped it on her ottoman.

Jif took a place beside us as Marguerite, Harriet's grandmother, instructed us in the dos and don'ts of curtsying, first toward our fathers as they held our white-gloved hands in the spotlight, then toward our mothers and the Camellia Club board, who would be seated in Queen Anne chairs in front of the guests on both sides of the red velvet carpet in the center of the ballroom. We watched successful curtsies as well as several faulty attempts from videotapes of past balls; then Marguerite modeled it for us gracefully a few times before asking each of us to stand up and give it a try.

I got as much of a kick out of Mrs. Marguerite Hartness as Harriet did. She had to be pushing eighty, but she'd been giving this curtsy lesson for fifty years. She was as spry and physically capable of bending down to the floor as any twenty-year-old deb in the room. She reminded me of Katharine Hepburn in her final films: elegantly sturdy even as her head trembled with Parkinson's.

Harriet was proud of her vivacious grandmother, who sported an up-to-date sarong and DKNY pumps, and she had every right to be. Marguerite brought the class level in Williamstown up several notches, and she even had a way of making the place seem livable.

"My cousin, the governor, has just accepted the invitation to the ball, and so has his dashing son, Paul, who is a senior at USC," Marguerite announced after winking in Jif's and my direction before dipping down to the ground again.

Yes, she had to be the most poised woman in all of South Carolina. Rumor had it that Strom Thurmond had proposed to her once and she'd said, "I don't think I can put up with you, Senator."

"Let's see y'all do it," she said as we all stood up to attempt the curtsy. We chuckled clumsily through the remainder of the afternoon as we each attempted to place the ball of our right foot just so behind our left and bend gracefully down to the Oriental rug without showing our cleavage or toppling over headfirst.

"I figured this might be a tasteless vegan meal," Jif said when Harriet opened Marguerite's garland-draped door in ratty blue jeans and a hooded sweatshirt a few hours later. Jif lifted up two chocolate Slim-Fast bars and said, "So I brought my own food."

"What food?" Harriet said, looking her up and down. "By the looks of you, you haven't eaten in months."

Jif grinned with pride as the scent of freshly cut pine and toasted pecans wafted through the doorway. That was just what she wanted to hear.

Harriet rolled her eyes. She hadn't wanted to encourage her.

"Gaunt must be in," she said, snatching the bars out of Jif's hands. "We're having Marguerite's homemade spaghetti with marinara sauce and a Greek salad sans the feta, all right? If I weren't a Yankee, I'd be offended by your bringing a prepackaged meal when you'd been invited to dinner."

"No kidding," I said, nudging Jif into the grand home, which was the picture of a Southern Christmas, with a fresh balsam-and-pine garland winding its way up the grand stairway and a wall of poinsettias lining the entrance hall.

"Besides," Harriet said, "the menu is entirely vegan and low-fat, so everybody should be happy."

"Welcome, girls," Marguerite said as she brought out a tray of freshly poured Co-Colas in crystal tumblers with a handful of salted peanuts, which she dropped into each glass before inviting us into her living room. We took a seat on the velvet Martha Washington chairs and watched the angel-abra carousel on the coffee table propel the brass angels around and around the gold star as the bells chimed.

"This is the way your mama used to drink them when she was a teenager," Marguerite said to Harriet as we sipped the sweet and salty froth.

"Why didn't she stick with these?" Harriet whispered with a momentary forlorn expression as Marguerite left the room to stir the sauce. She informed us, "Mom checked into the Betty Ford Center in October. Seems my stepfather found her passed out in the hot tub one afternoon when he came home early from work. She's always tipped the bottle, but it had gotten a lot worse in the last few years—what with my stepfather taking a little trip to the Bahamas with his personal assistant, and his perfect offspring turning into little devils. The one at Andover was kicked out for cheating on his finals, and the one at Yale was arrested for possession of cocaine. I don't care if I *ever* go home again."

The steam from the pasta curled out the kitchen window and into the night air.

"Thank goodness for Marguerite," Harriet said, and we all agreed.

"She's like your true mother," I said.

"You said it," Harriet agreed. "We're as thick as thieves, and we're going to spend this coming summer in Nice. Might even try Tuscany after that."

Marguerite's dining room was inviting. Magnolia limbs lined the fireplace, where a porcelain crèche decorated the mantel, and in the center of the dining table was a Williamsburg apple tree with a pineapple on the top, its spiky leaves fanning out and leaving pointed shadows on the linen place mats and china.

"Where's baby Jesus?" Jif asked as she peered into the empty manger.

Marguerite answered after passing the pasta. "Oh, my family had a tradition of hiding Him away from the children until Christmas morning. We'd all try to guess where He was throughout December, but we never could find Him. I think my mother kept Him in her underwear drawer."

"Why did they hide Him?" I asked. I had been a Christian for less than a week, and Christmas was becoming real to me.

"Oh, for a sense of expectation, dear," the beautiful lady said, her head wobbling on her neck. "When we woke up on Christmas morning, instead of racing down to check our stockings, we would gather around the crèche to see if He was there. How I remember picking Him up and cupping Him in my hands as a young girl on those mornings. I had been waiting and waiting on Him, and now He had arrived, and there was nothing so satisfying as His perfect little body in the palm of my hand."

I nestled myself beneath the blanket of Marguerite's memory and the earthy scent of freshly cut pine and pasta, and I pictured the Christ child on my own family's mantel. Yes, the dog had chewed up one of His legs, and there was a waxy mark from a purple crayon across His shoulder, as well as a seam down the side, evidence of the machine that had pressed him together. But His newborn eyes were like two perfectly formed pearls, and His arms were open and reaching out for an embrace that I had not returned until now.

"That's my mother," Harriet said, pointing up to a portrait above the fireplace of a pale young woman in a beaded gown, holding a single pink camellia in her lap. Her head was tilted slightly toward the ground, forbidding anyone a look into her eyes.

"That was when she made her debut at the Magnolia Club," Marguerite said, "some twenty-five years ago."

"And there is Marguerite," Harriet said, pointing to a smaller painting that hung between two windows on the opposite side of the room. "She made hers in 1930."

"You're stunning," Jif said.

And I stared into the painting at Marguerite, who was looking the portrait artist straight in the face with her black eyes. Her shoulders were draped with scalloped white lace, and her gloved hands were empty and resting, palms up, on her knee as though she were waiting for the world's gift, the baby Redeemer, to appear in her hands.

~

After a delicious dinner, we went back onto the porch to drink decaf coffee and eat vegan raspberry sorbet, compliments of the health-food store in Charleston.

As an owl hooted from the top of the magnolia tree, Harriet asked, "So what's been going on at NBU?"

"Quite a bit," Jif said, looking at me. "None of it has been good unless you count Adelaide becoming a Jesus freak and me losing five pounds."

"Five pounds?" I said, sizing Jif up and down. "I think you weigh less than I did in third grade."

We all laughed.

Then Harriet turned to me. "So you found religion up there? That's what's changed. I knew it was *something*."

"You could say that," I said. "I got in a tough spot, and it became my hope."

"Mmm," Harriet said, raising her dark eyebrows so that three clear lines stretched across her forehead. "You're talking stranger than the vegans in Bronxville, my friend."

She sucked down her coffee with soy milk and licked the bottom of the sorbet bowl as we inquired about her fall at Sarah Lawrence.

"I saw the Grateful Dead in Central Park," she said, lifting her sweatshirt to reveal a silver loop that was piercing her belly button. "That's where I got this," she whispered, then brought her finger to her lips and looked toward the kitchen, where we could hear Marguerite stirring her coffee. "She doesn't need to know. It's not exactly deblike."

Jif and I grinned at each other. Harriet was so out there, and we loved every refreshing minute we were with her.

"And I took a Flannery O'Connor story and turned it into a play for my theater class," Harriet said.

"Which one?" I asked.

"'The Life You Save May Be Your Own.' And there's a chance the theater club will perform it in the spring. You'll have to take the train up if they do."

"Cool," we said, and I could see Jif was already imagining what a trip to New York would be like.

"Could we go into the city to shop?" she asked.

"Why not?" Harriet said. "I mean, I personally loathe Fifth Avenue, but I'd go along if you guys made the trip."

"I'm turning in," Marguerite said as her head bobbed behind the screen door.

"*Bonsoir*, Grandmama," Harriet said in a French accent, and we all blew her a kiss from the porch swing after thanking her for the delicious dinner.

~

On my way home, I parked at the boat landing along the Waccamaw River and walked down to the bank to watch the moonlight on the water. What a long way I'd come in the few days since my conversion. No way would I have ventured to the river by myself just a few months earlier. My anxiety would have convinced me that someone might be hiding in the woods, planning an attack, or that I would somehow slip down the bank and into the current, where an alligator would seek me out.

The kudzulike fear had been burned back through the prayer I said with Shannon, and I imagined its black vines smoldering in a vacant field as I slid off my loafers and let the water rush over my toes toward the harbor.

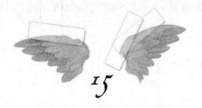

*15*

## Broken Loaf

Early the next morning, I received a hysterical call from Harriet.

"Marguerite didn't get out of bed when I called to her. An ambulance is here and taking her to Charleston."

I rushed over to pick Harriet up, and we followed closely behind the flashing lights as she bit her nails and pushed back the tears with the backs of her hands.

It was a beautiful winter day. The white morning light was blinding as it burned through the cloud covering above the rickety, rust-encrusted Cooper River Bridge. One bump from a barge below, and it would surely collapse into the harbor.

We took our seats in the emergency waiting room of the Medical University amid a crying child who had stapled his fingers together, a homeless lady with three Piggly Wiggly bags of clothes, and a cheesy green-tinseled Christmas tree with plastic candy canes, as a jazzed-up rendition of "Walking in a Winter Wonderland" played over the intercom system. It was seventy degrees outside, and Charleston wouldn't see a flake of snow for another ten years.

After three hours, the doctor came out to confirm that Marguerite had suffered a stroke, a fairly severe one, and her condition was uncertain. She was unconscious and had a week to regain consciousness before the likelihood of her coming around again became extremely slim.

Harriet called her mama at Betty Ford and her mama's brother, Uncle Fin, who lived on a commune in Arizona. They were both indisposed, so they left the details in Harriet's hands. She really was all alone.

I sat on a chair, thinking, *God, give her strength.*

The next thing I knew, Governor Maves, Marguerite's cousin, walked in with his entourage and told Harriet he would put his assistant, Lester Hayes, in charge of the details.

"Don't you worry," he said to her. "Marguerite's tough, and I'd bet the state she'll pull through."

Sure enough, Marguerite regained consciousness the next morning, Christmas Eve, and insisted with great vehemence that Harriet continue with the deb engagements and stop blubbering at her bedside.

I agreed to stay with Harriet in Marguerite's house for the rest of the Christmas break. Harriet didn't drive, so on Christmas Day I drove her in Marguerite's silver-blue Cadillac to the hospital, where Father Simmons from St. Anne's gave us Holy Communion at her bedside and we sang terrible a cappella renditions of "Hark! the Herald Angels Sing" and "Joy to the World!"

By day Harriet and I would suck in our bellies for our final fittings, smile in front of the portrait taker, and practice our curtsies in front of the president of the Camellia Club, and at night we would sit on the porch, eat vegan pasta, and talk.

"You're giving me the Heisman," Randy said when he called to ask me out for the third time. "I really have something I want to show you."

"We'll have plenty of time together come January," I assured him. He knew about my failing grades, and he had put me in touch with a football player's girlfriend who was looking for a roommate at USC.

Harriet and I conversed about literature, life, and God. She was open to the whole religion thing, and I read her the journal entries that I'd written to Mr. Lewis last semester, before giving her my copy of *Mere Christianity*. Harriet finished the book in less than twenty-four hours; then she made me drive her to the Williamstown Public Library, where she checked out *The Great Divorce* and *The Screwtape Letters*.

⁓

Harriet and I both had these overwhelming bursts of energy in the evenings that led up to the deb ball. We would drink wine from Marguerite's cellar and cook casseroles and soups into the wee hours of the night, carefully packing them in the freezer for Marguerite upon her return from the Medical University (which wouldn't be until after the New Year).

One night I wrote a letter to Peter Carpenter in which I told him that I missed him and hoped he was all right. Cringing, I even called his mama to ask for the penitentiary address.

⁓

"Marguerite is my little piece of mercy," Harriet said suddenly, looking up from one of her Lewis books as I fumbled through the drawers for a stamp. "My undeserved gift from God."

She put the book down and said, "I can't do this, Adelaide. There's too much water under my bridge."

"Not true," I said before opening the contemporary Bible Shannon had given me for Christmas to read aloud a passage from Hebrews I'd just stumbled upon: "'Let us go right into the presence of God, with true hearts fully trusting him. For our evil consciences have been sprinkled with Christ's blood to make us clean, and our bodies have been washed with pure water.'"

"Sprinkling? Full-fledged immersion wouldn't get me clean!"

As two moths gathered around the porch light, Harriet spewed,

"You know I've done drugs. Not just pot, but heavy stuff. And every now and then, I get this funny feeling in my gut and go to Hardee's and get a *big, juicy cheeseburger*. Plus I've slept around."

As Harriet watched the moths dance around the heat, she took a deep breath and kept going. "One time when I didn't have a ride home from a show, I shacked up with a forty-year-old deadhead who ran the falafel stand, and I wound up with genital warts." Then she raised her eyebrows as if she had trumped me and this sprinkling notion with just the beginning of her list.

She turned away from the light to look me head-on as she made her way farther down her list. "My oldest stepbrother—the one who ignores me—I even slept with him once. We were on a family ski trip in Austria, and we'd had too much to drink. I mean, that's pretty bad, isn't it?"

The moths were buzzing now, singeing their wings as they touched the bright light.

I didn't know what to say, but that had never stopped me before. "Well, it's definitely not in the 'all things bright and beautiful' category, Harriet, but from all I can figure, there's *nothing* that can't be forgiven."

"Oh, come on. Do you really buy that?"

As much as I could figure, with the exception of her relationship with Marguerite, Harriet had concluded that she wasn't worth a thing, and it would take more than me to persuade her otherwise.

"Yeah, I do," I said. "And a sin list as long as the Great Wall of China can't nullify the sacrifice made on mankind's behalf."

Harriet crinkled her face. She inhaled several breaths of the winter air before shooting an arrow.

"Did you forgive that law student who raped you last spring?"

My face reddened. I didn't know that Harriet knew about that, and I wondered if it was common knowledge. My throat burned with anger.

"Jif told me one night when I asked her why you always freaked out when someone came up behind you. It took me awhile to get it out of her, too, so don't think that she's spilling the beans around town."

∽

I thought for a moment about Harriet's question. Had I forgiven Devon Hunt? No. And I wasn't sure that I should. That sly predator.

"I haven't gone that far," I said to Harriet as I pulled a porch blanket tight around my shoulders. "Don't know if I will."

"Hey, I understand. I mean, I don't know if I can forgive my mother for not being a mother. Truthfully, the *worst thing* I've ever done, if I had to name it, is wishing that she would die. I mean, I have fantasies about her drinking herself to death."

My heart ached for Harriet. "I'm sorry" was all I knew to say.

"Yeah," Harriet said as she flicked out the porch light. The two moths thumped their bodies against the hot bulb even after the glow had disappeared.

∽

After we made our way up the grand staircase and to our separate rooms, I heard Harriet's muffled cries from across the hall.

When I closed my eyes, I could still see Devon Hunt pinning my neck down with his forearm.

I had my own fantasy. The details weren't clear, but I pictured him trapped in one of the old wooden coffins they buried Nathaniel Buxton in on the cemetery hill. A group of men had lowered him into the ground, and they were lifting their spades up and down as they covered the wooden case.

I was the only one who knew he was alive in there, but I didn't tell a soul.

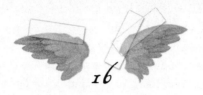

# First Love

At our morning hospital visit the day before the ball, Marguerite announced that her doctor had approved her request to attend the presentation the next evening and that the governor and his entourage would pick her up and see to it that she had a front-row seat for Harriet's debut.

"Get going," she said as she pointed toward the door of her room with her elegant arm jutting out of the hospital gown, a thick antique gold bracelet dangling from her wrist. She sent Harriet and me scrambling out of the Medical University parking lot to run her errands before our rehearsal that afternoon. We had to pick up Marguerite's royal-blue gown from the Santee Cleaners and her raw silk shoes that she'd ordered from Bob Ellis Shoes. Then we made a mercy call to her hairdresser, Nadine Bugbee, who agreed to cancel her customers' appointments for the next day so that she could go over to the hospital and get Marguerite's hair and face into shape.

Life was buzzing all over Williamstown as the out-of-town kin and escorts arrived with their floor-length gowns, kid gloves, and white-tie tuxes with tails. I hardly had time to say "boo" to Randy before we were walking down the aisle of the ornate Magnolia Club ballroom during the rehearsal—Randy stepping back as I practiced the curtsy toward the mothers on one side of the aisle before turning to the other side to the board and the would-be guests and onlookers.

The ballroom was absolutely stunning with thirty ten-foot Fraser fir trees entwined with thousands of small white lights and enormous urns strategically placed down the red velvet runway, with an explosion of white roses and Queen Anne's lace bursting out of their tops. The stately Queen Anne chairs were lined up perfectly on each side, and the red silk sashes on the doorways and the gold rope marking off the aisles were already in place. The marshals were marking off the parade course with black tape that would not be noticed in the darkened room the next night when the only light would come from the bulbs on the trees, the small lamps on the orchestra's music stands, and the spotlight trained on the debutantes as we marched up and down the aisle.

But the perfect decor couldn't subdue the undercurrent of nervousness that flowed through the setting as we debs rehearsed our individual presentations, our group parade, our curtsies, and then the meticulously executed first dance with our fathers before the escorts cut in. This would all take place as the who's who of Williamstown lined the other side of the aisle in observance of this rite of passage—the next generation of well-bred young ladies who had officially come of age.

I was sort of looking forward to the pomp and circumstance of it all. Of wearing Adelaide Rutledge Graydon's lace gown from 1899. But ultimately, it was a charade. A ritual passed down from our plantation forefathers, who sought to protect the bloodlines by setting the land gentry apart.

Poor Winkie Pride never mastered the curtsy, and at the rehearsal, her back foot slipped and she actually landed with her backside on the red velvet carpet. The escorts tried to muffle their chuckles, but I wondered if she would actually be able to make it through tomorrow evening without keeling over. She scurried back to her place with her head to the floor before Mrs. Kitteridge, the president of the club, asked her to try it again.

～

The next morning Harriet and I raced out to the hospital to deliver Marguerite's precious ball duds. She thanked us both, and before we left, she called us over to her bedside, where she presented each of us with a white box in the shape of a heart; we opened them to find a perfect strand of pearls. Harriet's clasp was a bumblebee with two emeralds for eyes and a body of sapphires between gold spread wings, and mine was an open flower with four little rubies of nectar in the center.

"Bitsy Stillwell picked these up for me in Japan last spring. I thought the second strand could be for your daughter someday, Harriet, but when Bitsy told me she was going back this summer, I told her to get me a third strand so that Adelaide could have one too. She's been a good friend to you in all of this. And I know you two will be the most beautiful debs Williamstown has ever seen."

"*Merci*, Grandmama," Harriet said, and she squeezed her grandmother until Marguerite announced, "I can't breathe, child. Now, get going."

"Thank you so much, Mrs. Hartness," I said, completely stunned by the generous gift.

"Don't look so surprised, dear. It makes an old woman happy to give a nice gift."

～

The rest of the day of the ball was a complete blur as Mama spouted orders at my siblings and sent Daddy to pick up the debutante gown at the seamstress. As if it were the Queen of England's inaugural gown, Mama had taken the Country Squire to the car wash so that no piece of dirt could possibly smudge the long white dress. Then she lined the trunk with two layers of sheets. She gave Daddy stern instructions about how to load and unload it. She even went out to the garage with him and asked him to practice using an old prom dress. Daddy rolled his eyes and reminded Mama that he had only one working arm, and if she needed more than that, she'd best do the job herself.

By lunchtime Juliabelle and Mae Mae had set up Randy and all of the out-of-town family with a lunch in the backyard that included chicken casserole, fruit salad, and lemon squares, while Mama, Harriet, and I excused ourselves for our afternoon grooming appointments.

"Adelaide," Randy said, racing to catch up with me as I bolted toward the car.

A little piece of biscuit was caught in the right corner of his lip, and he had cut his chin shaving, but he was still as handsome as ever.

"We need to talk."

"After the ball," I said, smiling at him. "I'm sorry I've been out of the loop. I promise you the whole day tomorrow."

"Okay," he said; then he lifted a piece of folded notebook paper out of his shirt pocket and handed it to me.

*Oh heavens, another poem,* I thought.

"I'll read it while my hair is setting."

"Okay." He grinned. "I'll see you tonight on the red velvet."

"It's a date."

Harriet, Mama, and I each had a manicure, a makeover, and a hair-setting appointment with Felix Idlewine, the owner of the elegant Felix's Hair and Beauty Salon, who had recently taken up residence in a lovely Victorian home on the National Historic Registry. His assistant, Tanya, pushed down my cuticles as Harriet selected her makeup colors and Mama was over getting her shampoo. When my nails were dry, Felix led me over to a big leather chair, dipped my feet in a little whirlpool, and handed me a thick magazine that had all sorts of buns and French twists to choose from.

"Up," he said, pulling my hair on top of my head. "Pick the style, and I'll make sure that beauty mark of yours can be seen. It makes you."

"Thanks," I said, rubbing my index finger over my jewel.

After I picked a French twist with subtle wisps framing the model's face, I pulled the note from Randy out of my pocket.

Sure enough, it was a poem.

> What flower blooms in the thick of winter
> To remind us that spring is coming?
> Oh, camellia, you make the sacrifice!
> Your white bloom fills my heart with hope!

Oh, good grief.

Randy was gifted at kicking the ball and catching spot-tailed bass in the creeks. He was good at looking good and being a gentleman who honored loyalty and faith above anything. But his poetry—oh, his poetry was so bad!

〜

When we arrived at the Magnolia Club, perfect from the neck up but still in T-shirts and blue jeans with our slips in tow, that undercurrent of nervousness from yesterday's rehearsal had turned into a full-blown hurricane of anxiety.

Mrs. Kitteridge rushed us up the grand mahogany stairs to the dressing room, where she instructed the mothers and daughters to throw on their gowns and dash down to the ballroom for the group and family photo shoots.

"Only an hour and a half before the guests will arrive, ladies!" she cried.

And the mothers were worse than anyone as they hurriedly poured themselves into their girdles and barked grooming orders at their daughters.

"The only thing worse than a nervous deb is a menopausal mother of a deb," said Harriet as she turned her back for me to button up her gown.

"You can say that again," Jif said, dabbing her eyes after her mother's scornful words about a run in her hose.

Jif looked beautiful, but thin and weary. I walked over to her with a Kleenex and told her how stunning she was.

"What does that beauty queen want from me?" she muttered, blowing her nose before powdering it again.

"She wants to be you," Harriet said.

∽

Mrs. Kitteridge had brought her walkie-talkies from home—the ones she kept in her bedroom and kitchen to call her housekeeper up when need be. She set one of them in the deb dressing room and another outside the ballroom so that she could greet guests while reminding the girls of the ticking clock before the procession.

Now her stained-glass voice came over the fuzzy machine. "Ladies, please come down for your photos. Time is of the essence."

As I made my way down the stairs, I stopped to peer into the candlelit ballroom at my parents, who were awaiting my arrival. Their handsome appearance simply took my breath away, and I had to get a good look at them before I was swooped up in their conversation.

Mama had never looked better. Not even in her wedding pictures. Her dress was wine colored with a satin off-the-shoulder neckline and a snug velvet bodice that showed off her petite figure. The double-strand pearls and teardrop earrings seemed to make her black eyes sparkle, and she looked like a precious gem that someone had carefully taken out of its case.

And Daddy looked so dapper in his white tie and tails, his hair greased back with a touch of pomade and his cheeks blushing with pride. He wore the prosthetic and the plastic cover instead of rolling up his arm sleeve and pinning it under his elbow. The white glove over the prosthetic cover made him look as though he had two healthy hands and arms. As if he could pick me up like when I was six and spin me around and around until we collapsed back into the salt water together.

Mama and Daddy rose to the occasion, and they appeared to be a couple with a picture-perfect marriage. How I wished that were so, and though it was out of my hands, I hoped what they had together would survive.

Heavens knew they had gone through worse than this. Once I snooped and read Mama's journal about the time when she knew Daddy was wounded in Vietnam and the trip she made to the hospital in Virginia to greet him and begin the long road of rehabilitation. She had seen other wives and girlfriends take one look at their husbands through the glass of the hospital window and run away, refusing to face their men and the mangled bodies they had come home in. But Greta was determined to love Zane, one arm or not, nervous breakdown or not, and she had done beautifully until this point in their lives.

I walked through the door and into the ballroom after Mrs. Kitteridge nudged me with her miniature flashlight, and I ran toward them and hugged them and took my place between them in front of the Christmas trees.

"You look radiant," Daddy said as he beamed with pride before the flash.

"We love you," Mama said, squeezing my waist, and we looked again toward the camera to document the moment.

Out of the corner of my eye, I glimpsed myself in the giant gilded mirror—my made-up face and artfully constructed French twist with little wisps framing my hairline and the back of my neck, then the silk cap sleeves and the one-hundred-year-old sweetheart bodice of lace and pearls from the late Adelaide Rutledge Graydon that the seamstress had measured over and over again at my fittings.

I didn't know if it was the dim light or the pride of standing by my handsome parents, but for the first time since I could remember, I felt beautiful.

~

"Thank God you're my date," Randy said as he looked me up and down.

"Stop it," I said.

He laughed and reached his elbow out for me to take. "Miss Adelaide Rutledge Piper, I am stupefied."

"Thanks for being here, Randy," I said to him. (I hadn't so much as sneezed his way in the last week.) "You look incredibly handsome in your white tie and tails."

My parents hadn't officially weighed in on my romance with Randy, but I knew Daddy loved how he treated me, and he was grateful to Randy for considering filling his shoes at the Piper Mill.

All in all, he was a man after Daddy's own heart—the Gamecocks second-string kicker, though he hardly ever got called into the game. But when he did, he loved it. This fall he'd kicked the winning field goal against the University of Georgia and replayed the video for me and Dizzy over and over, saying, "Check me out now, gals. That form ain't too shabby, eh?"

~

As the camera flashed on all the smiling parents and debs, I noticed Harriet standing in the corner, staring at the ceiling and waiting until she would be called over for the group photo. Her escort, Rod, would be rushing in at the last minute from Blockbuster, and Marguerite and Governor Maves (who would stand in as her father) wouldn't arrive until the procession. No other family member was present for this photo op, but Mrs. Zapes suggested that she, Jif, and I have our picture taken together.

After all the photos, we debs were rounded up like cattle and hurried up the stairs to spend the last hour touching up before the guests arrived. We took off our gowns as instructed, then snacked on finger sandwiches and Co-Colas behind the heavy closed doors in our bras and slips.

The last half hour before we were to make our way down for the procession was chaotic and stressful. Our mothers were sent downstairs, which was probably for the best. Marny was about to drive Jif over the edge with her nitpicking. Jif ran to the bathroom and stayed there for a good fifteen minutes until eventually poor Winkie had to bang on the door, she had to go so bad. Finally, Jif came back with watery eyes and two breath mints in her mouth. Harriet's and my eyes met after sizing her up.

Next, Jif and I ran into a variety of cover-up and powder issues as we tried to conceal the top of Harriet's tattoo that peeked out from the center of her back when she lifted her dress to curtsy.

Perky Nan McCant seemed to be the only one taking the evening in stride. The whole Kappa Nu house from Wofford was going to be there to cheer her on, as well as a slew of Converse College comrades.

The weak link was Winkie. It was obvious that she was on the verge of an anxiety attack over her curtsy, and we all knew that her misstep could turn the elegant evening into a laughingstock, if only for a moment, if she tumbled again.

When Mrs. Kitteridge announced the ten-minute mark over the fuzz of her walkie-talkie, there was a flutter of last-minute grooming. Girls spit out their chewing gum in napkins and put the final coat of lipstick on before suiting themselves up again in their white gowns.

In the midst of this last-minute rush, I looked over to Jif. As if in slow motion, I could see her eyes suddenly glaze over before she swayed once, then flat-out fainted into the communal vanity, sending two containers of powder, one open tube of lipstick, and a recently coated blush brush flying across the room.

The blush brush landed in the center of Nan's gown as Winkie was buttoning her up, and it left a streak of dark pink and beige from her hips down to the floor.

Nan shrieked with horror as I picked Jif up off the Oriental rug. Harriet ran to get a wet towel and the smelling salts from the first-aid kit in the bathroom as Winkie tried to calm Nan down.

She was literally shaking with rage.

"My gown! My gown!" Nan screamed as tears brimmed in the corners of her eyes. "Curse you, Jif Ferguson," she said in her direction as Jif started to regain consciousness. "You probably haven't eaten in the last forty-eight hours, and now you've gone and ruined my gown, not to mention my entire night!"

Winkie started to look as though she might pass out, too, when she realized that the stick of dark pink lipstick had gotten caught in the back of her dress and left a smudge the size of a plum on her derriere. Jif sat up after another whiff of the smelling salts as Mrs. Kitteridge fired the five-minute warning for the presentation over the walkie-talkie.

I stuffed a pimento cheese finger sandwich into Jif's mouth as I ordered Nan and Winkie to dig for the extra tube of concealer Mama had hidden in my bag.

"Everyone just get a grip!" I said. "The lights are dim down there, and you know our parents are so anxious themselves, they won't notice a thing. Beige is better than red, so let's do the best we can with this." *God, help us!*

As we paired up and coated the stains with a layer of concealer goo, the walkie-talkie sputtered before Mrs. Kitteridge called, "One minute until presentation time, debutantes. Come down, now!"

I looked around at the group of young ladies before me. Quite frankly, they all looked pretty good. And even though the circles of concealer stood out on the white dresses, a strange peace had entered the room.

Winkie looked at the front of Nan's gown and said, "It's not that bad. Half of it is in the fold."

Nan breathed a sigh and apologized for what she had said about Jif.

"Yours has faded some," Harriet said, opening the back of Winkie's dress. "Like Adelaide said, it's dark down there."

"Let's go!" I said, stuffing another pimento cheese sandwich down Jif's throat before taking my place in back of the line.

Jif wiped her mouth and walked to her position at the front with a sure-footed strength from her brief bites of sustenance.

As we all made our way down the mahogany stairs, I thought about Christ's very first miracle. I had just read about it in the Gospel of John earlier in the week. How He turned the water into wine at His mother's urging to spare a newlywed couple from their first social embarrassment.

*Who knows, maybe God does care about these silly little details,* I thought as I made my way behind the others and down the velvet-lined stairs before Mrs. Kitteridge handed me a bouquet of white roses, their stems wrapped in white satin.

"I'm a convert," Harriet whispered back to me before we lined up in the hallway to make our grand entrance.

"Are you joking?" I said.

"No. It happened when we were getting our hair done this afternoon. Sort of like C. S. Lewis on his ride to the zoo. When I walked into Felix's salon, I was agnostic, and by the time I walked out, I was a Christian."

"C'mon," I said, squeezing her shoulder. "Tell the truth."

"Well," she said, blowing a piece of hair out of her face, "I figured, what do I have to lose? Marguerite's sick, and everything else has gone down the crapper, so why fight something that's going to be positive in my life?"

I nodded as the orchestra finished "The Rite of Spring" in the ballroom.

"It was hubris that was keeping me at bay," Harriet added.

Mrs. Kitteridge was whispering directions to Jif, so we knew we had a few more minutes until showtime.

"Elaborate," I said as Mrs. Zapes and a few other older ladies lined us up and positioned us just so. Bitsy Stillwell wiped another crumb out of the corner of Jif's mouth with her handkerchief and asked Nan to blot her lips because they were too glossy.

"It was pride that said, 'You're too bad to be forgiven.' I mean, who am I to think that the sacrifice isn't powerful enough to cleanse me? So I said, 'Okay, God is sacred, so why shouldn't He have a crack at this?'"

Mrs. Percy tapped all of our shining foreheads and noses with her powder puff, and I grinned at Harriet.

"Now," the elderly Mrs. Zapes said, removing the silk sash at the doorway and nodding her head at Mrs. Kitteridge, who entreated us to enter the room as the Charleston symphony orchestra played "The Entry of the Guests" from Wagner's *Tannhäuser*.

Mrs. Kitteridge sent her flashlight signal, then pushed Jif toward the spotlight as a deep voice announced her full name over the microphone.

"Miss Jennifer Louise Ferguson, daughter of Dr. and Mrs. Theodore Foster Ferguson, presented by her father."

Jif took her father's hand, then smiled up at him as she gently curtsied down to the floor. When she stood, she took his elbow and walked down the center aisle, taking her place in the figure in front of her escort.

With the advantage of being at the end, I watched each young lady present herself to her father, her mother, the governors of the board, and the audience with a stroll down the aisle and two more curtsies to the ground.

Adjusting my posture as it came my turn to step into the spotlight, I breathed in the fresh Fraser fir–scented air, and I couldn't help smiling wide as I performed a curtsy for my father at one end of the aisle, then two more in the center that would be used as the model on the videos from that day forward and for many years to come.

No, I wasn't land gentry, nor was I an unblemished flower that was ready for the picking. I had been plucked before, and the world had slapped its ugly hand at me. And I had slapped my hand at others too.

But the sprinkling of the Messiah's sacrifice was upon me as I moved up and down the darkened aisle, and it had the power to make all things new again. I would be a fool not to let it cover me.

Smiling earnestly at Mama and the board and the audience, I stopped before Daddy, who stepped back out into the center for the first dance. He took my gloved hand in his and twirled me round and round across the velvet before Randy made the customary tap on his shoulder.

As I spun in the shadows of the tree lights, I made out Shannon in a champagne dress beneath a candelabra, and she was grinning at me. And I spotted Papa Great and Mae Mae, too, clapping their gloves together on my behalf. And Marguerite Hartness and Governor Maves, and even Ruthie, along with Dr. and Mrs. Baxter, who had made the trip all the way from Gastonia.

I shut my eyes as Randy led me in the dance, and I listened to the cupped sound of the white-gloved applause up and down the ballroom. It was the flapping of dove wings over and around me.

17

# Out of the Shadows

Life moved steadily forward until the end of my junior year at NBU.

Over the fifteen months that followed the debutante ball, I recalled with precision and frequency my dance with the divine across the Magnolia Club ballroom. Despite the sad events that commenced shortly after, that moment was branded on my heart. I often read this passage in Isaiah 49:16: "See, I have written your name on my hand." And to Professor Dirkas's poetry writing class, I submitted this:

> He fought
> for me—
> lifting me up
> out of the miry clay.
> He wooed me
> from my youth—
> waking me
> with the dove song
> and shading me
> at the riverside.
> Look into His palm
> and you will see

> *my very name*
> *carved*
> *with the edge*
> *of a rusted nail.*

The sadness was this: my parents separated shortly after the debutante ball, and in March 1992, they officially filed for divorce.

Mama had been wholly enraged at Daddy's behavior the night of my debut. After a few glasses of champagne, he'd made quite a scene by calling a number of Williamstown businessmen around the ballroom bar, where he drew circles of the Bizway business plan on cocktail napkins and challenged them all to discard their dead-end careers and join him on the path to untold wealth.

Papa Great had stormed out of the Magnolia Club, and as far as I knew, he hadn't uttered a word to Daddy since.

Dizzy and I had to drive Daddy to a motel room late that night, balancing him up the stairs and into the room where he collapsed with his head between his knees and stared longingly at the pyramid image on the cocktail napkin as if it were his own salvation tract.

We had to help him out of his tux and into his pajamas as he drooled and said, "I've got the plan. Why does Mama doubt it?"

Mama refused to go along with his plan once and for all, and after a few failed attempts at reconciliation, she asked him to leave for good. After their separation, Mae Mae and Papa Great tucked all of Zane Piper's girls, including Mama and me, under their financial wing while Daddy moved in with Uncle Tinka above the automotive shop to scrape and claw his way up the pyramid.

I couldn't pin the full blame on either of them. I knew Daddy had been miserable in his work life from the moment he returned from Vietnam, and so I understood his longing for a change. And as for Mama, who was emotionally distant but devoted in every other manner, I couldn't understand why she so vehemently abhorred the new business venture. Why she simply refused to give him an inch of support in his desire for a fresh start. They were both in the wrong, I supposed—selfish, prideful, and simply unwilling to compromise.

"Why can't you just *try* to step out of the box?" I asked Mama when she called early one morning to warn me about a snowstorm bound for Troutville that she'd spotted on the Weather Channel.

She kept quiet on the other end of the line.

"You've got to meet Daddy halfway. He's been doing what you wanted him to do all of his life; now it's your turn."

"Don't you think I've tried, Adelaide?" she said in the most forceful voice I could ever remember her mustering. "He's gone and done a 180-degree turn on us all, and he won't even look back to see the damage."

"Mama—"

"Never you mind," she said. "Just promise me you'll wear your down jacket, and don't forget about that long underwear in your top drawer."

⌒

Despite the tumult between my folks, the last year had been an extended honeymoon with my Maker. As I began reading the Bible and attempting to pray, I could look back and see how God had been courting me from my earliest days in the form of familial love, natural beauty, and countless acts of mercy that had spared my very life.

Everything had clicked during the last year. When I'd have a question or a thought, what I can only believe was God would confirm it at once either in Scripture, in the classroom, in a conversation, or in Mr. Lewis's books, which I continued to devour, one hearty steak meal after another. God seemed as attentive as a new husband to me that year, and I thought the foundation of my faith was being laid in granite.

One of the astounding acts of mercy that I had been the recipient of was Dr. Shaw and Professor Hirsch's success at convincing the dean of Undergraduate Studies to give me another chance (after failing my calculus exam sophomore year). The dean consented as long as I agreed to work off part of my scholarship as a dorm counselor. So for the second half of my sophomore year, I underwent training, and at the start of my junior year, I became the RA to an eclectic group of freshman girls who were trying to make their own way at NBU.

Not only that, but Whit and some of the other religious studies majors invited me to a study of the book of Acts, and by the end of the year, I declared a double major in English and religion. I was already beginning to research my senior thesis, which would be a study on the religious symbols in the short stories of Flannery O'Connor.

Ruthie Baxter had taken a semester off after the Christmas of 1990 to undergo outpatient psychiatric treatment and take part in a support group at the local crisis pregnancy center. She said she'd had a dream during that time at home of a precocious two-year-old girl peering around a doorway at her before running away, her laughter echoing down a hallway. And after that, she felt that the life connected to the heart on that fuzzy ultrasound screen was now in the care of God. And this brought her an immeasurable kind of relief.

And when NBU led a plant-a-tree campaign for the south side of campus, which had been hit hard by Hurricane Hugo, Ruthie and I combined a few months' spending money to buy and plant a white elm tree on the back quad in memory of the short life that had permanently changed us both. The tree grew and blossomed and provided shade for many a student in the years that followed.

I had spent the summer between my sophomore and junior years backpacking across Europe with Harriet, thanks to Marguerite's generous financial travel aid. (She was still recovering from her stroke, and the doctor had strongly advised her not to spend the summer of 1991 in Nice.) Harriet and I figured out the train system and successfully made our way through Italy, France, Germany, Austria, Hungary, and the Czech Republic on fifty dollars a day. In each new city and village that we visited, we lived on wine and bread and sought out the grand cathedrals so we could gander and pray in the massive structures that had taken lifetimes to build.

Dizzy had gotten into the cooking school at Johnson & Wales and seemed to be excelling in the baking department. She was leaning toward a major in pastry making and had FedExed a half dozen of her original almond croissants to me. I ate one with great pride as I sat on the porch facing the front quad and sipped my cappuccino. Who'd have thought that Dizzy, in all her black clothing and makeup, would be the creator of such a sweet and delicate treat?

It was Lou I worried about now. She had been hit hard by Mama and Daddy's separation. Not only did her speech impediment worsen during high school, but a rare learning disorder akin to dyslexia had been identified, and she was forced to enroll in a special-needs academy outside Charleston. Mama dutifully rented an apartment for she and Lou near the academy, and they would spend their weeknights there before heading back to Williamstown for the weekend. You had to give it to Greta—she was one devoted mother.

When Daddy wasn't traveling with Bizway, he'd take Lou in at Uncle Tinka's apartment, and she hated sleeping on the pull-out sofa in the dust-encrusted bachelor pad, listening to two men snore like beasts in their separate rooms.

As for Randy, he moved up to first-string kicker his senior year, and he hit the road with the Gamecocks all fall. What he wanted to show me that winter of 1991 was that he'd put the money he'd inherited from a great-uncle down on a deepwater lot on Pawleys Island. The lot had a rickety cabin on stilts and a crumbling dock that snaked its way out into the marsh.

"I'm going to rebuild it all," he said to me the day after the debutante ball. He pulled me in beside him. "And I hope you'll be the one sharing a life with me here."

"I just don't think—," I said, but my uncertainty about our romantic life never seemed to slow him down. "Let's see how this summer goes, okay? I'll be home, and we can really see where this thing is going."

"You're on," he said.

Now, instead of the bad love poetry, he mailed me photos of the island property with his step-by-step restoration plans for the house. He was putting a cupola up on the top, and from it you could see the beach on one side and the creek and marsh on the other.

"Not bad, eh?" he had written on the photo. "A poet could get inspired here. You can test it out come June."

As for Frankie Wells, he became the assistant editor of the campus paper and joined Harmony. I didn't know if this meant he was gay or just supportive of the gay society, and I was trying to get up the nerve to ask him.

Whenever I saw him, he was smoking a cigarette and scribbling something down in his little notebook. We still had lunch together when the paper had been put to bed and midnight study breaks along the colonnade. But, like many a friendship, we were adept at avoiding certain subjects.

Jif had rallied for a while. She'd gained back the fifteen pounds she needed to look remotely healthy, but after turning Harriet and me down on the European backpacking adventure for a summer internship at *Vanity Fair* in Manhattan (thanks to one of the Northeastern girls' contacts), she slid back into her old habits. The hollowness reappeared in her cheeks, and she was always chewing gum. Ned Crater had finally broken up with her because it killed him to see her wasting away, and she had gone through a string of good-looking frat jerks to satiate her desire for attention.

I continued to call her and invite her to the campus coffeehouse or to Sunday night vespers, but she usually declined. Sometimes I could hear her drunken and flirtatious laugh from my cracked dorm window late at night. I'd smile longingly for my friend and peek out the window to see her flip her cashmere scarf around her neck and lean on a boy's arm.

On these occasions I would picture her at the midnight breakfast following the debutante ball the previous year. How she had devoured the egg-and-sausage casserole, fruit, and muffins as we recounted the grooming mishaps that nearly prevented the presentation from taking place. She ate like there was no tomorrow that night, and she laughed and hung on Ned's arm. He had grinned as though he was the luckiest boy in the whole wide world, and I breathed a sigh of relief, because it seemed that her relationship with food was on the mend.

I never heard from Peter Carpenter, who was locked away in the Virginia State Penitentiary outside Richmond. Frankie said he'd heard he wouldn't be up for parole for another two years. And according to Mama, his mother rarely came out of her Williamstown house.

When I thought of Brother Benton grinning at me on the grass that day at orientation, it still sent a coldness into my bones. Two promising lives had been demolished my freshman year that I knew of. But I imagined there were others whose stories were hidden in shadowy places, covered by the tight-lipped administration, who shielded themselves behind the colonnade on the hill in hopes that no one would shine a light in the crevices.

College was a scary place at times. It was a safe haven for young and privileged criminals, and if you came up against one, it could mess you up for good. "This," I wrote in a creative nonfiction essay for Professor Dirkas's workshop, "is not something that they tell you in the gold-lined promotional materials or in the admissions office or on those quaint little campus tours in which only the attractive, clean-cut type take part."

That is why I enjoyed being a dorm counselor. It was like being a bossy big sister to sixteen other women, and I felt as though I had a little role in combating the dark side of campus life. I helped my freshman girls with their English papers and scolded them when their music blared at 3:00 a.m. I offered advice on how to cure their acne and thwart the freshman fifteen that crept up on them unawares.

At least one Saturday night a month, I'd pop popcorn and offer a movie so they might have another alternative to a trip down to fraternity row, which I still considered to be the noose around the place. I even bailed two of my girls out of jail when they were caught singing show tunes on the roof of an old apartment building downtown with some guys in the chorus. I laughed when I entered the jailhouse to learn that the girls had not been drinking. They had just wanted to sing at the highest place in the city, but their show had woken up a little old lady who did not like their rendition of "Oklahoma" or their footsteps plodding overhead.

Once a week I would hold a hall meeting they nicknamed "Piper Pipes," where I'd bring the girls up to date on campus events and invite them to share whatever was on their minds. I would remind them of ways to stay safe, blending some of my own philosophy and religion into the agenda: go out in groups; don't find yourself alone with someone you don't know well; know that there are consequences to actions; take Dr. Shaw's social justice class.

Two of the girls on my hall were from Tupelo, Mississippi, and they reminded me of Jif, Ruthie, and me our freshman year. They weren't as cultured or polished as the rest of the crew, and they had found themselves on the fringe of the social life and struggling to make the grade on the academic side. I tried to look out for them— invited them to vespers and even on a community service trip that Whit and some of the others were putting together over spring break to help with the cleanup in the aftermath of Hurricane Andrew.

One of the Tupelo girls, Cecelia Honeycutt, reminded me of myself. Cecelia was the only one on the hall who went to Florida on the relief trip and was a tremendous help, but she had a complete wall up when it came to religion, and she could not be persuaded. She struggled with weight gain and social rejection, and when I tried to reach out to her, to even share hints of my faith with her, Cecelia reared back and said, "Don't strap that Bible Belt on me. I came up here to get away from all of that."

"Simmer down, Honeycutt," I said with a grin, and I felt as though I were looking into my own fiery and discontented eyes of two years ago. "From now on I'm going to call you Jalapeñocutt. Or Peño for short."

"Whatever, Adelaide," she said, and I grinned when I heard her say under her breath, "Bossy dork."

I never officially laid eyes on Devon Hunt during the rest of my college career, though I assumed he was on and off campus from time to time since his father still served as the provost. Jif said she'd heard he was working for his local congressman in DC, and that really chafed me. A rapist aiding a representative on Capitol Hill. Humph.

Once I thought I saw his figure in the dark, walking with a group down the hill toward town, but I couldn't tell for sure. At this point, I couldn't really picture him in my mind's eye, but I knew that if our paths crossed, I would recognize him. Often I pondered the question Harriet had posed to me over a year ago—about whether I had forgiven him—and I still didn't know how to respond to that. Thankfully, I didn't replay the event in my mind. That part was a blessed side effect of the passing of time and the hope that came from my new faith. It wasn't an escape trick to suppress the pain, like Mama had taught me. It was just that somehow I had been released from the most acute trauma of the rape. But I didn't think I could ever *forgive* him, and I knew I never would *forget*.

Though I had received relief, something else continued to haunt me about the rape. The farther I got away from it, the more I wondered why I never reported the crime to campus security. I also wondered why the security guard who picked me up that night and Nurse Eugenia never asked me to do so. It seemed evident that I was not the first one they had seen abused in this way, and yet there was no real acknowledgment of the crime by either of them, and this bugged the heck out of me. I wondered sometimes how many others it had happened to.

A freshman girl in the hall above us had attempted to commit suicide by swallowing a bottle of Tylenol, but her roommate found her in time and rushed her to the hospital. And a fellow classmate of mine, Jane Avery, had successfully hanged herself toward the end of our sophomore year in an off-campus apartment. As with the case of Peter Carpenter and Brother Benton, the administration quickly covered up Jane Avery's suicide and stonewalled giving out information to the press and even her family.

I had known Jane Avery distantly after having taken an American lit class with her our freshman year. She had seemed strong, bright, and self-assured, and I wondered sometimes what had happened to her. Could she have been assaulted too? Or had she wound up in that abortion clinic in Roanoke, care of Nurse Eugenia? No one knew for sure.

Nonetheless, I was curious about it and concerned for the girls on my hall. I would eavesdrop in the bathroom and the hall from time to time—picking up bits of freshman-class tales. How a classmate they knew had been cornered by three freshman pledges in the basement of the frat house until her friends broke a window and pulled her out. And how another girl had been walking down frat house row late at night when a boy jumped off the porch and grabbed her forcefully by the arm. Luckily, a security guard had come along at just the right moment, and the offender acted as though it had just been a joke.

At the end of my junior year, I began to write candidly about the crime committed against me and the emotional aftermath I had experienced, and I submitted the piece to Professor Dirkas toward the close of my creative nonfiction class. Dirkas was troubled by my story, and he was obligated to show it to the administration. He encouraged me to speak to the dean and explain my experience in hopes that a stronger awareness about this sort of student-to-student crime could be raised and the crimes themselves dealt with in a just manner.

Upon my agreement, he gave the story to Dr. Josephine Atwood, the dean of student life, who knew me from that "pig's head on a stick" remark my freshman year. She called me promptly into her office and, to my disappointment, tried to squelch the matter.

"Miss Piper, the statute of limitations has nearly run out on this so-called crime that you wrote about in this essay. I doubt you would have a case with no evidence, but you may exercise your adjudication right before May if you wish. Otherwise, I strongly encourage you to put the matter behind you."

Dr. Atwood was the quintessential young administrator trying to mask her age and inexperience. I could see that now that I had a few years of college under my belt. Everything about her was navy-blue professional and toned down so as to dull her youthful appearance, from the light brown lipstick that left a ring on the rim of her coffee cup to the dowdy square heels and travel buff hose. Though the doctorate diploma from the University of Michigan in the brown frame behind her desk read 1982, her dark hair was pulled back tightly in a low, inconspicuous barrette, and she might as well have been menopausal.

The freshman me had been somewhat intimidated by a power-house woman like Dr. Atwood making the mock slash across her lips the day Peter was arrested, but the junior me, the one who wasn't on my own anymore, wanted to push.

"I don't wish to exercise the adjudication right, Dr. Atwood. What I want is to bring my experience to your attention so that the administration might understand the kinds of crimes that have been committed here in the past in order to better protect the students who will follow in our footsteps. I'm here on behalf of the freshman girls on my hall and the freshmen to come next year, in hopes that a general awareness might be heightened and a clearer policy might be created to aid victims of campus crimes such as this."

Wow. Polished. Not the muddled stuff I used to spit out when McSweeney asked me to dissect a Stevens or Frost poem on the spot. Every time he cornered me like this, I'd had difficulty collecting my thoughts, and I always thought of the brilliant conclusions I could have communicated two hours later over supper in the dining hall.

"The policy exists, Miss Piper, and it is quite adequate, I can assure you. You must do your homework before you criticize the system."

She tucked a pen behind her ear and began to scan a file on her desk.

"Where can a student find out about the policy?"

"In the handbook, of course," Dr. Atwood said as a strand of her stiff hair loosened and fell lightly across her chin. She quickly tucked it back into place and took a call on the speakerphone from her assistant.

I walked over to the handbook, which was on a coffee table in the office, and flipped through it as Dr. Atwood swallowed a moan of frustration.

When she hung up, I held up the open book and said, "There is nothing specific in the handbook about reporting an assault. The only 'crime' that is specified in the handbook is the violation of the honor code, which strikes me as ironic—the fact that one can snitch on someone for copying their French homework, but there is no clear outline of procedures for an assault victim or the potential consequences facing a rapist."

Dr. Atwood looked out the window onto the pristine quad. A vine of wisteria was draped across her thick pane, and the purple buds were beginning to bloom.

She winced after taking a sip of cold coffee and looked back to me.

"Also, I just want to know this: are the campus health-clinic employees and security employees aware of the definition and policy for student-to-student assaults? And if they are, are they encouraged to report the crimes?"

Dr. Atwood took a deep breath. I suspected that she was adept at dodging bullets, and I watched her scan the pile of files on her desk before responding.

"If what happened to you is true, I am sorry, Miss Piper. I have rarely heard of such an incident at an institution like ours. Consider your case extremely rare, because that's exactly what it is. While I find it admirable that you want to help your fellow students, I can assure you that this is *not* a common occurrence at Nathaniel Buxton University."

I was about to thank her for her time and forget the whole matter. Maybe Dr. Atwood was right. *It would be just like me,* I thought, *to be the only one in the world to have such a freak thing happen to her.*

*Push on,* I heard that third voice say. The one that Mr. Lewis spoke of in *Mere Christianity*—not the conscience that wants to do right or the lazy side that wants to forget about it all and relax. But the third voice—the one that whispers.

Suddenly it came to me, and I said, "May I conduct a campus survey to find out if anyone else has been sexually assaulted?"

The glare on Dr. Atwood's face assured me I was disrupting her afternoon.

"I don't think that would be a good idea, Miss Piper. Your viewpoint would be subjective, and there is simply no need for a survey since no one else has brought this matter to my attention. Now, if you'll excuse me, I need to prepare for a meeting with President Schaeffer."

I marched over to the library with my disk, sat down at the computer, and put my final touches on a poem for Dr. Dirkas.

### Honor Code

*You're sent packing*
*if you fib*
*at NBU—*
*I've known*
*four*
*convicted*
*of such crimes*
*here.*
*But you can assault,*
*defile,*
*maim*
*a fellow classmate's*
*heart*
*and no one*
*so much as says*
*"boo."*

I had left the dean's office in a cloud of frustration and defeat, but as the weeks passed, I let it go, thinking, *Well, I tried.* Maybe my role had been to be a flag raiser. One of several voices who would eventually convince Dr. Atwood and the college to strengthen their policy against this brand of campus crime.

It was two weeks before finals and the last summer break before my senior year, and I had to get planning for my future. I was looking forward to spending the summer in Williamstown with Randy. I was going to study for the GRE and hang out with the Pelzers and

Shannon. Harriet was going to come down for the month of August after her internship on the set of *The Comedy of Errors* at the Shakespeare in Central Park production.

Also, at Professor Dirkas's encouragement, I wanted to pursue an MFA in poetry, and I would spend a good part of my summer filling out the applications and creating a fresh portfolio to send to the graduate schools in the fall. Randy had sent me the information about the University of South Carolina graduate program, and it actually looked pretty impressive since they'd hired Julia Rodriquez, a Pulitzer prize–winning poet from the Dominican Republic. And Josiah Dirkas said that one of his favorite American poets, Donald Halstead, was taking a three-year stint there as writer-in-residence.

~

One afternoon when I was lounging on the dorm piazza, I read an anonymous letter to the editor in the student paper about a student's rape experience. The student was a senior, and her offender had graduated a year ago. She had kept the rape a secret for two years, but she suddenly wanted to speak out.

*What's going on?* I thought as I read the words twice over. Goose bumps were forming on my arms as the last mountain chill before summer swept through the piazza.

I was on my way to call Frankie and ask him about this, but I stopped short of dialing his extension.

*Wait,* I thought I heard the third voice say, and that's just what I did for the next week until I heard the thump of the newspaper at my dorm-room door. I opened it to find two additional anonymous letters to the editor about similar sexual assault experiences on campus. One went:

After admittedly drinking one too many gin and tonics the night of the Heritage Ball last year, my date (who was actually a gentleman) locked me in the room of his off-campus house and went down to the river for the bonfire. While he was gone, I became vaguely conscious of someone else in the room, and I woke up some time later to find his roommate on top of me, having his way. I called his name and told him to get off, but I was weak and weary and he knew it. He climbed out of the window when it was over, and when I woke up the next morning and confronted him, he said I was delusional. I know what happened to me. The physical evidence existed. He's avoided me ever since.

The other went:

I was attacked by my lab partner in a study room in the library. It was a Wednesday night around 1:00 a.m., and he dropped by with a cup of coffee and a fantasy I did not share. He locked the door— did I mention he's a good-sized rugby player and I'm just under five feet and 100 pounds? No one heard the desk topple over or my repeated calls for help.

"I'm not the only one," I said to Ruthie that night at the dining hall as I slapped the paper down in front of her salad bowl.

The next day Dr. Atwood met me in my dorm room and accused me of starting the whole thing. Several strands of the dean's hair had fallen down and were framing her face with frizzy wisps.

"It wasn't me," I said. "I haven't even sent my story in."

Dr. Atwood didn't believe me, and neither Frankie nor the senior editor of the paper were giving out any names to her.

"You could be in violation of the honor code if you aren't honest with me," she said, nervously tapping the rolled-up newspaper against the palm of her hand.

"I know that," I said. "I'm telling the truth."

"According to the records at the dean of Undergraduate Studies, Miss Piper, we gave you a second chance to work off your scholarship due to your poor academic performance your freshman and sophomore years. I would caution a student who is on unsteady academic ground against causing trouble when she still has another year to go before obtaining her degree."

"So that's a threat?" I said.

"You are overstepping your boundaries, young lady," Dr. Atwood said as she tucked the newspaper under her arm and turned to walk down the hall toward the spring sunlight that was sifting through the screen door.

"And you are looking the other way," I said to her.

She turned and raced back to me, working her bony jaw back and forth. "The *Princeton Review* is on their way to do an updated study about the campus, and I implore you to keep the lid on this."

I nodded twice out of fear and reflex, then watched as she turned and walked briskly down the corridor, making eye contact with the freshmen who were lingering in their doorways.

∽

The next week the paper didn't publish any letters on the subject, and I still bit my tongue and didn't ask Frankie about it.

Not only was it the end of my junior year, but it was also the end of my term as a dorm counselor. I wanted to do the best I could by the girls the last few weeks before finals, so I edited their English papers and invited them to my room most midnights for a much-needed study break that consisted of chocolate-covered coffee beans and *Saturday Night Live* reruns I'd taped over the last few months.

The sixteen freshmen on my hall were turning out all right. They were all going to move forward to their sophomore year in one piece. No one had so much as failed a class.

I was looking toward life after NBU now. Toward my thesis and graduate school, and I asked God to guide me about Randy and my folks.

I still had my St. Christopher medal that Juliabelle had given me, and I kept it in my backpack so my fingers would rub up against it every time I fished for a pencil or computer disk.

"This busty cheerleader is totally after Randy," Georgianne had called to tell me.

She and Peach still went to the Gamecock games, and Peach was helping to landscape Randy's lot on Pawleys.

A small twinge of jealousy caught in my throat, but I didn't have much right to keep tabs on him.

"I'm three hundred miles away," I said. "It's out of my hands. But I'll be home for the summer in a few weeks."

"I'll keep you updated," she said.

"All right. So how's Baby Peach?"

"Talking up a storm."

"Give him a squeeze for me."

"I will."

"So what does this cheerleader look like again?"

"You can't get home too soon, Adelaide. Let's leave it at that."

On the Saturday night of the alumni weekend (just days before finals and the close of spring term), as Ruthie and I were in the dorm-hall kitchen waiting for our ramen noodles to go limp so we could have a little brainpower as we studied for our Advanced French final, I received a frantic call from Peño, my feisty Tupelo freshman, who was on her second date with a Kappa Nu senior.

Her words were slurred, and it took me a moment to understand her.

"Adelaide, I'm at the Kappa Nu house, and I'm fading. He must've slipped something into my drink. Please come get me . . ." Then the phone line went dead.

"Call Dr. Atwood at home and ask her to meet me at the Kappa Nu house," I hollered to Ruthie as I ran to my room to put on my shoes. "And call campus security too."

"Okay," Ruthie said as she picked up the phone and waited for the operator.

I bolted through the quad and down the hill to the grand fraternity houses where drunken alums and students were scattered about the green lawns.

*Be with her,* I prayed.

When I got to the KN house, there was a live band and music blaring out the windows. The floorboards were pulsing to the drumbeat in the foyer. Several tipsy graduates and students danced clumsily everywhere. All I knew about Cecelia's date was that his name was Kevin and that he was a senior.

"Where's Kevin's room?" I said to a freshman boy, who pointed in the direction of the stairs and slurred, "Attic."

Just as I was racing up the stairs, I looked back to see Dr. Atwood in an NBU sweatshirt and jeans and a security guard on her heels. They were both looking around for me amid the drunken haze of the party.

"Dr. Atwood," I called down to her, "attic. Follow me."

We raced up to the third floor, where I knocked hard on a locked door before the security guard took a hammer from the fire extinguisher window in the hallway and broke open the door.

"What the—," a boy's voice screamed as we raced up the stairs.

When we reached the top, we found Cecelia completely unconscious on a couch, covered haphazardly by a blanket.

The boy was in his boxers, and he was shielding his eyes from the security guard's light.

"Get dressed and come with me, young man," the security guard said as I hustled to Cecelia's side and took note of the blood streaming from her nose. I covered her up tightly with an NBU-crested blanket and looked up at Dr. Atwood, who was radioing for an ambulance on the security guard's walkie-talkie.

As the boy was bending over in the corner to put his jeans on, I bolted across the room and pushed him from the back with all my might. He flipped over and landed with his feet on top of a crate that served as a coffee table, and two glass mugs of beer wobbled before spilling over, drenching his pants.

Before I knew it, I had leaped on top of him and was hitting his face and chest with my fists.

"You predator!" I screamed as he shielded his face from my swings and said, "Huh?"

"How could you do this to her?"

Dr. Atwood and the security pulled me off him just as my nails were going for his eyes.

"Let's catch our breath, Miss Piper," Dr. Atwood said as she pulled me close and directed the security guard to handcuff the student. And I wept with rage on her stiff shoulder as she softened for a moment and stroked my hair while the steady bass from the music below made the wooden slats of the attic floor shift like an after-tremor of an earthquake.

Cecelia came to in the local emergency room, where a blood sample with traces of Rohypnol had confirmed that she'd been slipped a kind of date rape drug sometime during the night. She looked to me when the doctor asked if she would consent to the administration of a Physical Evidence Recovery procedure. Though she was still groggy, her anger was already building, and no matter how humiliating it was, she wanted to obtain the evidence of this crime.

"Yes," she said as the doctor explained the invasive and painful procedure.

Then she turned to me and reached out her arm.

I scooted toward her and locked our elbows as the nurse began to prepare the kit, and I whispered into Cecelia's ear, "I'm so sorry, Peño."

The examination was horrendous, but Cecelia bit her lip and squeezed my hand as the tears rolled down her cheeks.

Dr. Atwood was out in the hallway, pacing. She had phoned President Schaeffer and was waiting for his callback. When the nurse walked out of the exam room with her sealed bags of evidence, I saw Dr. Atwood catch a glimpse of Cecelia on the examining table. Her face was gray, and she was staring at a spot on the ceiling where a leak had left a ring.

Ruthie met us at the hospital with a change of clothes since Cecelia had to leave her jeans and shirt behind as evidence.

"The hospital will hold them for a month before discarding them," a local police officer told Peño. "During that time you can decide whether or not to press charges."

Cecelia nodded as she slipped on a pair of my khakis and a sweatshirt.

Dr. Atwood was on the phone with President Schaeffer, recounting what had happened.

"I want an adjudication hearing," Peño said to Dr. Atwood as we walked out of the exam room and into the hospital hallway.

Dr. Atwood nodded in agreement and helped us into the security guard's car.

By this time it was 4:30 a.m., and even the fraternity houses had turned off their lights to get some rest before the bright light of Sunday morning pierced through their windows.

As Cecelia slowly made her way out of the car, I watched Dr. Atwood pull up to President Schaeffer's house on the hill behind our dorm. His lights were already on, and he was sitting on his porch steps.

"I don't know if . . ." Cecelia's words trailed off as she hobbled up the stairs and into the dorm.

An early rising sparrow was warming up its voice, and the first hints of daylight were spreading up and over the mountains in a blanket of violet blue.

I grabbed her elbow and said, "I'll help."

# Change of Plans

*"Freshman Cecelia Honeycutt Files for Adjudication in*
*Sexual Assault Case Against Senior Kevin Youngblood"*
*Story by Frankie Wells*

I spotted the headline on the front page of the university paper as I walked across the quad on the way to my French final. A couple of boys were sitting on the rocking chairs, reading the article as their golden retriever knelt between them. The canine was cupping a tattered tennis ball in his mouth in hopes that any moment his master would put down the news and play a game of fetch.

After my exam, I raced over to the student center to grab a copy of the paper, then sat down on the grassy knoll beneath Ruthie's tree and read about my courageous hall mate's pending case. *Frankie is right on target,* I thought as I read the article, which explained the weak policy in place for such a procedure and contemplated the number of victims who never sought justice because there was no clear path by which to seek it.

Dr. Atwood had finally changed her tune after witnessing firsthand the aftermath of Cecelia's attack, and midway through the article, Frankie quoted her as saying, "We now understand that we need to have a hard line on assault procedures on campus, and we will take measures this summer to make sure that a victim can seek justice and that an offender may have a fair trial. We pledge to meet this issue head-on."

"Good for you, Josephine," I whispered as Ruthie's elm tree left an intricate pattern of leaf and fruit shadows across my paper.

Peño's bravery astounded me.

"He messed with the wrong person," she had said to me one night after the reporter called. "And you know what? I think I'm not the first one this has happened to."

"You're right," I had said before pouring her a cup of coffee and sharing my own story with her.

⌒

Now, as the students roamed to and from their finals, Dr. Atwood was walking toward me, her square heels sinking into the grass on the knoll.

"Miss Piper, I need to speak with you," she said, yards away, as she straightened her dark suit jacket. She was so official-looking and determined. Like a banker on speed. Before I could get to my feet, she sat down beside me beneath Ruthie's tree, and the pendulous branches cast shadows on her suit and hosiery. "I'd like you to change your summer plans," she said, looking me in the eye.

"I beg your pardon?"

"Whatever you had going on this summer, I'd like you to reconsider. I need a student representative to stay here and serve as a campus voice and consultant as we rewrite our policy on sexual assault. I remember how confidently you handled that reporter your freshman year despite my protest, and now I want to use you to *benefit* NBU's reputation."

You could have pushed me over with the point of a palm frond. My heart started to pound. How the tables could turn so quickly. One minute Dr. Atwood wouldn't give me the time of day; now she wanted me to serve as her trusted student voice as she combated campus assault.

Since I had taken it this far, I figured I might as well see it through.

"I'd be honored to," I said, and by the end of the afternoon, I had phoned Randy, the Pelzers, Shannon, Harriet, and my family to tell them why I wouldn't be coming home next week.

"I knew about it," said Randy. "Jif told me the summer you came home after your freshman year. It doesn't change things between us. But I really wanted to spend this summer with you."

It was painful to come clean with my parents and tell them what had happened at the end of my freshman year. But if Cecelia had the guts to go public on campus, I at least had to be honest with my family by letting them know why I felt it was important to stay at NBU over the next three months.

Daddy hit something in Uncle Tinka's automotive store when he heard—it sounded like a wrench banging into a hubcap. The poor Ice Lady wept uncontrollably in her prefurnished Charleston apartment as Lou napped over her open math textbook, worn out with learning.

"It's okay," I told both of my parents when I brushed over the details of my assault. "It was awful, but I'm so much better. And now I have the chance to help make the school a safer place. You know?"

"I'm proud of you," Dale Pelzer said when I told him. "You've come so far so fast. Just keep it simple, Miss Adelaide. Keep your eyes on Him, that's all."

Dale. Hmm. He was country, but he had smarts.

A heightened awareness of the mistreatment of women was playing out on the national scene in the early 1990s. The Anita Hill and Clarence Thomas trials had unfolded in a manner unpleasing to many a woman, and when *Thelma and Louise* won the Oscar for Best Screen Play, the country seemed to be issuing an outcry on behalf of abused women.

The Violence Against Women Act was being constructed in hopes that Governor Bill Clinton would win the 1992 election, and the act requested that a significant amount of resources be put toward stopping college-campus crimes.

The *Roanoke Times* had caught wind of Cecelia's story and a similar one at the University of Virginia, where fifteen women and two men had reported sexual assaults to their administration over the last year. When the paper came calling on NBU, Dr. Atwood and her student voice—*moi*—met with them to communicate what we were doing to fix the problem.

Over the summer, Dr. Atwood and our committee of administration and faculty reviewed other colleges' policies and attempted to re-create our own. I helped write a survey that went out to the alumni and researched where we might obtain funds for the following: training of campus security, strategic placement of help buttons around campus, education for male students on what constitutes a crime, and the creation of a hotline to volunteer advocates whom a victim could call after a crime was committed. These advocates would walk the student through her options for reporting a crime and seeking justice.

Somewhere along the way, *Newsweek* magazine picked up the story and decided to write a feature article on date rape on college campuses. They decided to focus on NBU, UVA, and the University of Tennessee, where a woman had been brutally raped and murdered by a fellow student in her dorm room. A reporter and photographer came down for an interview in mid-July, and they took photos of Cecelia, Dr. Atwood, and me standing before the pillars of the colonnade as we discussed the new policy that would be implemented in the fall.

I experienced mixed feelings rehashing the rape to a total stranger with a tape recorder. Sometimes I was ashamed, but more often than not, I sort of reveled in it, the way Daddy probably did when he talked about the Vietnam War at the Bizway meetings. At last, no one to say, "Pipe down, Piper!"

Yes, a peculiar brand of pride was creeping up on me. Was it bad? I couldn't tell.

By August 1992, sixteen alumni had written in, most anonymously, to say that they had been sexually assaulted by a fellow student. Many of them gave donations for the installation of the alarm buttons. And in almost all cases, the victim knew the student who had raped her. More than 50 percent were on a date at the time of the assault.

When Dr. Atwood called me to say that *60 Minutes* wanted to interview Cecelia and me for an upcoming show, I couldn't believe it. There was that part of me that had always wanted to be in the spotlight. That part that wanted out of Williamstown and into the great big enlightened world, but appearing on a national news show to talk about rape and campus policy wasn't exactly what I had in mind.

Now other things were falling behind. My GRE review book hadn't been cracked all summer, and my MFA applications were collecting dust on my desk. Then Georgianne called late on Friday to say, "The cheerleader asked him out, and he went."

∽

I could tell Dr. Atwood was pleased that NBU was smelling like a wisteria bloom in all of this since it was taking the initiative to create the policy. Other schools were still dragging their feet or flat-out ignoring the issue, and so she wanted me to be in front of that camera, telling all of America that NBU had pledged to stop these kinds of crimes.

It was all about PR for Dr. Atwood. Sometimes I couldn't tell if she was excited about addressing student crime or simply thankful for her role in turning a difficult situation into an impressive amount of padding for her vita.

"Make us look good," she said when she put me on an airplane bound for New York City for the interview. (Cecelia's grandfather was dying of lung cancer that very week, and she could not make the trip, but she had given me permission to share her story.)

∽

When I stepped out onto the curb at LaGuardia Airport, I gawked at the line of yellow cabs and the urbane people cued up to ride into the city with their dark, unshaven chins and weathered briefcases.

"I'll meet you at Marco's tomorrow," a tall brunette with wild hair said to a handsome guy in a gray T-shirt and tortoiseshell glasses.

He nodded and opened the cab door for her.

"I'll take the next one," he said.

I wasn't even in Manhattan yet, and I was completely enamored with whatever kind of life was pulsing around me.

Mae Mae had taken me once to New York when I was twelve years old, and we had seen *La Bohème* at the Met and *Cats* on Broadway, and I had never forgotten the wondrous spectacle of humanity on the streets that we raced down to make our shows in time. Harriet was already back at Sarah Lawrence, getting ready for her next O'Connor play that would be produced at the beginning of her senior year, and she told me she'd take the train into the city and meet me for supper that night.

As I hopped into a cab and told the driver the address of my hotel, I felt like a kid smitten with the biggest toy in the store. A secret fantasy was forming in my mind—MFA school in Manhattan and some sensitive, brooding poet to settle down with. Now, that was about as far away from Williamstown as I could ever hope to get.

As I filed through my policy notes, the cab raced toward the bright lights of the city. It was two in the afternoon, and I had to quickly check in at the hotel before heading over to the studio for a review of the interview, which would take place tomorrow morning. After dropping my bags in a glorious eighteenth-story hotel room, I met up with the other students—two from the University of Virginia and one from the University of Tennessee, and we hailed a cab bound for Rockefeller Center.

*Boy, could I get so used to this!* I thought.

As the streets bustled with life, I sensed that the whole world was at our fingertips, and all we needed to do was raise our hands and catch a ride into untold universes, brimming with culture, art, and life.

One by one we went over the questions with James Albright, then out for a bite to eat at a restaurant near the hotel. Harriet was running late and joined us at the end of the dinner for coffee. Leah, one of the girls from UVA, was downtrodden and could hardly look anyone in the eye, and the other girl, Allison, was flat-out angry. She said she fantasized about her offender's death on a daily basis, and she was not going to relent until he was behind bars.

"I hope someone rapes him in prison," Allison said before ordering her gnocchi with pesto sauce. "I hope he's afraid to go to sleep at night when he lands his sorry butt in there."

The other girl, Belinda, from the University of Tennessee, seemed frightened out of her wits. The city was unnerving her with its beeping horns and bustling pedestrians, and she seemed to have a case of post-traumatic stress syndrome, though her attack had occurred more than three years ago. When the waiter came up behind Belinda with our cappuccinos, she jerked back, and he spilled coffee and steamed milk on the wall and the floor in an effort to avoid burning her. It took the poor guy fifteen minutes and a half canister of salt to clean the place up.

Harriet nudged me throughout dessert as we each recounted our experiences and the resistance we'd met from our colleges, families, and friends.

"Let's go for a walk after you get these guys home," she whispered on the way back to the hotel. "You could use some fresh air and a tour of the city."

After I told the other girls good night, we walked south toward Times Square, catching up and breathing in the life. When we passed the theater where *Les Misérables* was playing, a high school teacher with a string of twenty kids behind her called to us. She had four extra tickets in her hand, and she offered us two of them.

"What a town!" I said as Harriet graciously accepted the freebies and we made our way into the darkened theater, where we watched the beautiful story of God's mercy unfold.

"Let's live here together after graduation," Harriet said later as I walked her down to Grand Central Station to catch the last train back to Bronxville.

"You read my mind. I'm going by Columbia and NYU tomorrow to pick up an application."

"Yes!" Harriet said as her train *eek*ed to a halt before opening its doors. "You can come up for my play in September and have interviews."

"You bet," I said, hugging her as the passengers stepped off and a few folks who'd spent the evening in the city shuffled inside with their papers and laptops and coffees to take their seats.

"I'm relieved, Adelaide. I mean, I didn't want you to get, like, sucked up in this rape thing forever."

"What do you mean, Harriet?" I rubbed my jewel and felt my ears redden.

She rolled her eyes, and I sucked my teeth before furrowing my brow. "You have a problem with the antirape stuff?"

She stepped back down from the platform toward me.

"Not exactly," she said. "I guess . . . I don't want it to consume you, okay? I mean, if you keep hanging out with loony-bin material like those guys tonight, you might unravel too."

Now I was ticked. This was the most valid thing I'd done in my college career, and she was making light of it.

"This is who *I am*, Harriet! This is, like, a critical thing to bring to light, don't you think? I mean, you're the one for chicken and egg rights—how about human beings? How about women?"

"Forget it," Harriet said softly, stepping back toward the train. "I'm not trying to minimize what happened to you. I just think, you know, it could become too much of a focus."

"It wouldn't be bad if it did," I said as Harriet checked her watch and blew a piece of hair out of her face.

"Do you know how to make your way back to the hotel?" she asked.

"Yeah," I said, feeling a burning in my throat. I looked away to read some graffiti on the train that read "Z-man," then back to her. "Why don't you think this is a valid pursuit?"

"Sure, it's *valid* stuff, but you don't want to see everything through the lens of a 'postrape victim,' do you? You're, like, a lot more than that, Adelaide. You're a poet and a Low-Country girl and a debutante. And more important than any of that, a recipient of God's grace."

"I know," I said. "I know that."

The train lights blinked, and the driver lowered his head to peer down the platform toward us.

"I've gotta go. This is the last train, okay?"

She stepped inside the doors, stretched her arms, revealing her hairy armpits, and waved good-bye as the compartments squeaked and rolled down the tunnel and the tracks toward Bronxville.

What was up with her?

⌢

Later that night, I threw open the draperies and sang the "Lovely Ladies" song from *Les Mis* as I danced and jumped from bed to bed. I wished I'd invited Harriet to spend the night, but then again, she was chafing me with her lack of support.

Out of breath, I stopped to look out at the digital view of midtown and downtown. I could recognize the Chrysler Building staring back at me with its silvery fans of light, and the red and yellow lights on the Empire State Building dwarfing the midtown apartments, and then in the distance the twin towers of the World Trade Center illuminating the tip of the peninsula with their 110 floors of glass and steel as if to say, "Welcome to the center of the world."

Harriet. Humph. She had some nerve questioning me. It's not exactly a walk on the beach telling a large percentage of America about your attack.

⌢

The next morning James Albright interviewed us separately; then we joined a panel of experts on the subject. There was a member from NOW who was lobbying for the Violence Against Women Act and an administrator at Syracuse University who had heeded the warning against sexual assault a decade before and had a successful system in place to aid victims. Also, there was a handsome twentysomething young man named Tobias Moore, who had just started his own nonprofit, Rachel's Rape, in memory of his sister, who was raped in her dorm at Columbia University in the middle of the night two years earlier.

She had committed suicide six months after the rape. Fear and sleep deprivation had ravaged her mind, and she couldn't face it another day.

As I stood with the girls in the hallway outside the studio, waiting for the elevator, Tobias made his way toward me and handed me his card.

"May I call you for an interview for our newsletter?" he asked. "I think your story is amazing. How you're helping to write your school policy after what you've been through."

He hesitated for a moment, rubbing his chin, and I guessed he was wondering if he should risk asking for my number in front of four post-rape victims. I smiled his way as if to encourage him. He was truly dashing—tall with wavy blond hair and fair skin, and attractively dressed in an urban-preppy blend of a tattered oxford and corduroy pants. "Do you think I could buy you a cup of coffee before you leave town?"

"Sure," I said, looking over my shoulder at the heavy burdens of the girls behind me. I was happy to have a great-looking young man take an interest in me, and maybe these gals needed to know that there was life after assault.

"How about now?" I asked.

His bright blue eyes lit up like the front of the subway trains, and he couldn't conceal his sheepish grin.

"Great!" he said as the elevator door opened. "Let's go."

It was a mild and beautiful August afternoon, and after ducking into a coffeehouse and getting two cappuccinos to go, we walked uptown to Central Park, where we meandered through the lush pathways of the circumscribed forest while we talked.

When we shared a mustard-smothered knish on the steps of the Metropolitan Museum, he told me about the pain of losing his sister. He had been a senior at Georgetown University when she passed away, and after graduation he called the big-name accounting firm that had promised him a job to say he was starting a nonprofit in her memory and he wouldn't be able to take them up on their offer.

He had created Rachel's Rape in a one-room "suite" in the attic of an old investments building on K Street in Washington DC, amid several other minor nonprofits, and he'd spent the last two years lobbying Congress for tighter campus security mandates as well as creating educational programs for campuses to use, particularly in the Greek and athletic worlds, to teach men about what rape is and what the consequences will be for them if they commit the act.

After we shared our stories, he admitted he was late for a meeting with a potential funder and needed to catch a cab downtown. "Can I take you out to dinner tonight?"

"Can we go to Chinatown?" I asked. "My friend Harriet said I have to try the dim sum at Little River."

"How about Little Italy?" he asked. "I can't do Chinese—digestive issues, you know? But Luigi's has incredible hand-rolled pasta and tiramisu."

He had noticed a smudge of mustard on the knee of his pants and took out a towelette like the kind they serve with lobsters still in their shells. Then he tore it open and rubbed it on the spot before pouring a little water from his cup over his knee.

I chuckled at his meticulous cleaning job before saying, "It's a date."

"Terrific," he said, smiling up at me. "Why don't I catch the first cab for you so you can get safely back to the hotel?"

"I'm fine," I said, "and I might as well check out the Met while I'm here."

He folded up the towelette, slid it into his back pocket, and shook my hand firmly good-bye.

"I'll look forward to seeing you tonight," he said, staring into my face as if I were the most extraordinary sight he'd ever seen. "I'll meet you in the lobby at seven."

I blushed and pointed out a cab that had just pulled up to let a lady out in front of the steps.

I met Tobias in the lobby of the hotel just as the sun was setting. As we walked out onto the street, I watched the windows come randomly to life in a cacophony of light. New York City at nightfall was simply magical, and I was delighted to see a place that lived up to its reputation.

"Isn't it amazing?" I asked Tobias as he stared at his map and tried to figure what route to take to Little Italy. "It exceeds all expectations," I continued before lifting my arms to embrace the air. I nearly whacked a short lady who was trying to pass us with an armful of groceries, and she grunted, "Watch it!"

He looked over his map and smiled longingly at me before his pale blue eyes glazed over with sadness. "It doesn't do that for me, Adelaide," he said gently. "My sister was raped here, and she died here. I can't walk up to Ninetieth Street without losing it."

*Of course,* I thought. *How insensitive of me.* It was my first real date in a while, and I was already bringing the poor guy to tears. This kind and serious fellow with towelettes in his pocket and a sensitive stomach. I smiled encouragingly back at him. With the exception of Frankie (who had the heart of a true reporter) and Randy (who was my second cousin, after all), I hadn't known any young man of my generation to be as tenderhearted as Tobias seemed, and it was truly refreshing.

"So you're dissin' us for that total stranger?" Allison had asked me in the elevator earlier as she and the other girls headed for the same restaurant we dined in last night.

"Let's meet up for coffee in my room later," I said.

"Whatever," she said.

"Be careful," Belinda whispered.

But I felt safe enough on the arm of an antirape activist, and even if I didn't, *I was going out.* So I talked on and on to Tobias Moore as if there were no tomorrow as he asked me question after question about my life.

He seemed to hang on my every word through dinner. He was a gentleman and completely transparent, and I was taken aback at the attention he was paying me.

He hugged me good night at the revolving door of the lobby, and I breathed in his delicious scent, a combination of fresh mint and aftershave.

"Have breakfast with me tomorrow morning," he said just as I was turning toward the door.

Before I could respond, he assured me, "I'll pick you up in the lobby at 7:00 a.m., and I promise I'll have you in a cab bound for LaGuardia by 8:00 a.m." He motioned to a well-worn diner across the street that was lit up and bustling with patrons. "We'll just catch a little bite there and have a few more minutes together."

Cabs were racing down Eighth Avenue as though the city was just beginning to wake up to the summer night. They were honking at one another as a traffic light turned yellow, and in the distance was the sound of a police siren. An elderly man with two Scotties walked by and tipped his hat toward us. Tobias was standing on the balls of his feet, waiting for my response.

"See you tomorrow, then," I said, tilting my head to the side before waving good-bye.

He stayed on the sidewalk, tapping his thumb against his thigh as he watched to make sure that I made it safely through the lobby and into the elevator.

⌒

That night the three girls made their way into my room. They sat along the edge of my bed and recounted the interview as I poured them decaf coffee from the hotel pot.

After a lull in the conversation, Allison said, "Don't you guys dream about castrating them?"

Belinda pulled her legs up in the fetal position on the opposite bed and rocked back and forth. She sort of smiled at the thought of it as she rested her chin on top of her knees.

Leah breathed a sigh and said, "Yes, I do."

*Mmm.*

I looked beyond Allison at the city view. My back stiffened when I pictured coming face-to-face with my assailant.

"I used to imagine I'd get him in his sleep," I said.

"Yeah, and he would never know what hit him, right?" Allison said. Belinda let out a peep of laughter.

"I'm going to video my interview and FedEx it to him," Allison said, holding up her cup for a refill.

"You know where he lives?" I said.

"Exactly," she said. "I've driven by there before, and once I stared him down when he was getting out of his car after a workday."

"What'd he do?" Belinda looked up to ask.

"He looked like he had no idea who I was, and then he bolted into the house."

We all chuckled sinisterly, and when I said, "Mine works on Capitol Hill," the laughter grew until Belinda and I plummeted back on our respective beds and held our aching stomachs.

Allison kicked in the air, and when we came back up again, she said sarcastically, "So how was your *date*?"

"Nice," I said. "You know, not every guy is an assailant."

She was biting the inside of her cheek, and I hoped she wasn't wishing some awful fate on me the way she had her offender.

But the other two—Leah with the depression and Belinda with the anxiety—seemed to look at me as though I had two heads. Leah's mouth was half open, and she was taking deep breaths, and Belinda was blinking her eyes over and over as though I were certifiable.

"*What?*" I asked. "Why are y'all staring at me?"

"How can you date?" Allison said.

"Because I'm not dead," I said.

I thought of a verse that Shannon had sent me, and I said it out loud: "'There is hope for a tree, if it is cut down, that it will sprout again, and that its tender shoots will not cease.' That's Job 14 something—"

Allison waved away the words and shook her head in a kind of bitter disbelief. "So you're religious. That explains it."

Leah and Belinda chuckled behind her.

"Back to my fantasy," she said. "I've got it all worked out in my mind." And she went through a step-by-step castration plan that would make Lorena Bobbitt look like a peacemaker.

We finally decided to call it a night.

"Keep in touch," Leah said to me, and then we all exchanged numbers and addresses.

After they plodded back to their separate rooms in their shackles of pain, I could hear Allison's television turn on in the room to the right of mine, then the squeak-squeak of Belinda rocking back and forth in what I imagined was the fetal position in the room to the left.

After crawling into bed, the hotel chocolate from my pillow melting in my mouth, I thought about Devon Hunt and his telescope and the stars on the campus hillside, as the sound of cab horns and screeching breaks wafted up and into my window. As I fell asleep, I wondered what had become of him.

∽

"May I write you?" Tobias asked the next morning after we ordered our pancakes and coffee.

He had been sitting in a lobby chair facing the elevators when the steel doors slid open at 7:02 that morning. I was blotting my lipstick on an old Kmart receipt when he stood up to greet me.

"Sure," I said. "I love to get mail. With the exception of bad poetry."

He reached out and took my hand before fixing his eyes on me. Either the poetry thing went right over his head, or he didn't give a hoot about anything other than my "Sure."

∽

Tobias wrote me every day for the next eight weeks before he and his communications director, Glenda Lyles, traveled down to NBU to interview Cecelia, Dr. Atwood, and me for their newsletter. When I was giving him the campus tour on the early October afternoon of his visit, he stopped as the fiery-colored leaves fell down and around us on the quadrangle, took my hand again, and said, "You're very important to me, Adelaide. I really want us to get to know each other. There could be something here between us."

I nodded and gave him a wide grin. After all, he was handsome, tenderhearted, socially conscious, and we didn't share the same gene pool.

"What's not to like?" I said to Ruthie and Jif after he left. They were lounging in the snack bar, watching *Thirtysomething* reruns and eating junk food.

"He's a looker, that's for sure," Jif said, sucking on a Tootsie Pop. "I mean, those cobalt eyes. C'mon!"

Jif was in a better place once again. She was not concerned about her weight, because it would be months before school was out. Also, she was making a real effort to circle the wagons and spend time with her old friends before graduation.

"Yeah, but more important, he's nice, and he seems to respect you," Ruthie added.

Jif pulled a bag of jelly beans out of her bag and offered it to us before declaring, "Go for it, Adelaide! You deserve a fresh romance, girl."

∽

*God, I really like Tobias,* I prayed as I meandered out of the library that evening and watched a couple embracing at the top of the colonnade.

I hadn't been writing my thesis or preparing my graduate-school applications. Instead, I'd been going over the campus map and marking off every twenty yards where an emergency "attack" button could be installed. The plan was due to the engineer the next morning.

As a couple walked arm in arm through the pillars, I thought of Tobias and his affectionate gaze that afternoon on the quad, and my heart leaped.

"Someone likes *me*!" I grinned. "Someone really wants to *get to know* me!" And I skipped (landing awkwardly and saving myself at the last second from a sprained ankle). It was a big-time confidence booster, and I welcomed it with open arms. It was about dern time!

*Wait,* I might have heard the third voice say, but I was too excited to tune to that station. Rather, I began to connect the loose dots in my mind so as to convince myself that a relationship with Tobias was right.

~

"He sounds neat," Shannon told me during a phone conversation halfway across the country. She had ended up at Wheaton and was majoring in theology. She was planning to serve with a team of inner-city missionaries in Colombia, South America, as soon as she graduated.

"How's your thesis coming?" I asked her.

"It's a breeze," she said. "You know, just a little ol' examination of the sanctification process."

"Sanctifa-who?" I said as I continued to picture Tobias saying, "I think there could be something good between us."

"Well, it's complicated. I mean, it's like after you receive salvation, then you go through a process where the Holy Spirit brings all that you are into obedience and conforms everything about you to the standards of His Word."

"Heady stuff," I said. "Fill me in more one of these days."

"You'd be fascinated by it, and it would make for great poetry."

"Really?"

"Yeah, it's rich. It's like the spiritual you has passed from death to life, and now the natural you—the human flesh part—has to pass from life to death. Or to put it another way, just like a tree has to shed its dead leaves in order to thrive, so we have to let the Holy Spirit subdue our fallen nature."

"Mmm," I said, not really attempting to comprehend the notion. My mind was still on my new romance, and I was a Homer Simpson, stumped in my thought processes by the image of a glazed donut. I blushed as I described Tobias's sweet, doughy goodness to my friend.

"Well, he sounds great," Shannon said. "But is he great for you?"

"Yes, he is!" I declared a few minutes later as I hung up the phone, and from that point forward I couldn't put on the brakes. Dr. Atwood was calling on me constantly, and I was reworking Peño's case before the first hearing in November. Tobias phoned me every night, and I melted into his warm voice at the other end of the line. It felt so good to be adored and to be on the front line of an important issue, and I couldn't resist falling in love with him and his role in the fight against violence.

While he was sensitive, he was also tenacious, and he found excuses to come down to NBU to visit. Also, he invited me up twice to DC when his organization needed a student to speak on behalf of the victims.

I almost breathed easy on that quick flight up to National Airport even though the landing and takeoff unnerved me. I still remembered the 1982 crash of Flight 90 into the Fourteenth Street Bridge. I was eleven at the time it aired on the nightly news as my family and I ate dinner on our den trays and watched the icy horror unfold. I'd had nightmares about the plane plummeting into the Potomac River, and if I closed my eyes, I could still see the rescue workers pulling the handful of survivors out of the freezing water.

"This is the shortest runway in the country," a businessman told me when my white knuckles clutched the seat beside him one Sunday afternoon just before the ascent that would deliver me back to Roanoke.

"I really needed to know that," I muttered, looking out the window.

Behind the thick airport glass, I could see Tobias, who was still pacing at the departure gate where he'd gently kissed me good-bye. He knew I hated the takeoffs, and he wanted to see me through it. How dear he was!

I had finally shared the story of my conversion with him that weekend after a Violence Against Women awareness dinner at the Watergate Hotel.

"I know you're spiritual," he'd said, squeezing my hand when I told him exactly how I'd become a convert.

"So, I haven't ever really heard from you on the subject. What about *your* faith?" I asked. I was a novice Christian, but even so I knew I needed to be with someone who was on the same page.

"Well, you know I don't go to church every week or anything," he said. "But I'm open to that. I grew up in the Unitarian Church, and I have good memories of my time there. But I think *doing* something is the best way to get in touch with the divine. And with Rachel's Rape, I like to think I'm doing something every day to help someone somewhere. I think God can see that, don't you?"

After he said this, he repositioned me on the inside of the sidewalk. He said he always wanted to be on the outside so that he could protect me from a speeding car or a daredevil cyclist. And he had practically shrieked with fear when I'd gotten turned around in the subway earlier in the day and nearly boarded a train for the rough inner-city neighborhood of Anacostia. I'd noticed that his forehead was wet with anxiety after he pulled me out of the train compartment just before the doors shut and prodded me down the escalator to the next platform. He had taken a towelette out of his back pocket and patted his forehead while we waited for the train to take us to Capitol Hill, where he had promised me a tour.

"I'm fine, Tobias," I'd said, sensing his shortness of breath.

Then he walked me to his coworker's apartment just off DuPont Circle. Glenda Lyles was a thirtysomething African-American lady who had worked at an array of Washington nonprofits from the Hunger and Homelessness Alliance to the National Organization of Women, and she had taken me in during my two visits to DC.

Glenda's spare bedroom smelled like cinnamon and Ivory soap, and I loved to stay with her because of this and because she kept the place so warm that you didn't even need to put on socks when your toes hit the tiles of her bathroom floor.

"Good night, Adelaide," he said to me before buzzing up to Glenda at the top of the brownstone steps.

"I wish you just lived here," he whispered, his voice making the edge of my ear tingle. "Wish you could just glide on home with me to Adams Morgan and stay there forever." His eyes glistened beneath the glow of the streetlight, and the laughter that poured from an apartment next door made me smile.

"Maybe one day," I said.

(Randy had been dating the cheerleader off and on at this point, and I considered Tobias and the cheerleader to be acts of grace that allowed us both to broaden our horizons. But then again, I didn't want to hear all the details from Georgianne.)

Tobias winked at me once, then squeezed my hand. "Breakfast before your flight, okay?"

"Sure," I said. "I'll meet you at Starbucks."

"Meet me, no. I'll swing by and pick you up at eight."

Feeling a poem coming on now, I closed the door to Glenda's guest room and fumbled through my backpack for a pencil. My fingers sifted through the crud in the front pocket: a handful of lint, three dull pennies, the last mint in a tube of Breath Savers, and the St. Christopher medal. I rubbed it with my index finger before it dropped back down into the pocket.

The poem was sappy and superheroesque.

> He worships
> with his hands
> on paper
> petitioning
> for protection.

(I trashed it.)

*Seek ye first,* the third voice surfaced as Glenda's guest-bedroom pillow cushioned my head, but I was intoxicated by the laughter from the apartment next door—trying to piece together the conversations as if they were the definition of bliss and well within my reach. I fell asleep breathing in the cinnamon and the romantic love that was saturating my heart with its gratifying scent.

At 4:00 a.m. I awoke in blackness, the hum from a busted street lamp
sounding off across the street. My heart raced as I suddenly pictured
Rachel during the last days before she took her life, and in the quiet I
wrote:

> The morning
> claws its way
> into your quiet room—
> white light
> through a thick pane.
> You wake as a child
> blinking twice
> before memory,
> the edge of a hoe
> in a fertile
> garden,
> digs up
> the blackest soil.

Tobias rang the doorbell at 8:00 a.m. sharp the next morning, carrying a bouquet of pink tulips wrapped in waxy green paper.

*Seriously perfect*, I thought, looking at his damp blond hair curling
up from the back of his neck and an overlooked tuft of shaving cream
tucked in the curve of his ear. When I hugged him, he smelled clean
and manly all at the same time, and I thought I might never let go.

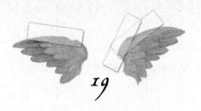

# Senior Year

I cringed when I received two letters from my professors one early December morning.

"The first portion of your thesis is overdue," Professor Dirkas had written me. "What's going on, Adelaide?"

And then another from Dr. Shaw, "You've skipped two classes in the last week. Are you all right? You'll need to get with a classmate to catch up before finals."

I had been so wrapped up in the campus-assault stuff—the placing of the attack buttons, the interviews, and the letters that came pouring in after the *60 Minutes* show aired in October—that I could barely keep up with my schoolwork.

Two letters had been slipped under my dorm-room door late at night. One said, "Thank you (from an anonymous victim)." Another said, "It still happens."

I took these victim letters as a sign to keep going, and I became consumed once again with my role on the student life committee and my budding relationship with Tobias.

"Randy's still waiting on you," Georgianne said when she called one night.

"But that cheerleader is bull-headed, and he can't hold out forever."

"I think I'm falling for someone else," I said.

"Well, don't expect *me* to tell him," she said.

By the end of the fall semester of my senior year, I received a C– in Dr. Shaw's Advanced Religious Studies class and a C+ from Professor Hirsch on the first installment of my Flannery O'Connor thesis. Then I botched my GREs and put a halfhearted effort toward applying to MFA school, and in the spring of my senior year, I received four complimentary rejection letters that encouraged me to try again in a few years with a larger body of work and, hopefully, a matured literary voice. *Ouch,* I thought as I read those words in the campus post office while sneakers squeaked across the linoleum and a small herd of senior frat boys guffawed in a corner as they read their own employment rejection letters before pinning them to a kiosk in the center of the hall. *Maybe it's not meant to be,* I said to myself as Frankie crept up behind me, resting his chin on my shoulder.

"Bummer," he said. "Let's get a pint of Cherry Garcia and rant on the quad."

"Let's," I said, handing the letter over to him. He ripped it into tiny strips before throwing it into the trash can on our way out.

Cecelia Honeycutt had won her case against Kevin Youngblood, and he was expelled in February 1993.

After his expulsion hit the local papers, Dr. Atwood lined up an interview with *Mademoiselle* magazine for Cecelia and me, and soon after, *Seventeen* magazine called to see if we would be willing to be on the cover of the "Off to College" issue that would be in print in June. Our story had an unusual hook: I had been quiet for two years until

I saw what happened to Cecelia, and we spurred each other on in the name of justice.

Yes, my fight against campus assault was my priority for now. And even though I went with Ruthie to vespers on Sunday night, the remembrance of my dance on the Magnolia Club dance floor, two years ago was tightly sealed in a box in my mind like the molded Christmas ornaments in the hot and humid Williamstown attic. Who had time to see about them?

I truly believed that my Maker wanted me to help make people aware of the crime. To have a little part in making men think twice and making women wise up and not put themselves in vulnerable situations. But when I missed both of Harriet's plays because of previous committee commitments and interviews, I began to wonder.

Harriet wrote in an e-mail marked "High Importance":

What is up with you, Adelaide? Even Jif made it up here for my spring play. And so did Marguerite avec walker, and even my mother, for God's sake! I was the writer and the director, and it was the O'Connor Redemption story this time. When you missed the one in the fall, I gave you the benefit of the doubt, but now that you missed the last one before graduation, I am truly bummed out and concerned about the ordering of your priorities. It sounds like I'm going to see your face on a magazine rack before I get to see you in person. What gives? And what did the MFA schools say? Are you going to move to NYC with me after graduation?

Harriet

The e-mail hit me between the eyes. I wrote back with a simple "I'm sorry. Rejected from graduate schools. Let's talk via phone."

What *would* I be doing after graduation? It was March, and the thought had just now occurred to me. Normally, my parents would have been pressing me on this, but the final divorce proceedings were drawing near, and their lawyers were keeping them occupied as they duked it out over their meager assets. No one else in the Piper family could see past April 25, when Greta and Zane would officially be torn asunder.

Now Jif was going to go home to Williamstown after graduation to get a boob job and work in her father's office until she could get back in at *Vanity Fair* in Manhattan. Marny wanted to spruce her up before she went back to New York, and she needed to earn some extra money so she could float as an intern for a few months before she got in on the payroll as an assistant to one of the editors.

"I can go for Diet Coke runs for six months if I save enough before heading back," Jif had said when we tried on our caps and gowns that spring. "As long as I land that job sometime after that, I'll be golden. Then I'm going to claw my way up to the feature section. Just watch me."

Ruthie was interested in teaching psychology in a high school, and she was applying for a Teach for America job as well as some in the Charlotte public school system.

~

Every now and then a collective female scream would breakout on the quad or in the dining hall as several NBU couples became engaged. It was sort of like a flu that was spreading around campus, and several couples that had been dating for six-plus months decided to band together and tie the knot shortly after graduation so they wouldn't have to enter the real world alone. I was surprised to see how quickly the frat-boy seniors followed the lead of their pretty girlfriends on this, but I guessed they were as scared and lost as everyone else, and they were willing to say, "I do," to make themselves feel better.

"I'm holding out," Jif said to Frankie, Ruthie, and me as we pic-nicked under the elm tree that March.

A Northeastern blonde named Porter had just strolled by us, staring at her own two-carat diamond as it caught the afternoon light. It was making little crystal-shaped rainbows on the sidewalk, and we were worried that she might bump into the next tree, she was so engrossed in admiring her finger.

"I'm not going to attach myself to one of these beasts," Jif whispered as we watched Porter run suddenly into the arms of her fiancé, an unshaven Sigma named Craig.

"Hey, what am I, canned spam?" Frankie said.

"What *are* you, Mr. Harmony?" Jif said. "That's the question we'd all like to know."

Frankie grinned and kicked at the green grass. "Wouldn't you, Beauty Queen. So what kind of guy are you holding out for?"

"After being in New York that summer, I saw that our options can be a lot better if we're willing to bide our time."

Ruthie, who ironically had her head on better than anyone else these days, said, "You know, I do think we should wait a few years. We might not even know what we want yet." She had not dated anyone seriously since Tag Eisley, but she exuded a rare kind of confidence and hope when it came to the subject. "It will happen."

"It is a predicament, though, isn't it?" Jif said. "I mean, once we've graduated, we're off the parental and scholarly dole. We have to make it on our own as single women."

"And men," Frankie said.

Jif continued, "It's easy to see why folks want to go into it together."

Of course, I was head over heels with Tobias and certainly fantasized about marrying him, though there were some things about him that were beginning to annoy me. First and foremost: his family. I met them for the first time over Thanksgiving break. Mr. and Mrs. Moore were benign, but they were astonishingly dull and somewhat morose. Each meal they had together was in near silence. All you could hear was the clink of flatware against porcelain and an occasional "Can you pass the salt?"

They had little to say to each other or to me, and this drove me wild. I had cleared my throat and tried to prod them into a conversation.

"Can you all explain to me the carpool lane into the beltline? I entered it by accident the other day and was afraid I'd get pulled over."

"Gotta have three passengers to enter during rush hour," Mr. Moore said between slurps of cranberry sauce. "Cuts down on vehicles in the city."

"Oh," I said. "Sounds like a worthy idea to me."

Tobias grinned in my direction. The Moores cut their turkey, and I went in again.

"Have you all taken in the Warhol exhibit at the National Gallery?"

*Chew. Chew. Swallow. Clink.*

"Come again?" Mrs. Moore said.

"Warhol, you know? The *Campbell's Soup, Marilyn Monroe, Twelve Electric Chairs* works?"

"Yes, we're familiar," she said. She studied me as though I had something black between my teeth. Mr. Moore cleared his throat and salted his potatoes.

"We've lived in Washington a long time," he said.

Mrs. Moore nodded, and I rolled my eyes.

"Oh, so you guys are, like, over the exhibits of world-renowned artists?"

*Swallow. Clink. Clink. Chuckle. Clearing of the throat. Silence.*

"Was your family always this quiet?" I asked Tobias later as we walked around the cul-de-sacs of the Vienna, Virginia, suburb where he'd grown up. "Or are they still in some kind of zombielike mourning for Rachel?"

"Adelaide!" he said. It was the loudest I'd ever heard him. He crushed the breath mint in his mouth instead of his usual sucking it to smithereens. "They're my parents. They are what they are, and they always have been. They're good people, you know?"

"I'm sorry," I said, a little surprised by my callousness. He had not yet had the opportunity to meet my folks, but I was relieved about that since they were in the middle of a bitter divorce (and fairly wacky to begin with).

He had met Dizzy, though, when she took a trip up to DC to study for a weekend with a pastry chef from the Vidalia restaurant. I had flown up to meet her, and we both stayed in Glenda's guest room, warm and snug in her aromatic digs. Tobias and I had taken her out to lunch during her class break. She had wanted to try the new Thai restaurant that the Vidalia chef had recommended, but since Tobias couldn't do Thai, we had settled for TGIFriday's and three orders of the grilled chicken salad.

"He's a nice guy," Dizzy said that night as we were crawling into bed. "And hot too. But it's just . . ." Dizzy hesitated.

"What?" I asked.

"He's kinda bland. And he probably, like, hates his blandness, and that's why he's doing this whole "stop rape" thing. To break away from his sensitive-stomach self. You know?"

"Maybe," I said, my wall of defense hardening like the curved back of a fearful cat. "He's a good guy. You just aren't used to it, that's all."

"C'mon, Adelaide," Dizzy said. "He's totally bland. Not that that's bad. I mean, it's safe . . . and predictable. Is that what you want?"

The other thing that rankled me about his parents was that they were neat freaks and experts in emergency preparedness, like him. If he carried towelettes in his back pocket, then they carried thick cases of baby wipes and Spray 'n Wash sticks in their briefcases and glove compartments. For Christmas they had given me a car escape hammer complete with a knife to cut my seat belt if I were trapped in an accident and a flashlight to help me see if I were underwater. The end of the hammer had a sharp-pointed metal knob that would effectively break through the thick windshield glass to allow escape. I thought this was particularly strange, since I didn't own a car, and even if I did, I was sure I would have lost the little contraption somewhere beneath the floor mats before I ever needed to use it.

Their house was boring too. A split-level with orange brick, and each room was lined with IKEA plastic cabinets and furniture that had surely been ordered in one fell swoop from Rooms to Go.

They were both government employees. Mr. Moore was an upper-level administration manager at the IRS, and Mrs. Moore was in accounting at the Social Security Department. Tobias would have been an accountant, too, if it hadn't been for Rachel's rape and untimely death.

Now, Rachel, on the other hand, had obviously been the one in the family who had the spark. I could see it in their childhood photos, where she made funny faces, her bright eyes monopolizing the camera. She was a thespian. A singer. And an art history major with a trip lined up to study for a semester in Florence just after she took her own life.

Mr. Moore blew his nose and Mrs. Moore did her crossword puzzle that weekend as the clock ticked away the Thanksgiving holiday. And I could see why Tobias had chosen to break out of the mold when the opportunity presented itself.

But had he really done it? Sure, he lived in the edgy Adams Morgan, but his apartment was as stale and antiseptic as his folks's place. If you went into his closet, you could see every suit in a plastic casing spread inches apart from the others and each pair of loafers lined up on the floor, their open mouths reminding me of a choir practicing its scales.

"Do you see that?" I asked as I stared down at his cognac, black, and chocolate shoes.

"What?" he asked, following my eyes toward his closet.

"Your shoes—the way they're all lined up like that, they look like open mouths singing."

He shook his head as if he didn't have the faintest idea what universe I was from.

To top it off, he had an equally boring roommate, Tom Rhys from Herndon, Pennsylvania, who was a public policy grad student at GW. Tom Rhys cleaned the apartment after breakfast every Saturday morning, and I always felt nauseous when I visited the place on the weekend because of the overwhelming fumes of Clorox and Comet seething up from the countertops.

Yes, the man who loved me was an activist with the soul of a bean counter, and sometimes I wondered how long before he'd revert completely back to the person he would have become had he not lost his sister.

⁓

When Tobias showed up unexpectedly on the NBU campus that April afternoon with a jewelry-box-shaped bulge in the side of his pants, I was floored.

We had been walking along the back quad when he simply knelt down on the knoll and proposed, just yards away from Ruthie's blooming tree.

"Adelaide, you know I'm in love with you. I believe in who you are, and your voice against violence is so sincere. Marry me and be my partner at Rachel's Rape as we fight this together."

As he knelt there, completely unconcerned about the grass stain that was surely forming on the knee of his khakis, I could sense a small crowd of girls and guys gathering around campus to watch this proposal.

These snapshots flashed across my mind: Luigi's kiss, Randy's cupola, and Brother Benton's proclamation about winning my hand someday.

I was shocked that this was actually happening. It was unexpected. My stomach was rising up to meet my throat.

I looked out at the folks on the quad, who were grinning and squeezing one another's arms in excitement. Then back to dear Tobias on his knee, looking up at me with those sensitive blue eyes that had shed many a tear over the victim letters I'd read to him over the course of the last several months.

Who'd have thought that I would be among those being proposed to before graduation? I could easily count my suitors on one hand my whole college career, and here I was with a handsome, tenderhearted twenty-six-year-old man who wanted to make me his wife.

Stopping for a moment to hear the third voice, a silence reverberated through my chest. Nothing.

Tobias looked up at me with such longing and expectation. He was beginning to wobble a little, and I knew I had to respond before he lost his balance.

I nodded in agreement to his proposal before he had to put his hand down to steady himself. Then he stood and placed the perfectly sized diamond platinum ring on my finger before picking me up and swinging me around as the little clumps of onlookers clapped.

"No way!" Jif Ferguson said on her way to her chemistry class. She let out a joyful squeal, followed by laughter and then a shout. "Adelaide Piper is engaged to be married!"

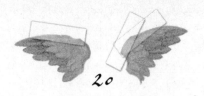

# Betrothed

When I called my parents to announce my engagement, they were shocked.

"We haven't even met him!" Mama said, and Daddy gave a steamy "That boy didn't have the grace to come down here and ask me for your hand? I don't know what to make of all this, sister!"

I tried to calm their nerves. When they wanted second and third opinions, I asked Dizzy to vouch for Tobias, as well as Ruthie and Jif. Mama's and Daddy's fears were assuaged when they rewound their videos of my *60 Minutes* segment and picked him out of the panel. He impressed them both with his good looks and with his sense of duty to fight for others on behalf of his sister.

So, in the end, they decided to let me make my own decision about whom I wanted to marry.

It was strange to be planning a wedding when my parents' divorce was almost official. Like someone dying and being born on the same day. It reminded me of how my great-uncle Graydon had died in the same hospital on the same day that Dizzy was born.

"They passed each other on the way," Mae Mae was fond of saying.

No, it didn't feel quite right to be picking out silver and china patterns when Mama and Daddy's court date was approaching at a rapid pace.

But Tobias wanted to be married before the New Year, and so the plans were well under way for a Christmas wedding at St. Anne's Episcopal Church and a reception at the Magnolia Club.

"Marrying a Yankee?" Papa Great said to me over the phone one morning when Mae Mae phoned me about the caterer. "Doesn't surprise me a bit."

Mae Mae jerked the phone out of his hand and said, "Adelaide, don't you listen to him. Tobias sounds wonderful, and Juliabelle and I will see to it that this wedding will be among the most elegant Williamstown has ever witnessed."

"Better now?" Juliabelle asked, picking up the phone somewhere else in the house. (We had never spoken long-distance before.)

"Yes, ma'am," I said. "You're going to like this boy, Juliabelle. He's a sweetheart."

"Well," she said, chuckling with hope, "this family needs something good to worry on."

⌣

Since I had so much on my plate with graduating and moving to Washington to start the new job at Rachel's Rape, I decided to leave the matter of the wedding in Mae Mae's capable hands. I was the first of the Williamstown debs in my set to get married, so my photo and engagement announcement were plastered on the front page of the local newspaper and listed as well in the state paper.

*Eat your heart out, Papa Great and Averill Skaggs.*

Harriet, Jif, Ruthie, and Georgianne agreed to be my bridesmaids, and Dizzy and Lou seemed happy to share the spotlight as the maids of honor. Jif had ordered several bridesmaid catalogs and circled some of the gowns she thought would be most flattering on the wide array of figures in the wedding party. She slipped them one by one under my dorm-room door so that when I returned from a night of

thesis research in the library, I could hardly cross my threshold without slipping on the glossy pages.

I was thumbing through a book of Watters & Watters gowns one
late April night when Dizzy called to say, "It's official. Mom and Dad
are divorced."

Was it April 25 already? I was angry at myself for not remembering the court date, and then I was surprised by the tears that followed.
They flooded my eyes, and my whole body shook with grief. The pink
and blue satin gowns in the magazine were turning a muddled shade
of gray from my tears, and I wondered why this was hitting me so
hard now. After all, it had been coming for more than a year.

"I freaked out too," Dizzy said. "Bawled right into my baklava,
and Professor Anatole, the pastry-making Nazi, told me to throw the
whole dish out."

I chuckled through my tears, but still it hurt. I supposed that no
matter how old you are, when your parents decide to rip apart the
one flesh that they once had become, you will inevitably find yourself in the center of the seam.

"You're lucky, Ad. At least you aren't down here with it in your
face all the time. You'll go from NBU to DC and never have to sleep
a night in that sad old house again."

*Sad old house.* I had never known it to be a sad old house. Sure, it
had been the place where I cultivated my desire to escape Williamstown, and it had also been the shelter where Dizzy hid her dark life
beneath the black clothes until the DUI made her come clean. But
that home had been a safe and nurturing womb for me, and it had
cradled me from my childhood.

"It's for sale, you know."

"Huh?"

"Yeah. The Ice Lady figured they should split the profit to cover
the legal fees. If it goes fast, you'll have to come down here sometime
before you get married and get your stuff."

Getting married. Though I had enjoyed looking at the china patterns and bridesmaid's gowns, I had pushed aside the actual thought

of the sacred event that was going to take place in my hometown church between Tobias and me eight short months from now. My heart had been on my thesis ever since the proposal. I was working hard on my second draft in hopes that I could bring my GPA up a smidge so that I could walk down the graduation aisle with President Schaeffer remarking, "With honors," after my name.

I had not let myself truly stop and think about the day after graduation and the new life that would begin for me in Washington.

"Fry one fish at a time," Daddy used to say to me when I'd get overwhelmed with my schoolwork. Once I had two tests and a term paper due my junior year of high school, and he told me to give him my backpack and ask for only one textbook at a time before moving on to the next subject. And that is just what was happening. My focus was on graduation, and I would deal with the rest of my life the day after I donned my cap and gown.

And while Mae Mae and Juliabelle were planning the wedding, Tobias was planning our new life inside the beltline. He had recently let me know that Glenda was downsizing to a studio apartment in her same building, and so the new plan was that I would live with his parents in Vienna, Virginia, until the wedding. They had a finished room over their garage that would serve as a suitable place for me to live temporarily.

Starting our married life in his hip city apartment would have been great with me, but he wanted to move to Arlington once we tied the knot. To settle down just outside the city so that we could enjoy a quick commute and a safer place to lay our heads. He planned to research the market over the summer so that we could get just what we wanted before the big day.

"Are you okay?" Dizzy asked now after the long silence of my reeling thoughts on the other end of the line.

Outside, a security guard was testing the new night lighting system that Dr. Atwood and I had designed, and the bright fluorescent lights flashed on and off on the quad like a silent warning.

"Yeah," I said, but I didn't know for sure.

Graduation was anticlimactic. It rained cats and dogs the day before, and instead of being held on the pristine quad, the ceremony took place in the gymnasium, where the muckety-muck keynote speaker's voice reverberated off the padded walls of the basketball court, and no one could understand a word of what he was saying.

A surge of terror rose up in my throat as I watched my parents sitting on opposite sides of the gymnasium and Tobias front and center, staring me down with his dogged adoration.

The night before graduation, my family had endured a painful dinner at Dr. Atwood's home on faculty row. The dean had offered to host us privately so that my folks could have a quiet setting in which to meet Tobias for the first time.

Daddy surprised everyone when he showed up with a black '64 convertible Mustang that he'd bought in Statesville on his way up the mountain.

Mama scoffed as he called us out the door to take a gander.

"Like he can afford *that*," she murmured, accepting a full glass of Dean Atwood's chardonnay. Mama never took a drink, and the acidity in her voice made me wince. For the first time I could really remember, a fury rose in my throat toward my father. Why did he have to slip the whole rug out from under her?

Then Daddy turned his attention to my fiancé. He put the metal-pincher grip of his prosthetic on poor Tobias's hand when they were officially introduced in the dean's living room, and I guessed that Daddy was getting back at him for not having asked him for my hand as Southern tradition dictates.

"Sorry," Daddy said as Tobias pulled his hand back and then down between his legs as he crouched over in pain. "I should have given you my good hand."

Then Daddy looked me in the eyes as Tobias inspected his throbbing red palm.

Mama shooed Daddy out of the way as if he didn't amount to a hill of beans, and she gave Tobias a well-rehearsed hug as well as a little gift bag that contained a framed photo of me as a young girl.

In the photo, I was four years old and sitting on the pine straw in the front yard, smiling up at the camera with my big, brown eyes. I was wearing an old-fashioned smocked dress, and my dirty bare feet were peeking out from beneath the hemline.

"Thank you," Tobias said as he rubbed his sore hand and smiled sincerely at Mama. "I will treasure this."

Then he looked to Daddy and back to Mama and said, "I love your daughter, and I always will."

"Dinner is served!" Dr. Atwood interrupted with a blackened spatula in her hand. She wasn't much of a cook, so we suffered through her tough pork tenderloin and crunchy risotto. My heart felt as heavy as the sheets of steel loaded onto the containers in the Williamstown port that night as I listened to the strange blend of voices that made up the different pieces of my life. Mama was talking up Dizzy's culinary prowess and Lou's rising grades at Trident Academy, while Daddy showed the Bizway plan to Tobias by drawing strange little ovals down the side of a paper towel and assuring his future son-in-law that the business was approved by the Federal Trade Commission.

Dr. Atwood talked over everyone about what I had meant to NBU and what we had accomplished together, but I was tired of thinking about campus policy and refused to contribute to the conversation.

Then Daddy and Mama got into it as we choked down the charred crème brûlée. Mama had mentioned something about Papa Great's role in keeping the unions out of the textile mills, and Daddy said that he was as happy as a clam to be the heck out of that doomed industry.

"So happy you were willing to dishonor your parents and give up your family?" Mama murmured, staring him in the eye as he attempted to get his prosthetic around Dr. Atwood's china cup for a sip of decaf coffee.

He spewed coffee across the table at her and said, "You wouldn't care a lick about what I wanted as long as it fit your perfect little picture of how life should be."

Then he looked over to Tobias, wiping coffee out of his eye with the corner of Dr. Atwood's navy linen napkin, and said, "She'd have me chained to some wall in a dungeon as long as she was happy!"

"Hush, Daddy!" I yelped midway between the sitting and standing position. I had jumped up so quickly that the table was rocking slightly, and Tobias thrust his hand forward to catch Dizzy's coffee cup before it overturned.

Dr. Atwood cleared her throat and looked conspicuously at her wristwatch, and Daddy looked me grievously in the eye as though the last member of his reconnaissance team had betrayed him. Had pushed him out of the foxhole, leaving his hide exposed.

He threw down his napkin on his dessert plate. "Thank you for the hospitality, Miss Atwood. Please excuse me."

Then he stormed out the door before anyone could call him back and sped down the hill, his Mustang sputtering over the speed bumps that led to the campus gates.

Now I felt completely alone in the gymnasium on my graduation day as I stared out at the faces that lined each row of bleachers. When they called my name up to receive my diploma, I was reminded of the .08 decimal point I lacked, and so instead of having "with honors" attached to my name, I walked up and across the stage as simply "Miss Adelaide Piper."

After the ceremony, I said my good-byes to Jif, Ruthie, Frankie, and my professors.

"Remember your poetry," Professor Dirkas told me as I hugged him good-bye. His recent chapbook about a couple adopting a baby from Guatemala had just been nominated for the Pushcart Prize, and I was thrilled for him.

"Dirkas is right," Dr. Shaw said as he and his toothless seven-year-old, Molly, ran over to tell me good-bye. "We expect to see *your* name in a publication soon."

"Can you write that on my next round of MFA applications?" I joked, and we all chuckled, knowing how disappointed I was that I had not been accepted.

"Hey, it took me three years to get into a program," Dirkas added. "The key to being a successful poet is acquiring thick skin."

"Thank you," I said to both of them, "for all you've done."

They both nodded, their humble way of saying, "You're welcome."

Molly broke the silence with, "Can I wear your dress, Dad?" in reference to Dr. Shaw's cap and gown.

What a beacon of decency those two professors had been to me when I was in my *Lord of the Flies* valley. They would never know how much their goodness had meant.

∾

I went back to my dorm room to meet my parents, who had to arrange separate times ten minutes apart to come by to bid me farewell.

*Daddy.* If it weren't for him, I never would have made it to NBU. Heck, I'd still be sporting my floaties for all I knew and staring at a storybook, wondering why the letters didn't make the right words.

When our eyes met in the dorm hall amid the pop of champagne corks and the squeal of packing tape being rolled across cardboard boxes, there was a double kind of shame between us. We both knew we had let each other down. Still, I hoped he would embrace me. Rub his good thumb across my jewel with pride.

"Good luck, sister," he said, getting only close enough to pat my shoulder.

He shook Tobias's hand with his flesh this time and turned toward the hall, looking back and forth in confusion before finding the back door that led to the parking lot.

∾

Tobias loaded up a U-haul with my stuff before we took one last look at the quadrangle and the colonnade. Though he was sensitive, my fiancé was still the possessor of a Y chromosome, and he rushed me into the car before I was ready.

"This is it, NBU," I mouthed out the window as two unhurried graduates threw a Frisbee back and forth on the hill, their black gowns split down the center to reveal their fraternity T-shirts, cut-off shorts and Tevas.

I rolled down the window to take one last breath of the pastoral scene. Out of the corner of my eye I could see the tombstones at the top of the cemetery hill, the dogwood blooms falling around them in a flutter of white. Then the grand Kappa Nu house with its Corinthian columns and rocking chairs, and I remembered racing there that spring night a year ago after Peño's distressing call and even farther back to when Peter Carpenter spun me around on the lawn my first night, freshman year.

And as we made the final curve before the exit gates, the image of Ruthie's elm tree appeared in the large side mirror on my door, its lush leaves swaying in the late-spring light. Just yesterday I had walked by it and seen the winged fruit forming beneath the blooms. In a few weeks the fruit would be carried off by the wind, and if one landed just so in a patch of fertile ground, the early shoots of another elm would appear, reaching up from the black mountain dirt.

When we turned onto the highway and away from the surrounding mountains that Daddy had named the "wise sages calling me to learn," a scream formed in my gut. I swallowed it, though, stuffed it down so as not to startle Tobias, and instead watched trancelike as the Blue Ridge gave way to the flat asphalt roads while we traveled the two hundred miles north to the Moore family F.R.O.G. (Furnished Room Over Garage) apartment at the end of a Vienna, Virginia, cul-de-sac.

"I'll see you at the office tomorrow," Tobias said to me after he settled me into my room above his parents' garage and prepared to head back to his apartment in the city. His blue eyes smiled straight through me, clueless to the terror written on my face. "It will be so amazing to work together, and I've already got you slated for a meeting with me on Capitol Hill with a senator who is fighting for us. I couldn't be happier, Adelaide."

I nodded quietly as a dark coolness filled my chest like the inside of a vault. Then I watched out the window as his sedan pulled out of the driveway. When he turned onto the main road, I looked up and out at all the cookie-cutter houses that lined the street. The walls in the F.R.O.G. were thin, and Mr. Moore was already snoring above the sound of *Headline News*.

The room was sparsely decorated with plastic furniture and a small bowl of potpourri that hadn't been refreshed in a year. I went over and took one whiff of it and smelled nothing. Then I wrote:

> Hurricane David
> lifted Papa's
> johnboat
> up and off
> the slip.
> It surely
> floated
> out of the river
> and into
> the Atlantic.
> We never
> saw it
> again.

Dare I say it, but I missed Williamstown. Missed Mae Mae and Papa Great's gracious home with the blooming magnolias adorning their garden, and the smell of pluff mud at low tide. If I closed my eyes, I could envision Mama's carefully tended hydrangeas and the yellow jasmine along the fence and the bees that buzzed around the summer flowers, gathering nectar. I missed Dale and Darla and Charlie Farley and the converted barbecue-joint church where I first learned about the plan of salvation. Heck, I even missed the stench of pulp and soot catching in my throat. It was terrible, but at least it was real.

*Snap out of it,* I said to myself, unpacking my cosmetic bag and lining the bottles of soap and hair products on the shelf over the bathroom sink. *Transition is always weird, but it'll get better.*

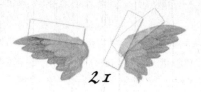

# The Singing Shoes

For the next month I boarded the subway and rode the forty-five minutes into the city to the office on K Street where Glenda, Tobias, and I fielded calls and researched campus policies on assault.

Everyone on my subway commute had to have been a government-employed accountant, I thought as they straightened their cheap ties and read their *Washington Post*s. I'd have preferred a straight shot into the inner city of Anacostia rather than the route from Vienna to McPherson Square. Just to glimpse a pocket of life. To see if the capital city had a soul.

After two weeks of meetings and long business lunches, Glenda presented me with a press release about my joining their team as well as my schedule of interviews. President Clinton was promising to sign the Violence Against Women Act, and NOW needed a handful of victims to speak before Congress, so Tobias was trying to arrange, through a sympathetic senator from his district, for me to be among that handful.

Glenda asked me to come up with an outline for my speech so we could present it first to Senator Carnes for his approval, and then she would coach me in the coming weeks before I gave my formal presentation on the Hill.

"Okay," I said, surprised by my lack of enthusiasm about speaking in the most powerful place in the known world. When I went to my little corner of the one-room office to brainstorm, I spent half a day staring at a blank page on an old computer screen.

I felt all talked out on the subject of campus rape and especially my own story, and after three false starts, I excused myself and ran out to the coffeehouse around the corner to grab a cappuccino and sit in the park, where I read the national section of a *New York Times* that I found between two slats on a bench. While four television networks had agreed to post warnings on violent shows and the Supreme Court ruled on the proper use of scientific evidence in the courtroom, the mighty Mississippi River was swelling uncontrollably and a five-hundred-mile stretch from St. Louis to St. Paul was closed down.

As I read, I thought of Frankie working as a reporter for his uncle at the *Atlanta Journal-Constitution* and Harriet in the Big Apple. She had gotten a job on the set of *Godspell*, which was playing in Soho, and she was having a ball as she served as the assistant director with one of her former professors. The professor had introduced her to Redemption Methodist, an exploding church that met in a downtown college auditorium and drew thousands of young professionals to its services. Harriet had sent me tapes of some of her pastor's sermons, but I hadn't had time to listen to them.

When I was on the streets of Washington, I felt best. Poems came to me instantly, and I scribbled them down in my little Rachel's Rape folder in my briefcase, though they had nothing to do with rape policy or even weddings and all to do with a deep-seated longing for something I couldn't quite name.

> As I ride
> the subway escalator
> up to street level
> the heat dissipates.
> On the corner
> there is the
> grind and dribble
> of an espresso

*machine*
*and a man*
*still snoozing*
*on the grate*
*which catches*
*my heel*
*as I pass.*

What was with me? It was a kind of restlessness. I had a strong desire to peel back the skin of the town to see if it had a pulse. I asked Tobias to take me to a poetry reading or out dancing or even to try a little exotic food sometime, but he was too busy assisting with the upcoming Violence Against Women Act to take a night off.

There was an Ethiopian restaurant that Dizzy had told me to try and a little place in Adams Morgan that was cooking the recipes from *Like Water for Chocolate*, a recent love story I'd devoured one night in the f.r.o.g. when I declined a dinner invitation from the Moores. (Instead of dining with the lackluster in-laws, I ate Nabs and drank Co-Cola and escaped into a beautiful Mexican world where unrequited love would not go quietly.)

"I'll go by myself, then," I told him one night as he walked me to the subway after a long day of work.

"Adelaide, that's not safe. I don't want you riding on the subway after dark."

Then I remembered Lazarus Greene from high school, and it took one call to information to get his voice on the other end of the line.

When we met at the Ethiopian restaurant, I threw my arms around him and he held me tightly for a moment. He still had that graceful gait, but he had filled out, and he pushed back his shoulders with a kind of self-assurance and strength. He sported a black oxford shirt and one small gold hoop earring in his left earlobe, and he had completely shaved the top of his head. It was smooth and perfect, like a bowling ball, and it caught the light of the afternoon sun as we sat beneath a blue café canopy and swept piles of beans and vegetables onto spongy bread out of a large, round pottery bowl.

"I'm glad you called," he said. He put his elbows on the table and clenched his fingers together, staring me in the eye. "I'm moving next month, and I would have missed you. I've thought about you a lot over the last few years, Adelaide."

"Really?" I said, grinning at his forthrightness and smooth grin.

"Yeah," he said, rocking his ball of hands between us. "You had *guts* to take me to that senior dance back in high school. I was probably a fool to go, but it's one of my best memories from Williamstown. And it helped me to see I had to get *out*."

"Yeah, well, you were the obvious choice," I said. "Bright, humorous, and handsome."

"So your fiancé must be all of those things?"

*Mmm.* "Bright and handsome, yes. But he's a little more on the serious side, I'd say."

"Well, it's a serious subject you guys are dealing with," he said. "Anyhow, most folks in DC are serious."

"Or boring," I said. "So where are you moving?"

"NYC. I was strong-armed by one of my English professors to be in a production of *Much Ado About Nothing* at the Kennedy Center my junior year, and it was the greatest thing I'd ever done. I had this epiphany, sort of, and I've been writing plays and acting in local productions since then. I still majored in journalism, but I want to give this theater thing a go and see what happens."

"That is really cool," I said. "My friend Harriet is in theater up there. I'll have to connect you."

"Sure," he said as he swiped the bill from the waitress before I had time to protest.

"You only go round once," he said. "Might as well make it count."

⌒

Lazarus walked me to the subway entrance that night, where a man playing the saxophone nodded as we exchanged numbers and hugged good-bye. Then he hopped on his bike and sped home toward his apartment on Volta Street. And I stood at the top of the escalator, watching him as he rounded the corner a few blocks down, dodging and ducking the honking cabs before pedaling smoothly away.

～

Like the kudzu that shrouds and distorts the trees and abandoned shacks along the Southern back roads, so the aftermath of an attack blurs the victim's sense of reality. She becomes a shaded tree buried in vines that keep her from seeing sunlight. But what about the kudzu itself? Does it know the damage it is doing?

The articles I was supposed to write for the Rachel's Rape newsletter became more and more creative, steeped in metaphor and symbolism, and, ultimately, tended to stray away from the subject.

"Your writing is beautiful," Glenda warned, "but this is going out to policy makers and campus administrators, so try to keep it concrete, okay?"

"Sorry," I said as Tobias and Glenda stormed up to the Hill to bend the ears of another congressman before the upcoming vote on the act.

I went back to the computer and changed the article to this:

Rachel's Rape supports victims and trains men in the prevention of sexual assault. We are proud to present the first national media campaign focusing on the role that men play in preventing crimes.

"Hello, Rachel's Rape," I said as I looked up from my computer screen to answer the phone.

"A-de-laide?"

The Southern drawl was unmistakable.

"Randy?" I said. I hadn't heard from him since he'd hung up on me when I told him I was engaged. "How in the world are you?"

"Good. Real good," he said. "How are you up there?"

"Oh, you know, it's kind of exciting working in the nation's capital and all."

"I know you always wanted an adventure like that," he said. "I'm proud of you."

"You aren't angry?" I asked.

"Not anymore," he said. "That's sort of why I'm calling."

"What's going on?"

"I'm getting married, too, Adelaide," he said.

My heart skipped a beat, and I felt the sting beneath my arms. Like a true Southern girl, I faked enthusiasm. "That's great! Who's the lucky girl? The cheerleader I've been hearing rumors about?"

"Yeah. Dodi was a cheerleader last year. She's from Greeleyville."

*Dodi is her name? Oh, good grief! It might as well be "Perky."*

"Greeleyville," I said. "The thriving metropolis. So when's the date?"

"I've got you beat there," he said, a hint of sadistic pleasure in his voice. "July 30."

"Next July?" I asked.

"No, this," he said.

"Good gravy, Randy! What—she knocked up?"

"Actually, she is," he said, and my face reddened with horror. That perky little cheerleader had his number, and there was no stopping this nuptial.

"Now, I know what you're thinking, 'cause I know you, Adelaide. You're thinking, *This is so Williamstown,* and you might be right about that. This isn't the way I always pictured things would end up, and that you well know. But this is the way things are, and after a lot of praying and talking to my folks, this is the right thing for me. She's a good girl, and I love her. I wanted you to know before I told anyone else in the family."

I blew a long, deep breath of something between acceptance and resignation. Randy was the kind of guy who loved to do the right thing, and I adored him for that. What did I expect him to do, wait for me forever? What a selfish you-know-what I'd been.

"I'm proud of you, Randy."

He chuckled faintly, as though he were on the other side of the world.

"I miss you, Adelaide. I wish you the best."

"Don't worry; I won't come to the wedding. I know that would be too weird."

"Yeah, I think so," he said.

"But I want to kiss that baby one day."

"You bet," he said. "He'll be here in October. Good-bye, now."

My office window faced the west side of the Hilton Hotel. Just above eye level I could see a housekeeping lady, fluffing up two pillows and folding down a bright blue bedspread before topping each side with a square of chocolate.

She looked up and squinted her eyes to see me. I was peering from around the computer at her, wondering how I ended up in this little office with a view of the fifth floor of a hotel.

When she looked away, I clutched the stapler by the phone and threw it, halfheartedly, at the wall behind me. It left a brown smudge above the fax machine before toppling off and into the recycling bin. Weeping into my palms, I pictured shucking oysters with Randy when I was thirteen and the cupola he'd built on top of his house that looked out across the sand dunes and into the Atlantic Ocean.

In my mind's eye I could see him cradling his baby boy in an elaborately embroidered christening gown, rocking him back and forth on the edge of Mae Mae's garden as the palmetto fronds rustled against one another and the Spanish moss swayed in the harbor breeze.

Tobias was focused on the cause. Day and night he wanted to discuss it with me. It was the very air he breathed, and he longed for it to be mine too. But on the days that he and Glenda left for Capitol Hill, I would turn on the answering machine and escape down to a pay phone in the lobby of the Hilton at the end of the block, where I tried to contact Harriet, Ruthie, or Jif to see how they were doing. (Shannon was out of reach in Bogotá, and everyone missed her.)

Occasionally I'd get Jif on the line, and she'd whine about how difficult the recovery from breast augmentation surgery was.

"Was it worth it?" I asked one afternoon, rolling my eyes. I loved Jif, but I just hated how her mind worked.

"Duh?" she answered with an unshakable faith. "They look great. You're going to be seriously jealous."

"Oh brother."

But usually I didn't get anyone on the phone, and instead I just sat down on the plush sofa and pretended that I was a tourist or the young wife of an ambassador. I'd order a white wine spritzer and watch the powerful patrons blaze in and out of the brass revolving doors in their muted silk ties and dark Italian shoes.

When that got old, I'd loll around the nearest blocks, gawking at the guards in front of the White House and the busy businesspeople everywhere pounding the blocks with their heavy briefcases, as if they had in their possession the very solution for world peace.

One afternoon, Tobias came up for air and took me out to look at potential newlywed apartments in Arlington.

As we drove over the Fourteenth Street Bridge into Virginia and exited off the GW parkway, we circled one high-rise settlement after another on the fringe of the beltline. As far as I could see, Arlington had all the leftover remnants of what is bad about the city (littered roads and smoggy air), with none of the beauty or energy.

"What's wrong?" Tobias asked when I pooh-poohed three different shoe-box apartments on low floors of the square high-rises.

The institutional-looking buildings reminded me of the communist housing that Harriet and I had seen on a train ride from Budapest to Prague two summers ago.

"Can't we find something with a smidge of character?" I asked.

He bit the inside of his cheek and looked at me as though I were a riddle he couldn't quite solve.

One Thursday in late July, when I was to present my speech to Senator Carnes in hopes of serving as a witness for the upcoming hearing, Tobias and Glenda left before me for the Hill so that I could have some time to rehearse in the one-room suite before showtime.

I started to practice, but when Mae Mae sent a mock-up of our wedding invitation through the fax machine for my approval, I tucked it in my briefcase and walked across K Street and into a lovely bookstore named Chapters. Randy's wedding was tomorrow night, and I didn't want to think about matrimony. My speech was polished, and I didn't need to go over it. With a whole hour before I had to be on the Hill, I granted myself a momentary bookstore escape.

The smell of Chapters reminded me of the NBU library, and I loved it. Tracing the outline of several new novels, I suddenly thought of Mr. Lewis and made my first journey over to the Chapters apologetics section.

It had been awhile since I'd read the Bible or even prayed. Things had been moving so fast between preparing for my speech and making decisions about the wedding that somehow I had distanced myself from God, and the void that I had known before was beginning to open up again.

*Remember me,* I thought I heard the third voice say as I picked up a copy of *Mere Christianity* and clutched it to my chest. *Refresh my memory,* I said. *I'm already forgetting.*

I closed my eyes and tried to think where I'd put my journal from sophomore year. The one that recorded my grappling with Mr. Lewis as he persuaded me to believe. Suddenly I realized that I couldn't recall one sentence or argument from those days, and I felt as frantic as a bee who is unable to enter the hive.

When I opened my eyes, the room seemed to darken, and the floorboards seemed to shift beneath my feet. Steadying myself, I took a deep breath and looked around at shelf after shelf of books and then back across the street to my office. It was swampy in the mid-day heat of the city, and the window air-conditioning units were dropping cold water on the heads of the passersby.

Before I knew it, a strangely familiar-looking young man in a suit and loose tie walked into the store and sat down at a table to thumb through a *Washington Post*. He took off his jacket, and two circles of sweat outlined his white shirt, and his hair fanned out at the ends like a rooster along the top of his collar.

When he sat back in the chair and folded the paper back, I remembered. It was Devon Hunt! What in the world was going on here?

I shifted my weight back and forth for whole seconds. Then I marched right over, sat down in front of him, and pulled down the newspaper.

He looked up at me in confusion. His eyes narrowed, and then it came to him, and his face morphed into the most terrified look I had ever seen.

He knew me. And by the look on his face, he knew I had spoken publicly about that night on the graveside hill.

My heart was thumping like a small bird's, and I pulled a Rachel's Rape brochure out of my briefcase and handed it to him.

"Read this, why don't you? And pass the word. Rape is a crime."

His neck stiffened, but his Adam's apple moved up and down as he swallowed. His eyes didn't follow me as I stood back up and walked toward the door. I still had a Lewis book in my hand, and the cashier said, "Would you like me to ring you up, ma'am?" as I headed toward the door.

I pointed toward Devon at the table, his hands running through his damp hair.

"He'll take care of it," I said, showing her the title.

*What a day,* I thought as my stomach caught in my throat and I tried to calm my beating heart. Funny, I didn't want to castrate Devon as Allison had suggested, and I didn't want to forgive him the way I knew Shannon thought I should. But there was a deep-felt satisfaction in confronting him, and I might have reveled in it longer if I weren't terribly confused about my feelings for Tobias and late for a meeting with a senator that had been set up for a month now.

I had to get to the Hill, but I was so disoriented that I kept walking straight down K Street. Two blocks down from Chapters was the White House, where the controversial President Clinton was conducting business behind a wall of security, and across the park a homeless couple was rolling their supermarket cart of essentials under a shaded tree for a respite.

As I watched a flock of pigeons take flight, I felt at war with myself, and I didn't know what to do about it. I was going to be late for my appointment if I didn't act fast, and so I walked out into the edge of the street and caught a cab over to meet Tobias and Glenda.

They were waiting for me on the other side of a security checkpoint in the Russell Building, and I slid my briefcase through the metal detector as Tobias waved me by the guards and onto the elevators.

When Senator Carnes's aide came out to say that we would have to reschedule because of an emergency session that had just been called, Glenda stayed behind to see if she could pop her head into some other offices, and Tobias and I walked to the subway so that he could help me get off early to Vienna before a business meeting with NOW and a few other activists that he was conducting in his apartment later that evening.

I held back from telling him about running into Devon. I was perturbed for some inexplicable reason, and when the escalator delivered us down to the subway, I could not suppress the desire to needle him.

"I don't know if I like living in Washington," I said as he slid my subway pass through the slot and the wall opened to let me through.

"We're going to live in Arlington, and it's much nicer there," he said as he pushed through the doors after me.

"No. I mean, I don't know if I like this whole area. You know I always wanted to live in Manhattan."

"Manhattan?" he said, rubbing his forehead in disbelief. "Are you serious?"

Then he took me gently by the arm and said through his concerned eyes, "That's one of the most dangerous cities in the world, Adelaide."

"Would you ever go anywhere else?" I asked, staring back at his sweet eyes. "I mean, is Rachel's Rape what we're going to do for the rest of our lives?"

"What are you saying, Adelaide?"

"I don't know," I said as I twisted my engagement ring around on my finger. A part of me wanted to take it off and throw it onto the third rail of the subway to see if it would melt like the pocket watches in Dali's *The Persistence of Memory*.

"Is everything okay, sweetheart?" he asked, leaning into me and brushing a strand of hair out of my face.

"I'm bored," I said, looking up at him. "I feel empty and sad."

He had not noticed that we had entered the wrong platform and would be headed southeast on the green line toward the inner city of Anacostia if we hopped on the next approaching train, instead of west on the orange line toward the Virginia suburbs. He bit his bottom lip in distress over our conversation as a train made its way toward us.

"Take me to the war zone," I said as the train stopped in front of us and I pointed up to the sign that revealed our mistake. I suddenly wished that my briefcase were full of St. Christopher medals instead of a presentation on date rape and that I could go skipping down the inner-city streets, throwing a medal on every doorstep.

"We're on the wrong platform, Adelaide!" he said as the doors opened and I stepped onto the train.

"I'd rather be gunned down than bored to death, Tobias," I said. "Come with me. Let's do something different for a change."

"It's dangerous," he said, and I thought his eyes might pop out of their sockets. I noticed for the first time a vein in the center of his forehead that was pulsing.

"Step back out here!" he screamed as the doors buckled before closing. I crossed my arms and refused to move, and his face turned a ghastly white.

"No!" he screamed as the doors sealed between us and the train barreled down the tunnel, leaving him behind.

~

*And there it was,* I thought, taking my seat next to a weary-looking African-American lady in a gray-and-white housekeeping uniform from the Washingtonian Hotel.

*Of course,* I thought to myself. *Why couldn't I have seen this?*

If Tobias couldn't bring Rachel back, he might as well marry someone who'd suffered the way she had. It was the closest he could get.

It came to me as I tunneled down the line, then rode the escalator up and out into the inner-city neighborhood, which, aside from some graffiti on the walls and some piles of trash that hadn't been picked up in weeks, looked the same as the rest of the Capitol Hill area. No, there were no bullets flying and no gang fights with switchblades hurling, and I made myself walk a few blocks around the area before I considered my next move.

A young boy looked up at me from beside his mother's arm. He had the most beautiful brown eyes I could imagine; I smiled at him, and he said, "Hello!" before walking by.

"Hello to you," I turned around to say, and I stopped and waved at him as he looked back over his little shoulder.

Hailing a cab, I uttered the name of the largest church I could think of: "National Cathedral." My plan was to sit there and pray, as Harriet and I had on our European tour, until I knew what to do next.

When I entered the grand sanctuary, dodging two pockets of tourists being led by two guides who were holding up tall and colorful umbrellas, I sat down on a pew halfway down the aisle and looked up at the altar for a moment before kneeling down in prayer.

The word *love* and a verse about first love that I'd heard before kept coming to mind. Was it from the Song of Solomon? Or Revelation? I grabbed a Bible from the pew, thumbed through the index, and turned to what I was remembering, Revelation 2:5: "Look how far you have fallen from your first love! Turn back to me again and work as you did at first."

With this, I fell down on my knees and wept silently as the small crowds of tourists snapped pictures all around me. How could I have forgotten what I had received a few short years ago? The One who saved my very soul and then danced with me down the center of the Magnolia Club ballroom. How could I have put that love on the shelf? Replaced it with human romance—and one that was a fraud at that!

I had missed the mark, almost imperceptibly, as I quietly ignored the red flags being raised around me. Once Dale Pelzer had asked me if God was in the driver's seat or the passenger seat of the car I was in, and my answer had been "Neither." Instead, I had tied Him on the roof like the Griswolds with their deceased aunt Edna, and I had put a gag over His mouth to boot.

*Does God take you back a second time?* I wondered as the tourists shuffled down the stone aisle toward the altar.

*Come back to me,* I prayed. *Have mercy.*

A kind of warmth filled my lungs as I prayed those words, and in an instant the prayer had been answered.

Outside the cathedral, the haze of the late-day city smog was hovering over the trees and the cars that lined Massachusetts Avenue on their brutal commute to the suburbs. I hailed the first cab I saw and headed straight to Adams Morgan.

When I reached Tobias's apartment, several other activists were arriving for the meeting.

He embraced me when he opened the door and asked me to sit in with them.

"No," I said. "We need to talk. I'll wait in your room until the meeting is over."

And there I sat for just over an hour in his little bedroom as Glenda, a sharply dressed woman from NOW, and a hippie-looking guy from Men Against Rape went over the upcoming vote.

I nearly hyperventilated when I fast-forwarded in my mind to what our life would have been like together: 2.5 children sporting Rachel's Rape T-shirts as we walked around some northern Virginia cul-de-sac.

When I looked down at the perfectly-lined-up shoes in Tobias's closet, I had to smile at what I knew was God's sense of humor making its way into my imagination. Instead of the shoes practicing their scales like last time, now they were singing a song written just for me, to the tune of "Dixie," and it went, "Oh, you wish you were the heck out of DC. There's not much soul and a lot of PCs. Run away, run away, run away, Miss Piper."

When Tobias walked into his room, I had already taken off my diamond ring and placed it in the black velvet box that he still kept on his dresser.

"What are you doing?" he asked as I gently handed it to him.

"This life is not for me, Tobias," I said. "You're a wonderful, caring man, but I don't want to marry you. And I don't want to work for Rachel's Rape or testify on the Hill next week. I just want to go home. And get back on my spiritual journey."

"Adelaide, I can't believe this," he said, rubbing his neck in frustration and defeat. "You know Rachel's Rape is my life, and I thought you wanted it to be yours too. If this is about religion, I'm willing to take you to church—"

"This is about my life," I said as I unloaded my briefcase and handed him my speech and brochures. "I know you miss Rachel," I said. "I'm so sorry about what happened to her. But I'm not your sister."

✑

As I rode the subway back to Vienna and packed up my meager belongings from the Moore family's F.R.O.G., I felt relief. Granted, I was terrified of what the immediate future held—I knew I'd go home to Williamstown, the very place I'd spent half my life dreaming of escaping. I'd have Randy and Perky in my face, with their happy little family, while I worked at some awful temp agency outside Charleston for the next year, as Winkie and Nan were doing. And Papa Great would surely declare me a lesbian. But in the end, I didn't care. I was running back into the arms of the One I had ignored most of my life, and there was nothing else more right than that.

That night I wrote the Moores a "Thank you, and good-bye" note and called a cab and charged a room at the Days Inn on my credit card, though I had no money to pay for it.

The next day I called Glenda to thank her, and I took one last walk around the Washington Monument and the Mall before Lazarus picked me up after work and took me to the airport, where I purchased a one-way ticket to Charleston, South Carolina.

He hugged me hard and said, "Maybe our paths will cross again."

"You never know," I said. "Thanks for helping me out."

When I walked into the terminal, I called my old house out of habit from a pay phone, and I was relieved when Dizzy answered.

"The wedding is off. I'm coming home."

She paused for a moment and then said, "Whew! Tell me what time your plane comes in."

"At 10:05 p.m.," I said. "United 102."

"I'll be there," she said. "You'll get to see Juliabelle too. She's here giving me a secret cooking lesson while Mae Mae and Papa Great are at the wedding."

When I hung up the phone, I made my way up the escalator and took my place at the boarding gate in front of the big, thick windows. It was 8:00 p.m., and the summer sun was just beginning to set behind the canopy of trees around the Jefferson Memorial. The pale pink in the last light of the day was glistening across the Potomac River, and the Fourteenth Street Bridge was still bustling with employees who had worked late on this random Friday night in late July. The businessmen and women filed in around me, opening up their briefcases with their important papers, and I closed my eyes and breathed a deep sigh of relief, in and out and in again, as the cell phones buzzed and the intercom announced the incoming flights.

When I opened my eyes, I saw that the sun had dipped, finally, below the green trees that encircled the city. And I spent the rest of the time before they called us to board watching planes ascend from the shortest runway in the country.

## 22

# Back Home

Dizzy picked me up in the Country Squire. She had a small gold ring through her nose and a Marlboro Light between her black finger-nails, but she was as sober as a Baptist preacher and grinning. She had a plan to borrow some money and open a Gullah restaurant on Upper King Street in Charleston, and she was learning all she could about Low-Country cooking from Juliabelle before her graduation.

"I just nearly made the mistake of a lifetime," I said as we sped past the "Holy City" and through the cypress swamp lining Route 39 toward Williamstown.

Dizzy knocked my knee with her elbow. "But you didn't." She cracked her window to ash out of it. "Know what I think, Adelaide?"

"Hmm?"

"Someone's looking after you despite yourself."

As she took another drag, I rolled down my window, leaned back into the soft upholstery, and let my arm out to feel the thick, moist air. It was a healing balm itself, like Juliabelle's well water hidden some-where back behind the cypress trees in the Francis Marion Forest, and I wanted to gulp it down. I stuck my head out the window and screamed along the dark, pine-lined road.

A fireworks stand marked the Williamstown County line, and at the foot of the bridge, three boys were smoking and shooting off Roman candles beneath the smoggy sky.

The mill village stirred with country music. Smoke spiraled upward from a bonfire in the center of the dirt alleyway between the two rows of houses. It was a Friday night, not to mention payday, so the men were sitting around the fire, drinking beer and rubbing their heels in the dirt, while the women put the children to bed.

Someone had added flower boxes with marigolds along the windowsills of Harvest Time, and the lettered marquee by the road was illuminating Dale's words of the week: "Refusing Jesus is a no-win situation!" No, they didn't mince words over at Harvest Time, and I couldn't wait to see Dale and Darla and get a tight squeeze from Charlie Farley.

∼

The rotten-egg stench filled our nostrils at once, and I pointed to the iron-ore soot as it poured into the starry sky. Main Street was dim, but I could make out the locked doors of Campbell's Pharmacy, Sugar's Funeral Home, and the mannequins casting their shadows in the window of Cato Clothes.

At the left turn toward the historic district, the grand Magnolia Club glowed with twinkling white lights strewn across the limbs of the live oak and palmetto trees for Randy's wedding. Through the tall windows, I glimpsed silver candelabras brimming with candlelight and champagne flutes and plates of sweet iced cake, and I imagined a guttural kind of laughter from the guests inside as they released their worries over this sudden union and plumb gave in to hope.

Randy's pickup truck waited in the center of the circular driveway, covered in shaving cream and littered with root beer cans. "Dodi and Randy" read a poster with glitter-glue script hung from the back gate of the truck. "Just Married!"

Dizzy gave a side-angled glance my way, and I gulped back my tears. "Well," I said, "can't unring that bell."

"Nope," she said. "He would've driven you nuts, anyhow. Like, way too stable."

When we pulled up to our picturesque home on the salt marsh, I pictured Adelaide Rutledge Graydon and the twist her life had taken, and I was grateful for the white clapboard house with its wraparound porch and dark green shutters and jasmine vines climbing the outside walls. It was the very thing that said, "Nobody can guess just how things will turn out."

The red magnetic SOLD letters slapped across the metal Williamstown Realty sign made me wince and say, "What's next for us Pipers?"

It was nearly midnight, and Juliabelle was smoking her pipe on the back porch between the crab dock and the hammock. The smoke of her burning tobacco billowed up into the Spanish moss above her head. When she heard us, she hurried in and hugged me tightly before pulling back to give me the once-over.

"Welcome back, child," she said. She looked older than I'd remembered, and her coal-black skin was beginning to sag below her sharp jawline. Her lips were cracked and her hair was graying on the sides, but her big black eyes still held a kind of vitality that glistened above the dusty lamps in our deserted home.

"Do I have a story for you," I said to her. "St. Christopher must be worn out with me."

She cupped her hands around my cheeks and said, "Not for now. Now's time for a midnight snack. Your sista's been cooking up a storm, and you got some samplin' to do."

"Check it out," Dizzy said, pulling me over to the stove, where she and Juliabelle had been filling the musty house with the sweet smell of shrimp and hominy grits, red rice with sausage, cheese biscuits, and banana pudding.

Dizzy loaded three plates for us, and we settled ourselves on the lawn chairs by the marsh dock while the mosquitoes nipped at our ankles. The backyard smelled like pluff mud and rotten tomatoes. The kudzu must have been taking over Mama's garden.

A car door slammed behind us. Then Daddy, still dressed in his tuxedo from the wedding, strode into the house, hauling an armload of Bizway vitamins. He stopped suddenly before walking over to examine the food on the stove, then peering through the back door in disbelief.

"What in the world?" he said, opening the screen door.

"Your oldest has come back home, Zane," Juliabelle announced. "Better get over here and tell her it's fine that she don't marry that sweet-looking Yankee."

"Thank You, Jesus!" Daddy yelled. Then he ran over, pulled me close, and rocked me back and forth, whispering, "You made the right choice, sister."

"You haven't eaten in a month of Sundays," Juliabelle said, looking Daddy up and down. "Want a plate?"

"I won't refuse it," he said.

It was a sweet reunion. Daddy smiling down on me. And no one questioning my decision to leave Washington and break off my pending nuptials.

The four of us settled into the lawn chairs, gobbling down the savory food and laughing while Daddy described Randy's wedding: the strapless white dress with the three-foot train his cheerleader bride had chosen to sport despite the obvious bulge of her belly, and the Carolina Gamecock groom's cake that had black icing on the outside with a field goal on top and red velvet cake in the center. Heavens to Betsy!

After Dizzy and Juliabelle went in to clean the kitchen, Daddy and I settled down in our lawn chairs, and I asked him, "So who bought the house?"

"Some couple from Chicago," he said. "It's going to be a second home for them, I reckon. We don't close for another three weeks, so you can get your feet on the ground here if you like."

"Thanks," I said, breathless from all the change around me. "You doing okay, Daddy?"

"Not really," he said, slapping away a mosquito with his stump. "I miss your mama, Adelaide, and I haven't talked to my own daddy in months." He lifted his eyebrows and said, "Some days I can't remember what in the world happened."

I nodded and bit my tongue, because it didn't feel right to say, "You and this new business were one of the things that made it all happen." There was a lot more to it than that, and I was finally beginning to see that sometimes it is better to just shut up and wait.

⌒

After the dishwasher was loaded, Dizzy turned in and Juliabelle shuffled between the pittosporum shrubs back to Papa Great and Mae Mae's as if she hadn't been up to a thing this evening.

Daddy loaded his car with some water filters and headed back over to Uncle Tinka's apartment, and I felt my way to the end of the crab dock and sprawled out across the musty ropes of the hammock.

There was a rope there, tied to a palmetto in the yard, and I pulled it and swung out over the marsh, looking up through the oak trees to the crescent moon beaming through the sooty haze. It left chips of light on the water churning in the harbor beyond me.

Before long the lights came on at Mae Mae's as my grandfolks returned from the wedding, but in a few minutes their house was dark again, and I imagined the ornery Hog with his usual whistle going through his nose and Mae Mae nudging him until he rolled over.

Well, I was back to where I'd started four years ago, I mused as I stretched out across the hammock. In my own yard with an itch in my soul and my family in a heap more trouble than we were in then. And I could already guess that it wouldn't be the last time I got off track.

But the way I looked at it, I was raw material. Leveled like the houses on Pawleys Island after Hurricane David pounded them when I was a child. It wasn't such a bad place to be. To be leveled. It might be the only place where my Maker could *make* something of me.

In the kudzu a raccoon scurried through the vines before plopping into the pluff mud, and his two iridescent eyes looked back at me before he turned and parted the tall marsh grass with his pointed snout.

There was a plan for me, I was sure. Maybe it contained a husband—a soulful, nonterrified one—or an opportunity to write poetry. But who was I to impose my will on everything?

In the backyard darkness a poem formed.

### Second Breath

*It starts*
*with a halt.*
*Not unlike*
*a mother's grip*
*on a boy*
*stepping*
*into the road*
*or a hare*
*just aware*
*of the bobcat*
*in the underbrush.*
*What precedes*
*resuscitation*
*is the stripping*
*to sackcloth—*
*the sitting down*
*in the cool*
*gray ashes.*

Now I rubbed my jewel, breathed in the moist air, and remembered *sehnsucht*. It was a German word I'd learned from Mr. Lewis, and the idea of it was coming back to me. Akin to joy, *sehnsucht* was a wistful longing. A yearning like the itch of the soul.

In one of his books he described it as "an unsatisfied desire which is itself more desirable than any other satisfaction." It was like poetry—how a few words pieced together in just the right sequence could pierce your heart for a moment with a kind of truth.

I was weary to the bone as I pulled my rope and swung in the hammock out over the marsh, but I had *sehnsucht* beneath the crescent moon on the crab dock, and I was waking up from a kind of sleep I'd never fall back into.

Mr. Lewis believed that our human life is just the first page of the first chapter of a very long book. And I considered this, my eyes darting back and forth in the darkness, while the crickets called and the furnace melted the iron ore, and the four converging rivers pushed their way out to sea.

# Acknowledgments

I am heartily grateful for each member of the Westbow Press team, especially my editor, Ami McConnell, whose direction significantly improved Adelaide's story. Thanks also go to my literary sounding board: Rebecca Kurson, Lisa Hughes, John Pelletier, and my husband, Edward B. Hart Jr., who has skillfully mastered the tricky technique of critiquing with love.

I am indebted to the best group of babysitters a working mom could come by: my parents, Betty and Joe Jelks, and my in-laws and friends, Ed and Mary Hart, Mary Boyd Hart, and Bitsy Andrews.

In addition, I want to thank the following South Carolina bookstores that have greatly supported these efforts: The Cozy Corner on Edisto Island, The Open Book in Greenville, Litchfield Books on Pawleys Island, and the Barnes & Noble booksellers in Mount Pleasant and Charleston.

My utmost and final thanks go to the One who called me to His marvelous light at Adelaide's vulnerable age.

# Reading Group Guide Questions

1. Adelaide is a risk-taker, a pot-stirrer, and one determined debutante poetess. She's interested in justice almost to a fault, but she has a tender side that sympathizes with her peers and their mutual struggles. In what ways do Adelaide's passionate attempts to "force things back to where they belong" and to "scratch the itch of her soul" (p. 34) contribute to her sufferings and her occasional loss of control throughout the novel?

2. Consider the "itch of your soul" or to put it another way — the yearning in your heart for a deeper meaning. How do you attempt to satisfy this desire?

3. What does Adelaide's poetry mean to her? How are her poems used during the course of the story to underscore the arc of her character's development?

4. Adelaide muses that there are two sides to Williamstown: When she looks out over her crab dock, she sees a subtropical Eden of converging rivers, rice fields, and barrier islands, but when she glances back over her house and toward the center of town, she sees the two

fingers of smoke blowing smog into the air. In what ways are there two sides to Nathaniel Buxton University? Do you think the underbelly of college life is accurately depicted in this novel?

5. Consider the fraternity hazing incident and the fate of Brother Benton and Peter Carpenter. Discuss how one choice during youth can have a dramatic impact on the rest of one's life.

6. Trace Adelaide's response to her rape. What does this tragic event do to her sense of self? How does Adelaide feel about Devon Hunt? Do you think that her confrontation with him at the end of the novel will further her recovery process? Why or why not?

7. Discuss the doubts that Adelaide faces before her conversion. Can you empathize with her struggles regarding the authenticity of Christianity? In what ways did the following events contribute to her spiritual awakening and subsequent conversion:

The HIV test
The trip to Harvest Time Church
Juliabelle's incantation and the tonic from Huger Creek
The conversations with C.S. Lewis
Ruthie's abortion

8. Why does Adelaide consider the debutante season a charade? How do the generation gaps between her grandmother and her mother contribute to her belief that making one's debut is an outdated ritual? After an unexpected turn of events on the night of the debutante ball, how does Adelaide's formal presentation to Williamstown society become linked to her new-found faith?

9. After the initial "honeymoon with her Maker" following her conversion, why does Adelaide's faith begin to wane? Does she make a conscious decision to distance herself from God?

10. Consider the personal struggles of the following characters:

   Zane Piper
   Greta Piper
   Dizzy
   Ruthie
   Jif
   Harriet
   Tobias

   What does this novel say about the effect of loss on the nuclear family?

11. Do you think Adelaide and her friends are any closer to finding the answers to the questions that she posed in her valedictorian speech?

   *Who am I?*
   *And where am I going?*

12. In the final poem *Second Breath*, what does Adelaide suggest one must do before starting over?

13. Picture Adelaide ten years from the end of this story. What do you envision her adult life looking like?

# Southern Fiction

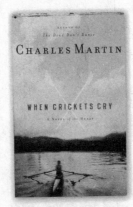

*available in bookstores
September 2006

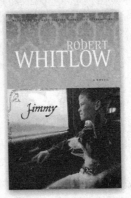

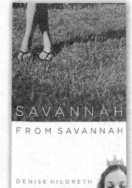

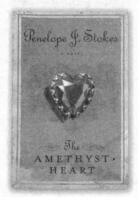
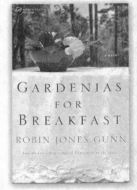